10 SIGNS *You Need* TO GROVEL

KELLY SISKIND

Text copyright © 2023 by Kelly Siskind
All rights reserved.

No part of this book may be reproduced, or stored in a retrieval system, or transmitted in any form or by any means, electronic, mechanical, photocopying, recording, or otherwise, without express written permission of the publisher.

Published by Montlake, Seattle

www.apub.com

Amazon, the Amazon logo, and Montlake are trademarks of Amazon.com, Inc., or its affiliates.

ISBN-13: 9781662505669 (paperback)
ISBN-13: 9781662505676 (digital)

Cover design by Caroline Teagle Johnson
Cover photography by Michelle Lancaster
Cover images: © sakchai vongsasiripat / Getty Images;
© Brian Koprowski / Stocksy United

Printed in the United States of America

10 SIGNS
You Need
TO GROVEL

ALSO BY KELLY SISKIND

Bower Boys Series

50 Ways to Win Back Your Lover

One Wild Wish Series

He's Going Down
Off-Limits Crush
36 Hour Date

Showmen Series

New Orleans Rush
Don't Go Stealing My Heart
The Beat Match
The Knockout Rule

Over the Top Series

My Perfect Mistake
A Fine Mess
Hooked on Trouble

Stand-Alones

Chasing Crazy

Sign up for Kelly's newsletter and never miss a giveaway, a free bonus scene, or the latest news on her books: www.kellysiskind.com.

10 SIGNS *You Need* TO GROVEL

ONE

Death by paper, that's what my tombstone will read. My fingers are cramping, I have four paper cuts, and if I keep staring down at this uneven mess of folded edges, my neck might fossilize at this torqued angle. The kicker? This origami project was rated for kids age twelve and up.

"Goddamn it." I go to crumple the mutant triceratops but fist my hands instead.

"Language," Mirielle says, eyeing me over the perfectly folded edges of her velociraptor. "These are virgin ears."

There's nothing virgin about Mirielle Allard's ears, or any other part of her. She's a seventy-eight-year-old Black woman who smokes a pack a day, blasts French music from her record player, and dishes about her wild days singing in jazz clubs, where men literally fought each other for her number. But my neighbor loves to bust my chops.

"My fingers are too thick for this." I lob the deformed dinosaur into my growing box of unfinished crafts. "I was better at the decoupage."

She raises a penciled eyebrow. "This from the savage who threw a tantrum when he couldn't get pieces of glue and paper off of his hands. Truly, David, you are *drôle*."

"Name's not David."

"Gaspard?"

"Still wrong." And I never should've told Mirielle I used to be in witness protection or that I've been using the alias Daniel Baker for eleven years.

Unfortunately, she heard me stumble into my place seven months ago, shout a bunch of heartache about the woman I loved and lost, and then punch the wall. Instead of bolting her door, she pushed her tiny self into my open apartment and tended to me. Cleaned up my hand. Bandaged it while humming, showing zero fear in the face of her six-foot-two, long-haired, tattooed neighbor with the permanent scowl.

Ever since, she's shown up several times a week with crafts and pastries and stories about her glory days, wearing colorful headscarves and flowy dress-shirt things—apparently, they're called *caftans*—while trying to guess what my name used to be before my family got shoved into WITSEC.

"Are you nervous about seeing your brother today?" She also loves nagging me about unpleasant subjects.

"Did you receive the yarn I ordered for you?"

She lifts her chin. "Deflection is a sign of weakness, *chéri*."

I grunt.

"As is not using your words." She methodically folds an edge of the paper, her attention flicking to me.

I scowl at her, but Mirielle doesn't even blink. Honestly, she could topple a dictator without smudging a stitch of her red lipstick.

I pick up another piece of origami paper, ready to try for serenity again, but my eyes stutter on the impressionist-style brushstrokes filling the page. My throat pinches. My heart rate picks up. If the woman I once loved hadn't studied art history, I wouldn't know impressionist art from cubist. Sadie was always flipping through her art textbooks, lying on her stomach while I'd kiss a line down her neck, lift up her shirt, lick those sexy dimples above her ass.

"Quit it," she said one night, laughing, trying to shake me off.

I gave her side a playful nip. "You taste too good, Sprite."

She shivered on a breathy sigh. "Quit calling me Sprite."

"Quit being so little and cute, and I'll quit calling you Sprite."

She shoved her books off the bed and tackled me, giving me a hot pout. "I'm sexy and mysterious, not cute."

That's it. The end of that particular memory. Simple and silly.

Flays me every damn time.

I rub my temples, unsure whether these relentless memories will ever end.

My phone rings from the coffee table, and I stiffen. The sight of my youngest brother's name has the cold pizza I ate this morning threatening to mutiny.

I haven't puked since I had the flu at age thirteen. Line up shots, and I'll drink you under the table. A fifth of whiskey? I won't even burp. I don't drink as much as my family seems to think, but my gut is made of the same material as my heart: cold, hard metal. The past week, however, I've hovered on queasy, all thanks to today's impending meet and greet with E. And that Sadie flashback isn't helping.

"Answer it," Mirielle says.

"I'm meeting E later. There's no point."

"For such a brawny man, you really are quite terrified. Jack," she adds, watching me for a reaction.

I give her a reaction, all right. Dialing up my glare to eleven, I snatch up my phone.

"What?" I say to my brother, the barked word sounding ruder than intended.

Mirielle rolls her eyes at me.

"Good morning to you too," E says, extra chipper.

"Are you calling to cancel?" Restlessness edges my movements, like I *want* him to say no. Like I need this meeting as much as him, when I've avoided him and my family for the past eight months.

"Just making sure we're on for today," he goes on. "One o'clock at"—a pause—"Down in the Hole?"

I relax slightly, but something's off. This constant pushing from him is unpleasantly excessive. "Tell me again why you need to see me?"

"It's Dad," he says quickly, a hint of strain in his voice. "He asked me a favor, and I can't discuss it on the phone. You're the only one I can talk to about it, so just make sure you're at the bar at one p.m. In two hours. Thirteen hundred hours military time, and don't be late."

Yeah. He's full of shit.

This mystery meeting has nothing to do with our waste-of-space father, the Worst Human Ever, who decided it would be swell to launder money for a drug cartel and ruin our lives. The tightness in E's strained voice and ridiculous babbling means something unpleasant is most definitely up.

"I'll be there," I say briskly and end the call.

Mirielle tilts her head, her dainty dinosaur held in her lined hand. "You have that mad-at-the-world look about you, *chéri*. Actually, *non*." She peers closer at me. "That is your regular face."

"Thanks for always making me feel better."

"That is not my job. That is *yours*."

I grunt, knowing it will irk her, but she's not wrong. *And* I've been trying.

Since learning the Quintero cartel wiped out the Becerra cartel in a bloody massacre eight months ago and my family no longer needed to be in witness protection, I've slowly come out of my angry fog. Ditched the bad crowd that led to drunk tattoos and infected piercings. I've been hanging out with my seventy-eight-year-old neighbor instead. In exchange for her teaching me crafts—which I suck at, but they do sort of clear my mind—I help out as a handyman around her place and help her navigate online purchases. (We will *never* discuss the underwear-and-bra-shopping incident.)

Work has been better too. Bartending isn't my dream job, but I've even been enjoying it more. Still tossing snarls out to annoying drunks, but I've been showing up early and getting more creative mixing drinks. I even called my brother back.

After so long being angry or plain apathetic, I finally have the itch to live more fully. I want to wake up looking forward to my days, my future. Normalcy. Optimism. Figure out what career might suit me better. Make an effort with my family.

I was hoping this meeting with E would be a leap forward, but life for me is a slippery slope. One wrong move and I tend to go off the deep end. E's odd behavior is a billowing red flag that screams Family Drama.

"I'm getting my life together," I tell Mirielle, trying to shake that troubling call. I point at my face. "This is my slowly-picking-myself-up expression."

She lets out a tittering laugh. "That, *chéri*, is your barely trying expression. Last I checked, you haven't made new friends."

"Am I talking to a ghost?"

"And your apartment still looks like you have only just moved in." She waves her hand extravagantly at my empty beige walls and sparse furniture.

Lips flat, I cross my arms.

"*And* you're not dating."

"Neither are you."

She blinks at me blandly. "I do not believe the online market is clamoring for widowed Frenchwomen who excel at decoupage. And I do not do that right swiping." She lifts her head as though affronted.

I have no clue how a producer hasn't turned Mirielle into a star by now. "I'm happy being on my own."

"*Non.*" She shakes her head. "Not according to the night we met."

This grunt turns into more of a hiss. "Haven't we talked that night to death?"

"But you were so broken, Edward." She stares at me.

I glower harder. "Wrong again."

She sighs dramatically. "You were just so *triste* that evening. So, so sad. Going on about the love of your life and how you had lost her once and for all. A man who feels that much should not be alone."

What I was that night was *destroyed*, because I'd done the one thing I promised myself I'd never do: search for Sadie Jones.

The love of my life had disappeared off the face of the earth (and internet) after *I'd* disappeared, and I knew looking for her was a horrible idea. If I found her and she was with someone else, the knowledge was bound to crush me beyond recognition. Still, I caved. I'd recently learned we didn't need to stay in WITSEC, and I hired a PI before I could overthink the choice. A week later, the man came to me with a phone number and an address—digits in an email that held more power than nuclear codes.

Lacking the courage to drive to Sadie's home in Tennessee, I called the number . . . and breathed in her ear like a pervert while she said hello three times.

Then a little-boy voice called "Mom" in the distance, and Sadie replied to him, "I'll be right there, sweetie."

I swiftly hung up and nearly shattered my no-puking streak, then proceeded to go on an epic bender, after which I stumbled home drunk, punched the wall, and blabbed my sob story to Mirielle while she tended my cut-up knuckles. Ever since that disaster, she's been up my ass about dating and finding my next true love, when all I've done since hearing Sadie's voice is miss the hell out of the woman who owned my heart.

"I should head to work," I tell Mirielle, standing unceremoniously. A man can only handle so many blunt pep talks. "I have a feeling E will show up early."

"Say *bonjour* for me. And next week we'll try crocheting. It might suit you better. Clear that busy, busy mind of yours."

"Sure," I say gruffly. "We'll surf the net tomorrow. Choose the sets you want."

"And I need more of my Bahamas Fever lipstick."

I walk her to my door. "We'll get that too."

"And we'll sign you up for dating sites. Walter," she adds as she sails out the door, her colorful caftan flowing behind her.

"Walter?" I call, bristling. "What part of me looks like a Walter?"

"The part that no longer knows how to have fun."

Fun? I know how to have fun. I was the definition of fun in college. I'm the guy who swapped my roommate's laundry load with a bag of old lady's undergarments. That was hilariously *fun*. Except it makes me think of underwear shopping for Mirielle, which was definitely not fun.

Grumbling under my breath, I tidy my small place, which does look half-vacant and maybe not very fun. I move the book from my bed onto my nightstand and stare at the title, *Eleanor Oliphant Is Completely Fine*, feeling a pang behind my ribs.

I started reading book club books to discuss them with my mother. A couple of years into WITSEC, after I moved out on my own, I'd surprise her at her regular coffee shop to perk her up. Distract her from her sadness by talking about books. Until the day she took one look at me and burst into tears. I wasn't sure what set her off, but seeing me made it worse. So I stopped going.

Even though I've avoided her coffee shop for the past year, she still emails me which books she's currently reading, and I still read along. But I don't reach out. The last thing I want is to make my mother cry.

I knot my hair on top of my head and grab my keys, needing air and a walk before meeting my brother. But the air doesn't clear my head. My mind is *busy, busy*, as Mirielle would say, picking over E's worrying call. Missing my mother and our book club talks.

When I arrive at my latest place of employment, Down in the Hole, I pause at the trampled cigarette collection outside the front door. The cancer-causing stubs overlap in a mess of white and yellow. A flattened pile that resembles a slightly deformed dolphin. The title *Mutant Dolphin Attacks Bystanders* pops into my head.

My stomach churns again.

Sadie used to do ridiculous stuff like this, point to gum on the sidewalk or bird shit on a window and pretend it was art. She'd give the piece an elaborate name—*Solar Eclipse Monsoon* or *Parody of Swan Lake*—describing the nuance and depth of the nasty splotch, while I'd tickle or kiss her, daring her to eat the stepped-on gum. I was an unabashed pest back then. She was light. Playful, creative, clever. No clue how she put up with my idiocy.

Not that it matters now. She's living a full life, and I need to do the same. Forget her the way she's forgotten me. Find my fun. Quit dodging my family. Date properly again, even though the thought makes me itch. Prove to Mirielle I can do better so she quits calling me Walter. Be a source of happiness for my family, not a source of tears.

Determined to make this meeting with E pleasant, I yank open the bar door. In the early-afternoon light, the wooden bar top looks like it got mauled by a bear, and the dark stains on the scuffed floor appear more suspect than usual. Half the lights on the bathroom sign are burned out, so the sign reads B RO M. Run down or not, the place is jam packed at night.

My coworker Frankie glances up from scrubbing one of the tables by the dartboard, her lined eyes doing a sweep of my face. She grunts at me. I grunt back. Frankie is my people.

I glance at the bar, ready to work on a new cocktail. Something to share with E when he shows up, but my eyes lock on a six-foot-four wrench in that plan.

"You're early," I tell E.

"Happened to be in the neighborhood," he says with false cheer.

Liar.

He slides out of a booth near the back, approaching me like I'm the rabid bear who tore into the bar top. The guy must've been hiding in here, waiting on me, ensuring I couldn't ditch him. And hey, I get it. I've done nothing but prove to my family I'm volatile and unreliable.

Fixing that starts now. "It's good to see you."

He startles, like he expected to be hit, not greeted. "You look better, except for the subpar ink, which still sucks."

I smirk. "You look like you still can't catch a football."

He laughs haltingly. "Guilty, but I can run you into the ground."

He can. Where I hit the gym to work out my angst, my youngest brother is a runner. He also wears his emotions on his sleeve. When we were kids, I'd rib him mercilessly for drawing instead of playing sports, tease him about his given name—Edgar Eugene Bower—and goad him into fights over his ongoing Delilah Moon infatuation. Still, if I got injured in a football game or received a bad grade in school, E would get this look on his face like he was absolutely crushed. Like he couldn't stand seeing *me* hurt or disappointed.

Today his face is all taut lines, like he's dreading telling me something.

I run my tongue over my cracked tooth. "You need to talk about our sperm donor?"

"He's a dick." He rakes a hand through his brown hair, his eyes darting over my shoulder.

"Not a news flash." Following his eyes, I glance behind me. No one's there, and I didn't agree to meet him to play games. "You're not here about him, E. If you came to give me shit about ignoring the family and pushing you guys away, save your breath." I rub at the twinge in my chest. "You're right. I'm tired of missing you all. I want to do better with you, but don't ask me about Sadie. I'm not going looking for her."

Been there, done that. E doesn't know I found her, but after the cartel got wiped out, he badgered me about searching for her. Told me to beg her for a second chance. I don't have the energy to discuss that heartache again today.

"That's great," he says, but he doesn't light up the way I expect. "Mom will be thrilled. As am I."

Unsure what's up with him, I nod to the bar. "Let me make you a drink. We can hang out."

Move this reunion along. *Fun* brother-bonding time, here we come.

"Um, no." He tugs at the back of his hair again, his eyes still shifty. "I mean, *yes*, I want to stay. But no to the drink. You were right before— about me not needing to talk about Dad. I'm here about something else."

I know E's tone. The nerves in his twitchy moves. He's about to tell me news I don't want to hear. I gnash my teeth, feeling like I'm standing on a sinking ship. "Let's just have a drink. Whatever you want to discuss can wait. I want to hear about your life. What you've been up to."

I start for the bar, sweat gathering along my neck. I can't handle another Bower disaster today. How the hell am I supposed to be fun when I'm constantly getting stuck under avalanches?

"We can't put this off, Des."

"Sure we can."

"I honestly wish we could, but it's not that simple."

The compassion in his voice has my feet faltering, and I forcibly hold in a growl. Can't catching up be reason enough to see each other?

"I really don't have time for drama. Let's just hang out." I march for the bar, determined to have a nice visit with him.

"I'm not here about Dad," he repeats.

I keep strutting, not bothering to turn around.

"It's about Sadie."

The air jets out of my lungs. My throat tightens. I swivel toward him, panic mounting. "Is she okay?"

"She . . . yeah." He nods and swallows slowly. "She's good."

I'm not good. Today's persistent nausea increases. Bringing up Sadie means avoidance is no longer an option. Not when she's involved. "Spit it out, E. Whatever it is, waiting to tell me won't make it easier. It'll only earn you a black eye."

"Yeah, so." He shifts nervously and glances toward the entrance.

Two guys who look a lot like our brothers pass by the window. The door stays shut, but a screech and whine from my left indicates our emergency back exit has opened. I check, and Jake is there, blocking the path.

This is *not* fun. No part of me is having a good time.

If all four of my brothers are here, whatever's happened with Sadie, it can't be good. Maybe it's her parents. While they weren't physically abusive with her, they were emotional terrorists, issuing passive-aggressive insults on a whim, using her as a pawn in their endless fights. Or he's here to tell me he found Sadie in Tennessee. Warn me not to look for her. Explain that she has a husband and kids and a happy life without me. Which would actually be for the best, considering the last time she saw me, I was finishing my first year of Duke Law, top of my class, no crap tattoos in sight.

I squeeze my tremoring hands into fists. "E, what's going on?"

Sadness swimming in his eyes, he approaches slowly and grips my shoulders. It's our oldest brother's signature move—arm gripping to keep us together. My anxiety doubles. "Sadie came to find me in Windfall, Des. And she wasn't alone."

So it *is* the husband thing. I slump, actually relieved. Better that than hearing her parents did something reprehensible or that she's hurt. I try to wrench away from E, but he digs his fingers in deeper. "She has a son, Des."

"Save your breath. I know. And I don't wanna talk about it."

He rears back. "You *know*?"

I huff out a harsh grunt. "I hired a private eye about a month after the Becerras were killed. Called her and heard a kid in the background, then hung up as fast as I fucking could. So yeah, I know she's probably married and happy and living her best life, but thanks for coming and reminding me of everything I've lost. Always a pleasure."

I tug out of his hold.

One step away, he says, "He's *your* kid, Des. The boy you heard is yours. You and Sadie have a son."

My chest caves. Spots flash in my periphery. I must have heard him wrong. I must have fallen asleep earlier into some kind of origami trance. Or I got in an accident and have been in an eleven-year coma.

I swivel and search E's pained face. Forget general nausea. My dormant gag reflex tests its strength. "I don't have a kid."

He smiles for the first time, his expression amused but still strained. "His name's Max. He's ten and has the unfortunate luck of looking like you."

I heave. Almost throw up on his face.

Tripping over my feet, I run to the "b ro m," drop to my knees, and empty the contents of my stomach into a toilet, abolishing my no-puking streak.

TWO

At some indiscriminate time later, while I'm still heaving and dying a violent death, I hear scuffling and talking.

"Is he puking?"

"It's Des. Of course he's not puking."

"He's definitely puking."

"He hasn't puked since we were kids."

My brothers' voices drift more firmly into my consciousness while the room spins and my insides revolt.

"I've never seen someone heave that intensely." E, sounding concerned.

"It's the shock. Get him water." Jake, the oldest, always telling us what to do.

"I think he just hurled up a lung. We should video this." Lennon being Lennon.

"No one's videoing anything. Leave him be." Callahan the Peacekeeper, here to rein in the Bower boys.

A few dry heaves later, one of them tosses a paper towel at my face. I wipe my mouth, somehow manage to crawl out of the bathroom stall, and sit my ass on the floor. When my head becomes too heavy to hold upright, I drop it forward into my hands.

Max. My son. Mine and *Sadie*'s son.

My gut twists again. Worse than the day I was told I had lactose intolerance and Lennon dared me to drink a carton of milk.

Jake crouches in front of me and shoves a glass of water in my hand. "Sadie heard about Dad's tell-all book deal and tracked E down in Windfall, where he's living now. She wants to talk to you and introduce you to Max."

I blink the burn from my eyes and sip the water, functioning by rote, trying to focus, even though it means remembering Dad's infuriating book deal. The news shouldn't have been a shock—some tell-all biography about what it was like working with the cartel, our father's way to earn more money off of our pain. I have no clue what lies he'll tell or what new truths will hurt our family and Mom when the book comes out at the start of next year. I can't rehash his latest betrayal. Panic overrides my anger and nausea.

"How can I be a father?"

"Well," Lennon says, giving me the condescending expression E calls his hipster smirk, "when the penis goes into the vagina and there's rubbing, you—"

Jake punches his arm. "Now's not the time."

Lennon shrugs. "He was probably too busy preening for girls in sex ed. He needs to learn the basics." And Lennon covers his discomfort with bad jokes.

My coping mechanism is more of an explosion.

"Fuck off," I tell him while wincing. A sudden headache grips my temples. Maybe it's a tumor and I'm hallucinating.

"Wait until you see Max." E nudges my shin with his foot. "He has your thick eyelashes. Kid's gonna break hearts."

I try to latch on to that visual, but my body isn't communicating with my brain. I grab the gross garbage bin and dry heave again. Fucking gag reflex making up for twenty-one years of slacking off.

"At least Des is sporting the man bun and we don't have to hold his hair back," Lennon says, snickering.

Without looking up, I give him the finger. I'm not sure what's more shocking about Lennon, the fact that he started an outdoor education program and hasn't earned a lawsuit with his blunt jokes, or that parents trust him with their kids.

A few more empty retches and stomach spasms later, I wipe my mouth. Get to my feet and pace, alternating between crossing my arms and uncrossing them, then glaring at each of my brothers, while the flickering light above the cracked mirror simulates the stroke I feel like I'm having.

Sadie must have gotten pregnant one of the last nights we were together. She was on the pill, but those things aren't foolproof, and there were plenty of times she'd forget to take them. Evenings where she'd jump suddenly and rummage through her purse, laughing with an "I can't believe I forgot again."

She didn't care. I didn't care. Mostly out of the notion of youthful invincibility. In high school, I was voted Most Likely to Drink a Fifth of Vodka without Puking. While I've upheld that badge of honor, I was also voted Most Likely to Drive a Porsche and Most Likely to Grace the Cover of *Forbes*. I worked my ass off and planned my perfect future—finish Duke Law, land a job at a top firm, buy a swank house, escape on Caribbean vacations—never contemplating Sadie getting knocked up along the way. Mostly because I wouldn't have been upset if we'd gotten pregnant.

Now? As horrible as it was thinking she had a family with some other guy, this jolt of fear is a whole other beast.

I stop my frantic pacing and stare at my fractured face in the cracked mirror. My mess of brown hair is knotted on my head. The left side of my neck has the blurred lion tattoo I acquired in a bathroom similar to this. The other side is cleaved by a scar I got in year two of WITSEC. That bar brawl started when a guy told me I should smile more. I'm not sure which fight broke my tooth or when the frown lines on my forehead became permanent. Nothing about me looks like the guy who surprised Sadie at her home with flowers, a cocky grin, and tickets to see Darius Rucker.

Except maybe my soot-colored eyelashes. Those haven't changed.

The ones my son apparently inherited.

"Is he okay?" I manage. "Happy and healthy?"

E rubs the coiled muscles of my back. "He's a great kid. Smart and sweet."

"And happy?" I ask again. The strain in my throat is growing, and I can't swallow. Max grew up without a father. I have no clue what Sadie told him about me, but he must have felt abandoned at times. Alone. Angry.

E's hand presses heavier into my back. "He's okay, Des. We've only met him a few times. He's been a bit quiet and reserved with us, so I don't know him super well yet. But on the surface, he seems happy."

I nod, still barely able to swallow. I keep picturing what he might look like, worrying that my absence in his life hurt him deeply, scarred him in some unseen way. Or maybe Sadie fell for someone else, a man who loved Max and helped him thrive.

My stomach twists, and I grip the sink, refusing to turn around. "Is Sadie seeing someone?"

The scrawled writing on the plaster beside the mirror reads *Go home, you're drunk*. Above that sage advice is a blotch of water stains. I squint at the splotches, picture them as one of Sadie's silly art pieces. I'd call it *The Cliff's Edge*.

"Funny thing about that." E's hesitant reply forces me to face him. He shrugs a shoulder, as though his next words don't have the power to annihilate me. "I don't know if she's seeing anyone."

I fist and release my hands. "How could you not know?"

"I didn't ask."

"Why didn't you ask?" I move to crowd him, grab him, shake him.

Callahan steps his big body in my way. "E was understandably shocked when Sadie found him. He didn't think to ask."

Yeah, okay. That makes sense. *Kind of.* My first ten minutes with this knowledge was spent with my face in a toilet. But E's been after me to call him back for *five months.* They've all clearly met my son and Sadie during that time. Mom would have been dying to meet her grandson.

Mom. I squeeze my eyes shut, clenching my fists until my jagged nails cut my skin. Mom lost everything: the husband she falsely trusted, aspects of her kids when our innocence and happiness were put through a trash compactor. Her friends. Her life. Now this?

I can't ask about Mom and find out if this news was the last straw. A guy can only take so much. And my brothers are toying with me. I force my eyes open and scowl at them. "You've all seen Sadie and met Max, yeah?"

"We have," Cal says.

"And none of you thought to ask if she's single?" Swear to God, my head might explode from this piercing headache.

"Oh, no. We did." Lennon grins. "We decided it's not our business."

I curl my lip. "Which one of you wants his teeth knocked out first?"

They all point at Lennon, who balks. "What did I do?"

"Look." Jake intervenes, clasping the back of my neck, forcing my likely wild eyes to meet his. "We're done with lies in this family." His grip on my neck tightens. "If she's with someone else, we figured you'd cut and run again. E thought it was better if we didn't ask and open up that possibility. So while we've seen her and Max a few times, and she's always come alone, we haven't asked specifics, and she didn't offer. Whatever her relationship status, you need to swallow this pain, step up, and be a father to your son. If you want to know if Sadie's single and you three can be a proper family, you'll have to ask her yourself."

A proper family. Has this guy seen my face? The horrible ink forever etched into my skin? And I'm not exactly flush with cash. I have savings from earning tips and living small, but not enough to pay for a kid's sports programs and college tuition.

Another glance in the mirror has a worse thought sucker punching me. Of the five of us, I'm the one who looks most like our father, the man who lied to us for years, made the Everest of selfish decisions, and ruined our mother's and our lives. What if I inherited more than a strong jaw, thick eyelashes, and lactose intolerance from him?

I mean, Jesus. I'm standing here thinking about Sadie's relationship status, how that affects *me*, when all I should be worried about is my kid.

Unable to handle another "You can do it!" pep talk, I shove past my brothers and bolt from the bar.

THREE

For as long as I can remember, my outside hasn't matched my inside. In my early twenties I was all jock, clean cut and cocky and put together, but I still worried I'd blank in a courtroom.

During my nights with Sadie, we'd sometimes lie on my bed or outside stargazing, wrapped around each other, talking quietly about our hopes and dreams.

"I applied for the summer internship at the Contemporary Art Museum," she whispered one night. "The one in Raleigh."

We lay on the rocky edge of Bear Lake, listening to the murmur of the water as I stroked her soft hair. "It's the perfect fit for you, but you sound nervous?"

"I just want it so bad. I mean, I'd basically be a glorified coffee fetcher, but it's a start. And I'd be around such creative people. Hopefully prove myself enough that they'd hire me for a real job after school. And I could work my way up. Maybe even curate art one day, build the kind of exhibitions that change how people think." She slumped into me on a sigh. "I hate wanting something this much, even though it's not even a real job."

"You, Sadie Jones, are clever and creative. Anyone would be lucky to have you, and it *is* real. It's the start of your dreams. But yeah, I get the fear. I feel like that about Duke."

"You're worried you won't get in?"

"I *have* to get in." I'd recently sent in my application. Had worked my ass off and was sure I'd be accepted, but I'd been uneasy since, something bigger than the admissions process making me edgy.

"There are other schools," Sadie said. "It doesn't matter where you study."

"Duke is the real deal, Sprite. The best law school in the state. It'll change our future." Allow me to give her everything she deserved. Security. Happiness. A pretty house with beautiful artwork on the walls. No yelling parents and sleepless nights. "Getting in will set us up for life. It's Duke or die."

"So dramatic," she teased, then ran her nose up my neck. "I have no doubt it'll be Duke."

"But what if I graduate and realize I'm not smart enough in the end?"

It was dark out, the moon brushing Sadie with a faint glimmer. She pushed up to her elbow and gazed down at me. "Not smart enough for what?"

"To be the kind of lawyer who makes a difference. I have these nightmares sometimes—panic dreams where I'm standing in a courtroom and can't speak. Or when I *do* speak, garbled words come out." Stupid words. I could picture myself in a courtroom, commanding attention the way I commanded a football field, but the reality of being a lawyer felt out of reach.

She flattened her palm on my chest, could probably feel the nervous pound of my heart. "The smartest men are the humble ones who don't expect the world to fall at their feet."

"But what if I can't do this? What if I learn this stuff but blank when it matters?"

"Well"—she pressed a tender kiss to my cheek—"starting anything new is daunting, but you're a hard worker. No matter how tough law school is, your determination will lead you to success. And we can practice. Rehearse the vocabulary you'll need, stuff a lawyer might say."

She tapped my temple. "Give this big, beautiful brain of yours more confidence."

Sadie Jones, forever my best friend.

I cupped her gorgeous face, my chest so chock full of emotion I couldn't name the tight pull behind my ribs. The harshness of my breaths, like Sadie's kindness and love singed the air, filling my lungs with a hot rush of devotion so strong it threatened to burn me up. "I love you, Sprite. So damn much."

I kissed her deeply, needed to share my building fever before it incinerated me, leaving nothing but the remnants of my Sadie-filled heart.

Two slower kisses later, she nestled against my chest, tucked her head under my chin. "I didn't know love could be like this."

"Like what?" I said roughly.

"Unconditional. So . . . big. I didn't know what family was until I met you."

"I'm your family now," I growled with protectiveness. "Not your folks." The assholes who fought ceaselessly and dragged Sadie through their animosity, or her sister, who was a lot older and rarely around, leaving Sadie to deal with their parents alone. "You need anything, you come to me. You feel unloved or sad, you call *me* or turn up at my door, day or night, and I'll show you what real love is."

She hugged me hard enough to bruise my ribs. We didn't kiss again. Just held each other tighter than tight, leaving no room for anything but our love and mutual support.

So consumed and happy with Sadie, I bought her an engagement ring the next year, three months before my WITSEC vanishing act, but I never proposed. Because, deep down, like before law school, Cocky Clean-Cut Me was a showboat who worried about failure.

These days I look like a meth dealer. I'm the scowling guy you'd spot and quickly cross to the opposite side of the street. *Dangerous*, that's what my blurred tattoos and resting pissed-off face read. Yet here I am, standing across from Rituals—my mother's local coffee joint—drowning in Sadie memories, on the verge of an internal meltdown.

It's been two hours since my brothers rigged me with C-4 and lit the fuse. I've been walking the streets since then, occasionally pulling out my phone and staring at Sadie's number, unable to dial, low-grade panic simmering in my gut. I walked here instead. To Rituals. The place I always find my mother, even though she's only ever inside in the mornings.

Today, she's here at this late afternoon hour. Like she's clairvoyant. Or maybe she just has a mother's intuition and knew I'd come to search her out.

I push into the familiar café, my head hung low and hands stuffed into my pockets. Chelsea Bower takes one look at me, and her eyes fill. She doesn't ask if I've called Sadie. She doesn't yell at me for ignoring the family or say she's sorry for this latest crushing shock. She stands, fits herself against my chest, and gives me a hug.

A sound escapes me. I'm not sure what it is. But . . . fuck. I think it's a *sob*.

Mom rubs my back. Another horrible sound moves through my chest.

"Sorry. Rough day." I try to push away from her.

She hugs my waist harder. "This isn't a rough day, Desmond. It's a devastating decade and a shocking surprise."

I hug her back. Squeeze her and make a few more embarrassing sounds. Jazzy music plays, reminding me of Mirielle's record collection. Only a few other tables are occupied, and I sense their attention on us. When I gather the few remnants of my composure, I kiss the top of her head and sit at her table.

"I'm glad you came here," she says softly.

I grunt and discreetly wipe at my eyes.

"I'm guessing you haven't called Sadie yet."

This grunt sounds strangled.

Even though I practiced law words with Sadie—*usufruct, prima facie, peremptory*—I've learned to appreciate the nuance of a grunt. Not only has the clipped sound kept people from asking about my past and forcing me to lie, but one guttural noise can mean so many things:

Hi

Bye

Yes

No

Fuck off

Fuck you

Fuck *yes*

Get out of my fucking way

Or in this case, *I'm terrified and have no clue what to say to Sadie.*

Mom's hair is in its usual ponytail, pulled back to reveal every earned stress line and the darker circles under her eyes. Her coffee mug is empty, the napkin beside it shredded to bits. She's obviously been here for a while, waiting for me, unsure if I'd turn up. Her son, forever making her life harder. I ready myself for a reprimand, annoyance that I've been avoiding her and my brothers so long.

She studies me for an unnerving moment, then she does the last thing I expect. She smiles. "Why do you think Eleanor relied so heavily on her routines?"

I startle at the question, then feel my facial muscles shift, the tension from my frown easing slightly. I guess we're doing book club. "I think it was a way to manage her stress. Her crosswords. Eating the same foods. Doing the same job in the same way. They were things in her life she could control." I'm talking about Eleanor in *Eleanor Oliphant Is Completely Fine*, but an itch forms under the crew neck of my black T-shirt. I'm also kind of talking about me. "What I don't get is how Raymond could be so patient with her."

"I think Raymond could see beyond Eleanor's practiced facade. I think he knew, deep down, she was uniquely special."

The way her expression softens, I think she's talking about me too.

Regardless, we go on like this. Asking and answering book questions, like I haven't just received terrifying, life-altering news. Because this is what we do.

Or more specifically it's what *I* do.

Before we learned the cartel got wiped out, I kept tabs on my four brothers from afar, walking by their apartments, making sure all looked well, even when they thought I was incommunicado. When it came to Mom, I'd covertly check up on her by staking out Rituals.

Every morning, she'd visit the coffee shop and sit by herself, glancing wistfully at tables of laughing friends. Like us, she never formed relationships during WITSEC. Lying about who you are doesn't foster closeness or true happiness, and her husband's deception made her feel naive and small, destroyed her trust in people. She even abandoned her career as a science teacher—the job she put on hold to raise us—opting for tutoring in smaller controlled environments instead.

On her particularly wistful days, when the sadness on her face was too much, I'd walk into Rituals, sit with her, and say things like, "I thought us boys were as bad as siblings got. Lakshmi and Radha had us beat" (*The Henna Artist*) or "If I was Afi, I'd never have married Eli" (*His Only Wife*).

A lengthy book discussion would ensue. We wouldn't mention WITSEC or poke and prod each other's emotional bruises. We'd just sit and talk and pretend like I wasn't a mess and like she wasn't a mess and like our family wasn't a mess. Until the day she took one look at me and burst into tears. I've never told my brothers about our book club of two. Pretty sure she hasn't either. There's no question I'd get the ribbing of the century.

"I think moving forward is what's hardest for her," Mom says, explaining why she feels Eleanor has spent so much of her life stuck. "I think she's scared to depend on others. That if she looks too deeply at why she acts the way she does and keeps people at a distance, she'll lose what little control she has and fall apart."

Yeah, we're definitely talking about me. *Me*, stuck. *Me*, shunning my family. *Me*, afraid to fall apart. Which is really fucking close to happening.

Leaning my elbows on the small table, I rub my forehead. "I don't know how to process all of this."

"Of course you don't. But that's what you have family for. We want to be here for you, Des. Help you any way we can. That's all we've ever wanted."

An uncomfortable twinge twists my gut. "Are you sure about that?"

She sits straighter. "Of course we do."

"Seeing me just adds stress to your lives," I say through my clenched jaw. "Everything about me pisses off my brothers. When I'm around, I know they feel furious. Want to murder our father for all the shit he pulled. I'm a constant reminder of how much we lost, how much he messed up our lives. And I don't want that for you all."

"Desmond." She clutches her chest. "Is that why you've pushed us away so much? Because you think being around you hurts *us* too much?"

"I don't know." I rub my face, wanting to scrape off a layer of skin. "I made you *cry*."

"And I told you afterward that it wasn't your fault. I was having a bad day, and you happened to be there at the wrong time. Truth is"—she gives my forearm a squeeze, stilling my fidgeting—"the less we see you, the *more* we hurt. We need you in our lives, no matter what shape you're in, so we can feel whole."

For a decade, I've assumed they were better off without the reminders I bring them. The day Mom broke down and apologized, I assumed she was lying about the *why* of it, trying to ease my guilt. I look most like Dad. I lost the most when I raged at the world and gave up on life.

With how hard E searched for me this time, and Mom's vehement words now, I'm no longer sure that's the case.

I pass my hand over my mouth, too goddamn overwhelmed. Sadie. Having a kid. Facing my family for the first time in too long. I also want to drop napalm on my father's house for taking everything from me: Sadie, law, happiness, a son I didn't get the chance to raise. But prison isn't high on my bucket list.

"I don't know the first thing about kids," I force out. "What if I'm terrible at being a dad? What if I mess him up somehow or hurt him?"

"As scary as this is for you," Mom says evenly, "there's only one wrong move here."

I tongue my cracked tooth. "What's that?"

"Doing nothing."

I stare at her.

"Not calling Sadie is doing nothing. Running off and ignoring your family is doing nothing. Pretending you're fine when you're not is doing nothing. All of that only leads to loneliness and heartache."

"But what if doing nothing is the best thing I could do for Sadie and Max? I'm not the man she knew, or the driven lawyer she expected me to become. Do I look like a responsible adult who can take care of another human being?"

"You, Desmond, look like a man who reads books he doesn't always enjoy just to make his mother happy and take her mind off her troubles. Does that sound like a bad man to you?"

The sentiment makes a dent in my turmoil, but she's simplifying things. Me. My nature. I've apparently become a Walter who doesn't know how to have fun. A guy who no longer laughs in the face of challenge or takes bad news well.

In the early days of WITSEC, I worried myself into a frenzy. Panicked over how Sadie was coping with my sudden disappearance, wondering just how devastated she was, unsure who she'd call when her parents dragged her into the middle of one of their fights.

Forbidden to reach out, I stomped around our house viciously, yelled more, got into bar fights, ranted that I didn't care about the fucking cartel and fucking death threats. But I did. We were under strict orders not to contact anyone from our past. One wrong move could paint targets on all our heads, and I would *not* let anything happen to my brothers or Mom. But shutting Sadie out?

I didn't know a living heart could turn to ash.

All the while, I had no clue she was pregnant *with my child.*

"You've seen her," I say hesitantly. "Sadie seems good? And . . . Max? E said he's a sweet kid but didn't mention much else."

"Max is amazing." Mom grins the widest I've seen in eons. Must be a grandmother's grin. "He's creative and smart, although on the quiet side. And Sadie is a sweetheart, as always. She seems like she's doing really well."

Probably because she has a man in her life. Some other guy who's loving her and raising our son, giving her the family love she never had.

A tornado of emotion whips through me. "I just . . ." I look at my stalwart mother, barely able to speak through this suffocating ache. "I loved her so much, Ma."

So *goddamn* much.

The creases by her mouth deepen. "I know. What you two had was incredibly special."

"I've wanted to see her for so long, talk to her. Now the idea has me nearly passing out. And that's without adding a *son* into the mix."

"Because there's so much unfinished history between you two. I can't promise you'll get her back, but everything with Max is bigger than that. You have to call her. Waiting won't make this easier."

I work my clenched jaw and grunt.

Translation: *It's time to ditch Daniel Baker for good and figure out if Desmond Bower still exists.*

"Think I'll call her outside, but I promise to be in touch."

"You better."

I kiss Mom's temple and head for the street, feeling on the electrocuted side of frazzled. There's a small park a block down. I walk toward it, mentally talking myself up to the task. I may not be the put-together guy of my early twenties, but Mom's right. I *have* taken care of her and the family in my own way. And Mirielle wouldn't have befriended a total fuckup, even though she loves to torment me. If I can learn a thing or two about kids, I might not even be a disaster with Max.

That's what I need. A plan. The past decade has been nothing but rash, knee-jerk decisions. Being a father will take dedication and preparedness. I have no clue how I'll handle seeing Sadie and facing the intense emotions she inspires, but there are more important factors at play.

First, I have to call her.

I sit on a park bench and run my thumb over my phone, my heart pounding faster the longer I wait. A kid glides down a slide into his father's open arms. My chest spasms, and my palms turn sweaty.

Taking a huge breath, I dial Sadie's number.

It rings once, and my thudding heart shoves into my throat.

The second ring has my lungs swelling so fast I'm sure they'll burst.

The third ring—

"Hello?"

At the sound of Sadie's voice, something in me *does* burst. I think it's my brain, the part responsible for speech. I make a garbled sound, like my courtroom nightmares have actualized, and I can only mumble unintelligent nonsense.

Planting my elbows on my knees, I clear my throat. "Hi, Sadie. It's . . ." *Daniel,* I almost say. The name I still use. But nothing's the same anymore. "It's Desmond."

Her breath catches. "Des? Oh my God. Is it really you?"

My stomach drops to my feet. Then plummets through the earth's crust. I somehow move my hand and massage my brow. "Yeah, honey. It's me."

I wince at the endearment. I have no right to call her honey. At least I didn't slip and call her *Sprite*. That nickname's too *us*. Too fun loving and cute. "I'm kind of freaking out here. I can't believe . . ." That I'm hearing her ethereal voice again. That we have a son.

The words dry up on my tongue.

"I know. God, I know. When I heard about your dad's book and put two and two together—Des, what you've been through. I was so mad for so long. Now . . ." She doesn't finish either. There's too much that's too hard to say. Eleven years of hurt and confusion.

I swallow past the razor blades in my throat. "How is he? Our . . . son. Is he okay? Happy and healthy?" I keep asking everyone the same damn questions, struggling to believe each reassuring reply.

"Tries my patience like you did." A watery laugh slips through the line. "And he's kind of going through a rough patch with friends and finding his confidence, but he's great. He's my everything." Her voice catches but also softens with fondness.

Relief should have me smiling. A portion of my ruptured heart should regenerate. Instead, it feels as though something's crushing my windpipe. The extent of what I've missed is staggering—Max learning to talk, walk, make friends, fight with those friends. Max hurting, crying, laughing. I wouldn't even recognize him if I saw him on the street. "I'm so sorry, Sadie. For everything. If I'd known . . ."

What? What would I have done? Risked her *and* our child just to be together?

I bite my cheek, blink to clear the sting from my eyes, because my tear ducts have suddenly become Niagara fucking Falls.

"Getting pregnant was a shock to me at the time too," she says softly. "I mean, it was the pill. I was never good at taking it on time. I just never expected that surprise."

Silence descends. She breathes quietly in my ear. I focus on the grass, brush my boot over the spiky blades, my stomach spinning from the mere sounds of her muffled breaths.

"We just moved back to Windfall," she finally says. "I missed it so much, and it makes sense with E here, finally having family close, although we haven't seen him since we got back. Things have been so busy. And I tried to wait, not introduce Max to your family before he met you, but finding you took so long."

She's probably busy because she's married or in a relationship, doing her best to navigate that guy's feelings while bringing my family into Max's life. Sadie is smart, fun, creative, gorgeous. A woman like her doesn't stay single for eleven years.

I jam my elbow into the bench back, mumble "*Fuck*" under my breath.

"What's that?" she asks.

"Nothing." Just me being too chickenshit to ask if she's single, and I'm focusing on the wrong thing again. *Me.* My selfish desire to have a second chance with Sadie, when our son is who needs my focus. "I have some stuff to deal with here before I come, but I want to meet him as soon as possible."

"Actually . . ." A different hesitation tinges her voice. A hint of reservation? "Is it okay if you and I meet first, without Max?"

"Of course. Whatever you think is best." But apprehension simmers in my gut. "Are you worried about how he'll react?"

"Sort of. Like I said, he's going through a tough time with his friends and his confidence. He's very reserved with your family and has been off lately. He's had a lot of change in his life recently, and I want to find a way to ease him into this."

A stab of helplessness slices through me. Worry for the son I don't even know, but I'm flying blind here. "If you think that's best, sure. We'll figure this out together."

"Thanks," she says softly. "And, Des?"

"Yeah?"

"It's so great to hear your voice."

Her husk-tinged voice has dismantled me, but the connection has also reignited my determination. Based on Sadie's hesitancy to introduce me to Max, I was right about needing a plan before meeting him. A strategy to ease him into this new transition. Keep him safe emotionally. Figure out how to be a good dad in the process.

An idea forms. One that will take a ton of work, along with a shot of optimism. The largest obstacle, though, will be getting Lennon on board with my ramshackle plan.

FOUR

You know that saying "Time flies when you're having fun"? Fun fact: it also flies when you're scared shitless. It's been three weeks since I spoke with Sadie. We've texted since then, but she's been too busy with work and Max to meet me sooner. Although disappointed, I've used my time wisely. I bought a *How to Parent for Dummies* book. When I read the chapter that said kids react positively if adults share their "feelings," I started to sweat. While I feel more panicked than dad ready, I'm running full-steam ahead with my potential meet-Max plan.

In three nerve-racking days, I'll be facing the love of my life for the first time in eleven years to share said plan. Today, I'm facing my family, asking for help, also for the first time in eleven years. Milestones abound these days.

We're in our usual meeting place, Lennon's equally bland Houston apartment. Like my stark place, the sparse furniture is function over form, most of it acquired through garage sales or IKEA. The only aspect that makes his apartment nicer than mine is his vintage *The Invisible Man* movie poster on his wall. Wish I came up with that WITSEC zinger.

"So." I eye my family, unaccustomed to being the convener of our gatherings.

Callahan, Jake, and Lennon are squished on the couch facing me. Mom's sitting on Lennon's small end table. E's leaning into the wall, his arm wrapped around Delilah, the two of them so happy together some of my anxiety ebbs.

While Delilah was a pretty girl back in the day, she's a gorgeous woman now, with big curly hair and those vibrant blue eyes. And she appears happy. Regardless of how E's disappearance hurt her, she seems to have grown into herself and thrived. Knowing my determined brother, he likely fought tooth and nail for her.

Channeling some of his strength, I clear my throat. "I'm meeting Sadie in a few days."

"With that hair?" Lennon shades his eyes like he's watching a horror film.

I snarl, already losing my cool.

"No, seriously." He turns to E. "He's cutting the Fabio locks, right?"

"It's kind of grown on me." E twirls one of Delilah's curls around his finger. "I like how the loose pieces cascade around his face."

Jake spreads his legs into Cal's and Lennon's space. "When it's down, it does cover the hairy amoeba ink on his neck."

"It'll give him and Sadie something to talk about," Callahan adds. "They can swap hairstyle suggestions."

I clamp my jaw so tight my ears hurt.

"The long hair softens his face," Mom says, grinning the way she does when her boys are joking instead of scowling or fighting. And I can't stay annoyed. Not when Mom's happy.

If being the butt of everyone's jokes makes her smile, my idiot brothers can take their shots. "Are you assholes done being assholes?"

Lennon scratches his reddish hipster beard. "For now."

"Right. So." I roll my shoulders back and crack my neck. "I need your help."

No one moves. The apartment's AC kicks on with a whir.

"We're here for you," Cal says, breaking the silence. "Whatever you need."

What I need is a crystal ball. "Like I said, I'm meeting Sadie in a few days. She's not bringing Max. Said he's going through a tough time, and she's worried meeting me could set him back. I'm dying to meet him, but the last thing I want is to hurt him in any way. So . . ." I turn to Lennon and huff out a sigh, knowing he'll be insufferable about this. "I need you to start a branch of your kids' camp in Windfall and hire me to lead hikes."

The bastard smacks his leg and grabs his ribs, cracking up. "Sorry, I—" He laughs harder, tipping over. "I thought you said you want me to—" And again. "Hire you to work with *kids*."

I glare at him.

"That's enough." Mom's firm tone silences Lennon's snickering. "What exactly are you wanting, Des?"

They all stare at me.

Feeling twitchy, I shove my hands into my jean pockets. "I haven't spoken to Sadie about this yet and don't know the details of what's going on with Max, but I was thinking he might do better meeting me without knowing who I am. Pressure-free time for us to get to know each other. So when he does learn I'm his father, he won't be so over-whelmed. Since Lennon already has these outdoors programs, I thought leading hikes with Max in the group would be a great way to make that work, but only if Sadie agrees. And if any of you see him during that time, you'd have to play along with the plan."

"So you want to *lie* to your son?" E narrows his eyes. As do the rest of my brothers.

Even Mom's face pinches. "Lying is no way to start a relationship with Max. You should know that better than anyone."

The rebuke stings, but I'm not a criminal using my family to cover my money laundering.

"I'm trying to do *right* by Max. Find a way to make this transition go as smoothly for him as possible. And I don't know anything about kids. If I accidentally do something to hurt or disappoint him, make whatever he's going through harder . . ." I blink hard, trying to clear the burn behind my eyes. "I *won't* hurt or disappoint him. One wrong move could scar him for life. And like I said, Sadie gets the final vote on this, but it's important you're all on board."

When no one speaks, I force out a quiet "*Please.*"

Lennon massages his beard, taking his sweet-ass time. "Just to be clear, you want me to move my business so I can hire a tattooed alcoholic who just admitted he knows nothing about kids?"

Cal smacks Lennon's head. Jake smirks.

I consider knocking the know-it-all look from Lennon's face, but I unclench my fists. "I know you all think I'm some raging alcoholic, but that's because you barely see me. Which is my fault," I add before they pipe in. "Yes, I used to go on benders and graced you with my worst, but most of that time I was just hanging out alone in my apartment, *sober.* I barely drink these days, and I took classes the past month. First aid, CPR, and an eight-day outdoors instructor course. I even earned a babysitting certificate with a bunch of little girls. Since hiking is another version of walking, I consider myself fairly qualified now."

"I'm thrilled you took courses," Lennon says, gesturing wildly as he talks, "but this is my business reputation. When you lead kids on hikes, you can't just grunt and glare. A team leader's job is to build self-esteem. You have to make it *fun* for them. Offer interactive nature lessons and keep them on track. It may sound easy, but it takes work and patience. Do you honestly think you have the patience to handle a group of obnoxious kids?"

"I used to take Cal frog catching. This is just like that."

"Yeah, but . . ." Cal gives a sheepish wince. "You used to nail me with rocks."

"I won't do that part."

"Um." E raises his hand. "Did no one catch the fact that Des took a *babysitting* course?"

They all snicker. Except Lennon, but I don't waver. For ten years of witness protection, my choices were ripped from me. I barely remember what it's like to have a goal and work toward it, but this determination feels good. Important.

I square my chest and stare him down.

Jake gives me his oldest-brother look—stern brown eyes boring into me. "Taking on part of Lennon's programming is no joke, as is being responsible for a group of kids. You're sure you have your shit together and won't mess this up?"

"I'm sure," I say, but a tremor runs through my hands. If this happens, I'll have to buy more dummy books about being around kids.

Mom stands from the end table and comes to my side. "If this is what you need, we'll support you. Lennon." She runs a hand down my back and faces my infuriating brother. "You've talked about how your programs aren't as busy in Houston as you'd like. Moving things to Windfall could help. Or you could set up a separate operation there for this one program."

He doesn't answer, but he doesn't say no.

E rubs the small scar through his top lip the way he does when he's nervous or thinking.

I gave him that defining mark the day he drew a picture of me with an inflated head. In retaliation, I threatened to tell Delilah he had wet dreams about her. A few flying fists later, E's face went through the glass coffee table, and I was grounded for a week. Although the two of us laughed about it afterward, I snuck out that night and fixed E's broken bicycle. He assumed Callahan, who was always quick to be the family pacifier, had done it. I never told him otherwise, and I don't have it in me to tell him how on the edge of splintering I am now.

He stares at me another beat, then drops his obstinate chin. "I don't love the lying part, but it sounds like this might be best for Max. As long as you protect Lennon's business and Sadie agrees, I'll play along."

Jake and Callahan grunt their agreement.

"Have you all forgotten about me." Lennon waves at us. "I'm the one you need to convince, and I'm not going to Windfall. I have no interest in living there."

"But Maggie asks about you all the time," E says, his tone antagonistic. Like he's got dirt on Lennon.

Lennon's neck flames red. "Like I said, I'm not going there."

Unsure why those two are having a stare-off, I move between them and focus on Lennon. "You don't need to be there. Like Mom said, we'll keep it as a small satellite operation. One summer program and that's it. *If* you trust me to not sink your reputation."

I wouldn't trust me, but this is all I've got. A Hail Mary pass snapped into the end zone, with the clock running down and the opposing team in the lead.

Lennon's eyes dart to each of us, squinting as he breathes loudly. "I don't have a say in this, do I?"

"Depends if you value that hipster beard and those eyebrows." Jake makes a razor-buzzing sound.

"For the millionth time, I am *not* a hipster." Lennon's nostrils flare. "But, fuck it. Fine. You're hired. If we do this, though, he has to listen to everything I say and follow all my rules. If he tanks my reputation, you're all responsible."

We mutter our assent.

Lennon steeples his fingers. "And you all have to quit calling me a hipster."

Jake snorts. "Forget that."

E downright guffaws. "Not happening."

"But he *is* a hipster," Cal says with exaggerated confusion.

"The clothes speak for themselves," I say, gesturing to his skinny jeans and short-sleeved floral button-down, which he for sure bought at a thrift store.

He mouths, *Fuck off,* then points to his room. "You and I need to have a word in private."

He marches ahead of me and swivels once we're alone, pointing at my chest. "This is my livelihood, and those kids' parents will be putting their trust in you. So I need a promise that you feel capable. That those courses you took sunk in."

Instead of slapping his pointing finger away like I normally would, I blow out a rough breath and pull him into a hug. "Thank you for this. I know it's asking a lot, but I took those courses seriously. I won't let you down."

He sags into me and hugs me really fucking tight. "I've missed you, man. *This* you," he adds.

"Yeah." I pound his back. "Me too."

We step apart, and his hipster smirk returns. "Please tell me there's a picture of you at the babysitting course."

I raise my middle finger. "I've rented a small house in Ruby Grove. It's an hour from Windfall. Close enough without inviting a shit ton of gossip, and most hiking trails are between the towns. Figured I'd put flyers around that area, and I'll ask E to put some up in Windfall. Get as many kids involved as possible. Do you have something standard you do? Or should I make my own?"

"I have stuff. I'll email you the basics, and you can fill in the dates. With the shorter notice, enrollment will likely be small, but"—he nudges my shoulder—"I appreciate the effort, brother of mine."

"Like I said, I'm taking this seriously. Hopefully Sadie agrees to the plan."

Her potential reaction is one of a million concerns that's stolen my sleep recently. When texting each other the past weeks, I kept my intentions about our meeting vague, preferring to broach this proposition in person. I've also refrained from asking about her personal life. Max is my focus. I'm a new dad trying to navigate new-dad difficulties. There's no reason whatsoever—absolutely *none*—to get personal with Sadie at this juncture. If she's dating someone, I doubt I'll even care.

Frowning, I rub the twinge in my chest.

Lennon scratches his neck, his attention darting between me and his hipster shoes. "You must be losing your mind about seeing Max." His eyes flick up to catch mine. "You doing okay?"

On the verge of puking again most days—my new super fun, stress-induced habit. Thankfully, Mirielle has been extra pushy with the crocheting, which is a disaster for my thick fingers, but the focus occupies my mind. "The lead-up is a lot, but I'll be fine."

"What about Sadie?"

"What about her?"

"Have you asked if she's single?"

The turbulent seas in my stomach take an uneasy sway. "It's not important right now."

He narrows his eyes at me. "Because you're worried about what she'll say?"

"Because"—I lean into him and curl my lip—"*it's not important right now.*"

And why does it suddenly feel so damn warm in here?

"You know . . ." Lennon clasps his hands behind his back and sways slightly. "I'm sensing a pattern with you."

"Funny, I'm sensing you might get punched in the face."

He waves his hand vaguely. "Your whole tough-guy thing, shutting out the family for months at a time, pretending you're not dying to find out if Sadie's single."

"Is there a point to your useless observations?"

He struts leisurely toward his window and stares out of it a moment. "Truth or dare?" he finally says.

His abrupt turn in conversation has my abdomen flexing with dread.

As a teen, Lennon loved playing truth or dare. Being the cocky troublemakers we were, we played along, dares being the only obvious choice. Lennon's provoking games led to Jake stealing Mr. Hatcher's doorbell (Hatcher the Hatchet owned the local slaughterhouse and was always carrying bloody cleavers). Cal streaked across Kemani Tatum's (former Miss Virginia's) lawn. E put Krazy Glue on my hairbrush and got a black eye for his efforts (I wound up having to shave my head down to stubble). The endless games also led to lactose-intolerant me drinking that carton of milk.

And here Lennon is, asking me to play truth or dare. "I'm not playing your childish games."

He nods. "Dare it is."

Without another word, he marches back into the living room before I can sit on him and force him to share what horrible idea he's planning.

Whatever. I have too much on my plate to worry about his schemes. Tomorrow, I'll be driving to North Carolina, where I'll eventually be seeing Sadie for the first time in eleven years. Somehow, I have to face the woman I loved without falling apart or puking in a toilet again.

FIVE

Anxiety has become my persistent sidekick. Although I haven't seen Sadie yet and asked her to okay my Max-hiking suggestion, I'm moving ahead with my plans. Even if she doesn't like the idea of hiding who I am from Max, I'm hoping she'll still let him join the hikes, give us that time together. Since I promised Lennon I'd help boost his business, I've been walking around Ruby Grove all morning, putting up flyers.

The start of my outing went okay. This picturesque town where I'm living is nestled among the Rough Ridge Mountains, with cobbled sidewalks and old-fashioned lampposts like Windfall, but without the landslide of memories. I've been getting plenty of questioning glances, but I've gone about my business. Stayed focused. A man with a plan.

Now I'm dissolving at a rapid pace.

Lennon's flyers are partly to blame. Each paper reads, **Littlewing Outdoor Camp! Sign up for wilderness learning and adventure! Fresh air and fun for all!**

The number of exclamations alone have me sweating, and this is the last one I'm putting up. Outside of Biff's Diner. The place where I'm meeting Sadie in ten pulse-racing minutes.

Anxiety Central, *party of one.*

With the last flyer secured, I store my supplies in my Camaro—yes, I drive a rusty yellow Camaro, not the Porsche from my high school's Most Likely To list—then head for the area behind the diner.

To protect Max, I suggested we meet outside of Windfall. If Sadie wants to delay him meeting me, the last thing they need is the town's rumor mill catching wind of my return. So here I am, lurking around the diner's outside back corner, like the seedy meth dealer I resemble, staring at the entrance to the parking lot. I can't allow Sadie to see me before I see her. There's no question my first glimpse of her will flatten me. I'll need a minute (or ninety) to recalibrate.

A car pulls into the gravel lot. I attempt to see through its dusty windshield while my heart trains for a heavyweight match against my ribs. A woman's driving, but I can't make out her features. She parks, finally shoves open her door, and . . . it's not her.

I suck in a ragged breath. Can't hear anything but the deafening pound of my heart. One glimpse of a woman who isn't Sadie, and I'm a minute from passing out.

Not cool.

I bounce on my toes and shake out my body, like I'm sparring in my gym's boxing ring. I throw some jabs and try to find the toughened survivor I am under all this feverish anxiety.

Another car pulls in. A red Honda. It drives slower, its tires crunching over the gravel as I tuck back behind the diner's corner and squint. The car parks too far away to see much. Nothing happens. The door doesn't open. Whoever's in there doesn't get out. And somehow, I know.

Sadie's in there.

She's nervous and frazzled, like me, unsure how it'll feel to see me again. Except I'm not unsure about that part. I know seeing her will knock me on my ass. A one-two punch that ends with me in the dirt.

A couple of minutes later, about two seconds before the arrythmia I've suddenly acquired causes me to pass out, the Honda's door opens. A woman gets out. And *hell*.

It's my girl.

She's still tiny and ethereal looking, with big eyes and the delicate cheekbones of a Tolkien elf. Her hair's more sun-kissed blonde than honey, with darker roots. But her lips—they're still kiss-pink and perfect.

I slam my hand against the diner's exterior and brace.

A few harsh breaths later, I stretch my neck and gather myself. The fact that Sadie's still gorgeous and my insides are doing some kind of circus act doesn't matter. We're simply here to discuss our son, not us. If I could lead my high school football team to the state championship and ace first-year law, I can surely walk into a diner and face the woman I once loved madly.

Fists clenched, I round the corner and freeze.

Sadie hasn't walked in yet. She's standing outside the door, her back to me. I debate returning to my hiding spot, but there's no point. Dragging out this meeting won't do either of us any good.

Two steps toward her, I realize she's on the phone. When I'm a few feet away, I hear her say, "What if this is a bad idea?"

My muscles fuse. I suddenly regret not hiding.

"No. Not like that," she goes on. "Just . . . E keeps being vague, not telling me much about Des except that he's been in rough shape." A pause. "Maybe. Things are just so fragile with Max. And I'm nervous Des has changed so much I won't recognize him, or that I won't like who he is now. Or he won't be good for Max. Or maybe I won't recognize myself around him. I've worked so hard to rebuild my life, and everything with Des was always so intense. Amazing and perfect, but I'm not sure I can be strong around him." She slumps forward, seems to rub her eyes. "Or I'm overthinking everything."

I have her beat on overthinking, and aside from *amazing* and *perfect*, every word she uttered was a shot to my chest.

Won't like who he is now.

Won't be good for Max.

Won't recognize myself around him.

An irrational fear of losing her all over again roars to life, but there's no point dwelling on my tangled emotions. She's not mine to lose.

She's making soft sounds of agreement, acknowledging whatever it is the person on the phone's saying.

I clear my raw throat and say, "Sadie."

She swivels and jerks. Goes completely still, then mutters something into her phone. She tries to put her cell away, but there's no missing the way she fumbles getting her purse open. I shift on my feet, unsure what to do, hating how jittery she is.

She breathes harder and presses one hand over her mouth, as though she's struggling not to cry. And I can't take it. I step toward her and . . . nothing. I can't do a damn thing. Hug her. Console her. I lost that right eleven years ago.

"Sadie, honey. Please don't cry."

She doesn't remove her hand from covering her mouth. "Des."

Her glassy eyes move over me, from the messy bun on my head, to the jaw she used to call my "superhero jaw," to the tattoo on my neck, all the way down to my scuffed boots and back up again. Slowly, she uncovers her mouth and reaches toward me.

When her fingers graze my bearded chin, I flinch. Nearly fall to my goddamn knees. I close my eyes instead. Can't handle looking at her while she traces the edge of my jaw, the line of my neck, over the scarred side.

"I can't believe it's you," she whispers.

Her hand leaves my face, and I almost grab her wrist to put her fingers back, tuck my arm around her waist and pull her against me. Bury my face in her hair and weep.

But.

Won't like who he is now.

Won't be good for Max.

Won't recognize myself around him.

I shove my hands in my pockets. "Yeah, uh. It's me." Except ineloquent and desperately needy. "We should go inside. Sit down for a chat.

Which is actually a serious talk, not a chat. About us. I mean, about our *son,* since he's both of ours."

Jesus Christ. I've swapped my former cockiness for a raging case of Kill Me Now.

She moves toward the door, then glances back like I might have vanished in the span of that nanosecond. Not surprising, considering our history. She gives her head a little shake and leads us inside.

Like when I was hanging up flyers, the few patrons in the diner scrutinize us. We're strangers to town, but we're also an odd pair. Sadie's a gorgeous woman, put together in slim blue jeans and a pretty pink tank top. I'm muscled and intimidating, with a decade's worth of resentment on my weathered face. My neck bristles, the area with the ink feeling particularly prickly.

When we're finally seated across from each other in a red vinyl booth, she doesn't glance at her menu. I have no clue what to do with my hands or legs or general body.

Her huge Disney-princess eyes finally lock on me. "This feels like a dream."

More like one of my heart-wrenching fantasies. "Seeing you is beyond amazing, but yeah. Kind of an out-of-body thing." I spin my bundled fork-and-knife set in restless circles. Our eyes meet briefly, then dart away. "Guess it's hard to catch up on eleven years."

She laughs. "Cue cards would be helpful."

"Three things to say when you're faced with your ex who disappeared into witness protection?"

She covers her mouth again, giving her head a bewildered shake. "God, we're a pair."

"What can I get you?" Our waiter smiles down at us, giving me a moment to get my bearings. Soak in the fact that Sadie's here, sitting across from me.

We order coffees and ask for waters. He leaves. The awkward silence resumes.

When my ribs feel like they're about to cave in, I lean my elbows on the table. "I have so many questions. About you—how you're doing, *what* you're doing. About Max and whatever he's going through. Is he okay?"

"He is, but he's changed so much recently. Become introverted to the point I'm a bit concerned. And I'm so sorry it took so long before we could meet. Work's been crazy. I'm finalizing a project, and I had sitter issues, and . . ."

"And?" I prod, not liking how guilt ridden she sounds.

"I was also delaying, I think. Hoping Max would have a turn-around, and I'd be able to bring him with me."

"Sadie, it's fine. Don't apologize for being a good mom. I'm slotting myself into *your* schedule, not the other way around. If you have reservations about me meeting Max right now, I'm sure you have good reason. Can you tell me more about him?"

"What do you want to know?"

"What kinds of food does he eat?" The simpler stuff to start. Let Sadie relax into this talk.

She smiles. "Carbaholic like you, but experimental. Loves all mushrooms. Even the weird ones."

I like that he's an adventurous eater, like his mother. Curious and open minded. "Is he good in school?"

"His reading was delayed, but he's zoomed past kids his age now. Reads all sorts of books that kind of surprise me. I should probably enforce more parental controls, but I'm so happy whenever I see him with a book. Can't bring myself to take one away."

I picture Max joining my book club of two, discussing the marzipan from Denise Mina's *Deception*, analyzing if sugar can enhance an erotic experience—Mom's horrifying contribution.

Might be too young to join.

Our coffee and waters are set down as I ask Sadie more questions. I grill her on what Max was like as a baby (cried nonstop), if he's big for his age (skinny but tall), if he's lost his baby teeth (all but three). I steer clear of landmines like *Does Max have any father figures in his life?* but I can't gather enough other details. I'm on the brink of starvation, living off of nothing but Max Minutiae.

Even the parts that are more worrying. "Him becoming more closed off—any idea why?"

She takes a slow sip of her coffee. "I get the sense that he feels like he doesn't fit in with other kids. We moved to Windfall recently, and I think he was happy to make the change. But moving is also tough. It takes time to make friends and adjust, and starting a new school when the year's almost done isn't easy. Kids get mean and—"

"Kids are mean to him?" The snarl in my voice is impossible to suppress. My arms instantly flex. Is this what they mean when they say a parent would do anything for their kid? I haven't even met Max. Already, I'm bristling to take names and terrorize.

"Maybe. It's hard to get a straight answer out of him. He's quieter than he used to be, won't let me in his room. Spends lots of time drawing."

"Like E." I smile at the notion, then slowly frown. All I did growing up was goad E. Torment him for drawing instead of tossing a football with his obnoxious brothers. Probably exactly what Max is going through with his friends, and *I'm* supposed to be the role model.

"So . . . meeting me," I hedge, feeling less secure in my plan, "you're worried whatever's keeping him closed off will get worse?"

"Maybe? I took him to a counselor before we moved to Windfall, but it didn't help much, and I haven't found someone new who has time yet. He just seems so fragile right now. As much as I hate making you wait, I was wondering if you mind delaying meeting him a bit longer."

"Actually," I say through my buzzing nerves, "I have another suggestion."

She nibbles her lip. "Okay."

"If you want me to wait, I'll wait. The final decision's yours, but even if we wait, I imagine he'll feel a lot of pressure around me. The buildup to meeting me will create more stress for him?"

Sadness seems to weigh her down. "It will."

"But if he meets me without knowing who I am, we might be able to bypass that anxiety. If he already knows me when we tell him I'm his dad, the transition might go more smoothly."

She frowns but doesn't interrupt as I explain about the hikes I'll be leading, that if she signs him up, I'll have time to build trust with him. Develop a gradual bond.

"So," she says slowly, "if he asks about you during that time, we'd tell him your family still can't find you?"

I nod. "They agreed to the plan. The hikes start in two weeks."

Brow pinched, she focuses on the table and blinks for several slow beats. When she looks back up, there's more color in her cheeks. "I'm a bit nervous about lying to him, but I think it actually might be a good way to do this. Let him get to know you without all the anxiety that comes with such a huge event. Thank you, Des." She dips her head shyly. "For thinking of this. For thinking of *him*."

A familiar burn tightens my throat, but a rush of relief has me relaxing. "He's all I've been thinking about these days."

She sniffles and nods. "When we do tell him, Max knows the whole witness protection story. I explained it to him before meeting your family, so we don't have to navigate that."

"That's good," I say quietly. "Do you two need money? Anything at all?"

"Thank you for offering, but we're fine. What I want is to know more about *you*." Her gaze drops to my neck, lingering on my tattoo, then drifts to my lips. For a second her eyes seem to flare with heat, and my body reacts like it always did—desire licking up my spine—but she flicks her attention to my eyes. "How did you get through it all?

Witness protection is only this crazy thing I've seen in movies. It must have been horrible."

"Horrible?" I laugh, but there's zero humor in it. WITSEC talk is an excellent libido killer. "There isn't a big enough word to describe what it's like to learn your father's a criminal who lied to you for years, but *you* get screwed for it."

"But why? I don't understand *why* he did it."

"Greed? Narcissism? Ego?" I force my locked shoulders to lower. "I honestly don't know."

"And his tell-all book—the articles about it said your dad's testimony sent Victor Becerra's son to jail. That he was killed there and Victor put out hits on your whole family as retribution. You must have been freaking out."

"Me? Nah." I go for unaffected, but my shrug is more of a jerky twitch. "What's a death threat or fifty?"

The corners of her lips lift. "I forgot you watched the Rocky series in one night. You could totally take down a hitman."

"In my sleep."

"With one hand tied behind your back."

"While blindfolded," I add, doing a half-ass karate-chop move.

Her small laugh cracks me open in the best and worst way. Joking with Sadie is a breath of fresh air, but I can't evade the tough stuff. Not with our messed-up history.

Spreading my thighs apart, I lean my elbows heavier on the table. "We were obviously all rough for a while. Mom put on a brave face. Kicked Dad out once the US Marshals got us settled in Houston and did her best to provide some normalcy, but none of us left the house much in the early years. We got pretty reclusive."

"God, Des. I'm so sorry."

No one's more sorry than me. "We moved on with life eventually. Got jobs and our own apartments. But none of us made any real friends. Trusting people was hard, and having to lie about our pasts was a conversational dead end."

I had my book club of two, though. Days and nights where I'd read a bunch of sometimes boring but usually thought-provoking books so Mom and I could gossip like a couple of middle-aged housewives about the juiciest parts—"Any dude who proposes on a jumbotron deserves to be ditched" (*The Proposal*).

"E's doing great now," I say, steering us to less morose topics. "He's back with Delilah, and his graphic novels are incredible, which you probably already know. Lennon runs his outdoor camps for kids. Jake and Callahan work together doing construction. They seem happy staying in Houston."

"And you?" she asks hesitantly. "Are you happy with your life?"

"Me?" I lean into my bench seat, still going for cool. "If I were any happier, you could use my energy to power a space station."

She stares at me, no lip twitch in sight. Guess she doesn't buy my bullshit.

"Missing you, Sadie . . ." I close my eyes briefly, my heart feeling like it's covered in paper cuts. "It sucked the life out of me."

She makes a tiny sound, and I meet her pained gaze, wishing I could erase her hurt, but I need to hear her story too. Face the heart-wrenching history I've tried to bury. "What about you? How did you deal with everything?"

The only connection I had to her at the time was social media. Her worried and angry posts were similar to Delilah's and broke me word by word:

If anyone hears from the Bowers, I need to find Desmond.
Desmond, you have to call me.
If this is some kind of joke, I don't understand it.
You're a pathetic coward. How could you do this?

I hit the bottle hard after that last one and got my first tattoo—a knife over my heart. It was supposed to be realistic, showing the knife in three dimensions, as though halfway through my chest, but I was drunk and wandered into a subpar shop. The finished piece looks like a penis lying on my pec.

I breathe through the memory, wait for her to tell me about those horrible days.

"At first," she finally says, "I was more scared than angry. Didn't believe you'd leave without a good reason."

"You have to know—I almost called you a thousand times. It was a physical effort holding back."

The gold flecks in her brown eyes shine with sadness. "I slept outside your old house for two weeks. Set up a tent."

Jesus. I pass my hand over my mouth, can't even drink my coffee. "You were all I thought about. All I cared about. I knew you must have been freaking out. I obviously didn't know the extent of"—I gesture toward her stomach, feeling like my lungs are underwater—"what you were dealing with. But—"

"Des, stop." She presses her fingers to the inside corners of her eyes and blinks. "I've spoken with E and your mom a lot. I know none of what happened was your fault. I won't lie and tell you I wasn't shattered back then and furious. It's just not something I want to rehash. Not right now, at least. We've both been through hell, and we both survived. Our son is what matters now."

She's right, but a tear pushes from her glassy eyes. And dammit. I hate seeing her cry.

I was always there for Sadie when she was having a rough time. Especially with her folks. The night her father yelled at her mother for spending too much money and her mother lied, blaming the spending on Sadie, her father had shouted that Sadie was a mistake who never should've happened—the surprise child they hadn't planned. I kept Sadie on the phone afterward, listening to her quiet sobs, telling her funny stories about my brothers until she was tired enough to fall asleep.

Making Sadie happy made me happy. Seeing her hurt made me hurt.

Like now.

I don't know where her family fit into her pregnancy and her early years with Max. She hasn't mentioned them, and I'm scared to hear they were cruel. Still, my tear ducts react, burning and watering, as I ready myself to ask the tough stuff.

But a pint-size Black girl appears next to our table. "Did you know forty-one percent of male air travelers cry while on an airplane?" Her braided hair is in a complicated twist, her bright outfit has a nineties vibe, and she's scrutinizing us like she's peering through a microscope at a rare cell mutation. "It was in a Virgin Atlantic survey. Some people think it's the slight oxygen deprivation. I think it's all that thinking time. People get weird when they have time to think." Her alarmingly wise gaze lands on me. "Have you had a lot of time to think?"

Jesus. Who is this mini Freud? "My bet's on oxygen deprivation."

"Except sixty-seven percent of men say they feel more emotion than they let on. Which basically means sixty-seven percent of men are liars." She stares at me, unblinking.

I'm shuttled back to high school, sitting in front of Principal Osorio, telling her it wasn't me who toilet-papered the girls' locker room overnight, when we both totally knew it was me.

"Maybe you should mind your own business," I tell the kid.

"Maybe you shouldn't lie to your friend."

Okay. We're done here. I tip my head to the side, as though I hear something fascinating. "I think that's your mom calling. She said to quit bothering the nice people at this table."

"Nice people don't lie about hearing things and their repressed emotions." She looks at Sadie and smiles pityingly. "Make good choices."

Sadie sputters out a laugh while I search the diner for a hidden camera. Maybe Lennon sent this miniature tormenter to get back at me for infiltrating his business. A pint-size spy to ensure I toe the line.

Or she's a run-of-the-mill kid, one of the billions of know-it-alls who can see right through me. I wouldn't know. I've spent zero time with children, including mine, and I'm suddenly regretting putting up flyers around here. What if this girl joins my hikes?

The smells of fried potatoes and searing burgers suddenly make me queasy. My T-shirt's crew neck feels too tight. Learning secondhand details about Max won't erase our years apart. Reading books and taking leadership courses won't prepare me for face-to-face interactions with kids. And here I am, planning to lead a troop of preteens, including Max—who might be as terrifying as that little girl—on hikes like I'm some granola-eating, nature-loving molder of young minds. Just me and a gang of preteen psychotherapists.

And I'll have to be *nice*.

Sweat slicks the back of my neck. "Is this what all kids are like?"

Sadie's hand lands on my knee, sending a wave of awareness through me. My stomach flips. Honest to God. Flips like I'm a lovesick pancake.

"Is that part of why you want to meet Max without him knowing who you are?" She glances toward the bathrooms, where the girl went. "You're worried you're not good with kids?"

More like petrified. "No. Not at all. I just think it will be best for Max."

Those 67 percent of male liars have nothing on me.

Sadie doesn't call me on my partial falsehood. Her thumb moves, rubbing the inside edge of my knee. Forget a lovesick pancake. My stomach's a malfunctioning Ferris wheel, spinning in wild circles. Her eyes flick to mine. For a second, I think I see heat in their depths again—longing, like the times I'd catch her watching me when I'd be studying.

I'd nudge her those days and say, "Stop being a creeper."

She'd go all moony and kiss my cheek. "I just can't believe how lucky I am to love you."

That was then, this is now.

Her gaze drops back to my neck. My ink. My scar.

"Good choices." Our little nemesis walks by again, coming from the bathrooms.

I swivel, unable to control my dirty look. (*Hiking leader* is sounding dumber by the second.) With my abrupt move, Sadie's hand slides higher up my thigh, and my leg jerks, slamming her hand into the underside of the table.

"*Ow.*" She winces.

I mumble apologies and reach under the table to grab her hand, make sure she's okay.

I am not okay.

Our chests are pressed to the table's aluminum edge, our hands linked underneath, both of us breathing hard. My heart beats wildly. Sweat gathers between our palms. I have no clue if Sadie's having I-miss-the-love-of-my-life sweats or how-do-I-politely-let-him-down sweats.

Unable to face the possibility of the latter, I extricate my hands from hers. "I should go."

She leans back and touches her clavicle. "Right, yeah. Me too."

I shift on my bench seat, unsure what to do with my too-big body in this too-tight space.

Another stretch of uncomfortable silence later, Sadie's uncertain gaze slides back to me. "But I'll see you again soon, right?"

"If you want." I've never heard my voice like this. Soft, tender, needy. "I still have lots of questions I didn't ask you."

"Me too," she says quickly. "I mean, as long as you have time. I'm sure you want to know all about Max."

"Yeah. Sure. Of course. We'll talk about Max." At least Sadie won't be on the hikes with me. Any chance of me acting normal and impressing my son would be toast.

Even thinking about finally meeting him has my nerves rioting, but I need to buck up. This hiking ruse is about his mental health, not my dad deficiencies. I have to earn his trust. Build a foundation with him so when he learns who I am, he won't shut down further.

I've already planned fun outings for him and my troop. The activities should give him a boost to his days. I've researched the best trails to hike and explore the area. I've reviewed my leadership material, even the babysitting stuff.

Operation Inspiring Hiking Leader and Dad Whisperer is underway.

What could possibly go wrong?

SIX

I check my backpack for the seventy-ninth time, ensuring the first aid kit and emergency supplies are secure. My nature-inspired coloring books and baggies of snacks are lined up on the picnic bench—six baggies for the six kids who signed up for my hikes, zero peanuts in sight, in case one of them forgot to alert me to an allergy. I'm wearing cargo shorts with plenty of pockets for pens and my cell and quick-access bandages. Unfortunately, I'm also wearing Lennon's company Littlewing Outdoor Camp T-shirt.

First, yellow is not my color.

Second, the shirt's too tight. He claimed it was the largest he could get, and the tag does read extra large, but it feels like an extra large in Ken-doll size.

Third, thanks to the too-tight T-shirt, some of my tattoos are visible. Not the phallic-shaped knife on my pec, but the blurred bleeding rose on my right forearm and the scythe-wielding skeleton on my left, which looks more like Casper the Friendly Ghost playing baseball, are on display, proving how poor some of my choices have been. Not much to be done about that.

Or about my brother.

"Your cell phone is charged, right?" Lennon asks as he digs through my backpack for his fourth time.

I pat one of my pockets. "Still charged since you asked five minutes ago."

"And you have the extra maps and flares?"

"Still in the pack, yeah."

He closes my bag, then grabs me by the front of my nearly suctioned shirt. "Those kids are your responsibility. One of them gets hurt, it's on you. Pay attention. Stay focused. And, for the love of God, do not get lost."

I knock his hands off me. "I have this under control."

I know what's at stake here. I wouldn't hurt Lennon's business, and I sure as hell plan to impress my kid. It's been two weeks since I've seen Sadie. Fourteen days to prepare myself for meeting Max and to organize a kickass hiking program.

"Right. Also." He runs a hand through his wavy hair. "I hired an assistant for you."

"You did *what*?"

He steps back from me, the skin around his beard getting blotchy. Lennon is the fairest of us Bower boys, his emotion often betrayed by his coloring, but he's still tough to pin down at times. Aside from his paler skin, he has a reddish beard, blueish eyes, brownish hair, and an *ish* personality. He was the type of teen who flitted between styles and personas, moving from hippie to rocker to cowboy to hipster. Like he's just . . . *ish*. Not fully formed and comfortable in his own skin.

He folds his arms and takes another step backward. "Figured you'd want to spend more time with Max than the other kids. Since they'll all need attention, I hired someone else to work with you."

It's not the worst idea, but he's acting cagey. His truth or dare taunt from the other week has me on the offensive. I'm about to box him against the closest tree and demand answers when a car pulls up and parks. According to the reconnaissance I've done, none of the parents who signed their kids up for the program are from my past. Still, I adjust my baseball hat and sunglasses, feeling weirdly exposed.

Lennon scoots around me, waving at the newcomer as he goes. The second I recognize the girl in the passenger seat as the mini Freud, I curse.

"Look who we have here!" Lennon's all smiles and gyrating hands. "Thrilled to have you join Littlewing."

I'm not thrilled. I'm downright petrified. This is the first kid I'll be responsible for, and she's one of the reasons I swapped crocheting for an attempt at needlepoint this week. Have I been fretting—yes, *fretting*, like an eighty-year-old grandmother—over meeting Max? Painfully so. Have I also been stressing over whether this little therapist would see my flyer and join my hiking troop? Absolutely. My newest crafting exercise was supposed to distract and calm me. All it did was puncture my finger with tiny holes, while also puncturing my patience. My pitiful efforts have joined my box of half-finished relics.

Now this kid's here.

Lennon chats with her mother, then gives me an intense act-your-goddamn-age look. "Why don't you introduce yourself to your first recruit." He gestures toward the little gremlin. "This is Olivia."

Right. Yeah. Happy Hiking Leader, here I come.

I grab my clipboard and pen and meet her by the Hood Rock trailhead sign. "Nice to officially meet you, Olivia." I attempt a smile, but my lip curls of its own accord. "I'm Daniel."

My WITSEC name still comes easily. Especially since I can't have Max realizing who I am.

Committing to her role as most terrifying child ever, Olivia doesn't say hi in return. She stares at me, her shorts and T-shirt and stack of bracelets as bright as the outfit she wore in the diner. At least it'll make losing her tough. Preferring to avoid her unnerving stare, I find her name on my list. She's apparently twelve and the oldest of the group. I give her name a forceful check. *Worst nightmare, present and accounted for.*

She blows a bubble of pink gum and pops it. "Approximately a hundred people a year choke to death on ballpoint pens."

And we're off to the races. "Probably best not to scare the other kids with your plentiful knowledge of death traps."

"If you're worried about scaring kids, I'd consider wearing long sleeves."

Why. Why. *Why.* Of all the summer programs, *why* did this kid have to sign up for these hikes? "I'll take that under advisement."

"You do that, Daniel. And just so we're clear, I hate hiking. I'm not here by choice."

Fantastic. This program is eight weeks long, two hikes per week, each outdoor excursion lasting three hours. That's forty-eight hours with this firecracker. "Anything else you hate that I should know about?"

"The shirt you're wearing is questionable. Yellow is not your color."

"Not a news flash." I'm about to sidestep Olivia when a red Honda pulls up.

I freeze, but my heart thinks it's blasting off on a rocket.

Seeing Sadie is partly to blame, but it's the young boy beside her that has me in turbulence. Max. *My son.* I strain my eyes. Try to see what he looks like, the smallest glimpse. He doesn't get out when Sadie parks, but she does.

And she's wearing the same yellow T-shirt as me.

I make a garbled sound and search frantically for my asshole brother, unsure what the hell he was thinking. I can't lead hikes *with* Sadie. I'm a mess around her. Awkward. Frazzled. When I finally spot Lennon, I catch his hipster smirk as he makes a mad dash for his truck, disappearing inside it before I can burst his head with my eyes.

I am so screwed.

"Maybe hiking won't be so bad," Olivia says, way too amused for my liking. Her eyes dart between Sadie and me.

"Do not ruin this for me, kid."

"Ruin what?"

"Nothing." It's the first time I've seen Olivia smile, and I don't like it. There's evil in this child.

"I'm sure you'll ruin whatever this is just fine on your own." She slides another knowing look to Sadie, then back to me. "Men generally do."

I'm not sure how this twelve-year-old wound up as pessimistic as me. I'm not sure why Lennon thought hiring Sadie would help me, when what I need is to focus on Max. The only thing I do know is I am not prepared for this.

Thanks to this warm June day, the sun's shining through the forest canopy, and Sadie's wearing cute shorts that dry my mouth. Her yellow T-shirt's even worse. The fit is snug like mine, but where my shirt makes me look like a gym bro who was dressed by his mother, hers is perky and cute and showcases the feminine dip of her waist. She's as tiny as ever, with slender arms and delicate features, but there's a softness to her body that wasn't there a decade ago. The softness of a woman. Of a mother.

I blink hard and dart my focus to Max, try to see him more clearly.

Finally, he pushes his door open, and I hold my breath. His head is hung so low I can't see his face, but my insides go berserk. I bite my cheek, attempt to stem this wave of emotion from knocking me over. He looks up, and it's no use. My eyes burn. My throat attempts to crush my Adam's apple.

My son.

Max is skinny, like Sadie said. And tall. Not that I know how tall a ten-year-old should be. Or anything about age-related norms. But yeah. He's tall with hair the same dark brown as mine. He's tentative, barely moving from the car. My cheek hurts from biting it, and my throat burns hotter. I want to weep for the years I lost. Sadie. Max. The family that was supposed to be mine. But this isn't the time or place to fall apart.

Max starts walking my way, and I stand straighter.

Aside from poking holes in my skin while needlepointing this week, I've practiced this moment—finally saying hi to Max and introducing myself.

I actually stood in front of the mirror and rehearsed lines.

Max, hey. Thrilled to have you join us.

Hi, Max. We're gonna learn so much together.

Hey there, Max. You sure are tall for your age.

It was as pathetic as it sounds, but I will not falter. Lennon's stunt bringing Sadie here doesn't matter, especially if he's trying to push us together. Whatever happens or doesn't happen between Sadie and me is separate from being a dad.

More cars arrive and park. Max wanders forward on his own, squints at the sun. He glances at the towering trees and trailhead sign, his attention settling on the picnic bench with our supplies.

Ready to own this moment, I swallow the emotion crowding my throat, walk right up to him, and say, "Max. Hey. Hi."

Clearly, I should have practiced more.

He looks up at me, his attention darting to the ink on my arms. His eyes widen, and I consider lodging a complaint with the health board to arrest all seedy tattoo artists who prey on angry-at-life drunk idiots like me. I'm also struck by just how similar Max's eyes are to mine—dark and intense, thickly lashed. A fresh wave of heartache blindsides me. *So many years lost.* My clipboard tremors in my grasp.

Keeping my shades firmly in place, I crouch in front of my son. "It's great to meet you, Max."

A hiccupy gasp comes from my right—Sadie. Her lips are pressed tight, her eyes so wide I bet they sting as much as mine. Abruptly, she turns and fumbles for something in her purse. And hell. I hate seeing her like this, upset because of me. Our whole tangled situation is beyond messed up. We still have so much talking to do, mountains of baggage to unpack. For now, it'll have to wait.

I blow out a breath and focus on my son. "Glad to have you with us, Max. I'm . . ." *Desmond,* I want to say. Give him my real name. But my insides go haywire. "I'm Daniel," I force out.

"Hey." He scratches his skinny arm. The mosquito bites there are already red and inflamed. I used to scratch my bites raw too. Never listening when Mom told me to stop.

Since I'm a practicing parent, I say, "You shouldn't scratch those bites. It'll make them worse."

He curls his hand into a fist and drops it to his side, looking chastised.

Immediately, I want to take back my words. Let him scratch to his heart's content, anything to wipe that sadness from his face. His focus slides to something beside me, his glum expression mixing with resignation as he mumbles, "Great."

The other kids have arrived—two boys and two girls, all standing with their thumbs hooked through their backpack straps. The boys are talking loudly and laughing. The opposite of Max's frustrated *great*.

I gnash my teeth.

Maybe these are the jokers who've been giving Max a hard time. Maybe I'll be losing some kids on this hike after all.

The two new girls are chattering to each other, apart from Olivia, who's tossing rocks at a tree. If Lennon were still here, he'd be doing his congenial thing, buttering up the parents, adding implied exclamation points to everything he says. He's good like that. Mr. Positive, exuding fun-loving energy. I'm as naturally chipper as a storm cloud, and this whole Sadie wrench has thrown me further off my game.

Max stands awkwardly. I stand awkwardly. Neither of us speaks, which is my fault. I'm the adult. I should ease him into this new program, especially since he seems put off by the other kids. Yet I'm standing like a mute schmuck in a too-tight, yellow gym-bro shirt.

"Max." Sadie joins our painfully somber duo, witnessing my instant dad failure. "Why don't you go on over and say hi to Carter and Jun? Daniel and I need to have a word."

I tense, unsure if she wants to have a how-come-you-look-so-bad-in-yellow word, or a you're-clearly-unable-to-make-basic-conversation-with-your-son word.

Max slouches and drops his head back. "Do I have to?"

"Sweetheart." Her tone softens with concern. "Did something happen with you guys? I thought you hung out with Carter at school this week?"

"Nothing. It's fine." He blows out a long-suffering sigh and trudges over.

I glare at the little bullies, who've for sure done something malicious to upset my son. Believe you me, I will discover what it is.

"Des?" Sadie says softly.

"Sorry, yeah." I hug my clipboard against my chest, attempting to cover the loud thud of my heart. "Lennon hired you to help lead the hikes?"

She freezes a moment, then frowns. "He didn't tell you, did he?"

"That would be a no."

She huffs out a laugh. "Guess he's still a troublemaker."

"It's in his DNA."

Neither of us offers up a guess as to *why* Lennon pulled this ruse. My infuriating brother is playing cupid, even though I don't even know if Sadie's single.

She fixes her ponytail and shifts awkwardly on her feet. My body decides it's a human sauna, overheating in seconds. Goddamn my brother.

"You're sure you have time for this?" I ask, filling the awkward. "You're not too busy?"

"My schedule can be flexible, and I just finished a big project. I thought it was a good idea to be here for Max, in case anything goes wrong. As for us, I told Max we knew each other as teens. Figured we wouldn't be able to hide our"—she grazes her teeth over her bottom lip, being sexy without even trying—"familiarity."

I nod quickly, still at a loss around Sadie—overwhelmed by her nearness, the ache that moves through me at the sound of her voice. A warbler flies overhead, a bird I recognize thanks to my nature readings the past month. Its song is sweet and piercing and does zilch to calm me.

"Also," Sadie adds hesitantly, "Lennon said you've been struggling. That you're basically terrified to meet Max."

Forget busting Lennon's head with my eyeballs. I'll be dragging him up to Hood Rock and dropping him off the edge. "He doesn't know what he's talking about."

"Wow." She reaches for my face but doesn't touch my cheek or jaw like I crave. She lifts my sunglasses and peers into my eyes. "You really are terrified."

Yep. Lennon's a walking corpse. "I'm nothing. I'm fine."

I'm the opposite of fine, especially staring into Sadie's eyes, trying to breathe through the flutters—swear to God, actual *flutters*—invading my stomach.

Her gaze falls to my lips. My lungs pump too fast.

She drops my shades and huffs out an amused noise. "You sound like my lying ten-year-old son."

My son. Not *our* son.

It's fine. I get it. She's been a single mother for ten years. Comments like that are habit. Still, her words dampen the fizziness crackling through me.

Needing a moment to collect myself, I glance around the clearing. Olivia's closer than before, no longer maiming trees with rocks. She's standing there watching us, for sure Freudalizing our every mannerism.

"Is that the girl from the diner?" Sadie asks.

"Unfortunately, yes."

She laughs. "This might be more entertaining than I thought."

"Yeah, no. No part of her is entertaining."

Sadie tips her head, scrutinizing me again. Her attention drifts to the ground, to a pile of branches at our right. "*Hidden Sparks of Life*," she says.

Anyone else might give her some serious side-eye, unsure what nonsense she uttered, but I know Sadie. At least, I did. She's playing her game, studying random patterns, imagining them as art.

All I see are a bunch of broken branches. "There's nothing there but dried wood."

"But if you light dried wood, it sparks." She picks up a stick, runs her fingers over the peeling bark. "These sticks build into a fire. They create heat. Warmth. Food. Light. They start out as rough and broken and become life." She drops the stick and dusts her hands on her shorts. "Don't sell yourself short, Des. Being comfortable around Max might take time, but you'll get there. Doing this for him was a great idea."

She walks off to talk to the other kids.

I alternate between freaking out and freaking out. When my phone rings and I see Lennon's name, I storm off toward the trees and jam my thumb on the answer button. "What the fuck?"

"Truth or dare, my friend. You chose dare."

"I chose nothing."

"Exactly. If you don't choose, I choose for you. And I dare you to ask Sadie if she's single."

My long hair is down today, covering my neck tattoo and adding a layer of heat to the fury burning me up. "It doesn't matter if Sadie's single."

"I beg to differ."

Is this why he's pushing me? He learned details about Sadie's love life and is forcing me to face truths I'd rather ignore? "Do you know something I don't?"

"I know you're a coward who will never ask her, so I decided to do something about it."

I growl. He didn't overhear that phone call—Sadie worrying she wouldn't like who I've become or that I wouldn't be good for Max. He has no clue what I'm up against.

"Fact is," he says, "you have to stop pretending you don't care. If she's single, you need to start making up for lost time. If she's not, you need to find a way to put your feelings aside so you can coparent Max. It's time to pull up your big-boy pants."

My growl graduates to a snarl.

"You should thank me," he says. "I got out of there before Max recognized me. He might've put two and two together."

The last thing he'll get is a thank-you from me. "Fuck off with your meddling."

"Anyway, I'm heading back to Houston, so the program's now in your hands, as is your future. Don't mess this up or hurt my business. And quit being a quitter. I've never known you to welch on a dare."

"I didn't accept the dare!" I whisper-yell.

"Exactly," he says and hangs up.

Feeling unhinged, I pull up Mirielle's contact and shoot my former neighbor a text. She asked for regular updates, and I'm a minute from losing it.

Des: Lennon hired Sadie to lead the hikes too.

Mirielle: I like this brother of yours, Walter.

Des: Told you my name isn't Walter.

Mirielle: It is until I decide otherwise.

I glare at my phone. This name game is becoming less fun.

Des: How am I supposed to focus on Max when Sadie's around?

Mirielle: Chéri. Sadie needs you as much as Max does. You are the father of her child. She needs to get to know you again. Trust you. That means spending time together. And you should cut your hair.

Des: What does my hair have to do with this?

Mirielle: It's your security blanket. And it's not attractive.

Maybe I should have texted my mom.

I'm still wound up, and a group of kids is waiting on me. But Mirielle is *partially* right. I do need to re-earn Sadie's trust, which means this might not be so bad. I can rebuild our friendship while I get to know Max, as long as I can stop thinking about Lennon's stupid dare.

SEVEN

This hike is off to a painful start, and we're still in the parking area. "So," I say to my kiddie troops, who are in a semicircle looking half-asleep.

One girl yawns.

Olivia mumbles, "Awkward."

Sadie rolls her wrist patiently, suggesting I say something more.

Right. "I'm Daniel. I'll be your hiking leader for the next eight weeks. Behind you is Sadie." The woman I loved more than anything, who may or may not currently be single. "She's my assistant."

"Coleader," she pipes in. "Daniel can be athletically challenged."

I quirk an eyebrow at her. "Sadie's actually here to scare off wildlife. The sound she makes when she laughs is terrifying."

The kids laugh. *My son* laughs. I suddenly feel ten feet taller.

"He also has a horrible sense of direction," she adds, clearly fighting a smile. "I suggest following me."

"She speaks the truth. I'd follow Sadie anywhere."

Affection sparks in her eyes, and heat suffuses my face, like I might be *blushing*.

I snap my focus to the kids and clap my hands loudly. "Let's hear from all of you. Tell everyone your name and one thing about yourself." When no one speaks, I jut my chin toward Max. "Why don't you go first."

Hunched slightly, he drags his shoe over the gravel. "I'm Max." He eyes the boys nervously and tucks his hands into his pockets. "I like to draw."

For some idiotic reason, Carter snickers.

I make a plan to find poison ivy and dump him in it. Until then, I need to do something about my face. This perma-scowl is the opposite of the Happy Hiking Leader I'm supposed to be. It's like I have no control of my facial muscles, the way they harden and pinch every time these kids test my patience.

Even though nothing's funny, Sadie laughs, the sound too loud and overly bright, probably to draw attention away from my glare. "Thanks, Max. Let's go clockwise."

The two girls beside Max are wearing similar crop tops in different colors, their jean shorts are ripped and frayed in the exact same places, and they both have high ponytails and similar headbands, like they're part of a Barbie gang. The girl closest to Max stands taller, with an air of self-importance, clearly the leader, while the smaller girl keeps tugging down her top and fidgeting with her hair.

Sadie points to the alpha girl. "You're next."

She lifts her chin. "I'm Jasmine, and I know every word to every Camila Cabello song." She beams like she won a spelling bee.

"I'm Zoey," the girl beside her says, sassing out her hip to mimic Jasmine's pose. "I own every Camila Cabello album."

Yep. Follower central.

Annoying Carter smirks. He announces his name like he's royalty and says, "My dad owns a Porsche."

There goes my face again. Sadie gives another bubbly fake laugh.

Jun introduces himself next and tells us about his new dog, Newton.

Olivia is last, taking her time, looking concerningly smug. "I'm Olivia," she says bluntly, "and over six hundred thousand people go missing in America every year. To date at least sixteen hundred people who vanished in the wilderness still haven't been foun—"

"Okay then," I blurt before she tells us there's a serial killer loose in the woods, "we'll be hiking the Hood Rock Trail today. The first half hour is mostly flat, then there's an incline to the lookout point. We'll take a break before the harder climb, where we'll have snacks. And"—I settle into my role, feet planted firmly, proud of the planning I've done—"I have coloring books for each of you, highlighting some of the fun stuff we'll see along the way. And we'll play catch my shadow for the easy part of the hike."

They stare at me blandly.

I scratch my beard. Maybe they've never heard of the game. "Catch my shadow is when I'm in the lead, and you try to keep up and—"

"It's a stupid game for little kids." Carter elbows Jun. "Told you this would be dumb."

If this is dumb, I am screwed.

Jun yawns. Jasmine rolls her eyes. Max shares a look with Zoey and shakes his head, like he can't believe what a numbskull I am. Olivia makes a crash-and-burn sound effect with her mouth.

Yep. Screwed.

The past two weeks, Lennon busted my balls, asking if I needed help planning the hikes and organizing activities. Each time I told him to get lost. I feel competent in terms of safety and outdoor prepared-ness, and I was determined to do the activity planning on my own. I read nature books. I scrolled through blog posts and found one titled "Hiking Fun for Kids." Nowhere on that post did it list the appropriate age for the suggested games. I assumed the term *kid* was universal. I mean, Max is a kid. Carter is a smart-mouth, but he's a kid. Olivia's kid status is questionable, but none of these little humans are even teens yet.

Now I'm getting eye rolls and head shakes.

"Daniel was testing if you were paying attention," Sadie says smoothly, coming to my side. "We'll be playing other fun games along the way, and the coloring books are to help with a free-drawing exercise we'll be doing. Head on over to the picnic bench. Load your backpacks with the snacks, books, and colored pencils. And no phones in your hands. They're on lockdown while we're hiking. Once you're all set, holler and we'll be on our way."

Zoey, Jasmine, and Max peel off first, chatting as they go. Carter and Jun body-check each other, half jogging and half stumbling toward the table. Olivia gives me a thumbs-up, then dramatically mimes flipping her thumb upside down.

I scrub my hand over my face. "That went well."

"It could've been worse." Sadie pats my back, her small hand lingering on the muscle I've spent years building at the gym. Her fingers widen and dip into the groove of my spine. I control my breaths, try not to get lost in the feel of her when today's spiraling out of my control. But she's so close. She smells like the early days of summer—soft and breezy and slightly sweet. New smells I don't associate with Sadie.

"Guess I need to learn more about kids," I say. And more about her. What summery soap she uses, if she still dreams of owning a cute pygmy goat, if she works with art like she planned or gave up her career to raise Max. Eleven years of blanks to fill in.

"My advice," she says tenderly, keeping us connected with her light touch, "is not to underestimate kids. They're generally smarter than people give them credit for. Except maybe Carter. And ten-year-olds think they're verging on adulthood. Max is always telling me to stop treating him like a little kid."

Exactly what I did. Coloring books. Catch my shadow. I shake my head and groan.

She moves closer, just a partial step. Close enough for me to feel her breath on my neck. "You'll get better at this. Give yourself time."

Her hand is still on my back, the tips of her fingers spreading wider along my spine. My pulse reacts. My internal temperature reacts. Every fiber of my body *reacts*.

A throat clears. Olivia is a foot away, grinning an I-caught-you-sucker grin. "We're ready for this incredibly exciting hike you planned." Sarcasm is strong with this one.

Sadie's hand slips off my back.

I attempt to regain my equilibrium. "Then let's get to it."

The first section of the hike is relatively easy. Trilliums and blood-roots blanket the forest floor in swaths of white. Dark-pink rhodo-dendrons and small white silverbells decorate the understory, while warblers, tanagers, and vireos sing and flutter above us.

No, I'm not imagining myself in a Disney movie, with swooping birds and Technicolor forests, while a singing squirrel twirls through the leaves. I'm focusing on my surroundings, forcing recall from the books I've read, to distract myself from the uncomfortable twinge in my chest. Sadie has taken over the group. She's in front, playing a more appropriate game with them called "and then." It's a creative thinking game where she begins a story, and the next kid needs to improvise and add a new line starting with *and then*.

The first story went like this:

Sadie: I bought a ticket to go on the first rocket to Mars.

Jasmine: And then Camila Cabello shows up and tells me she loves my shoes.

Zoey: And then Camila Cabello asks if we can be best friends.

Max: And then Camila Cabello discovers a hidden gem beside the rocket glowing with power.

Jun: And then aliens come down and laser everyone in half and destroy the rocket's engine.

Carter: And then Max farts and the rocket takes off.

We're on story four. I have no clue who Camila Cabello is, but she stars in each adventure—Jasmine, Zoey, and Max appear to be obsessed with her. Max displays his impressively vivid imagination. Jun keeps blowing things up. Carter adds farts or burps or puking, targeting Max and Jun as the butt of his moronic jokes. Olivia refuses to play and walks at a snail's pace, so I'm kicking up the rear, ensuring she doesn't become one of the 1,600 people who've vanished in the wilderness.

She's been blessedly quiet, but she keeps glancing at me. Each penetrating perusal has me getting antsier. When she walks even slower, forcing us into a near crawl, I debate pulling the flare from my backpack and signaling for help.

"There's major tension between you and Sadie," she says.

Oh, hell no. We are not going there. "You're imagining things, kid."

"Is she your wife?"

"No."

"Ex-wife?"

"No."

"Tinder hookup who ghosted you?"

"What the—" I stop myself before I say *fuck*. But come on. What is wrong with this child? "You need to hang out with kids your own age."

She shrugs. "Kids my age don't like me."

Shocker. "You shouldn't even know what Tinder is."

"My mom's single." She kicks a rock, still barely walking. "So . . . is Sadie, like, your high school sweetheart and you broke her heart or something?"

I choke on nothing and almost trip. I'm not sure what's more maddening, this nutcracker's quick diagnosis of my horrible love life, or that I planned kiddie activities for a bunch of preteens. I breathe in deeply, inhaling earthy scents and hopefully a teaspoon of patience. I keep my mouth shut, praying Olivia will quit grilling me.

We follow the winding trail through towering oaks and hickories, passing truck-size boulders I'd like to crawl under. Sadie and the group are well ahead, but she glances over her shoulder and nods to me. I nod back. Her attention slides to Olivia, and she offers a compassionate smile. *This kid's as painful as you imagine,* I think and find myself grinning back. Like we're twenty again. Like we're in love with our own secret language of looks and inside jokes.

"So she's definitely an ex," Olivia says.

"It was a long time ago," I snap, immediately regretting my tone and giving her even a morsel of truth.

She makes an *oooooh* sound, showing what looks like genuine excitement. "Did you cheat on her?"

"No."

"Did you take your anger out on her and hurt her?"

Jesus. "Of course not."

"Did you disrespect her life choices?"

How does a twelve-year-old have a degree in couples counseling? "Quit with the badgering."

My steps are more like stomps, this volatile energy jacking up my blood pressure to Hades levels.

"Did you have gambling or money issues or get up in her face about her spending habits? Because seventy percent of couples fight about money and—"

"I was shoved into witness protection for ten years and left her without a word." I slam to a stop and almost puke out a lung. And yeah, *this* face I'm making isn't pinched and glary. I probably resemble a terrified cartoon sketch of myself: bulging eyes, paling skin, the edges of my lips dragging my mouth open into a silent scream.

"Ha ha," I say. My impression of a strung-out comedian. "Just kidding."

I pick up the pace, nowhere near as fast as my pounding pulse, intent on losing my shadow.

"Holy." She jogs, catching up with me. "Were you seriously in witness protection?"

"Nope."

"Oh my God. Is Daniel even your real name? Or is it an alias? What was the program like? Did you kill someone? Were you part of a mafia? Did you get caught hiding a body? Did you—"

"Look." I give up speed walking. There's no escaping her inquisition and the truth bomb I exploded. The only option is damage control. Ensuring the group is still far ahead, I lower my voice. "Yes, I was in WITSEC. No, I didn't kill anyone. My father laundered money for a drug cartel and ruined all our lives. While we're in the clear now, I'm still using my alias, Daniel, not my real name. And this topic is not up for discussion. Do not breathe a word of it to the group."

She stares at me, her dark eyes wide with . . . wonder? Shock? Villainy?

I rub the back of my sweaty neck. "Are we clear?"

"I thought my dad cheating on my mom with her best friend was bad." She blows out a kind of whistle sound. "You got me beat."

I wince at that sad peek into her life. Unfortunately, I've got most people beat on degenerate dads. While Raymond S. Bower and I had what I thought was a normal, although distant, relationship growing up—tossing the occasional ball around outside, laughing together when I made fun of my brothers, fighting over my curfew—he lied and schemed for a solid portion of that father-son time. My family tolerated him for the first six months of WITSEC. Me? I opted for volcanic rage, spewing my hate as often and as loudly as possible.

The day he took me aside and said, "If you want the family to get through this, you better get your attitude in check," my inner volcano had an extinction-level event.

"*I* need to get myself in check?" I shoved him. Screamed. A feral roar without words as my face nearly exploded from my fury. "*You* are a disease. A fucking cancer, and the sooner we cut you out, the sooner the rest of us will start to breathe again."

I was twenty-three and wrathful. He was a lowlife who laundered money, but he dropped his head, wouldn't meet my eyes. The first hint of remorse I witnessed. That was the last time I saw my father. Mom said they fought that night and she kicked him out. I think he put us first for once and realized staying was slowly killing us.

"Sorry about your dad," I tell Olivia. My father may beat hers in a scumbag contest, but I'd bet the bulk of her sarcasm and prickliness comes from hurt. "Must've been rough."

"Fifty percent of couples divorce. No biggie." Her tone is as cavalier as ever, but a sheen glosses her eyes. She looks up at the bird's nest above us and crosses her arms. "You know what would make me feel better, though?"

When I don't reply, she shifts her focus back to me, the sadness in her eyes replaced with craftiness. Not good.

I resume walking, unsure how to regain control of this volatile situation. "Whatever it is, the answer's no."

She meets my quickened pace. "But I have so many questions."

"That's nice for you."

"How about one per hour, and you have to reply with more than one word." *Her* words are a mile a minute now, higher pitched, and bursting with glee.

I step over a fallen branch, wondering what would happen if I dropped to my knees and crawled into the thick underbrush. "This isn't a negotiation."

"I mean, it kind of is. You don't want me telling anyone about your secret seedy past, so . . ."

Of all the kids in all the world, how did this Tasmanian devil wind up invading my life?

Maintaining my determined pace, I say, "One question a day. That's it. Take it or leave it. But you can't ask my real name, and it starts on our next hike." Once I've had the chance to come up with all possible questions she might ask and all neutral replies I can muster.

"Deal," she says, practically skipping now.

The group is waiting for us around the next bend.

I'm not sure how my current face looks, but when Sadie sees me, she laughs and says, "Let's break for a drawing exercise, shall we?"

EIGHT

Sadie gets the kids working on an art project, using my kiddie coloring books as inspiration for a more age-appropriate exercise. They'll trace the birds or bugs or butterflies from the book, then add their own imagined forests around their drawings, giving them freedom to create. She even has a stack of tracing paper she magically pulled from her backpack.

I'm not surprised by her quick thinking. In high school, she developed an art-inspired board game for her history class, using the playing cards and landing spots to teach the class about Greek and Roman art. Predictably, she aced the project. I have no doubt today's nature activity will be a similar success.

Of no use to her project, I hang back, reviewing all the ways Olivia will torment me with her question extortion.

Prying into my father's cartel ties.

Asking how I crushed Sadie's heart.

Grilling me about my bad tattoos.

There's also the possibility she'll ditch our deal and tell Max about my past before I tell him who I am. A prospect I can't let happen. So far, he's been as withdrawn as Sadie described. Building a relationship with him won't be easy, but I will not fail. I need to use my time with him to my advantage. Form a gradual bond as I planned. Organize less pitiful games that add some fun to his day.

Maybe I'll even learn how to keep secrets from a freaking twelve-year-old girl.

Max is sitting with Jasmine and Zoey, the three of them on a fallen log. The other boys are on the opposite side of the trail. Olivia's on her own, in a more secluded spot, leaning her back against a tree. I've sequestered myself on a boulder, far enough away to freak out in private.

When Sadie's done ensuring they're all occupied, she joins me on my freak-out rock. "You look like that time Justin Bernardini barfed beside you at the fair, and you nearly broke your nonpuking streak."

I broke my nonpuking streak the day I found out I had a son. Information Sadie doesn't need to know. "Olivia is special," I say.

Sadie grins at my discomfort. "She's something, all right. Her mother pulled me aside before she left. Said she's been going through a rough divorce, and it's been hard on them both. Be patient with her."

Better plan: find a way to neutralize Olivia's vocal cords, thwarting her promised interrogation. "Thanks for stepping in with the art stuff. They seem engaged."

Especially Max, who's hunched over his book, tongue poking out of his mouth, utterly focused on his drawing.

"I always have papers and activities with me. Nothing's worse than getting stuck somewhere with no way to entertain a kid."

She shifts on the rock, and our arms brush. The tiniest contact, but I swear I have a head rush. Instead of draping herself over me the way she would have a decade ago, Sadie sits posture-perfect and rests her hands on her thighs, seeming tense. I'm stiff and aware of my every breath, doing my best to keep my knees from splaying out and hitting hers.

I clasp my hands together and massage my palm, needing a start. A way to rebuild a friendship with Sadie, like Mirielle suggested. Put her at ease. We have to coparent Max. The last thing I want is for her to feel awkward around me.

I inhale her summer-fresh scent, watch the wind play with the loose hairs around her face. So damn beautiful. "Art," I say roughly.

She frowns at me. "Art?"

"After I left and everything, your internship at the Contemporary Art Museum in Raleigh was supposed to turn into a full-time job. Did you take it?" Assistant to the head curator, a boost to her future career, where she hoped to eventually move up, plan inspiring exhibits, open people's minds with thought-provoking installations.

She picks at her nails, everything about her tensing further. "It was too much. At first, I was terrified you'd come back and I'd miss the chance to talk to you and tell you I was pregnant. When it was clear that wasn't happening, I kind of fell apart. My sister was busy with her own life and nursing career. I pushed my friends away. Refused to tell anyone in town I was pregnant, dreading the pity and gossip. So when my dad got a job in Locklear a few hours away, I just . . ." She lets out a long sigh. "I thought going with them and starting fresh somewhere would help."

"*With* your parents?" The narcissistic assholes who cared only how the world affected them? Who never once considered how their careless words and fighting tore down their daughter? "Sadie, why would you move *with* them?"

She goes quiet at the question, and regret slams into me. She stayed because I was gone. Because she was alone. Because the hardship you know often feels safer than the hardship you don't.

"I'm sorry," I say quickly, putting the weight of my heartache into the words. "I get it. You were scared."

"Yeah, well." She chews her lip. "It didn't take long for things to go south. Money was tight. Dad lost his new job, and the fighting got intense, but the wild thing, the thing that kind of shook me, was how I gradually started to feel stronger." Even now, her spine straightens. "Like, having Max gave me perspective. I realized being around my parents was toxic for both of us, and I had no choice but to leave their home. Figure things out on my own."

Because she's a strong, capable woman, but her confession carves another scar on my heart. "What did you do?"

She plants her palms on our shared rock and leans back. "Remember that day when I picked up the phone at home and overheard my mom talking to my grandmother?"

"Your grandmother was trying to convince her to leave your dad."

She nods. "My grandmother got it—how unhealthy their relationship was. And I remembered loving her from when I was little, but my parents had cut her out of our lives, and it had been so long. Anyway, I decided to find her, let her know she was a great-grandmother. Maybe move near her to have some family support. And Des"—her shoulders lower as she tips her face up to the sky—"she was so sweet. Wouldn't let me get my own place. Insisted I move to Tennessee and move in with her."

She tells me about the joy of finally finding love in her family, how doting Celia was with Max, how helpful to her. Turning all that struggle and fear into hope and happiness.

"She had a heart attack last year, died in her sleep, but even now she's still giving to us. Left everything to me—her home and more savings than I would have guessed."

"Then you moved to Windfall," I say. The final puzzle piece that led to us sitting here, sharing a rock and our trauma.

She gets a faraway look on her face. "Her farm felt lonely after she was gone. More isolating as Max got older, and he started struggling with friends at school, coming home brooding and sad. So when I learned about your dad's book and that E was back in Windfall, moving felt right. The inheritance and sale of her land took the pressure off me financially." She dusts some dirt off our rock. "I decided it was time to face my past."

"You're amazing, Sadie. To do all of that on your own." Leave everyone she knew. Start fresh. Search out a grandmother she hadn't seen in years. "I'm *amazed* by you."

She exhales and nods slightly. "I'm pretty amazed by me too."

"I hate that you lost that job, though. The museum work. I know how much you loved the internship, how excited you were for the promotion."

"It was a blow for sure, but . . ." She smiles at the kids busy doing their art. Except Olivia, who's breaking twigs and stabbing the earth. "I started an online business a few years ago—a more accessible space for regular people to shop for great artwork at affordable prices. I focus on uplifting new artists, giving them a wider audience. I've even started working for larger offices, building their corporate collections. And I have an incredible opportunity on the horizon." She elbows my side. "What about you? E said you didn't go back to law school."

I could change the subject, evade the details of my fall from grace, but she's sitting primly on her part of the rock. I'm sitting like someone shoved a wire rod up my back. If I want to earn Sadie's trust and rebuild our friendship, truth is the only answer.

I wipe the sweat from under my sunglasses, lift and replace my ball cap. "Like I said at the diner, losing you was beyond rough. I could barely breathe, let alone concentrate long enough to study. I was angry all the time, furious at everyone and everything. So." I sigh and grit my teeth. "I just gave up in the early years. Felt out of touch with people. Tended bar because it was easier than school and earned decent cash. Hung out with a bunch of idiots, provoking fights just to feel something besides dead, and I got a bunch of ink no one would call art."

I glower at the bloody rose on my right forearm. The shading is atrocious. "Later on, I stuck with bartending because it was familiar. Made friends with an eccentric neighbor who lives to give me hell. Her name's Mirielle, and you'd love her sass. But I mostly stopped thinking long term, planning ahead, and being more productive." I run my tongue over my cracked tooth. "It all just messed with my head."

Sadie presses her hand to my thigh, the tips of her fingers landing past the edge of my cargo shorts, grazing my skin. I practically faint from her light touch.

"What you went through was unimaginable. Your father broke your trust, tore you from your life and everything you knew. But you're here now, trying to get to know your son. Putting him first, instead of barreling ahead with introducing yourself. I bet you've been stronger than you think."

"I mean, I *have* been working out a ton." I flex my arm dramatically, the cuff of my yellow gym-bro shirt straining with the effort.

She snorts. "I've noticed."

"Have you?" I resuscitate my dormant smolder, enjoying this. Us being light together.

Her smirk is pure teasing. "That shirt doesn't hide much."

"Fucking Lennon," I grumble. "He needs new company shirts."

She laughs at my annoyance. I finally relax more, but there's no missing how her lips part. Her gaze lingers on my chest. With interest? As though she's still attracted to me?

She readjusts and gives my thigh a tender squeeze. "When things were toughest with your family, I bet you helped look after them."

I frown, unsure how she'd know about that—my book club of two with Mom, keeping an eye on everyone, even when they thought I vanished. "A bit, yeah."

"Because you're a good soul, Des. You might have postured a lot with your brothers, but you'd go and fix E's bike after fighting and pretend it wasn't you. When Lennon got sick with mono, you ran around school collecting all his schoolwork for him and let him think Callahan did that. The day your mom got in that car accident with your brothers and everyone turned up late and exhausted, you cleaned the house and had dinner waiting for them, but you told your mom Delilah's mother made it."

I smile. "My chicken, tomato soup, and rice casserole." A can of tomato soup, frozen vegetables, rice, and chicken baked in the oven. A dish I learned when my mom had been sick with the flu, and I'd taken over cooking duties for a few days.

Sadie nudges my foot with hers. "Still the only thing you can cook?"

I chuckle. "Sadly. Mirielle tried to teach me crepes. It didn't go well. What about you? I bet you're a Michelin-starred chef by now."

"Hardly, but Max likes cooking. It's fun to experiment together."

I watch him a moment, how utterly focused he is on his art, and the strangest pressure winches my chest. "Maybe I could take him to a cooking class eventually. Do something fun with him one on one, after he knows who I am. Get him busy and out of his head."

"I bet he'd love that. And that's exactly what I'm talking about— how you think of what others need when they're down, what will make them happy. You cooked for your family that night because you wanted to ease your mom's burden, and you hid doing it because you worry people will think you're soft. Truth is, you've always been soft, Des. The tattoos and hard exterior are just a disguise."

"Maybe." But the heat of her this close settles me in a way I can't quite describe. Attraction is there—always there with Sadie—but I suddenly feel more grounded too. Almost at peace. "Guess it's time I quit pretending I don't care, which includes caring about you. I know I said this before, but if you need anything at any point, please ask. Even if it's just to talk through things about Max, or if you need to vent. Or if other life stuff is stressing you out. And I have some money I want to give you. It's not optional this time, so please don't make me slip it under your door."

"Okay." Her eyelashes flutter as she blinks up at me. "I appreciate that more than you know, and"—more blinking—"I've really missed this."

"Missed what?"

"Having my best friend."

I exhale for what feels like the first time in eleven years. "Me too."

A canopy of leaves dances above us. Birdsong carries on the breeze. Her spine softens, as does mine, the two of us leaning toward each other in a portrait I'd call *At Long Last*.

Then someone shouts, "Give it back!"

NINE

Max is on his feet, fists clenched at his sides. Carter's holding what looks like Max's artwork, saying something I can't hear, while the others form a semicircle of captivated spectators.

I don't know what's going on, but I'm up and stalking toward them in seconds. So quickly they all step back. Except Olivia—always *except* Olivia—who looks like she wants to pop popcorn and watch the action.

"You." I point to Carter. "Hand it over."

He leans away from me and holds out the thin tracing paper. "I wasn't doing anything."

"Looks to me like you took something that wasn't yours."

"The paper fell, and I picked it up."

Possibly, but the red flush on Max's cheeks says otherwise. "Max," I say more gently, "did your paper fall, or did Carter take it without asking?"

Max purses his lips and digs his sneaker into the earth. "The paper just dropped," he mumbles.

Nope. Judging by Carter's penetrating stare at Max, and Max's sulking, Carter definitely snatched the page. And my kid doesn't want to tattle.

With my hands tied, I give Carter a hard look. "Would it be okay if I went to your house and took your dad's Porsche for a spin without asking him?"

His nostrils flare. "That's stealing."

I shake Max's page. "So is this, even if it fell on the ground. If you didn't have permission, you don't have the right to take something. Now you're gonna sit back down on the other side of the path and finish your drawing like the mature ten-year-old you are."

His thin lips flatten until barely visible, his eyes shrinking into I-hate-you slits. Whatever. The kid can hate me all he wants, as long as he doesn't pull a stunt like that again.

Carter and our audience resume their seated positions, hunching over their work. *Except* Olivia, who resumes breaking branches and tossing them around.

I look at Max's page for the first time, and I'm at a loss.

He chose to trace the California condor—an almost-extinct vulture with a massive wingspan. Instead of drawing basic trees or mountains for scenery like the other kids, he added a boy on top of the bird, the pair flying toward the sun, fury etched on the boy's face. At the base of the page is a small forest and tiny people drawn with harder, angrier strokes—more abstract than realistic—as though the flying boy is escaping the darkness of the world.

The work isn't as jaw dropping as E's graphic novel illustrations, but holy shit. It's incredibly emotional, evoking a sense of adventure, but also fear and displacement.

Feelings I know well.

If I were to name it, I'd call the piece *I Don't Belong Here.*

Shaking off the intensity of his work, I crouch in front of him. "Max, this is incredible. Like, insanely good."

He blushes and ducks his head. "Thanks."

His modesty also reminds me of E, who got embarrassed when people complimented his art. A trait I'm pleased Max shares with him. "What does the picture mean to you?"

He hunches forward and shrugs. "I don't know."

"Well, what were you feeling when you were drawing?"

"I don't know," he says again, kicking at forest debris. "I just drew it."

When visiting art galleries, Sadie and I used to dissect art. Stare at one piece at a time, then swap interpretations, sometimes ridiculous and fantastical, other times taking the exercise more seriously, trying to understand the artist's state of mind when creating.

At one exhibit there was a small painting of a girl petting a dog. It was sweet and serene but blurred slightly. Sadie studied the small painting and said, "I think she's struggling financially. That she can barely afford to eat and is hungry and at her wit's end. She's trying to remember simpler times as a child, when life was easier."

I stared harder at the work, attempting to absorb the artist's intent, and said, "I think she suffered a tragedy—the loss of a parent or grand-parent. I think she's trying to keep good memories alive, but they get overshadowed by her sadness."

I watch Max now, worried about what inspired his character's slashed eyebrows, angry scowl, and flying escape to the sun. More evidence that Sadie's concerns about our son are warranted.

"It's a pretty awesome piece," I say carefully. "I'd love to see more of your work sometime, if you're willing to share it."

His face brightens a fraction. "Yeah?"

"Bring it next hike. And don't worry about guys like Carter. They talk big because they're small. He's probably jealous of your talent. Just wait until girls get a look at your art. You'll be fighting them off."

He drops his eyes and scratches his mosquito bites. I'm back to shifting on my feet, my tongue feeling swollen in my mouth, worried I'll say the wrong thing.

I walk with him to his spot on the log next to Jasmine and Zoey. The girls both traced the red fox and drew a girl beside the fox with big hair and big eyes—for sure Camila Cabello—surrounded by trees. The drawings are flat and crude compared to Max's masterpiece but better than I can do. Max sits near them, and I analyze his spot for clues to his emotional state. *Is he drawing sad pictures because he doesn't have a dad?*

Did a person he trust hurt him the way my dad hurt me? All I see is the bag of carrots and celery I made for each kid. Based on this evidence, I deduce that Max likes celery more than carrots, since those are almost gone.

Top-notch private-eye work.

Whatever fears or sadness lies behind his art, it'll take more effort on my part than doing a visual sweep of his drawing area. Effort I want to put in, help him some way. Do something to make his life happier, because I missed ten years of doing somethings for him.

Unfortunately, we have no alone time for the rest of the hike. Olivia keeps pace with the group. We play word-association games, where Sadie names something she sees, then the next person says a word that links to the last one, no repeats allowed.

The first round goes like this:

Sadie: Butterfly.

Jasmine: Camila.

Zoey: Cabello.

Max: Superstar.

Jun: Alien.

Carter: Farts.

As usual, Olivia refuses to play. We hike and take a couple more breaks, staying on time. I also spin over ideas, ways to entertain these preteens on our next hike. Make the outing more fun for them and Max. Better activities to make up for today's fail.

On the home stretch, I find myself watching Sadie, how easy she is with the kids, the sway of her hips. Her bright smile. She glances at me, and my face heats, because I'm already watching her. *Caught in the act.* I expect her to look away, but she doesn't. Her attention lingers, and I swear her cheeks flush.

I dare you to ask if she's single. For the first time since Lennon's dare, hope thrums in my chest. A steady soundtrack to an imagined future with my family—Sadie, Max, and me together. There are miles to go before that could become a reality. Work on my end to connect with Max, and Sadie and I have to get to know each other again, but it feels like something's there, a connection still between us. As long as I get the right answer to that tough question.

We're at the parking area too soon. Carter and Jun are in one carpool together, as are Jasmine and Zoey. After they leave, another truck drives up—a dirt-covered Ford I don't recognize from this morning's drop-offs. A Korean man gets out, who's as far from dirt covered as possible, exuding confidence and success, dressed sharply in dark jeans and a button-up short-sleeve shirt. He's the kind of handsome that inspires women to use words like *snack* and *thirsty* and *unf.*

He scans the area. When his eyes light up, I follow his line of sight to the worst possible place: Sadie.

"Joseph, hey!" Sadie beams and waves, running over to meet him.

I quit breathing. Quit blinking. *Dearly beloved, we are gathered here today to witness the death of my heart.* All I can do is stare at this *GQ* guy, who probably earns a living as a Calvin Klein model, and fight the urge to punch a tree.

Max joins them, smiling his face off. The guys high-five like they're best buds.

Forget tree punching. I'm a melting wax sculpture titled *Demise in a Yellow Gym-Bro Shirt.*

Olivia appears beside me and clucks her tongue. "If you want to compete with that, I suggest a haircut."

Of course Olivia has the same blunt advice as Mirielle. "He's not that good looking."

"He's smoking hot."

Dammit. The familiar urge to take the easy road strikes. Resume my steady life of hanging out with Mirielle and mixing drinks, no rejection or new losses to cut me down. But I'm done with easy. With or without Sadie, my life is here now, with Max. I need to get my act together. Be as strong as the mother of my son, who started fresh with nothing but her determination. And, strangely, my hair could play a part in that future.

Mirielle wasn't fully off base with her hair "safety blanket" jab. For years, the long mess has been a curtain to hide behind. My way of blocking out the world, shielding myself from judging looks, including my own over my lack of progress. Maybe I do need to cut it off. Shed this symbol of my past. Figure out exactly who's under all this hair and ink so I can excavate who I'm meant to be, starting with the makeover of the century.

TEN

I should've thought through my makeover location more thoroughly. I'm once again hiding. Instead of being lodged behind a diner, terrified to see Sadie for my first time since WITSEC, I'm in Windfall, shoved behind a lamppost, feeling like I'm in a time warp.

Windfall's central grassy square hasn't changed. The mermaid fountain and large oak at the center still draw lazy readers and loungers. The low bushes, where Sadie and I often stopped to make out, look thicker and higher, but kind of the same. Massive barrels punctuate the surrounding streets, overflowing with colorful flowers and greenery, the historic buildings and shops as brightly painted and well maintained as ever. People smile and talk to one another as they pass. Dogs bark, tongues lolling.

And Jesus, who would have guessed I'd miss this place so damn much?

I stand incognito, hat pulled low, long hair pushed forward, covering as much of me as possible, but there's no covering the emotion trembling through my chest.

A woman walks by and tugs her son closer while eyeing me warily. Two other townsfolk stop and stare at me, then lean together and whisper.

There's no way they recognize me, but I take that as my cue to depart.

I drove here from my rental in Ruby Grove for a reason. It wasn't to fall apart in front of this gossip-hungry town. I strut through one of the narrow walkways that lead to the alley behind the town's stores. The back entry to Delilah's coffee shop, Sugar and Sips, is easy to spot. I hightail it up the stairs to her and E's apartment above, but music and laughter are drifting out.

When I called E and told him I was coming over tonight, I didn't bring up my makeover plans, just that I wanted to stop by. He didn't mention company. Or a party. I debate turning around, driving the hour back home, doing this makeover thing myself. But I came here for a reason.

I knock loudly.

Dogs bark. Footsteps hurry closer. Delilah swings the door open, while talking to her dogs as she invites me. "Stay, Mac. *Stay.* Don't clobber him. That's a good boy, just—"

The big fluffy one jumps on me, paws planted at my waist, tongue and mouth reaching for my face. I smile and rub his head. "I think he wants to eat me."

"Macaroon shows love with licks. Just shove him off. The polite girl is Candy Cane."

I angle away until Macaroon's paws hit the floor. Candy Cane pants and wags her tail a mile a minute. I crouch and give her some pets, both dogs crowding and licking me until I'm chuckling. Maybe this is what I should've done during the past decade. Bought a dog to keep me company and slobber all over my face.

A final rub later, I stand. The second I'm on my feet, Delilah wraps me in a hug. "So good to see you, Des."

It's pretty damn good to see her too.

E waves. "Nice to see you smile." He gestures to two other guys, who are sitting at their kitchen counter. "Not sure if you remember Ricky—front man for the infamous band the Tweeds. That's his husband, Aaron, who can't hold a tune and is not allowed to do karaoke when we go out. They stopped by for an impromptu drink."

Aaron rakes his hand through his dark hair, his light skin blushing at E's teasing. I don't remember him from our Windfall days, but I remember Ricky and his garage band. E talked about them a bunch, and Ricky often came to my football games, cheering and heckling loudly. He's bigger than he was as a teen, broad and fit with a beard now, his reddish-blond hair shaggier. I had no clue he was gay back then, but I'm sure it's one of a million revelations I missed the past decade.

"If I'm intruding, I can go," I offer. Mellow acoustic tunes are playing. Wine is open. The four of them are relaxed and happy, enjoying a postdinner drink, planting me in fifth-wheel territory.

"We're the ones who showed up unannounced," Ricky says. "Had to share our good news that Aaron made dinner tonight and didn't burn it."

Aaron drops his head back. "That was one time."

"I bought those steaks from Hatcher the Hatchet. I could've died, and you ruined them."

I laugh, remembering Lennon daring Jake to steal Mr. Hatcher's doorbell. Jake's scream when the slaughterhouse owner came from his home's back shop carrying a bloody cleaver was priceless. "Hatcher's still alive?"

"He has a store in town now, but he's scarier than ever." Ricky shivers dramatically. "And we should go, leave you all to catch up."

The last thing I need are witnesses to my plans for this evening, but Ricky and Aaron seem nice enough. They might even be able to lend some male-grooming expertise. "No need," I say as they start standing. "I could actually use some help."

They get comfortable again. The dogs are flopped on the floor. Delilah and E lean against the kitchen counter, tucked close as usual, waiting on me.

Sweat dots my brow.

"We can play charades," E says and sips his wine. "Try to guess what help you need."

"I'm on Ricky's team," Delilah says quickly.

"Excuse me?" E does a crap job of looking indignant. His eyes are all moony for Delilah.

She pats his stomach. "You suck at charades, babe."

"I'm excellent at charades. Aren't I?" He looks to Ricky and Aaron for validation. The two men alternate between studying their nails and the walls.

"Traitors," E mutters.

I rub my sternum, overwhelmed by the good-natured teasing. Sadie and I used to have nights like this, getting together with friends, separating during the night, always seeking each other out with flirty looks and private smiles. My football buddy Kyle Jackson and I joked around like E and Ricky. Once college started, I drifted from him and my high school friends. Met new people. Had fun with them. Drank beers together. Watched sports. Good times, most of them. But in the aftermath of WITSEC, I didn't miss any of my crew all that much. I was either too self-absorbed to form deeper connections or, more likely, too happy with Sadie, investing my emotional energy in her.

As I watch E, I'm so damn proud of what my brother has rebuilt for himself. Taking life by the horns, not giving up when things got hard. Six years younger and a hell of a lot stronger.

Guess I better start learning from him.

"I need help," I repeat, zeroing in on Ricky and Aaron. Who better to help me find a sense of style and purpose under all this hair than two gay men? They make shows about this stuff. I remove my hat, place it on the counter, and say, "I need a makeover."

No one moves. Delilah bites her lip. E barely covers a muffled snort. Ricky and Aaron exchange an is-this-really-happening look.

"Just to be clear," Ricky says, "you think because we're gay, we can go all *Queer Eye for the Straight Guy* on you and transform you into a dashing prince?"

"Maybe?" I hedge, but I already know how idiotic I sound. On top of losing my sense of style, I've become a moron who latches on to the stereotypes of a TV show out of desperation.

E's full on laughing now. Delilah's muttering at him to stop. Ricky rubs his face and shakes his head.

Aaron gestures at his own styled hair and striped shirt. "I mean, I understand why you'd ask *me*. I do give good style. But him?" He plucks at Ricky's threadbare T-shirt. It's way nicer than mine. "This man only goes shopping when I secretly toss his ripped, ten-year-old clothes."

"Actually." Ricky perks up on his seat. "Don't let my outfit fool you. I *am* excellent at styling and makeovers. It's my favorite pastime. Someone pass me scissors and a razor." He claps his hands and rubs them together a tad too eagerly.

"Yep." E presses his lips flat, but there's no hiding the twitching. "He really is quite good."

Delilah doesn't add her two cents to their jabs, but her face looks ready to burst from suppressed laughter.

"He'll make you the belle of the ball," Aaron says.

Unable to maintain character, he coughs, then cracks up, covering his face as he loses it. The rest follow, snickering and making half-choked sounds.

I cross my arms. "Look. I get it. I'm sorry. All gay men obviously aren't into style and makeovers and grooming." Candy Cane whines. "Not dog grooming. I mean people grooming. Or both." Jesus. I'm talking myself into a sinkhole. "No clue why I said any of that. I'm just nervous and really need some help."

Ricky approaches me and places his hand on my shoulder. "You said that because media often feeds stereotypes compartmentalizing gay men as flamboyant, style obsessed, and over-the-top outgoing. Your job as a human is to educate yourself and understand that just like straight men, who stretch the gamut from quiet to loud to confident to insecure to stylish to this"—he points at himself—"we're not defined by our sexuality." He gives me a light punch and resumes his seat.

I hang my head, properly chastised. "Dude, I'm really sorry."

"Already moved on," he says affably. "While I don't suggest you let me near your hair, I do have some beard oil that's great if you plan on keeping the face fuzz."

"Should I?" I ask tentatively, touching my beard, unsure when I became this guy. An insecure, bumbling idiot.

Delilah shakes her head. "I say off with the beard. Your jaw's too good to hide it."

"It is a good jawline," Ricky agrees.

"Yeah, okay. A shave." I grab the mess that is my hair. "What about this?"

"Oh, I know." E studies me with an impish gleam. "I vote for one of those hipster Viking cuts with shaved sections and braided parts. Then you can get your scalp tattooed."

I lift my middle finger.

"What? Think of how jealous Lennon would be."

Delilah gives me an encouraging smile. "I cut E's hair sometimes and could give it a shot, but don't you want a professional working their magic?"

I considered booking an appointment at a salon. An anonymous visit where no one would make fun of me to my face, but the idea of being in public for this overhaul made me antsy, and part of this makeover is about my inside—the invisible stuff underneath my resting I-hate-the-world face. That starts here. With E. As hard as I've worked to alienate myself from my family, pushing them and the memories they inspire away, worried my appearance made them angry or sad, they've never given up on me. They keep turning up for interventions, hiring me to lead hikes, even though I'm pitiful at it. They've been there for me time and again, and I'm tired of missing them.

"I'd rather do it here," I say roughly and look at E. "With you."

Emotion turns E's face red, as usual. The guy can't hide a thing. "Yeah, of course. We'll all help."

Delilah comes over and takes my elbow, guiding me toward what looks like their bedroom. "Let's go find the old Desmond under all that mess."

The old Desmond's buried so far under this ink and tangled hair no makeover will uncover him. That's okay. This isn't about excavating Cocky Superhero Me. This is about discovering who I am now.

An hour later, I'm standing in front of the bathroom mirror, feeling naked. It's wild what a safety net hair is, as Mirielle said. My easy air of I-don't-care-what-I-look-like chopped off. I rub my smooth jaw, drag my hand up the short buzz at the back of my neck, through the longish brown strands on top.

My personal makeover team hovers at the doorway.

"You look hot," Delilah says. "Even the neck ink is cool in a blurry retro way."

Aaron assesses their work. "I second the hotness."

"As do I, but not the ink part. The ink still sucks." E, always there to give me a hard time.

Ricky smirks. "I still think we should give him a Mohawk."

They'd worked as a team to delouse me. Delilah washed my hair and chopped off the bulk of it. Aaron helped with the final styling of the top. E shaved the back of my neck. Ricky heckled us and kept the mood light.

When they're done praising their work, they leave. Except E, who puts his hand on my shoulder. "You really do look good. Clearer, if that makes sense. Your eyes are more alive."

I stare in the mirror and try to see what he sees. My eyelashes look thicker without everything to distract from them, and yeah, my eyes maybe appear more awake and purposeful. I also look younger but harder. Or maybe *hardened* is the better word.

In my early twenties, when I'd step in front of a mirror before going out, I'd lift my chin, confident in my appearance. While I still have the same features, I also see my resemblance to my father and feel a twinge of hate. I see fractions of me—a man whose identity was sawed into jagged pieces and tossed in an incinerator, then hastily reassembled and slapped with a presentable cover. Like my inside still doesn't match my outside, and I'm not sure how to get all parts of me in sync.

At least I look less like a meth dealer.

"Thanks, E." For calling me and being the one to tell me about Max. For talking to me when I'm at my snarliest and the rest of my family backs off. For being a great brother. "For everything," I add quietly.

"Always," he says, ducking his head. "Also, if you have any issues with Lennon, mention Maggie Edelstein's name. It shuts him up every time."

I don't remember Maggie or what her deal was with Lennon, but I tuck that intel safely away.

E leaves, and I stare at my reflection a moment longer. I think back on the good parts of today's hike. Meeting Max. Spending quality time with Sadie. I don't know if this GQ Joseph guy is a friend of hers or more, but being around E and Delilah, absorbing their happiness and rightness together, has a familiar determination taking root. The quarterback I once was. The tenacious law student.

Max is still priority one, but I want to be part of Sadie's life too. Have a second chance with her. Make them both the happiest they can be, and I'm ready to fight for that chance.

Sadie and I have talked through a lot of our toughest history, acknowledged our hardest days. We have more to discuss, but I've also been gifted time with her, thanks to Lennon's meddling. Hikes to remind us how much fun we have together, and there's nothing stopping me from returning to law school. Reenrolling. Showing her I'm still a responsible guy who can provide for his family.

But I'll start small.

Our hiking program runs two days a week, Mondays and Fridays. This week's second session is in four days. I have a solid idea on how to keep those Camila-Cabello-and-fart-humor-loving kids entertained with more age-appropriate games. I'll spend more time with my son, hopefully uncover why he's drawing angry boys zooming away from Earth. I also have the added bonus of showing off my makeover to one Ms. Sadie Sprite Jones.

ELEVEN

I don't remember the last time I woke up at the crack of dawn bursting with energy. I don't remember the last time I woke up at the crack of dawn, period, but I rushed around this morning, brushing my teeth and getting dressed, practically tripping over myself in the process, eager to start my day. While I'm dying to see Max and Sadie again, my scavenger hunt is also to blame.

I hit up Ruby Grove's main street yesterday morning, buying knick-knacks at their cheap-and-cheerful dollar store: buttons, stickers, glow sticks, bubble wands, and the like. I'm not sure this stuff classifies as "fun" or "cool." I mean, I'm thirty-four, and I still like playing with bubble wands and glow sticks, but I'm not a prime example of adulthood. There's a chance my crew of preteens will scoff when they find the loot I've stashed in the woods. My hope is the searching and discovering will overshadow any Desmond-screwed-up-again eye rolls.

So here I am, at the start of today's loop hike—the Cove Forest Trail—in my yellow gym-bro T-shirt, sunglasses and baseball hat omitted to flaunt my new look, double-checking the treasure-hunt package I prepared. And get this. I've been *smiling* since I got here.

Lennon calls as I finish. The sight of his name kicks my good mood up a notch. Keeping in mind E's wonderful intel, I answer the phone and say, "How are things with you and Maggie?"

"How . . . *what?*" he says, whisper-hissing the last word.

"Maggie Edelstein. Rumor has it there's history there."

"Fucking E," he mumbles. Then louder, "I barely know Maggie. All *you* have to worry about is not losing kids and not screwing up my business. And don't you dare say anything to Maggie about me." He hangs up swiftly.

Gotta hand it to E. I've never shut Lennon up that quickly.

I relax even more, until I see today's first arrival. The sight of Olivia is a pinprick to my newfound enthusiasm, my positivity slowly leaking out. She bounds out of her car with such enthusiasm I recoil.

Her mother waves at me. "I have to thank you."

"Yeah?" I say tentatively.

"Haven't seen Olivia this excited for anything in ages. Whatever you're doing with these kids, keep it up. Oh, and"—she gives me a flirty once-over—"like the new look."

She leaves with a wave.

I revert to the anxious version of myself, my natural state around this kid. The only reason Olivia's excited is because she has a question prepared for me. Her once-a-day interrogation, as per our deal.

She clasps her hands and blinks up at me. "Don't let my mom's flattery go to your head. She flirts with everyone."

Charming as ever. "Thanks for the boost to my confidence. Now hit me with your question." Best to get this over with, save myself from stressing over when and where she'll attack.

She rocks on her heels, doing a fantastic job of getting under my skin without uttering a word. "Did you know that statistically men lie twice as much as women?"

"Is that your question?"

"Did it sound specific to witness protection to you?"

Honest to God. She does not give me an *inch*. "What's your point, kid?"

She chews her gum, her pink top and turquoise shorts as bright as the mischief in her eyes. "The makeover's a good start. Just don't be a statistic."

I have no plans to lie to Sadie. No matter what happens between us, she'll get only the truth from me. Olivia, however, will get a pack of lies if she asks a WITSEC question at an inopportune time. I also came prepared for her today. Aside from creating a kickass treasure hunt, I did some statistical research of my own. "Did you know women talk three times as much as men? It's tiresome that you're so predictable."

Take that, mini Freud.

"Did you know the average woman can only keep a secret for forty-seven hours and fifteen minutes?" She taps her chin. "I'm not even a woman yet. Must be half that time for me."

My eyelid twitches. Palpitations overtake my chest. "We have a deal, Olivia."

"That we do," she says sweetly as another couple of cars pull up.

Carter and Jun spill out of one carpool vehicle, looking half-asleep and groggy. Jasmine and Zoey pop out of the second in another matching outfit—jean skirts with leggings and a different version of Monday's crop tops. They look more prepared for a mall expedition than a hiking trail. At least they aren't sleepwalking like the boys or staring at me unnervingly like the exorcist otherwise known as Olivia. The last car to arrive is the worst. Sadie and Max don't pull up in her red Honda. They get out of the muddy truck driven by none other than GQ Joseph.

Max hikes up his backpack and smiles at the girls. He walks over and chats with them animatedly. Probably about Camila Cabello, but he seems more upbeat than last time. As does Sadie. She's wearing another pair of mouthwatering short shorts, the yellow hiking leader shirt that flaunts her softer lines, and a smile aimed at her chauffeur. "Thanks again for the lift."

Joseph leans his elbow on his window rim and flashes his dimple. "Back here at noon, right?"

She fixes her ponytail and nods. "You're the best."

Actually, he's the worst. No man should be that attractive. And there goes my face again, doing its pinching thing. Olivia snickers.

Sadie's attention grazes over me, then she does an exaggerated double take—her eyes flaring, mouth dropping open, color rising to her cheeks.

Point for the makeover.

Pleased with my effect on her, especially in front of Joseph, I stand taller. "Okay, swashbucklers." I march toward the picnic bench by the trailhead sign. "Who's ready for some hiking fun?"

Jasmine and Zoey cross their arms. Max clings to his backpack straps like they're life preservers. Carter and Jun yawn and scratch their heads. They better not have lice.

"I'm ready, sir," Sadie says brightly and salutes me.

Damn, she's cute.

I hold up one of the activity packages I made. "There's treasure in these parts, mates."

They trade confused looks. Rightfully so. My pirate accent sounds less Captain Jack and more like a disgruntled lumberjack. I ditch the act. "Each of you will get one of these packs. There are six clues in each that'll lead you to something I've hidden in these woods along the trail. When you find your treasure, you have to flip through the provided nature book and list at least two trees, birds, or flowers you see in that area. I'll keep track of who finds each clue first and give you points depending on the order. Whoever's fastest will have the most points by the end and wins."

Carter scrunches his round face. "What do we win?"

"You get to keep the treasure I hid."

"So . . ." More face scrunching and judging from Carter. "The rest of 'em have to give it back?"

"No."

He scoffs. "Then the winner is basically the same as the loser. That's not fair."

He has a point, albeit an obnoxious one. The only rebuttal I can think of is regurgitating lines from one of the old Bill Murray movies Sadie and I used to watch on the regular, *Stripes*.

"Fair?" I say, my voice booming with melodrama. "Who cares about fair? The world isn't fair. Life isn't fair. The lines at the DMV aren't fair."

Sadie makes a cease-and-desist hand gesture across her neck.

Point taken. I was messing up the lines anyway. "Fact is, treasure hunting isn't about fair. It's about following clues and finding loot. *And it's fun.*" When the group still appears unimpressed, I cave. "The winner also gets five bucks."

"Oh yeah." Carter pumps his fist like a heavyweight contender about to hit the ring. "I got this."

"I am so winning." Jasmine snatches up an activity pack and reads hungrily, the rest crowding around the table and following suit.

Sadie moves beside me as we watch them analyze my clues. "Guess you still fuck up movie lines."

I huff out a laugh. "At least I'm consistent. And"—I pull a folded paper from my pocket—"this is for you."

Eyeing me quizzically, she unfolds the paper and squints at the name and number on it. "Who is this?"

"I did some legwork, found a counselor just outside of Windfall Max can see, if you're still looking. She works with kids and can fit him in."

"Wow, Des." She presses her hand to her chest. "This is amazing. Thank you."

"It's the least I can do. She has a good reputation." And will hopefully give Max the safe space he seems to need.

Sadie folds the note carefully and puts it in her back pocket. "I'll talk to Max about it, see if he'd be okay trying again. But this is a huge help."

I nod, feeling shy for some ridiculous reason.

She slides me a not-so-subtle perusal. "You cut your hair."

Instinctively, I touch the buzzed back. "I did."

"And shaved."

I massage my jaw, as though her words are guiding me, making me very aware of myself. "I did."

I'm also aware of Sadie's nearness, can't help imagining how my smooth cheek would feel brushing against her neck, the curve of her belly, the clover-shaped birthmark on her hip, the soft skin of her inner thigh. I stifle a rising groan.

"You look . . ." She trails off, her voice turning breathy.

I lick my lips, feeling suddenly parched. "I look what?"

"The same but different."

I angle toward her fully, let her look her fill. There's no hair hiding my scars and painful past, my ink and the slow progress I've made this year. I have no secrets about where I've been or who I've become. "Is that good or bad?" I ask.

Her chest rises and falls deeply. "You look *really* good."

Goddamn it, how can one woman affect me so intensely?

Red splotches decorate her chest, a telltale sign she's turned on too. Sadie's whole body used to blush red when I'd kiss her lips or nip her ear or run my nose up her neck, at which point my body would hit hyperdrive. And yep. Still the same reaction. Everything in me flares brighter, and I can't look away. I soak in the bow of her soft mouth, the constellation of freckles—pale and sweetly innocent—decorating her slightly upturned nose, the natural kiss-pink of her lips, her blonde-streaked hair highlighting the myriad of colors in her gold-flecked brown eyes. I'm instantly addicted. So consumed that words push past the thickness in my throat. The dare. The question. The truth I no longer want to avoid.

"Sadie," I say, my voice a gravelly blend of raw and charged, "are you single?"

Her eyes flare, and her lips fall open. My chest spasms, a minute from rupturing.

"Yeah," she whispers, and a rush of relief winds me. She clears her throat, her breastbone rising faster as she searches my face. "Are you seeing anyone?"

I swallow, mentally restraining myself from touching her. "I haven't dated anyone long term since you." I drop my voice. "No one's ever held a candle to *you*."

She bites her lip and touches her clavicle.

I fist and unclench my hands.

Laughter comes from the kids, and we both glance at them. All seems well, but by the time I look back at Sadie, she's stepped away.

"So," she says awkwardly, "that treasure hunt? Great idea. Like, really great. It must've taken ages to hide that stuff. It's such a great activity."

There's nothing great about Sadie repeating the word *great* three times. Maybe blurting the single question right before our hike, in front of a group of kids, wasn't the smoothest move.

"Yeah, well." I reach to tug at my long hair, only to remember it's gone. "Had to make up for my last pathetic attempt at fun games. Spent most of yesterday hiding stuff and getting attacked by trees." I hold out my arms, showing off the scratches.

She glances at my forearms, and more red dots her chest. She quickly crosses her arms and focuses on the kids. "I'd say your work's paying off. They're already engaged."

I'm certainly engaged in Sadie's reaction to me. She used to tell me my forearms were sexy. *Forearm porn* were her words. With the hours I spend working out, seems I've given her a little extra eye candy. Maybe flustering her in front of our audience isn't so bad.

Quitting while I'm ahead, I face our group and am unprepared for the sudden warmth that fills me. Carter and Jun are comparing sheets. Jasmine and Max and Zoey are guessing what I've hidden in the forest. Even Olivia's perusing her nature booklet. I rub my chest, unsure what this weird pressure is. Probably lingering heat from learning Sadie's single.

I nod at my group. "Let's get treasure hunting."

The first third of the hike runs as smoothly as I hoped. I haven't lost or maimed any kids. None of them exhibit signs of boredom. Olivia hasn't even cashed in today's owed question yet. They're following my handout closely, each clue giving them the approximate time and distance between the next one. Some find their treasure easily, some take longer. We wait at each junction, and I record the order in which they discover their trinkets, preparing to tally the scores at the end. When Max finds a glow stick and whoops, my chest spasms so intensely I'm worried I'm having a heart attack.

"Seriously, Des. This hike is the best," Sadie says.

While keeping the kids engaged means I haven't had alone time with Max yet, Sadie and I have spent the last forty-five minutes walking behind the group, reminiscing and catching up.

I step over a branch and match her stride. "Remember that time in Windfall when you were so busy telling me about an art exhibit that you walked right into a telephone pole?" I nudge her arm. "*That* was the best."

Laughing, she gives me a friendly shove back. "Not as good as the time you slipped at the spring fair and fell in that pile of cow shit."

An incident that still has the power to test my no-longer-ironclad gag reflex. "Never happened."

"I have photographic evidence."

I replay the day, how much fun we had watching the horse jumping, holding hands as we ate candy apples, then licking each other's sticky fingers. After which I slipped and fell in cow shit. "You don't have photos. You were too busy helping me up."

She covers her face with one hand, muffled noises slipping through. "Actually, I do."

"Sadie." I stop walking. "Did you take advantage of me when I was in a horrendously vulnerable state and take a picture?" I had cow shit in my hair, down my back. Every-fucking-where.

Forget muffled. She's full-on cackling now. "Oh my God." She tips forward, bracing her hands on her knees, tears leaking from her eyes. "You were covered in shit. How could I not?"

I force my amusement into a fake scowl. "You deleted them, right?"

"Um." More laughing and eye wiping. "Yes?"

She was always a horrendous liar. I'm laughing with her, though. It's impossible to keep a straight face when she's this unabashed, her wide grin infectious. As much as I hate having that mortifying moment immortalized in a picture, I'd bathe in cow shit again if it meant having a front row seat to Sadie's joy. I also have my own set of embarrassing photos.

"Guess it's a good thing I still have those pictures from the night you drank your weight in boxed wine and decided it would be fun to drag me through a sex shop."

She stands abruptly, eyes wide. "You do not."

"Oh, I do." The one where she's miming giving a dildo head. The one where she's tangled in bondage straps. The one where she mistook anal beads for a necklace.

She momentarily appears shell shocked, then she laughs again, the two of us losing it, trying to walk on the trail, practically doubled over . . . and I smack into a tree.

We laugh harder, making sounds that no doubt terrify the birds and wildlife. The kids are stopped up ahead, staring at us with confused what's-wrong-with-them looks. I make a shooing motion with my hand, gathering my composure. "Treasure awaits. Move along."

They turn. Except Max and Olivia, who both stare at us an extra beat. While those long perusals make me edgy for different reasons, I don't remember the last time I've felt this good.

Just over the halfway point, we stop for snacks and leisure time. Sadie steps away, visiting each kid to chat about their nature booklets and treasures. I grab a crushed beer can from the ground, annoyed with people for being people. Littering in nature is reprehensible.

As I shove the can in my backpack, a small shadow slashes the ground. "Did you have to wear a disguise in witness protection? Is that why you have those tattoos and had the bad hair?"

Honest to God. I look at the ground for one minute, and there's Olivia, cornering me while I'm distracted. "Nope. Those bad choices were all mine."

I should buy a T-shirt: I Survived WITSEC and All I Got Were These God-Awful Tattoos.

"Okay, but—"

"Nope," I repeat and bare my teeth in a saccharine smile. "One question per day."

She makes a grumbly sound. "Fine. I'll do better next time." Her threatening tone doesn't bode well, and she's lingering. "Also, just so you know, this hike doesn't suck."

There's that strange warmth again, pushing at my ribs.

Feeling on top of my game, I decide to search out Max. He's not with Jasmine and Zoey this time. He's on a lone tree stump, hunched over his sketchbook. So much like his uncle E, always with a pencil in his hand, imagination running amok. Also like his uncle, he might not appreciate being interrupted, but my time with him is limited.

I approach slowly and smile at the glow stick protruding out of his backpack. Beside it is the corner of a book. Now *that* has promise. Sadie mentioned he reads tons, that some of his chosen novels are more adult in nature, beyond his age range. While I only read school-assigned books growing up, my book club with Mom pushed me to explore literature, delve into character motivation the way Sadie pushed me to examine art—the women in my life always making me a better person. Maybe my efforts with Mom could be my in with Max.

"Reading something good?" I ask.

Pencil stilling, he frowns. "What?"

I nudge his bag with my foot and get a better glimpse of the upper part of the cover: *Simon vs. the—*

Max tugs his bag closed and shoves everything deeper inside. "Don't go through my stuff."

His cheeks flush, his thick eyelashes lowering as his shoulders curve forward, like he's both embarrassed and mad. Remorse winds me. A whole walloping of guilt that makes me want to hit rewind and get a do-over. Honestly. How do parents do it? I wasn't even reprimanding or disciplining him, and it feels like someone's stepping on my lungs. But I'm done running scared. If I want to get to know Max better, I have to roll with these punches.

I crouch beside him. "You mentioned showing me more sketches last hike. Can I check out your work?"

He pauses, grips his pencil tighter. Eventually, he says a tentative, "Sure."

He holds out his sketchbook hesitantly. I'm not hesitant. I take it and flip through the pages, examining his work intently. Some of his sketches are quick and rough, others more detailed. In one a boy stands by himself with a crudely drawn crowd on the other side of the page. No other details, just a desperate sense of apartness. In another a boy is on the ground in pieces. It's not a gruesome sketch with blood and guts. The boy looks toylike—a wooden boy who's broken apart, unable to put himself back together. A third is filled with a number of smaller sketches, each with two hands clasped. Some hands are only outlines, others have warped proportions—studies of what makes a hand a hand, maybe? There are also pages of birds and rockets and planes. Flying is obviously a thing with Max.

"Am I sitting next to a future pilot?" I ask.

His face lights up. "The Cessna 195 is the coolest. Super vintage with radial engines and cowling bumps." While I hold his book, he flips pages back and forth until he hits an impressive sketch of a fifties-style small plane. "Mom says it's a class act."

This kid is a class act, rambling off airplane terminology I don't even understand. But I understand the brightness in his eyes. This is what he loves. Still, the intermittent drawings in his sketchbook reminded me of the angry boy he drew zooming away from Earth. "Gotta say, your art is amazing. As cool as that Cessna. Bet your mom's proud."

He takes the book back from me and slides it shut. "I don't show her my art. Just the school stuff."

I glance at Sadie, who's watching us but quickly busies herself with useless tasks. "Why don't you show her?"

"I don't know. She gets . . ." He trails off and flips the corners of his sketchbook pages.

"Too analytical?"

He nods.

An aspect of her that hasn't changed. Sadie breaks art into its base parts, delving deeper, excavating the artist's mind. He knows it and doesn't want her picking through his head.

If he knew I was his father, would he regret letting me in?

That prospect has me grappling for conversation, anything to start building more of a relationship with Max. The only thing that pops into my head is *Nice weather we're having*. Feeling antsy, I watch him set up to sketch again and remember an activity Sadie and I used to mess around with, where we'd stare at each other or at knickknacks or buildings, not our pages, drawing cool abstract images without breaking our lines.

"Want to play a drawing game?"

Max side-eyes me. "What kind of game?"

"A speed-drawing contest. We both have to draw blind without looking at the page, and—"

"We can't lift our pencil from the page?" he finishes excitedly.

I guess Sadie played the game with him too. "I see you know the rules. But I should warn you, I'm excellent at this game."

He's already moving, pulling out another pencil and sketchbook from his backpack and handing them over. Endless art supplies. "You won't be as excellent as me."

Seems Max inherited some of my cockiness. "I basically have a black belt in blind drawing."

"There's no such thing."

"I also won gold in blind drawing at the Olympics."

One corner of his lips kicks up. "Is that the same Olympics where you asked a bunch of ten-year-olds to play catch my shadow?"

I bark out a laugh. Kid has a sense of humor. "The exact one."

I get my phone set up, then we face each other, sitting cross-legged on the ground, pencils poised for our battle. "Ready?" I ask.

"I was born ready."

The comment is cute and confident and zooms me back to Sadie and me racing to go cliff jumping at Bear Lake, tripping over ourselves to get there first; the two of us at the Smash Shack, stuffing our faces with french fries in a french-fry-eating contest, cracking up the whole time.

All our contests started with me saying, "Ready?"

Followed closely by Sadie's brash, "I was born ready."

She's obviously played tons of games with Max. Hundreds. Thousands. Ten years of fun games. He's picked up her mannerisms and challenging quips and probably loads of other habits.

And I missed all of it.

Swallowing roughly, I say, "Ready, set . . . *go.*"

We stare at each other, our pencils moving over our pages. Max's tongue pokes out of his mouth—his concentration pose. Sadie used to say I looked constipated when I was focused, but I don't worry about my expression. I focus on Max, drawing his cute tongue, the slopes of his wide lips, his small but strong nose, then his eyes and all those thick eyelashes, never lifting my pencil, loving this game. I get to stare at my son and discover the dusting of freckles on his nose (freckles like Sadie's), and the slant of his ears (they stick out slightly like mine), and a subtle divot in his chin neither of us have. I get to stare and soak in how he really is a combination of Sadie and me and an X factor that's all Max.

My alarm goes. We lift our pencils and grin at each other.

"Mine's amazing," I say. It's not. I'm useless at drawing. My lines swoosh all over the page in erratic loops.

Max looks at it and snorts. "My head isn't that wide."

I hold the page next to his smiling face. "No clue what you mean. It's a perfect likeness."

His drawing of me is, of course, phenomenal. It's abstract and funky, my shorter hair done in overlapping strokes, and I do look kind of constipated. "Pretty sure I win," I say.

His retaliation: "You're a poor loser."

Nailed that one. "At least give me a rematch?"

"That tree." He points to a larger maple up ahead, its trunk swelled with a gnarly knot. "Think you can handle it?"

"I was born ready," I say, stealing his and Sadie's line.

Five drawings later, I'm still useless with a pencil, but Max and I have relaxed into this effortless banter. Joking together. Having a nice time.

He taps his pencil on his sketchbook after, alternating between blinking at his page and stealing peeks at me. "You know my mom, right? From when you were younger?"

Know is the understatement of the century. "I do."

He quits fidgeting and nails me with a curious stare. "You make her nervous."

"What makes you say that?"

"She takes way longer getting ready when we come here. She does that when she's nervous. Happy nervous."

Well now. Can't say that's unwelcome intel. "I bet you have lots of experience making girls happy nervous."

His eyebrows drop into sharp slashes. "Not really."

"In time, kid. Like I said, the girls will go nuts for your art."

He seems to sink more into himself, angling away from me, our easy banter back to stiff. Can't be comfortable for him discussing his mother like this, and our time is too precious to spend it discussing Sadie.

"So, Max." I try to catch his eye. "Do you do other art besides drawing?"

He perks up. "I did pottery once last year. Didn't like it as much, how squishy and messy it was, but the glazing part was cool. I made my mom a container for her pens."

I glance at Sadie, who's talking animatedly with Jasmine and Zoey. She probably loved that gift. Gave our son a huge hug and uses it on her desk.

A marble of affection knocks around in my chest, a game of pinball happening with my heart as I watch her and picture their loving home together. An imagined scene that makes me happy for them.

When I turn back to Max, his thick-lashed eyes are narrowed at me. He cocks his head in a way that looks eerily familiar. "You like my mom."

Jesus. Is it that obvious?

Sadie was right. Kids are way smarter than adults give them credit for.

"She's wonderful. A real great gal." My heart trips over itself as I push to my feet and dust nothing off my thighs, because *gal*. Who in the twenty-first century says *gal*? "Keep up that awesome sketching and your awesome treasure-hunting skills, kiddo."

I pivot and strut away before I say things like *way to go, daddy-o* and *you're a hip cat*.

At least I made progress with Max today. Already, I feel a connection with him. The beginnings of a true friendship. I might not even have to wait much longer before I tell him who I am, especially if he has a social worker he likes.

For now, I'll search for Max's book, *Simon vs. the* something, and try to create more common ground with him. And maybe I'll call Sadie tonight. Find out if Max is doing better at home. See if she thinks I can introduce myself sooner. I might even ask her on an official date, instead of mooning over her from afar, while our son sees right through me.

TWELVE

The internet is not my friend. During WITSEC, any and all social sites were torture chambers that shoved happy, smiling, oh-my-God-I-have-*the-best*-life people in front of my face. A bunch of bullshit mainly. No one's life is all filtered zit-free smiles and seaside vacations. I'm well aware that snippets on social media are designed to create the illusion of a good life. Even so, everyone's illusions were better than mine. They still are.

I'm on the Duke Law website, and all I feel is queasy. Every picture shows smiling students, younger than me, socializing together like it's so easy to make best buds the second you step on campus. Whatever. Once again, I get the act. Plenty of students show up in their introverted bubbles and barely talk. This website is propaganda, extolling the virtues of Duke Law. I click on the course browser link. No smiling freshman here, but my queasiness worsens.

Antitrust

Internal Arbitration

Conflicts of Law

Adjudication

Ethics and the Law of Lawyering

Twelve years ago, perusing these courses gave me a kick of adrenaline. The good kind. I was aware the work would be hard. I had some insecurities and knew I'd have to work my ass off, but I was up for the challenge.

Now? My pulse races and my throat closes, like my body's allergic to academics. Every word I read has me curving forward, my forehead feeling clammy. I have no clue if the take-no-prisoners guy who propelled me through college still exists under the scar tissue I've developed. I have no clue *why* I haven't reached out to Duke since deciding to better myself, attempting to get reinstated into the program.

Abruptly, I shut my computer and massage my brow.

My Ruby Grove rental doesn't come with a caftan-wearing neighbor who bluntly sasses me and calls me Walter, but it has more charm than my Houston pad. The maritime-inspired art on the walls isn't my taste—Sadie would call it motel chic—but it's better than the bare walls Mirielle loved to criticize. I even draped a quilt Mom made over the couch, adding a touch of hominess. And ugliness. My mother can't quilt or craft for shit, a lack of talent I've clearly inherited, but she loves making stuff for her boys.

The best part is the bare-bones gym in the garage.

I change into shorts and a tank top and spend an hour hitting the heavy bag and doing sit-ups and push-ups and pull-ups, then I knock out reps on the bench press until my chest aches. When I'm done and less agitated, I shower and take my laptop and e-reader outside.

The small bungalow has a private yard with a few skinny trees. I sit in the provided lawn chair and kick my feet up onto the metal coffee table, ready to look up Max's book. This I can do. Read a book at a ten-year-old level. I open my e-reader and type in *Simon vs. the*, hoping a slew of titles doesn't pop up. Only one does.

Simon vs. the Homo Sapiens Agenda

I frown at the odd title. It sounds more academic than simple plea-sure reading, which isn't bad. Maybe my son's a budding pilot *and* a budding evolutionary biologist, intent on discovering the origins of humankind. Pleased with the possibility, I click on the title and start reading the blurb. By the time I get to the end, I'm reading so slowly, so intently, each syllable feels like it's expanding in my brain.

This is clearly a teen book, not an academic dissertation on man's evolution. At least not *humankind's* evolution. It seems to be about a gay teenage boy struggling with his sexual identity, and . . .

I was not expecting this.

Hand covering my mouth, I reread the blurb twice. Yep, still the same. I'm not sure if a ten-year-old reads a book like this because he sees himself in the main character. Or is it simply popular, and my kid's open minded and curious about the struggles gay kids experience?

I think back to Max's art, how turmoil fueled some of it seemed: the angry boy zooming away from Earth, the sad boy separated from the crowd, the toylike boy broken into pieces, the page filled with held hands. I can't remember if the hands he drew all looked male, but what I do remember is how they seemed like a study. Sketches of what two hands holding are supposed to look like. As though he's maybe trying to figure out if the hand he wants to hold is okay and normal? Or I'm reading way too much into this book and those sketches, doing what I did with Ricky and Aaron, making sweeping assumptions without educating myself.

But if Max is gay, if he's struggling to understand himself or afraid to tell people, to even tell his mom, hiding his sketches from her the way he has, then I've already said insensitive, alienating remarks. *I bet you have lots of experience making girls happy nervous.*

I uttered that nonsense. Didn't even think twice. Just assumed my son was straight and his world experiences were similar to mine.

In time, the girls will go nuts for your art.

I said that too. Can't even claim I was joking. I certainly wasn't smart. Even if he isn't gay, I just taught him it's okay to assume everyone lives in a straight vacuum. That it's okay to not make space for other people's differences. May as well get a Closed-Minded Dad tattoo added to my stellar collection.

After a third read of the book blurb, I download the book, then open my laptop. I google *how to tell if your child is gay* and *signs your child is gay* and *indications your child is gay*. Covering all my bases. Some sites say boys who play with dolls or cross-dress or hang out predominantly with girls might be gay. As far as I know, the first two don't apply to Max, unless Sadie omitted certain details when I grilled her on our son. The last one, though. He definitely prefers Jasmine and Zoey to Carter and Jun, but I prefer Jasmine and Zoey to Carter and Jun, so not exactly a scientific study. One religious-based site uses words like *sissy* and *epidemic* and other slurs that make me want to slam my laptop against the ground.

What the hell is wrong with people?

When I'm a modicum calmer, I scroll and read the nonbigoted sites. The only undisputable fact I uncover is there's no My Child Is Gay checklist. And I need to do better. Apparently, if Max is struggling with his sexual identity, the sites say I have to foster an open relationship with him. Allow for communication. Let him know he can talk to me about anything, and make it clear I'm open-minded. (A.k.a., quit making assumptions he's straight.)

I need to show him my love is unconditional.

And yeah, *love*.

Pressure balloons in my chest, pushing at my ribs. Twisting me up inside. Not sure how this kid already has me worrying over him—this surge of protectiveness that has me ready to fight the world on his behalf—but it's there. Undeniable and emotionally driven. Max is a piece of Sadie and me. He's proof of how deeply we once loved each other, and I never want him to experience hate or hurt or ever dislike a part of himself.

So yeah. I'll be devouring *Simon vs. the Homo Sapiens Agenda* in short order, and I'll make damn sure I'm no longer careless with my words. First, I need to figure out if Sadie knows more about Max's life than she's letting on.

I hit speed dial on her number.

She picks up after one ring. "Des, hi."

"Hey . . ." *Sprite.* I almost used her nickname. Our history rolled into one cute syllable. I swallow and try again. "Having a nice weekend?" Painful small talk for the win.

"Quiet but nice."

I stretch out on the lawn chair, adjusting until the metal rim doesn't dig into my thighs. "Is Max around?"

"He's downstairs drawing with Joseph, but I can get him."

"No, no. I actually wanted to talk to you." Specifically without Max around, but not while Max is anywhere near Joseph. Sadie and I only scratched the surface of our are-you-single talk. The whole Joseph situation is still a blank spot. He obviously spends a lot of time with them. He could be into Sadie without her knowing. Or they could have a history together she didn't mention, and *single* means different things to different people. Hooking up randomly with someone doesn't classify as a relationship. Another topic I should probably address tonight. May as well start there.

I take a breath and say my favorite word. "Sadie."

"Yeah?" Her voice is soft, tentative. Maybe she senses how big this call is, all the massive topics I need to address.

I settle deeper into my chair, inhale the scents of charcoal and grilled meat from a neighbor's barbecue. Kids laugh in the distance. Happy families doing happy things. I grip the back of my neck. "You spend a lot of time with Joseph."

"Oh. Yeah." There's a pause, the sound of a chair scraping, like she's sitting down too. "I might not have mentioned it, but we work together."

"Doing the online art business?"

"Mostly. My reach was small when I started, then I did this one-off trip to New York and met Joseph at a gallery opening."

"You must have loved New York." A city exploding with art and artists. A city I'd love to explore with Sadie.

"It was amazing and crazy busy, but I didn't have a ton of time there. Joseph did, though. He travels a lot, networks with up-and-coming artists and at-risk kids in funded art programs. We're building a new arm of the business," she says, talking faster, livelier, "giving these young adults better visibility. An online venue to share and market their work. Shining a light on how they view the world, breaking down boundaries of sexuality and society's expectations, with a lot of focus on the immigrant experience too. And those corporate businesses I mentioned are eager to develop art collections in their offices with a slant to these unique perspectives."

"Wow." I love the swagger in her voice, her excitement as she talks about this career she's built. "You're actually doing it. Living and breathing art."

"I mean, sort of."

"Quit being so modest. You've built a business from the ground up and are helping support artists. It's what you always wanted." Makes me feel *slightly* less ill that she had to give up the gallery job when I left.

Her heavy breath pushes through the line. "I only focus on the behind-the-scenes stuff. Joseph coordinates our efforts, meets the artists, does the in-person presentations to the offices. He travels and takes videos of the corporate spaces to show me. So, yeah, I actually help choose the art and manage the business end of things, but I'm never in the spaces." Another weighted pause. "Sitting in my small office all day doesn't feel particularly creative."

Forget less ill. My gut does an unpleasant twist. Sadie's business may be thriving, but I'm not sure she is. Being a single parent steals your options, narrows your focus. I mean, Sadie wouldn't give up Max for anything in the world, but I hate that she's had to abandon a portion of her dreams—working in a gallery space, interacting with patrons and artists, seeing artwork in the flesh. I also can't even hate Joseph. He's filling in where she can't, being her legs on the ground.

I chew the inside of my cheek. "You mentioned something the other day about an exciting new opportunity. What's that about?"

"I don't want to jinx it." But a happy buzz returns to her voice.

"Because it's amazing?"

"Too good to be true, honestly. And I shouldn't talk about it yet, but . . ."

"But?" I prod, loving her barely contained enthusiasm.

"It's *unreal*. Sarah Lim is this billionaire hedge fund genius and major supporter of the arts. She's finishing construction on what will be *the* largest modern art museum in the United States. Like, absolutely state of the art. The type of place that'll draw millions of visitors annually, and I'm in the running to be part of the staff, along with Joseph. I'm not exactly sure of the position available, and it will be done remotely, but it's the kind of work I dreamed about in college. Impacting so many people through art."

"Sadie, that's incredible." I grin, so damn happy for her. "Of course she'll hire you."

"Like I said, I don't want to get too excited. We've been working on it for a while, and there are no guarantees."

"How about I get excited for you?"

She laughs. "Sounds good to me."

"Guess it's good you met Joseph. Seems like he's a big part of your career." And nothing more, if I have anything to say about it.

"He's wonderful," she says, clueless to my simmering jealousy. "He wanted to show me some pieces in person, which is why he's here. And my car needed work. He met me at our first hike so I could drop it off at the mechanic's. He's staying here and was nice enough to shuttle me around for a few days afterward."

An explanation I'd like to accept and run with, but I can't let this go without specifics. My imagination has become a living, breathing beast, picturing them enjoying a bottle of wine together, discussing art, their shared passion leading to shared smiles and occasional hookups, kisses and moans as they . . . nope. No thanks. I crack my neck.

"I know I have no right to ask this, and you already said you're single, but this Joseph guy." My heart thrashes wildly, trying to race through the phone line. "Is there something between you two?"

All I get is heavy breathing. Mine and hers. Then, "No." The word is whispered, so soft I have to press the phone harder to my ear. "We're just friends and coworkers."

Too relieved to speak, all I can do is grunt. Translation: *Thank fucking God.*

"Sorry to push the single subject." I'm whispering too. No clue why. "I just feel a lot when I'm around you."

She exhales softly, this conversation turning intimate. The setting sun makes me wish she were on a matching lawn chair, her feet kicked up beside mine, the evening opening up before us. Or maybe I like this better. Her soft voice in my ear, nothing to distract me from our words.

"I feel it too," she says eventually. "All our history. But yeah, the dating thing—it's always been hard for me. I don't let men meet Max. Not unless I'm sure it's long term."

"Has anyone been long term enough to meet him?"

Her pause lingers. "One guy."

The knowledge is a physical blow. A man shared her bed and her life. A man who maybe helped raise my son. "How long ago?"

"Three years, and losing him was hard on Max. So no, I haven't dated in a while. I'm not sure how to do both. How to be a mom and a woman with her own selfish needs."

"Honey, having needs isn't selfish. That's being human."

"Doesn't make it easy."

Her words sound like a warning of sorts. That she maybe wants to reconnect as badly as I do, but she's worried about what it all means for Max. I'm not just some random guy. I'm his dad. If Sadie and I date, and for some reason we don't work out, *he's* the one who'd be hurt the most. Implications I'll have to consider more fully. "You're an incredible mother, Sadie. Always putting Max first."

"He's an incredible kid, so it's not hard. Most of the time."

"Do you do anything just for yourself? Without Max?"

"Not often, but when we lived in Tennessee, I'd occasionally do a painting and wine class with a group of women. I'm not talented like Max, but it was fun to get out and talk with adults. And I'm really good at axe throwing."

"Axe throwing?" I picture tiny Sadie wearing camo, holding a massive axe, murder in her narrowed eye. "Moving targets or stationary?"

"Stationary, but I bet I could hit a moving target. That would actually be fun."

"So what you're saying is you love to imagine murdering people?"

"No! But I love the power of it. Feeling like I can control this primitive tool that can also be a weapon. It makes me feel strong. Unfortunately, there isn't an axe-throwing place in Windfall."

But I bet I could create something for her. "If I tossed an axe, I'd probably have to stick a picture of my father on the target."

"Count me in for that," she says, her voice harder.

I run my hand up the back of my neck. "I'm sorry. Really wish I could go back and murder him."

"I thought we were done with apologies."

"Right." I shift on my chair, still heart-deep in this moment, not ready to lose this connection. I need to think more on her worries about Max, how they relate to her dating. How we can test our boundaries while being careful with his feelings and making Sadie comfortable.

For now, we need to pivot. "I have some questions about Max."

"Of course. Ask anything."

I plant my feet on the ground and lean my elbows on my thighs. "You said Max reads a bunch, and I've been reading a lot the past few years. I'd love to see what he's into these days, if you don't mind sharing. Might help us find common ground."

"Honestly, I wish I could answer that."

"You don't know?"

She sighs heavily. "Like I've said, he's gotten pretty introverted the past year. We talk at dinner and have fun when we're out, but it's like a switch flips at times. He won't show me his sketchbook or talk about his books or friends. Just locks himself in his room for hours, and I made a promise never to snoop through his stuff. My mom did that, and it always felt like this huge invasion of privacy."

Her mother invaded more than Sadie's privacy, always finding passive-aggressive ways to make her daughter feel small. Even away at school, Sadie would get incessant calls from Mrs. Jones purposely bitching about her husband—*he never helps around the house, he refuses to look for work, he snaps at me for no reason, he has no right to go through my credit card bills*—knowing her daughter felt pulled to mediate. Be the buffer, even when their cruelty targeted her.

She's trying not to be anything like her invasive mother, but Max's self-imposed isolation suggests my gut feeling about him might be right.

I rub the space between my eyebrows, preparing to ask Sadie if she's ever questioned Max's sexuality, wondered if he might be gay. A sudden stitch cramps my side.

Max has been actively hiding his art from his mother. I might be the only adult who's seen his sketches. If I break his trust, or if I'm wrong about his struggles, he might quit sharing his work and thoughts with me. Become more closed off. Before that happens, I need him to know whatever he's feeling is okay.

"If you come across anything," I say, "let me know."

"Is something up?" Concern pitches her voice. "He showed you his sketchbook, right? Last hike."

"He did and nothing's up." *Men lie twice as much as women. Don't be a statistic.* Olivia, on the mark as always. "Max is insanely talented, though. Has a plane in there that's unreal."

"He loves aviation everything." I hear the smile in her voice.

"You've raised an incredible kid."

"You've already said that."

"I'll probably say it a million more times, because it's true. Did you talk to him about seeing the new counselor?"

"He doesn't love the idea, but he agreed to go. I'm hoping she's a better fit than the last man. And he's been a bit better recently. You two seemed to connect on today's hike."

"Have I mentioned what a great kid he is?"

This laugh is full of fondness. "I believe you did. The appointment's in a couple of weeks. Might be a good time to introduce you, when he has someone he can talk to about it all."

I nod, even though she can't see me. "I was gonna ask about telling him sooner, but that makes sense."

As tough as waiting is, the time will allow me to delve deeper into his mind, solidify our connection. Find a way to show him he'll have my love and support no matter what he's going through.

"Thanks for being so great with him," she says softly.

"Not a hardship." I exhale long and slow, not wanting this conversation to end. "Guess I'll see you Monday."

"Definitely."

I don't hang up. She doesn't hang up. The sun dips lower, brushing the sky in soft pastels—a serene painting I'd call *Possibilities*. We both breathe quietly, the elongated seconds adding to the tender ache I can't seem to shake these days.

Unable to handle this sweet agony any longer, I whisper, "Have a nice night, Sprite."

THIRTEEN

It's not sunny, but no one seems to care. We're half an hour into our hike, and once again the kids are engaged and excited. At least the three with me are. Max, Zoey, and Jasmine are following their map and compass, stopping regularly, discussing whether they're still on track. We're on an unmarked loop trail through forest and farmland. Sadie and I have GPS coordinates on our phones, but the kids are flying blind. I swear, every time they realize which way they're supposed to go and their eyes light up, I feel a little thrill.

My Happy Hiking Leader persona has taken over.

Sadie's three cadets—Carter, Jun, and Olivia—have the same map and compass, but I sent them in the opposite direction to us. When Olivia realized she wouldn't be within interrogation distance of me, she fumed and scowled. I retaliated with a full-teeth smile. The goal is to meet up with them at the midpoint—a lookout ridge where you can practically see all the way to Windfall. Until then, I have Max to myself.

"Let's take a break," I tell my troops.

The girls stop and drop, immediately pulling out their phones. Scroll and gossip central. At least I got them to unplug when on their feet. Max searches the grass, clears away some sticks, and settles down with his backpack.

This is my cue, why I split up the group. Alone time with my son.

I read *Simon vs. the Homo Sapiens Agenda* in one sitting. And cried. Then I watched the movie on my laptop—because who knew it was a movie too—and I cried. No, I won't ramble on about spoilers. Suffice it to say, navigating love and sexuality as a teen is some daunting shit. Also, I'm pretty sure the book isn't geared toward ten-year-olds. The amount of swearing and general musings on sex would have most adults slamming on the parental controls. I'm not enough of a parent to control anything, and Sadie said she made it a point of not snooping through Max's stuff. So here we are. Me reading and crying, while also laughing. Seriously, that Simon kid is hilarious. But I don't know if *my* son is gay. I just need him to understand that it doesn't matter who he loves or doesn't love. All that matters is he's okay and happy.

The gray sky stretches above us, a heavy awning casting a somber mood I will ignore. Stretching out my neck, I walk over and sit across from Max. He removes his carrot and celery sticks from his pack and offers me some. I grab a couple of carrots because I know he doesn't like those. We munch. We drink water. I pretend I'm not freaking out that I'll mess this up by saying the wrong thing and hurting him somehow.

A deep breath later, I say, "I read *Simon vs. the Homo Sapiens Agenda.*"

He freezes midreach for his water. "Why?"

Excellent question. Didn't plan for this, but I certainly should have. I rub my jaw and shrug. "Saw it in your bag and thought it looked interesting."

"Okay," he says guardedly.

Yeah, it was an unconvincing answer. A pathetically subpar effort on my part. I need to veer closer to honesty here. Honesty with some facts omitted.

"Truth is," I say, talking through the nervous vibrations of my heart, "I used to have this mini book club—just me and my mom. We'd pick apart novels, debating what we liked and didn't like. But we don't live in the same city anymore, and I miss those talks. When I saw your book last time, I thought it would be fun to read something different. Maybe talk about it with you, if you've finished it."

He picks at the grass, shreds a blade into thin strips. He grabs a broken branch next and picks at that. Eventually, he looks at me. "Did you like the book?"

"Like? Nope." Max's face falls, and I grin. "I *loved* the book."

"Really?" He's gawking so hard he's liable to catch flies with his mouth.

"What's not to love? I mean, that Martin guy deserves a shot to the neck, and I hate how social media like Tumblr tears people down, but the writing was brilliant. Simon was impulsive and funny and kind of broke my heart a few times." Hence the crying. "It was a fantastic book."

Brightness shines from his dark eyes, or maybe that's the sun finally peeking through the clouds. "You really read it." A statement still tinged with surprise.

"Hell yeah. What about you? Did you like it?"

He blushes. "I actually read it twice."

"Because you have killer taste." I wince at how over the top I sound. Like I'm an outcast desperately trying to be liked. I grab a matching stick to his, peel it like he's doing, going for nonchalant when I'm having an internal earthquake. "What do you say we ask each other questions about the book? Book-club-level questions only."

His stick stripping gets intense. "What are book-club-level questions?"

"Deeper questions, digging into how the characters felt. I can go first." He nods and lowers his shoulders a fraction. I forge on. "So, Maximillian."

He rolls his eyes. "It's just Max."

"So, Just Max. OREOs—why do you think Simon liked OREOs over all the other cookie options out there?"

He smiles, and my internal earthquake decreases from a five on the Richter scale to a four. "I think," he says, "it's having the hard and soft together. The squishy inside and crunchy cookie part. Simon is kind of deep, always analyzing stuff. He probably liked thinking about it, and how they separate is fun."

"Totally agree. Your turn."

He tosses his naked branch and grabs another. "Why do you think Simon liked listening to Elliott Smith so much?"

"Have you listened to Smith?"

He nods. I guess we both tried to get into Simon's head.

"Did you like it?"

"No?" he says on a question, like he doesn't trust his opinion.

"Not my favorite either. I prefer my music louder, but maybe that was the thing with Simon. The music is kind of mellow and sad, like it's one long exhale. Maybe he enjoyed it because the sound matched how he was feeling at the time. Or how he *wanted* to feel. Like he was dying to exhale."

Max chews his lip, as though deep in thought. The girls giggle at their phones. A yellow-bellied warbler flits in the trees.

I do the opposite of those Elliott Smith exhale songs and suck in a shaky breath as I prepare for my next question. "When the book starts, Simon's pretty secure in who he is. He's obviously stressed about coming out and all the change ahead of him, and I don't think he liked that his dad made all those off-the-cuff heterosexual comments, but how do you think Simon felt before the book starts? Like the years leading up to when we meet him?" When he was younger and closer to Max's age.

Max scrunches his face and absentmindedly taps his foot on the grass. "I think," he starts, then stops. The blush on his cheeks flushes redder. He eyes the Camila Cabello fan club, who wouldn't notice if pigs started flying around us, then shifts his focus back to me. "I think he probably felt . . . alone. And maybe scared."

"Yeah, I bet he felt really alone." I'm practically whispering, barely blinking, worried one wrong move will shut him down. "But why scared? What do you think he was scared of?"

"I don't know."

"I bet feeling different was scary. Maybe he was wondering if something was wrong with him."

"Maybe." His foot tapping picks up speed, and that red flush travels down his neck. "And of people not liking him, maybe. Of his mom not liking him."

I freeze midswallow. My insides shoot to a seven on the Richter scale.

If I had to guess, this is Max talking about Max. Not Max talking about Simon, who had a close relationship with *both* his parents, not just his mother. But that's all Max has—a mom. Not four brothers like me. There's no father in his life to worry about, although I'd take fatherless over a criminal asshole any day. He has one person in his corner, and I think he's scared if he's "different," she might like him less.

At the end of the day, his true sexuality doesn't matter. Max is ten. These are early days in his self-discovery. This conversation isn't about him coming out or fully acknowledging what he is or isn't feeling. It's about me getting across that I'm a safe place. That in time, when he knows who I am, he can tell me anything without fear of judgment and will hopefully walk through his life stronger.

"That makes sense," I say tentatively. "People in general can be uncomfortable when they meet others who are different from them. And Simon felt different from his family, but I also love that he still knew his family would support him. Like later, when we're in his head, he's still freaked out about saying the words out loud and changing their dynamic, but he's not worried he won't be loved."

"Yeah," he says, breathing harder. "I liked that part."

"If I was Simon's dad, I'd be sad if I knew he was sad or scared when he was younger, before the book starts. I'd probably wish I could go back in time and tell him he's loved unconditionally. Because he was, even if his dad made heterosexual jokes too much."

Max blinks a bunch, his attention firmly on the branch in his hands. I blink a bunch, willing my tear ducts to calm the fuck down. I want to fold Max into my arms, hug him fiercely. Give him nothing but love and comfort and unsay the careless *girls will dig you* comments I uttered.

"You're as good as my mom at book club," I say through the strain in my throat. "What should we read next?"

He twitches his nose and sniffles. "I just got *If We Were Us* from the library. And *Divergent*. And *The Hate U Give*."

He really is a reading machine. Hard to believe he struggled reading early on. "Since you did a bang-up job on the last book, it's your pick."

"*Divergent?*"

"*Divergent* it is. We'll convene for book club next week, same time, probably different place. Until then, I have another important question."

He scratches his ear. "Okay?"

"Is it the color or taste of carrots you don't like?" I steal another from his bag and crunch loudly.

He grins. "They taste boring."

"Celery is boring. Celery tastes like nothing."

"Not nothing. Celery tastes refreshing, like water. And sometimes it's bitter in a good way."

I make a face. "If you say so."

"What's with the weird ink on your neck?" His topic change jars me, but he smirks, blushing slightly. And wow. He's also part Lennon, going for the snide jabs.

"This?" I point to the blurry lion that I maybe like a little more in this moment. "You don't dig the dolphin on my neck?"

He rolls his eyes and laughs. "It's not a dolphin."

"You're right. It's a gorilla."

This giggle comes from his belly. "It's a weird-looking lion. And why do you have a ghost on your arm? Ghosts don't play baseball."

They sure did in *Field of Dreams*. Sadly, Max is smirking at the scythe-wielding skeleton on my left forearm, which looks nothing like a scythe-wielding skeleton. But hey. I'm actually coming around to my ink. I want to remember how angry and lonely I was the past decade. Remember to make good choices going forward. To always put Sadie and Max first so I don't end up with another head full of knotted hair and a gnarly personality to match.

The ink is also freeing. I don't have virgin skin I'm worried about marring. Having it means I can do what I'm about to do without a second thought.

"I'm actually due for a new tattoo." I look at the blurry, bloody rose on my right forearm. "But I need a better artist to design me something."

"You could ask Joseph. He's good at drawing nature. Or one of Mom's artists from her website."

Yeah, no. Joseph may be Sadie's business associate, but I don't trust him. I'm still worried he has designs on Sadie and she's oblivious. If he does, he'd for sure undermine me. Plus, I have someone else in mind. "Why would I do that when I'm looking at a talented artist right now?"

His jaw unhinges. *"Me?"*

"I mean, I could ask Jasmine or Zoey." I hook my thumb toward the duo still hunched over their phones. "But I'm not sure I want Camila Cabello on my arm."

He snort-cackles. "Camila Cabello is awesome."

I tried listening to her. It hurt my ears. "If you say so. But back to my new ink. You design me something *without* Camila Cabello, and whatever you create, I'll get tattooed."

"Seriously?"

"Seriously."

Max is a human version of his glow stick now, beaming and blushing all at once. "This is so cool."

Cool is how much I love this kid already.

FOURTEEN

As we finish the first half of our hike, I'm verging on gleeful. Max is having a blast teasing me with what he might design for my tattoo, even pointing to a pile of animal droppings without saying a word. Just making eye contact with me and laughing his butt off. Honestly, if he draws a pile of shit, I'll still get it inked. On the other side of my neck if it makes him laugh like that. I also have some thoughts on how to make his mother as happy as he is right now.

But the second I spot Olivia at the halfway meetup point, my glee slips. Thinking fast, I dodge her advance and tell Sadie we need to talk.

"Did something happen?" she asks, concerned, as I guide her away from my tormentor.

"Olivia happened."

She tips her head back and laughs. "What is it with you two?"

"She likes to practice her psychoanalysis techniques on me."

"She's a little intense."

Understatement. I check on our kids, who are all occupied. Max, Jasmine, and Zoey are standing in a circle doing some kind of interpretive dance where Jasmine makes a hand gesture and hip twitch and they follow her. Even Olivia joins in. Jun and Carter seem to be channeling their inner Rambos, holding invisible guns as they pretend to shoot the birds above, making *pew-pew* sound effects with their mouths.

"We need to take care of some adult stuff," I call to them. "Be back in a second."

They ignore us. I gesture ahead and lead Sadie behind a grouping of trees.

"Des. What—"

I cage her with my arms, giving her space, but not much. "I was thinking about what you said on the phone."

"Which part?"

"You're single," I offer roughly. A detail that stole my sleep all weekend. The kind of insomnia where my body burned, my cock hard from remembering the soft sounds of her voice through the phone Friday night.

Sadie doesn't speak. Her breasts rise on each heavy inhale, her skin flushing its telltale turned-on blush.

"I'm single," I say. A repeat of what she knows. Putting the facts out there, because I can't keep denying our chemistry. My morning with Max has me feeling invincible. The notion of us being together as a family is a possibility I've been terrified to imagine, but it's there now. A future I need to pursue. "I want to ask you out, Sadie. Take you on a date, but we're both worried about Max. About setting him up for hurt if we don't work out. So I was thinking we could take things slowly. Not let Max know we're testing the waters."

She glances in the direction of the kids, her forehead wrinkling. A moment passes with no reaction from her, then two.

Unable to give up just yet, I lean toward her ear, graze my nose against the delicate edge until her breath catches. "If you don't want to go out with me, I won't push. But I won't pretend I haven't been dreaming about you for eleven long years, or that my body and heart don't ache with missing you. I'm dying to take you on a date. Treat you to a nice night where you have no worries except what to wear. Make you laugh. Feed you good food. Afterward, maybe I'll lean over you like this. Run my hands through your hair. Drag my fingers along your scalp until you sigh, then press my lips to yours for a long, slow kiss. Or"—I pull back slightly, giving her space to think—"we can just stay as friends and coparents to our awesome kid."

I'm close enough to see the subtle shift in tones on her eyelashes, from dark brown to lighter at the tips. I can also see the indecision in her eyes. She trembles and worries her lip, and I kick myself for pushing too hard too soon.

"It's okay, honey." I give her arm a soft nudge. "Let's head back to the group."

I go to turn, but she grabs my hip. "Des?"

"Yeah?"

"Are you free this afternoon?"

A zip of adrenaline revs my pulse. "I am."

She looks mildly shell shocked, like she didn't plan to blurt that question, then she twines her fingers nervously. "This is super short notice, but Jasmine's mom asked if Max wanted to go there to play after the hike, and he was actually excited, which I'm thrilled about. She apparently has a trampoline he's dying to try. Anyway, work is slow for me this week, so we could hang out if you want, as long as I'm home to cook dinner. But if you don't, that's totally fine. You're busy, I'm sure. And I kind of spoke before I thought, which is something I never normally do."

She drops her gaze, adorably bashful and nervous.

I dip my head to meet her eye. "Did you miss the part where I said I've been dreaming about you for eleven years? Of course my answer is yes, but I have a request."

She blinks. "Okay . . ."

"Do you mind if I take you somewhere? Unless you had specific plans."

"I honestly hadn't thought that far ahead. Or at all, really." She shakes her head with a self-deprecating eye roll. "Whatever you want to do is good with me. But I really don't want Max to know, even after we introduce you next week. I'm hoping he takes that news well, but there's so much involved with him. More than anything, he needs stability."

"I understand and completely agree." Especially after today's talk.

I still don't think I should discuss our book club specifics with Sadie yet. At least not why they started. Max needs time to digest our chat. Feel what he needs to feel about that. Learn to trust me. Then, hopefully, when I tell him I'm his dad, he'll believe I'm no different than Simon's dad. A dude who will say stupid things but loves his kid, no holds barred.

Unfortunately, Sadie's "stability" comment is gumming up my throat. The only thing of value I own is a rusted yellow Camaro that occasionally decides driving is for suckers, and I doubt she thinks being a bartender is dependable work.

I scratch at my hair. "We should get back to the kids."

She nods, then heads toward the group. I take a fortifying breath before following. I'm pumped about having time with her later today, can't wait to surprise her with a fun outing, but her stability talk is lingering uncomfortably. I scrub my hand down my face, a mix of feelings making me dizzy. When I step forward, I nearly walk into Olivia.

She cranes her neck to stare up at me. "What job did you do during witness protection? Did they give you, like, a whole new life with new clothes and a new house and tons of new stuff?"

I swear this kid smells anxiety. I scan the clearing before answering her unpleasant question. Everyone's busy checking out the maps for our return trip. Except Olivia, who's busy driving me nuts.

May as well get this over with. "They helped us get settled with a house and furniture and stuff, and they gave us funds for school and living. After an allotted time, we were expected to fend for ourselves financially."

She pops a stick of gum into her mouth. "Okay, but that doesn't answer my question."

"Pretty sure it does. You get one question a day and you asked two. I answered one of them." The easier one.

"*Pretty sure* if there are two questions, and you can only answer one, you're obligated to answer the first one."

"Not in my world." And she's not the only one who has internet access. "Forgot to mention it, but did you know gum is basically a lump of soft plastic, and chewing it contributes to a hundred thousand tons of plastic pollution every year? Way to go on killing the planet." I give her a suck-on-that smirk.

She retaliates with a mad-scientist leer. "Did you know the color yellow creates feelings of frustration? It stimulates eye strain and fatigue." Her attention drops to my Littlewing Outdoor Camp T-shirt. "Basically, you're slowly killing *us*."

Dammit, how is she this good?

Whatever. Olivia's superhuman brain is the least of my problems, and the last thing I want to discuss with her is my job. Sure, I've earned good tips bartending, have been thankful for the work it's provided, but it's always felt like an escape. An easy out, instead of striving for something more fulfilling. And I haven't earned enough to save for the big stuff.

College funds.

Retirement plans.

Life insurance.

Medical coverage.

On the stability factor Sadie mentioned, I hover around 0.15.

My stomach becomes an origami project, folding in on itself. Loving Max and Sadie is only a portion of being part of a family. A real parent and partner would provide for them, offer permanent security, but I still haven't progressed past visiting the Duke Law website. I think my avoidance is fear of failure. Worry that I've lost my ability to study and focus. Maybe I'll flunk out and hit a new low. Or I've just become an expert procrastinator.

I return to the group and try to shake off my unease. Sadie's attention lingers on my face, her expression eager but still shy, like she can't believe she asked me out. Channeling my old cocky ways, I give her a wink.

"Can we go already?" Jasmine is shockingly not glued to her phone. She's gripping her group's compass, face intent. An explorer ready to venture into uncharted land.

Actually, all the kids are up and antsy, not rolling their eyes or sprawled over the grass half-asleep. Max is beside Jasmine, analyzing their map. He points to the page, then points toward the taller elevation at his right. She nods. Zoey crams herself between them to get a look as well. And I need a second. A moment to breathe through this rush of warmth invading my chest. The same sensation I felt during the glow stick scavenger hunt.

These waves of emotion could be Sadie and Max related, but they remind me of the thrill of throwing a touchdown, the blast of accomplishment I felt when I aced my LSATs. Like I'm *proud* of myself. Which is kind of sad. This is a group of preteens, who generally get under my skin and test my patience. I mean, look at Carter pretending his compass is a grenade launcher, making his *pew-pew* sound effects, while Jun pretends to get blown to pieces. Couple of idiots.

Anyone with a half a brain could entertain these kids. Stability and security. That's the tough stuff I need to figure out. This afternoon, though, all my time will be devoted to Sadie and the perfect impromptu date I have planned.

FIFTEEN

Sadie parks her car behind mine, eyeing the forest as she joins me. "Are we going on another hike?"

"Nope." I pull a bag from my back seat, swing it over my shoulder, and walk toward the woods up ahead. I couldn't have asked for a better afternoon for this surprise date—warm and quiet, without another soul around. The only downside is we're still wearing our yellow Littlewing T-shirts. Cute on Sadie. Not so cute on me.

She falls into step, her ponytail swaying with her eager steps. "Are you sure, because this feels pretty similar to hiking."

"Still *no*."

"Can I have a hint?"

"What's the fun in that?"

She slants me a cheeky look. "So now you're saying I'm not fun?"

"I'm saying you have to trust that I'll *bring* the fun. Your only job is to join me."

"Okay, fine." She adds a bounce to her stride. "But what's in your bag?"

I laugh at her impatience and knock my elbow into hers. "Quit it with the questions."

She hums under her breath, strutting so happily she's practically skipping. I expected Sadie to be a bit reserved for this date, still shocked she asked me out. Nervous and maybe shy. She looks like she's on her way to her favorite art exhibit. "Are you just excited for this incredibly fun, unbelievably impressive mystery outing I've spontaneously planned, or is something else putting that grin on your face?"

She lifts her head to the cloud-dotted sky and smiles wider. "I got good news on the drive over—about the modern art museum job."

I stop walking and face her. "You got offered the position you wanted?"

"Sarah's offering us something. No details yet, but we've booked a video meeting for later next week."

"Sadie." I pull her into a hug. Can't resist. I cradle her close, so impressed with her drive and ambition and relieved she's getting a chance to reclaim a part of her life she lost when raising Max. "You deserve every good thing. The best of the best."

"Thank you," she whispers and nuzzles in closer. Presses her face into my chest in a way that anchors me. Makes me feel like I have a place in this world. "It's all kind of surreal right now."

I release my tight hold on her and gently link our fingers together, testing whether this type of affection is okay. She glances at our held hands, and the quietest contented sigh escapes her.

I lead us into the forest. An environment that's starting to feel as grounding as Sadie. The leaves above cast shadowed shapes over the trail, the birds singing bright and clear.

I squeeze her hand. "Tell me more about the job."

"Like I said, I don't know specifics. She's obviously hiring curators—my total dream job—but I don't have enough experience for something that huge, and it wouldn't even work. I think she wants us to develop the mentorship programs we pitched to her. Outreach for at-risk youths, giving them access to spaces and established artists. Something collaborative. Not just teaching these kids," she says, her voice building in confidence, "but sharing ideas, learning from them too. The stuff we've seen, how emotional and raw their work is, shouldn't be overlooked. The shared experiences can lift up the whole art community and make a difference in so many lives. *If* she goes for the project as we pitched it."

As usual, Sadie's compassion and ability to think in bold strokes blow me away. "I knew you'd do it."

"What?"

"Change the world."

"A little overdramatic, and it's not happening yet."

"It will."

We walk on, chatting lightly, sometimes falling into an easy silence that settles my soul in a bone-deep way. Like we didn't lose eleven years together. Like the gaping hole in my chest isn't so wide.

I spot the tree I marked with a yellow ribbon last week and run my thumb over her hand. "We're here. Just around this corner."

When she sees where we are, she gasps. "Oh my God. It's stunning."

The small clearing is dappled in the partial sun, the area blanketed with white and yellow wildflowers. In the center is a willow oak tree, tall and leafy, its branches spread in invitation.

"Someone obviously cleared the area at some point," I say, appreciating the serenity of the peaceful land. "There's even the remnants of a stone house on the opposite side."

Releasing my hand, she wanders ahead, letting the tall flowers tickle her fingers. "Could you imagine living here? It would be like living in a fairy tale."

"Yeah." I picture Max and Sadie and me playing games in the grass, and warmth floods my sternum. "I was looking for the perfect place to take you at some point, and the blog I read didn't disappoint."

"Are we having a picnic?" She spins around, walking backward, her eyes sparkling.

"Nope." Unable to keep her in suspense, I unzip my bag and pull out one of the axes I bought last weekend. I've kept them in my car, hoping to have a day just like this. "You're going to show me what a badass you are."

Her mouth drops open. "You brought me here to throw axes?"

"There's a dead tree on the other side of the clearing. Seemed like a good target, and you can't beat this setting."

She does a cute little jump and races through the wild grasses and flowers, finding the decaying tree easily. I follow in her path. Magnetized. My body drawn to her radiant light.

She circles the tree's girth, letting her fingers drag along the bark. "This is the best surprise."

"I'm full of them."

"You are," she says with a bit of wonder.

That magnet pulls harder, and I clear my throat. "Sadie Sprite Jones, it's time to show me what you've got."

She joins me and examines the two axes I bought. She chooses the one she likes best, and when she steps back, I swear she looks a couple of inches taller. "Have you thrown an axe before?"

"Nope. I was hoping for a lesson, seeing as we're both on the yellow team." I gesture to our matching Littlewing shirts.

"Are we, though?" She smirks at the cotton suctioned to my chest. "I feel like I'm on the cute team and you're on the redneck meathead team."

I toss my head back, laughing from my gut. "I will burn this shirt one day."

She grins. "Lennon did shrink it, by the way."

I jerk my head up. "Are you shitting me?"

"No." She snort-laughs. "He purposely bought a small-fitting cotton shirt that wasn't preshrunk so you wouldn't question the size on the tag. He told me when he hired me."

"My fucking brother is going to eat my fist."

She laughs harder, tipping forward, nearly dropping her axe. "He was so proud of himself."

I glower, planning how to make his life miserable. The scheme will definitely involve Maggie Edelstein.

"Come." Sadie nods to the other axe, still laughing. "Let's start your lessons and never mention your shirt again."

Like that's possible. I'm a neon yellow sign that reads **MAKE FUN OF ME**. Whatever. Sadie can tease me all she wants. Watching her grin that wide is worth it.

I follow her, loving the confident sway of her hips in her short shorts.

When she reaches a spot she likes, she turns and faces me. "Are you ready to focus, Bower?"

I salute her. "Yes, ma'am."

"Keep your arms and shoulders as relaxed as possible, and don't throw too hard. A softer touch gives greater accuracy. Most men go for the single-handed toss, thinking it's the macho move, but two-handed over the head gives more consistency. Slow, steady breaths are your friends, and don't forget the follow-through. If you end your toss too abruptly, you tend to hit high."

"Two hands. Slow breaths. Follow through." I nod. "But I'd like to watch you first."

She doesn't need me to ask her twice. Chin ticked up, she takes a strong but comfortable stance, holding the axe with two hands behind her head. She plays with the weight of it—a slight pulse to her arms—then she steadies her breath, firms her legs, and lets it fly.

The blade bites into the wood, dead center of the tree, and I can't help my bellowed whoop. She pivots toward me, the exhilaration on her face nearly blasting me off my feet. I don't think I've ever seen Sadie this sexy. Powerful and commanding.

Axe throwing is some serious foreplay.

I wrangle my focus. Don't want to look like a chump in the face of her competence.

"Like this?" I plant my feet, trying to follow her instructions, but the axe feels gangly.

"Relax your arms."

I try, but my instincts don't like the instruction.

"If you do this . . ." She comes up behind me, presses her small hands to my triceps, positioning me until my arms soften slightly. Unfortunately, other things harden. I clench my ass, try to keep my body's reaction contained. The last thing I want is for the axe to go flying and hit one of us.

"Better," she murmurs close to my neck, not helping the situation in my cargo shorts.

When she steps back, I force more control into my breaths, attempt to maintain the posture she shifted, but I'm still wound up. My grip feels awkward. The second the axe leaves my hands, I know it's a lost cause. The blade misses the trunk and ricochets off a neighboring tree.

I shrug at her and point at my shirt. "I blame the fit. It cut off blood flow and my ability to focus."

She rolls her eyes. "Such a man, looking for something else to blame."

Grinning, I hold up my hands in surrender. "I take it back. I have no problems admitting a woman bested me at axe throwing. Or that watching you wield that weapon masterfully was really fucking hot."

She gives her ponytail a seductive toss. "I do give good axe."

So damn good.

We mess around a while longer, standing at different distances and angles. Sadie hits the trunk 95 percent of the time. With her teaching, I improve, but she's still better than me. We joke and heckle each other. I do a horrible impression of a crazed axe-wielding lumberjack, and she laughs so hard her axe doesn't land anywhere near the tree.

Eventually, we find ourselves sitting in the clearing, facing each other under the shade of the large oak. She's cross-legged, picking at the grass. I have one leg bent, my elbow resting on it while I watch the wind flirt with her hair.

She tosses a few blades of grass on my legs, smiling when they get caught in my leg hairs. "You seem really at home out here in the wilderness."

"It's surprising, to be honest. I've always considered myself more of a city guy. Never searched out trails or hikes in Houston. Just stuck to the concrete jungle. But I like this." I breathe in the scents of earth and grass and fresh air, taking in the peaceful quiet. "A lot."

"It suits you. In a rugged, stripped-down way."

"I feel calmer out here. Get less bogged down in my thoughts. But the gym is pretty awesome too. Pushing myself and sweating my ass off is a great stress reliever. What about you?" I take a blade of grass and use it to draw a line down her shin. "Did you get into axe throwing to destress?"

"Not exactly." She shivers but doesn't nudge the tracing grass away. "I can thank a horrible date for that."

My frown muscles kick in. "I already don't like the jerk."

"You and me both. His name was Derek, and he was a mansplaining idiot. Took me axe throwing to show off, but he wasn't great at it, barely listened to the instructor. I, on the other hand, followed everything she said."

"You were always a kiss ass," I tease.

"I like learning!" She tosses a stick at my stomach.

I mime being wounded, then take the branch and break it into smaller pieces. "You were a great student, so I'm not surprised you learned fast. But back to the jerk. I'm guessing he couldn't handle you being better than him."

"He pouted the whole night and never called again, thankfully, but I got hooked. Couldn't go often enough to join regular competitions, but I loved how empowered I felt when I hit the target. Like I could take on the world and win."

"Being around Max today made me feel something similar." I think about our book club talk, how deeply his reactions affected me. "Knowing him makes me feel bigger than I am. *More* than I am. Like I have a stronger purpose in my life." I scrape a hand through my hair and duck my head. "I already love him so much it hurts."

"Oh, Des."

Her hand comes to my knee, and I look into her eyes. A swirl of affection glows in their depths, filling my lungs with more than purpose. A deep well of emotion rises in me, achingly tender but also fierce. The urge to protect her and our son. To care and provide for them any way I can.

To love Sadie with my whole heart and body.

I catch a wisp of her loose hair, rub it between my fingers. "Can I kiss you, Sprite?"

Her breaths tremble, but she nods.

Heart beating a mile a minute, I cup her cheeks, tilt her face up to mine, and finally press our lips together.

Lightning. That's the only way to describe the feel of Sadie Jones. A crackling zing through my body. I kiss her softly, tender presses that turn my body hot and hard. I lick her bottom lip, a question. *Open up for me?* She does—fuck, *yes* she does—and she moans, unabashed and needy. Because *this.* This is us kissing deeply, feeling every hardship and memory we've earned, good and bad. We're a portrait of sadness and hope and missing and first loves torn apart too soon.

The Taste of Wonder, that's what I'd call this work of art.

Before I get carried away, I press my forehead to hers. "That was some kiss."

She rubs her nose against mine. "I think my stomach fluttered away."

My smile comes so easily it almost freaks me out. "I'll make sure to catch it for you."

And be the man she deserves.

If I want any kind of future with my family, I need to quit procrastinating. Switch gears from Happy Hiking Leader to Take-No-Prisoners Law Student. Give Sadie the security she's been fighting for since I disappeared, starting with a visit to Duke University.

SIXTEEN

Adulting is no joke. The past five days have been nonstop planning and doing. And stressing. I drove to Duke University and stressed the whole way there. I spoke with the dean and stressed throughout the whole meeting. I exhumed my sad story of my criminal dad and witness protection and—you guessed it—I melted into a puddle of stress sweat. I'm as exhausted as a test subject who's been forced to stare at the color yellow for hours, but sleeping's still been an issue.

It's nearly midnight. Bats are flying as I lounge in my backyard. I've already finished *Divergent*—book club with Max resumes Monday, after which I'll be telling him who I am. That upcoming confession is part of the reason I can't sleep. As is the slow pace Sadie and I have set with each other. Neither of us has pushed for another date yet. I'm letting that kiss and fun afternoon linger, living off of every remembered word and intimate moment. Hopefully Sadie is reliving our date too, settling into the idea of us. As consuming as those Max and Sadie thoughts are, school seems to be pushing to the forefront of my insomnia.

Feeling unsettled, I pull out my phone and text my caftan-wearing former neighbor, who is also a night owl.

Des: I found a craft I'm actually good at.

This week's effort is embroidery bracelets. Shock of all shocks, I'm not half-bad at them. I'm sticking to basic braiding patterns. Chevron V shapes that aren't perfectly uniform, but working with string beats origami paper cuts and needlepoint wounds. I bought green, pink, purple, white, blue, and orange thread—no exhausting yellow—and have already finished one.

Mirielle doesn't reply right away. Hopefully she's asleep, not chasing serenity like me. I pin the top knot of another bracelet to my sweatpants when my phone buzzes.

Mirielle: I'll be the judge of that. Photo please.

I snap a picture of the bracelet I finished and attach it.

Des: Not bad?

Mirielle: I believe you've found your calling. But

I stare at her text, waiting for her to finish. When the phone rings, I startle and answer. "Mirielle?"

"This texting is ridiculous," she says. "The buttons are too small. Tell me, *chéri*, why are you sad?"

"Who said I'm sad?"

"Your lack of sleep."

My lip curls of its own accord. "Then I guess you're sad too."

She huffs. "Was I the one who texted you? I think *non*."

Guess there's no arguing with that. "I miss Sadie and Max when I'm not with them," I grumble quietly.

"But you *have* seen them, yes?"

"Only on the hikes this week." And during my sleeplessness, when I'm alone in bed, thinking about what she and Max are doing, wondering if they miss me half as much as I miss them. "But we played name that tune on the trail yesterday. I busted out some Camila Cabello songs, so that entertained the shit out of them."

"Virgin ears," Mirielle says.

Not on her life, but yeah. Yesterday was a blast. I sang so loud and proud the kids were doubled over, laughing their butts off at me. Max had to stop and catch his breath. Sadie had tears streaming down her face. Naturally, I sang louder.

As much fun as that was, watching her and Max get in her car afterward and drive away shaved off a layer of my fortitude. "I haven't told her about school yet."

"Isn't this the grand plan? The big show to sweep her off her feet as a majestic lawyer?"

"Why do you have to make it sound so ridiculous?"

"Why do you have to wake up a sixty-year-old woman in the middle of the night?"

"*Sixty?*"

"Choose your next words carefully, Walter."

I chuckle quietly as Mirielle starts talking about a new record she bought. The outdoor light is soft enough not to interfere with the bat ballet. I place the phone on speaker and grab two threads of my new bracelet, fold them over another two, then tighten the strings and repeat the motion. Mirielle's accented smoker's voice is the soundtrack to the steady work. My fingers move as I try to figure out why I haven't told Sadie about school yet.

Gradually, my eyes settle on my wallet. "Money," I say when there's a lull.

"If you need money, I have some in my freezer."

I scrub my hand over my mouth, smiling to myself. Of course she keeps cash in her freezer. "Thanks for the offer, but no. I won't take your money. I'm just wondering if that's why I haven't told Sadie about school yet. Going to Duke will cost a ton of cash, and I'm not sure my mother kept my witness protection funds."

The school-specific chunk that she'd set aside for me. She pushed me year after year, sneaking in subtle probing, asking if I'd thought more about law, going back, reinvesting in myself. I'd deflect like the master deflector I am with one of my seasoned grunts.

Maybe that's why I can't sleep. She hasn't mentioned law to me in a few years. She probably spent that cash or spread it around to my brothers. The idea of incurring mountains of school debt is nauseating, to say the least, and it would mean not having extra money to help support Sadie and Max. Details I need to figure out.

"I gotta go, Mirielle. Thanks for chatting."

"The pleasure is mine, but you should spend more time with your family too. That brother with the letter for a name. Make more of an effort with him. If you can handle that, Arnold," she adds, hanging up before I can squash her latest name guess.

Shaking my head at her antics, I call Mom.

"Des?" she says, sounding half-asleep and worried. "Is everything okay?"

No idea why I thought calling her at bat-ballet a.m. was a good idea. It's past midnight now. Mirielle has me thinking everyone's awake at this hour. "Sorry. Everything's great. Go back to sleep."

"No, no." Rustling carries through the line, then a faint *click*, like she's turning on her bedside lamp. "I'm awake. What's up?"

The fact that I feel like I've been treading water. "Duke's willing to take me back."

"Des, wow. I had no idea you wanted to reapply."

"Yeah. I mean . . ." I run my fingers through the bracelet threads hanging down my thigh, spinning them around and around. "It's what I always wanted, right?"

"It is. I just . . ."

I still my fingers, wait for her to go on. To whoop and laugh and say *Finally* and *I'm so proud* and *I knew you could do it*, like the night she toasted my first Duke acceptance, crying as she told me what a great lawyer I'd make. "You just what?" I ask.

"Nothing," she says quickly. "I'm just thrilled you're looking ahead and finally following your dreams. So you need money, I guess. I can forward you the college fund." She doesn't have the enthused tone I expected, but I did wake her at a late hour.

I'm not as enthused as I expected. If she has that cash, taking classes won't bury me in debt. I can afford school, not begin my professional life on the back foot. I'd be able to help Sadie out. But I'm not punching the air and shouting my joy. A bat swoops so low I flinch.

"That's great," I say. "The money's great. I'll be starting classes at the end of August."

Which means figuring out living arrangements in Durham. Getting caught up on readings other than teen books. I'll travel back to Windfall on weekends to see Sadie and Max. Or maybe they'll come to Durham with me. If she wants that. If she wants me more permanently in their lives. But this—law. Proving how serious I am. Once she sees I'm working toward our future, she'll worry less about me derailing their family balance.

"Des," Mom says gently. "How are things with Sadie and Max?"

Hard. Sad. Amazing. Complicated. "We're taking things slow. I think I'll talk to Sadie tomorrow . . . which I guess is today now. Tell her about school. And we're telling Max who I am on Monday." A prospect that has my stomach hollowing.

Mom and I talk a bit longer, finalizing the money details, discussing all things Max, while I try to shake my unease. I debate asking her opinion on my whole Max-is-maybe-gay theory, seek advice on keeping lines of communication open. But in that Simon book, the main character didn't want his coming out to be a big thing. He was nervous about the drama that would unfold. Even the happy, supportive drama. I have no doubt my family would be happy and supportive, but they'd also be overbearing. Go out of their way to show their love excessively. Maybe say something before they should.

Eventually we say goodbye and hang up. Instead of turning off my phone, I take Mirielle's advice and send E a text: Can you and Delilah come for dinner one night soon?

He's geographically my closest family. Aside from asking for his makeover help, I haven't spent time with him, caught up on his life. I don't expect a reply now. My mind is just so on fire tonight, spinning through a thousand and one worries. Sending the invitation takes another weight off.

I go to turn off my phone, but dots bounce with an incoming reply.

E: Why? Is something wrong?

Des: Why are you awake?

E: Why are YOU awake?

I smile at our provoking exchange, worrying over each other the way we do.

Des: Busy mind. Sadie. Max. Other stuff. What's your excuse?

E: I was actually thinking about you, which is freaking me out. Maybe I have telepathy.

Des: Or you just miss me.

E: Is it OK if I drive over now?

I glare at the time on my phone.

Des: No. It's not OK. It's fucking late and you'll be fucking tired and I won't have you getting in an accident.

E: Cool. I'll see you in an hour. I have something to give you.

Growling, I almost dial his number to yell at him, but he won't listen to me, and I don't want to wake Delilah if she's asleep. I move inside to wait for him, busy myself with another bracelet. In my annoyance, my braiding skills take a nosedive. I'm yanking the strings too hard, and the knots are sitting awkwardly. Still, when I'm done, I grab an envelope and paper and write a short note.

> Mirielle—thanks for reminding me I'm not alone.
> Your surly neighbor,
> D_ S _ _ _ D
> P.S. You better quit calling me Walter and Albert
now.

I smirk at the hangman-style clue for my name, knowing she'll get a kick out of it, then I fold the note and stuff it into the envelope with my latest bracelet.

A knock jolts me. Not for long. I march to my front door and yank it open. "I told you not to drive at this hour."

E grins. "But I have telepathy."

"Or we're just a bunch of screwed-up guys who don't sleep well and often think about the family."

"Or that." He shrugs, pushing past me. "Nice place."

I grunt my thanks. "I wanted to have you and Delilah over to hang out, but at a reasonable hour. Why couldn't this wait?"

He rubs nervously at his neck. "It just couldn't."

I stare at him, waiting for him to go on.

"I can't stay. I have a busy morning with work, but I have this thing—something I've kept for a while. And ever since we found you, and you moved closer, I've been wanting to return it but wasn't sure you were ready. Then you texted tonight, exactly when I was thinking about you, and I know you've been spending solid time with Max and Sadie, and I just . . ." He pulls something from his back pocket and holds out his hand. "This is yours."

I blink at the small red box, and a wave of emotion pummels me.

The last time I saw a box like this was our first week of WITSEC. I was locked in a bathroom, crushing it in my hand, crying so hard I was heaving. Then I tossed the box in the trash and never looked back. Now it's in my hand.

SEVENTEEN

Slowly, I open the velvet box, and there it is. The engagement ring I bought for Sadie. Simple and elegant with a round-cut diamond on a slim white-gold band. My chest pulls tighter. So damn tight as a million memories, good and bad, overload me. "Jesus, E."

He shrugs. "Figured you'd want it one day."

I don't have words. None that are good enough for my brother, who fished this out of the trash and saved it for me.

He punches my shoulder lightly, his expression reflecting the choked-up feeling I'm fighting. "I hope you make good use of this."

I nod, too emotional to speak or say goodbye as he leaves. I can't quit staring at the ring or stop the memory that comes flooding back. That unforgettable night. *The* night I tucked this box in my pocket— my last night with Sadie before we were torn apart.

The two of us were walking through Windfall's town square, the only people out on the quiet night. I'd just aced my first year of law school. Sadie was about to start that killer job at the Contemporary Art Museum in Raleigh, no longer working as an intern. We had our eyes on swank apartments to rent, where she'd live and I'd move after I finished law school. I was driven. Put together and ready to tackle the world, my hair short and styled, my square jaw clean shaven. I wore designer clothes to portray the image of the man I wanted to be.

Honestly, if you looked up a picture of success in the dictionary, my all-American face would've been splashed across the page. I'd always imagined Sadie next to me in that shot, the epitome of success. Marrying a smart, fun, gorgeous woman who didn't let her volatile family steal her spark. I may have only finished my first year of law school. I couldn't afford us a house or lavish wedding yet. I didn't care. I was Desmond Bower, and I wanted to marry Sadie Jones.

Unfortunately, having cold feet is a thing. Personally, I prefer to call it Male Moron Syndrome.

Picking up on my uncharacteristic anxiety, Sadie rested her head on my shoulder as we walked. "You're being weird tonight."

"Weird?" My stilted laugh did me no favors.

"Just, different. Kind of . . . nervous?"

Unsure what was wrong with me, I tightened my hand around her slim waist, brushed my fingers over the soft fabric of her pretty dress. "Maybe you make me nervous, Sprite."

She flicked my abs. "The only thing that makes you nervous is pizza."

She had me there. Pizza downright terrified me. How could something so delicious be so vicious on my lactose-intolerant stomach? Compared to resisting the lure of pizza, proposing to Sadie should have been a cakewalk.

"I'm just distracted by your beauty," I said, trying to get my head right. I loved Sadie. Down to my marrow. Didn't doubt that for a second. I planned to propose that night, but questions kept filling my mind, a million what-ifs dogging me.

What if law school got busier and too demanding and I hurt her?

What if I got too wrapped up in Sadie and couldn't focus on school?

What if she got to the city and realized the world was much larger than me, and she met someone better suited to her before I got there?

What if we got married and everything that was so easy between us gradually got harder, forcing us apart?

What if marrying Sadie was *rash*? A bad choice that would derail my path to success?

The faster my mind spun, the twitchier I felt. I touched my pocket nervously, feeling the ring in there, hating the anxiety rushing through me.

Slowing our stride, I tugged her against my chest. "You know I love you, right?"

She tilted her head, searching my face. "I know, Des. I love you too. Even though you wear that blue plaid shirt."

She hated that ratty old shirt I refused to toss, but she was being cute and flirty. Perfectly Sadie. Instead of teasing her back the way I normally would, I kissed her hard and rough, on the edge of desperate, moving us as I licked into her mouth, tangled our tongues, held her ass so we were flush and grinding. I needed her. *Us.* To get as close to her as possible, leaving no room for my confused thoughts.

We were in the town square, near the mermaid fountain and towering oak. The area wasn't built for privacy, but the night was dark and quiet.

"Are we doing this?" she said on a moan as I lowered her down beside a row of bushes. The only cover in the vicinity.

"We're doing this."

I didn't care that we might get caught. I didn't hold back, shoving down my jeans and sinking into Sadie, growling in her ear, pushing hard and deep as she clawed at my back and met me thrust for thrust until we were shaking and coming.

She kissed me softly afterward, twining our legs together on the cool grass. I couldn't quit running my hands all over her, didn't want to get dressed or go home. I kept opening my mouth against her skin, tried to push out the words. *Will you make me the happiest man in the world and marry me?* The words didn't come.

After dropping her off at home, all I could do was kick myself for being a coward. I drove too fast, shaking my head, grinding my teeth, determined to propose next time I was home from school. I was so frustrated with myself I didn't notice the van and strange car at first. The men and women in US Marshal jackets attempting to corral my family out of our home. When the bizarre scene registered, I squinted through my windshield, confused.

E was yelling and shoving at a man, tears streaming down his face. Lennon looked shell shocked, standing statue still. Jake and Callahan were holding up their hands in supplication, trying to calm E down.

Unsure what the hell was going on, I jumped from my car and stormed toward the huge guy grabbing at E, ready to let the punches fly.

Mom ran in front of me, her eyes red and puffy. "Des, no. We have to leave. Your father . . . We . . ." She gulped, couldn't catch her breath. She looked *terrified*.

Fear sucked out my fight and froze me in place. "What the hell happened?"

Her teeth started chattering. "I don't know. Your father—they say he's been laundering money for a drug cartel. It doesn't make sense. But we're in danger. We don't have a choice. We have to go. All of us in that van. *Now.*"

I blinked at her, sure I heard her wrong.

E was still screaming and lashing out by the front door, fighting off that hulk of a man, while Jake and Cal tried lamely to intervene. A woman took Mom by her shoulders and led her away. Our farm was next to the Moons' chicken coops but far from their main house. Far from anyone who could hear us and know the madness that was going on.

When E made a pained sound and his knees hit the front porch, I reacted. Stormed over to them and shoved off the marshal while grabbing E by the arm. I yanked him up, held his shaking body against my chest. "We're getting in that van. All of us. You don't have a choice. Everything will be fine, but you're coming with me."

"No. Delilah." He sobbed, tried to punch me. "I can't leave Delilah."

I held him tighter, a full-body hold as he shook and gulped. "Get in the fucking van, E. You'll talk to Delilah later, explain what happened then." Even as I said it, I knew. Nothing would be okay. I didn't have details, but I knew this night would change everything.

The horror of my premonition sunk in on the drive away from our farm. The marshals started talking about witness protection and new identities and Safesites, and numbness seeped through me. Witness protection meant hiding. Hiding meant keeping my family safe, but Sadie wasn't my family. I'd never proposed. She wasn't allowed in the program with us.

When we got to our Safesite, I detonated. A roar of endless shouts that shredded my throat. I punched the wall over and over until my hand was bloody and my brothers were on me, holding me down, trying to calm *me*, telling me we'd be okay. A useless bucket of well-meaning lies. I knew I'd never have the chance to kiss Sadie again. Never get to propose and joke with her about what a nervous fool I was over it, second-guessing our undeniable future.

I tossed her engagement ring in the trash that night. Never expected to see it again. Now it's here, in my hand, and I can't put it down. Even for a second. This ring is proof Sadie and I aren't over. That the two of us are meant to be.

Max's health and happiness will always come first. We won't tell him we're dating until Sadie feels fully secure in her feelings, but I'm solid in mine. Sadie is the only woman for me, and I think it's time for a second date. To push a little harder at our boundaries. Visit her home today, even though she's not expecting me. Tell her about law school. Show her the man I can become. Hope to hell I get to offer her this ring one day and make our family whole.

EIGHTEEN

I'm exhausted from little sleep but also pumped full of optimism. I'm excited to tell Sadie about Duke and see Max outside of the hikes, something we'll hopefully do more often after I confess who I am Monday. I probably should've called, told Sadie I'm stopping by, but it was early and I was on the buzzed side of eager.

So here I am, driving down her street, checking the house numbers, my heart knocking a nervous beat. When I spot number thirty-seven—a blue Victorian home with white trim—on this quiet residential street, I'm seriously moved.

Sadie did this. Earned a living on her own. Fostered a beautiful relationship with her grandmother and used her inheritance to build this picture-perfect life.

Except.

Is that . . . ?

Sadie didn't mention that Joseph was still in town, but that's definitely his muddy truck parked on the street. Or maybe he came back so they could plan for that video meeting with Sarah Lim next week.

I park across from his truck and squeeze my steering wheel, practically crushing it. For coworkers who run an online business, he demands an awful lot of face time. I know seeing art in person is different than looking at images online, but is it really necessary?

He comes out of the front door, and I duck. He has an overnight bag in hand, as well as a large tube slung over his shoulder, likely filled with rolled artwork. The door closes before I glimpse Sadie, and I sink lower. Except screw that. I have no reason to hide. There's no one else on the street. If Joseph has his sights set on Sadie, it's time he learns he has competition.

I hop out of my ozone-depleting Camaro and slam the door. He glances at me but doesn't seem to recognize me from when he picked Sadie up at the hike. Must be the missing yellow gym-bro shirt. I opted for a threadbare gray V-neck tee today. It shows off my harder lines without suctioning to my chest. While I'm not as handsome as this guy, with his strong cheekbones and model lips, I'm taller and thicker and am happy to flex my arms as I lift my sunglasses on top of my head.

I nod to him. "You work with Sadie, right?"

He closes his trunk and studies me. "You're the witness protection ex, right?"

Okay, then. If Sadie gave him that background, the pair must be close. "I am." I cross my arms, giving him a prominent view of my biceps. "I thought you left."

"I did. Then I came back. There's been some ongoing work, and I hate online chats. Plus it's always great to see Sadie and Max. You have a fantastic kid."

Now I have to add *nice* to Joseph's list of attributes. "I do, thanks to Sadie."

He leans on his car and crosses his arms too. Unlike me, his stance doesn't read like Big Man Posturing. More like he's settling in for a friendly catch-up chat. "She's an amazing woman. Smart and kind. Incredibly creative. Considering what she's been through, losing you the way she did, it's a wonder she's built such a strong life for her and Max."

Maybe not so friendly. "I know exactly how incredible she is and how rough my disappearance was on her."

He taps his fingers on his elbow and flexes his jaw. "I'm sure you do, but sometimes it's easy to get caught up in reconnection. Don't forget what she gave up when you left. How long it took her to find her feet and fight for herself."

I stand taller, not liking his insinuation or the undercurrent I'm sensing. "You want Sadie." No point beating around the GQ Joseph block.

"You misunderstand." He kicks off the car and gives my arm a friendly-*ish* slap. "I want what's *best* for Sadie. Make sure you put her first."

His vagueness doesn't sit well. He also didn't deny his feelings. He probably thinks *he's* what's best for Sadie. Not as far as I'm concerned. E returned that ring for a reason. My brother sees what I do: that Sadie and I are meant to be. We have an adorable son together and undeniable history. I'm not going down without a fight.

Joseph gets in his truck and drives away. I scrub my hand over my head and get ready to do what I came here to do. Tell Sadie exactly what kind of put-her-first man I plan to be.

A doorbell ring later, Sadie opens the door. "Did you—oh, Des." She startles and presses her hand to her chest. "I wasn't expecting you."

I can't tell if that was a disappointed *oh, Des* or a genuinely surprised *oh, Des*, and I hate that I'm back to feeling unsure around her. Insecure. Goddamn GQ Joseph.

"Sorry to show up unannounced. Just wanted to talk and thought it was better to do it in person." She moves back, inviting me in. Once inside, I look past her, into the sunlit house, taking in the soft yellow paint brightening the hallway. "Max here?"

"He's outside sketching. Did you want to talk to him?"

"I'd love to see him for a bit, but I also wanted to see you." Checking that Max isn't in visual distance, I take her hand, run my thumb over the bumps of her knuckles. "How has Max been at home lately?"

"So much better," she says, her voice softening. "Jasmine invited him over again this afternoon, and he's been way more upbeat."

"Good." I nod a bunch, suddenly more nervous about Monday's big talk, unsure why. "That's really good."

She stares at our linked hands a moment and grazes the tips of her fingers over my palm. Something hot and fluttery tugs under my navel. I stretch my hand wide, let her explore the edges of my fingers, the creases between my joints. Unable to resist, I explore her hand too—the velvet softness of her skin, the pads of her fingers and crisscrossed lines of her palm.

For a beat, time seems to still. There's no law school or Joseph or challenging dad confessions on the horizon. There's just us. Tender strokes of our hands and tiny revelations. When my nail drags rougher, she shivers. When her thumb brushes mine, I damn near black out.

"Sadie." *Sadie, Sadie, Sadie.* Her name. Forever music on my tongue. "Just so you're aware, not kissing you is a form of torture."

Her eyelids slide closed, as though she's lost in the moment, but a furrow creases her brow. "I have to agree, but this all kind of scares me."

"Which part?" I ask, readying for bad news.

"The intensity of us, how much I think about you when you're not around. We still don't know how Max will react when he meets you or if the connection between us is the kind of chemistry that'll last. I know I'm the one who asked you out last time, and that afternoon was fantastic, but I'm still scared to hurt Max. And if we don't work out and I lose you again . . ." She breathes faster. "I'm not sure I can go through that a second time."

"What we have is real, honey. It's not fleeting chemistry."

"You don't know that for sure."

I sure as hell do, but she clearly doesn't. A reality that breaks my barely mended heart. "So you want to hit pause on dating?"

She chews her lip. Glances at the closed front door. Is she thinking about Joseph? Wondering which man is best for her and her life? "I'm sorry, Des. But—"

"Daniel!" The back door thuds closed.

We jerk apart. Some of me just *fell* apart. Hearing Max call me Daniel here is uncomfortable, and I don't know what Sadie was about to say. Starting with *I'm sorry* isn't promising.

Unwilling to believe she's giving up on us, I strut down the hall, meeting Max in the kitchen. "Max! How's my favorite artist?"

"I've been drawing all week." He clambers onto the island stool and spreads open his sketchbook, a different one than the book he shared with me on our hike. "At first, I was thinking nature stuff, since you do nature hikes. Like trees or flowers or butterflies. Then"—his dark eyes go wide and twinkly—"I thought since you're, like, big and strong, you'd want something big and strong." He flips the page and pushes the book toward me.

It's filled with a number of drawings. Rockets. Two different airplanes. He even drew a helicopter. Kid really loves aviation.

I love that I've given him this project, the excitement in his voice and the sparkle in his eyes. "These are all so good I can't choose. Final decision's yours."

"Really?"

"Really." I flip the page back, still awed by his talent. Strong linework. Soft shading that brings the images to life. "I also dig the flowers and butterflies. Maybe choose two images. One from each page."

"Really?" His jaw practically hits the counter.

I ruffle his hair. "Really."

"What's all this for?" Sadie rounds the counter and peers over Max's shoulder. "Part of one of the hiking activities?"

Max beams. "I'm designing tattoos for Daniel."

"Ha, ha." She makes an exaggerated isn't-our-son-the-funniest face at me. "What's it actually for?"

"I'm designing him tattoos," he repeats, then turns to me for confirmation. "Right?"

"Kid's got skills. I decided I needed Windfall's best designer on my next pieces." Max and I share a conspiratorial smile.

The only thing Sadie shares with me is a death glare. "Max. Why don't you take your stuff upstairs and get ready to go out? I need a word with . . . Daniel."

I mouth at him, *What did I do?*

He giggles and mouths back, *You're in trouble*, laughing under his breath as he heads upstairs.

"Desmond." Sadie crosses her arms, chin lifted, lips pursed.

I know that clipped tone and that your-balls-are-mine stare. I hold up my hands in surrender. "Sadie, look."

"Don't *Sadie, look* me. You can't make false promises to a kid. If you offer them something, they get excited. And this is Max. Drawing is his life. So when you tell him you were messing around, just bonding over art and ink, he'll be crushed."

I shrug a shoulder. "I'm not messing around."

"You're gonna let a ten-year-old kid design a tattoo for you. Whatever he wants. And you'll get it permanently inked on your body. Forever." Her sarcasm reminds me a tad too much of Olivia's ingrained snark.

"No. I'm letting my ten-year-old *son* design me whatever he wants, because he's talented and smart and I want permanent art from him on my body. Forever."

Sadie freezes. Something flicks across her face, an expression I can't quite place. Then she softens—her eyes, her posture, even the obstinate tilt of her chin. "You're serious."

"Of course I am. Serious about him, and about you. About us as a family. I've reenrolled in law, back at Duke. That's what I wanted to discuss with you. I'm staying in North Carolina and planning for my future. Finally picking up my pieces, but I can't imagine doing any of this without you."

She breathes harder, giving me nothing. I have no clue what's going on in her mind. If she's just nervous about setting Max up for failure if we don't work out, or maybe this has to do with Joseph or other issues she hasn't shared with me.

She covers her face with her hand, gives her head a small shake, then she looks at me with a cocktail of emotions I can't begin to decipher. "Okay."

"Okay?"

"I'll go out with you again. But I still don't want Max to know. I mean, we'll tell him who you are Monday. He needs to know that. But he can't know we're going on a date or doing whatever it is we're doing."

"Oh." I grin. "We're definitely going on dates. *Plural.*"

One corner of her lips kicks up. "I can't believe you're letting him design you tattoos."

"Well." I hold out my arms. "I've already set the bar low on quality."

"They aren't that bad. They're actually kind of hot." She licks her lips. "In a sexy bad boy way."

Well now. *Sexy bad boy* I can work with. I tap my left pec. "Wait until you see this one." Her expression turns hazy, color rising to her cheeks. Even though that particular tattoo is more comical than bad boy, I'm getting off on her reaction to me. I step closer and run my hand down my chest, over the bumps of my abs, settling by my right hipbone. "And this one."

"There's one there?" Her voice is all thirsty breath and throaty hum.

I lean down toward her ear. "Go out with me Thursday night, and you might find out."

Footsteps thud above us. I straighten, not missing the goose bumps decorating Sadie's neck.

She touches her collarbone. Another of her turned-on tells. "I can probably get a sitter."

"Then it's a date. And Monday, after the hike"—I rub the back of my neck, decidedly less confident—"we tell Max who I am."

She presses her hand to my shoulder. "I'll be with you, Des. It'll be okay. He already thinks you hang the moon."

"What if he's angry I lied to him?"

"The lie didn't serve you. You wanted to meet him sooner, but we both made this decision for *him*, so he could get to know you without worrying about what to say or how to act. And waiting until he starts with the counselor can only help him."

I nod, still not fully convinced. Max and I do have a good connection. I don't question if he likes me. Doesn't mean he won't freak out and shut down. A terrifying possibility, but Sadie's right. He'll have us and a counselor if things go south.

NINETEEN

I'm no less panicked today. We're nearing our halfway hike break, and I've spent each minute of the past seventy convincing myself Max will be furious I've lied to him this long. He's soon going to shut me and his mom out. The progress he's made will crumble. I keep reconfirming with Sadie that his counselor appointment is on for tomorrow, but no part of me is comforted.

If Max ends up upset, I'm not sure what I'll do.

We've stopped beside a creek. The water gurgles. A couple of butterflies flit about. It's a happy Monday with happy sounds and happy sunshine. I'm the lone gloomy cloud in a cartoon that follows a character around, raining on his head.

Forcing my jaw to unclench, I ready myself to approach Max. Not for my life-altering confession—that frightening confrontation will go down in another grueling seventy or so minutes of worry. Today is still book club day, our planned discussion of *Divergent*, and I need this. These last moments with him before my big reveal, at which point everything might change.

I attempt to suck up my nerves, ready to head over.

But Olivia.

There's no other way to describe her. But Olivia. *Except* Olivia. The perpetual thorn in my side. She's blocking my path, her face more stoic and intense than her usual rabid-for-more-dirt expression. "I have my question."

"I don't have time for today's interrogation."

I've avoided her until now. *Busy, busy, busy.* Explaining today's activity to the group, while stressing over telling Max I'm his dad. Dodging her proximity by chatting with the other kids, while stressing over telling Max I'm his dad. But Olivia. It was only a matter of time.

She fiddles with one of her many bracelets. "Fine. If you're busy or whatever." She sighs. "I'll just double down next time."

Not fine. There's a vulnerability to her tone I'm not used to. Her usual lioness flair is nowhere in that sad sigh. "Changed my mind. Ask now, but make it quick."

"Really?"

"Time's a-tickin'."

"So. Um." Accelerated bracelet twirling. "Did you forgive your dad after he hurt you and your family?"

Wow. Okay. I scrub my hand over my mouth, unsure how to navigate this familial land mine. Olivia must be struggling with her feelings toward her dad, torn between hating him for hurting her mom and maybe missing him. I mean, the guy's certainly not in line for any Man of the Year award. Cheating on your wife with her best friend is harsh. Still.

I crouch on my heels, lowering closer to her height. "Forgiveness depends on a lot of factors."

She digs her toe into the ground. "Such as?"

"Well, my dad was a good enough dad growing up. We weren't super close, and we fought plenty, but he showed up to some of my football games and helped me with homework from time to time." The basics of being a father. Never above and beyond, but he was present, any of his good intentions crushed under his irrevocable actions. "While I have some solid memories of him from my childhood, what he did later was worse. The bad outweighed the good."

"So you didn't forgive him?"

Not unless fantasizing about tying his tortured body to train tracks counts as forgiveness. "I didn't, but that's a case-by-case situation. If, for example, we're talking about a *guy* who cheated on his *wife* with his wife's *best friend* . . ."

She makes an irritated noise. "Way to be subtle."

"Not going for subtlety, squirt."

"Do *not* call me squirt."

"As I was saying, in your situation, you need to weigh a bunch of stuff. Was he a good dad to you before? Has he tried to apologize since? Will staying mad at him hurt more or less than forgiving him? Forgiveness is a big ask, but not forgiving someone is sometimes harder. Sits with you in a rougher way."

I see that roughness with Lennon. He may be the Bower jokester, quick to cover his discomfort with humor. Smiles and jazz hands at work. But I'd bet part of the reason he never grew out of his *ish* personality is because he was closest with Dad. The only Bower boy who fished with him. The one who was never on Dad's bad side, the two of them often in cahoots. I used to be jealous of them, unsure what I did or didn't do to miss out on the dad-son bond. Probably lashed out a time or twenty because of it.

Lennon, though. I'm guessing he's felt displaced in a different way since WITSEC, unsure how to forgive Raymond S. Bower, the father who singled him out as worthy, while still being furious with him.

As trying as Olivia is, I'd hate for her to lose her fire and become *ish*.

"At the very least," I tell her as I stand, "hear your dad out. Don't make any rash decisions. Also, I charge for advice by the minute. If you need more, it'll cost you, and I take payment in silence."

She replies with one of her this-adult-is-so-not-cool eye rolls and trudges off. For some reason, I smile. Now it's time to steal my last minutes with Max, before *he* needs to blackmail an adult to ask similar probing questions, including the zinger, Should I forgive my dad for lying to me?

Carter and Jun are tossing rocks into the creek, making *pew-pew* sound effects again. I don't know how I got lucky enough to have a kid who doesn't make *pew-pew* noises constantly. Small mercies. Max is with Zoey and Jasmine, the three of them glued to their phones. While the phone time would normally annoy me, their eager faces and busy thumbs do the opposite. Not only have I allowed them to use their phones on today's hike, but I've made it part of the activity.

Their task has been to snap pictures of as many birds and butterflies as possible. We'll tally them at the end and decipher which species we caught. Since bribery still motivates the heathens, I told them there was a prize for the kid who snaps the widest variety of species. They've been nature paparazzi the whole hike.

I could interrupt them, ask Max to attend our planned book club meeting. Discuss *Divergent* and which faction we'd each be in, while I silently plead with him to not freak out later at my impending confession. But he's smiling and laughing with the girls. Seems he's really coming out of his shell with Jasmine and Zoey, having fun the way kids should be having fun. I don't have the heart to take him away from that.

I join Sadie instead. She's leaning against a tree, looking relaxed, watching the water meander around rocks. I lean on the opposite side, anything but relaxed.

"Butterfly!" Jasmine calls. They all clamber to get shots, falling over one another, ending with Max on the ground, Zoey with one foot in the creek, and Olivia with her phone punched up in the air, yelling, "Got it!"

Sadie knocks her foot against mine. "You planned another fantastic hike."

I grunt.

Translation: *I can't form words when my insides are contorted into knots.*

She traces the bumps and grooves of our shared tree. "You're still nervous about telling Max?"

A deranged laugh almost escapes me. "Mildly."

Her fingers keep tracing the tree's gnarly surface. Fungus juts out from the bark between us in semicircular fan shapes, like spaceships got lodged in the trunk. "*Beauty in the Breakdown*," she says.

I frown, feeling the stirrings of a headache. "Isn't that a song?"

"I think so. It's also this." She taps the edge of a fungus fan. "Mushrooms grow on dying trees to help them decompose. Eventually, the trees become fertile soil."

I stretch my jaw, and yeah. Headache central. "Are you saying that when I'm dying"—which, judging by how I'm feeling, might be by the end of this hike—"you'll cultivate mushrooms in my body to speed up the process?"

"What I'm saying, smart-ass, is I can't predict how Max will react when you talk to him, but even if he's mad and lashes out, or if he shuts down, his hurt will settle. Love will grow. He just might need time."

Yeah, no. Her pep talk isn't making me feel *peppy*. Trees can take decades to decompose. A goddamn century. I'm not strong enough to survive without Max. "I know this isn't about me. I'm more worried about him than anything, but . . ." I trail off, afraid my voice might crack.

"You're also scared he'll push you away?"

I give a jerky nod.

She presses a reassuring hand to my forearm. "Give yourself a break, Des. You lost ten years of his life. It's only natural to think about yourself, how scary it would be to lose more."

If that happens, it won't be pretty. But I make a mental note to do a fungus-themed hike for the kids, get them running around, learning to identify different species. They'll probably like that.

Sadie and I don't talk more about Max. We watch the kids, while I continue my internal meltdown. I also laugh when Carter *pew-pews*

Max, and Max mimes a dramatic death. Even those two are getting along better. But in an hour, Max might revert to the timid, introverted kid I first met. He might be so distraught that he shuts out his new friends.

By the time we've finished our hike, my internal meltdown hits hyperdrive.

I collect the kids' phones, happy for the distraction. After a quick tally of the most pictures of birds and butterflies captured, I present Olivia with her winning prize: one of my recently finished braided bracelets.

"Oh, wow." Her face lights up, and she does a little jump. My insides mimic the move. "You made this?"

I hold up my callused hands. "These thick fingers made every knot. And you'll notice there's no yellow."

She laughs, beaming brighter than earlier, and a chuff of pleasure lights me up too. Not sure when she became less terrifying, but I'm actually digging that kid.

Unfortunately, my good mood dips quickly.

The kids start going home, eliminating the buffers between me and today's life-altering talk. When the last car drives away, all that's left is Sadie, Max, and my rattling nerves. There's a small pond and picnic area at the start of this trail. A family of ducks waddles along the pond edge. Clouds blow above with the steady breeze. Sadie and Max are skipping rocks, laughing and egging each other on.

I inhale deeply and walk over, hanging back when I reach them. Feeling separate from my splintered family.

I open my mouth and say *Max*. At least I thought I did. Only air came out.

I clear my throat and say, "Max," louder.

They turn, and my kid beams at me. "My mom can't skip rocks. They just sink."

She couldn't skip rocks when she was mine to love either. "Your mom only listens when strangers give her pointers. Like with axe throwing. If it's someone close, she hates admitting she's not the best at something."

She plants her fists on her hips. A study of indignation. "That's not true."

"Yes, it is," Max and I say in unison.

She laughs, her eyes darting between us. "You two are ganging up on me."

God, do I want more of this. Ganging up with Max to tease Sadie. Having them heckle me. "We call it like we see it, Sprite."

Her face goes soft. At her nickname or this perfect family moment, I'm not sure. She pushes her hand through Max's hair, focusing her attention on him. "Daniel wants to talk to you for a sec, if that's okay."

His eyes dart between us, his brow furrowed. "Sure?"

Already, my chest constricts. My headache from before resumes—a steady pulse behind my eyes that makes me slightly nauseated. Hands stuffed into my pockets, I walk to the nearby bench and sit at one end. Max sits in the middle. Sadie takes the far end.

Here we are. At my crossroads.

"Max." I angle toward him and remove my hands from my pockets, but I don't know what to do with myself. I place my hands on my thighs, then pick at my cuticles. "I have something to tell you, but before I do, I want you to know a bit more about me."

He glances over his shoulder at Sadie. She gives an encouraging nod. He turns back to me with a quiet "Okay."

"You know I have a history with your mom, but it was more than that. She was . . ." I lift my eyes from his for a moment, needing her to see this. To see me—the depths of my feelings for her. "I was in love with her," I say roughly.

She covers her trembling lips with her hand. I attempt to say *I still love you* with my eyes, but I probably resemble a terrified lamb about to be slaughtered. I return my focus to Max, who's looking slightly bewildered. "I loved her a lot, and she loved me. We were planning a future together, but things beyond our control tore us apart."

His dark eyes sweep my face, probing, analyzing. "So you wanna date my mom?"

I want to *marry* his mom, but that's a whole other conversation. I don't bother mentioning my asshole father and witness protection. Sadie explained the story to him before he met my family. He knows what I went through. He just doesn't know who I *am*.

"Thing is, Max. The reason I'm here, running this program. The reason I returned this close to my hometown is . . ." Goddamn it, these tears. Burning up the backs of my eyes again, threatening to fall. I glance at Sadie. My Sprite, who encourages me when I'm floundering. She's battling her own set of waterworks and losing. Tears drip unchecked down her cheeks. I push through the fire burning up my lungs and say, "I'm your dad, Max."

He blinks at me, doesn't speak, but he's breathing hard. Like, really hard.

I press my fist against my chest. Swear to God, my heart's about to bust through. "I didn't know, Max. Had no idea your mom was pregnant with you when we had to go into witness protection. Only found out about you recently. My real name's Desmond, and I'm sorry I didn't tell you right away. I was worried about you. Scared that the pressure of meeting me would be hard to handle, or that I might accidentally hurt you. Because honestly, I'm a bit of a screwup. But then I met you, and you're this great kid. So amazing and smart and talented and easy to be around. *You* make being a dad feel easy, and I'm so proud you're mine." My tears are everywhere, dripping over my nose, my lips. Total shit show. "I hope you can forgive me for keeping this from you. I want nothing more than to be your dad."

He still doesn't speak or move, and I start to cave. I'm buckling. A landslide of devastation I can't control.

Sadie's hands are on Max's shoulders. She's telling him "It's okay" and "We can leave if you want."

For the record, I am not okay. I can't leave. I will petrify in this spot. A tarnished sculpture with my insides gouged out, amid the hopping squirrels and green-green grass, titled *The Day Desmond Lost His Heart*.

Then arms are around my neck. Little-boy arms, hugging me fiercely. Max doesn't say a word, just cries and shakes and squeezes me, and I'm squeezing him back, burying my face against him, breathing him in, worried I'm holding him too hard.

"I love you," I choke out. "All of you, Max. No holds barred."

No matter who he loves or doesn't love. No matter what happens with Sadie. From here on out, I'll always have Max.

I open my sopping eyes and see her. Sadie Jones. The strong woman who loved her son so fiercely she cut off her parents and carved out a new life for herself. She's bawling and smiling and beaming, and I can't lie. I need her too. Us. This family together. Which means I have some convincing to do, starting with our second date this Thursday night.

TWENTY

Dates can be nerve racking. Dates with your first love, who raised your son and owns your heart, are a whole other beast. I'm pacing outside the entrance to a fun street food scene, alternating between crossing my arms and sticking my hands in my jean pockets. Since we're keeping our date secret from Max so he doesn't get his hopes up about us, I couldn't pick up Sadie at home as I would've liked. I got to our meeting spot early instead. I'd claim my eager arrival was so she wouldn't feel awkward waiting for me. Truth is, I'm mildly overexcited for tonight.

Before leaving my house, I tried on three different T-shirts—all plain black, but I swear each fits differently—and settled on the one that's softest. And yes, that's gel in my hair. I don't remember the last time I cared so much about how I looked or waited eagerly to glimpse a woman. Everything feels new and exciting. *I* feel new, all thanks to Max.

We've chatted on the phone every day since Monday. Probing talks where he asks me personal questions about my interests and hobbies (exercising and pitifully done crafts) and what it's like having four brothers (invasive and annoying). He also hit me with random doozies like, "Do you think dragons exist?" And, "If you were a french fry and you were starving, would you eat yourself?" His brain is ridiculous and awesome. I hate when I have to hang up with him, and I'm busting to see him tomorrow on our hike. I'm not sure if he'll feel awkward or shy in public with me. Whatever transpires, we'll work through it. I'm just excited to see him again.

And his mother.

Nearby vendors are selling mini samples of their street food concoctions, the mouthwatering smells of grilled meat, exotic spices, and caramelized sugar drifting from the festivities. A couple walks past me toward the action, holding hands and leaning into each other. The woman has a cool collection of tattoos that put mine to shame, and when the guy kisses her cheek, my stomach does this nervous, happy jump I can't even describe.

Then I smell the best smells: sunshine and citrus—my sweet Sadie Jones.

"Des?"

I swivel, and there she is, smiling shyly, killing me with her fluttery summer dress. The fabric looks thin, the barely-there straps exposing the freckles on her shoulders. The low front flirts with her cleavage, but her lips are what do me in: pink and shiny and begging to be devoured. At a loss for words, I do the only thing humanly possible—lean down to kiss her.

Sadie gives me her cheek.

I press a soft kiss to her cheekbone, unsure why she's holding back. We've already kissed once. She agreed to this date. Hopefully the fears she admitted at her home haven't returned.

She tucks her purse close and eyes the busy street. "I had no idea there were food festivals nearby." A family brushes by her. Instead of stepping into me, she steps away. "How'd you find out about it?"

I attempt telepathy to read her mind and figure out why she's putting up walls and awkward small talk between us. When that doesn't work, I fall back on my pre-WITSEC method of winning Sadie over. Shameless flirting. "I visited my pal Google and searched 'romantic venues where I can feed my date food and lick her sticky fingers.'" I wink at her.

She stands rigid, fiddling with her purse. "I'm sure the search results were plentiful."

"And alarming." Sticky anything in a search is a downward spiral to degenerate sites, but I thought I planned a great date.

Going out in secret meant we couldn't stay in Windfall. My temporary home of Ruby Grove was also out. We'd for sure run into Olivia, who'd then have new blackmail material, since I don't care about the witness protection leverage any longer. So here we are. At a fun event to promote the local restaurants, in a random town about a forty-five minute drive for each of us. Distance that comes with bonuses. No one here knows us. My plan was to be all over Sadie all night. Unfortunately, she's a wooden sculpture of herself.

"Is everything okay with Max? He said he liked his counselor, right?"

Her posture softens. "He's good, Des. Better than good. And Samantha seems like a great fit for him."

"Okay, good." But we're both saying *good* too much. Awkwardness that needs to end. "So, Sadie Sprite Jones. What should we try first?" I sound like I inhaled helium, suddenly nervous and twitchy. I'm not sure how to stop. "The tacos or falafel look good. Or do we skip dinner and go straight for those mini cupcakes with the ten inches of icing?"

Her face brightens for the first time. "They have cupcakes?"

Thank God for her sweet tooth. "Ten inches of icing it is."

I lead the way, needing to get this night moving, Sadie relaxing. Me not sounding like an overenergized chipmunk. I did a quick tour of the vendors online and try to remember where the cupcakes are, but she touches my arm, stilling me. "We don't have to have cupcakes. Something else is fine. They'll have dairy in them."

I love that she knows I can't eat dairy. Details a girlfriend would know.

"Actually." I move into her space and drop my voice. "They're vegan. Perfect for me to lick off of you."

She inhales sharply, her nostrils flaring wide. Instead of freezing up and creating space, she flexes her fingers in my arm. "You're forward."

"I know what I want." The dairy-free cupcakes were the clincher when choosing this outing for our date. I knew Sadie would want those treats, and I *maybe* planned to accidentally smear some on her neck.

She blows out a breath, then gives me those gorgeous eyes. "I'm sorry."

"For what?"

"For acting weird."

"Hey." I brush the backs of my knuckles down her arm. "All I want is for you to be yourself around me. If that's anxious or weird right now, I'll take it."

Her shoulders lower. "Why do you have to be so you?"

"So sensitive and thoughtful and handsome?" I shrug. "It's a curse."

She laughs and fits her hand in mine. "I particularly love your modesty."

"Modesty is for suckers."

A nearby busker strums for his audience, and Sadie sways slightly. "Can we start over? Pretend I didn't dodge your kiss and put on the brakes the second I saw you."

I want to ask why she put on those brakes, but we need to have a fun night out, and the busker switched tunes to a coffeehouse rendition of *Dirty Dancing*'s "She's like the Wind."

This is a sign. Divine interference, giving me the gift of obnoxiousness.

I stop abruptly and say loudly, "Sorry for the interruption, folks, but I always do the last dance of the season."

Sadie murmurs, "Oh my God." There's genuine fear on her face.

"My kind of dancing," I go on. Then I forget the rest of those infamous *Dirty Dancing* lines and shout, "Nobody puts Sadie in a corner." I hold out my hand to her, grinning.

Her cheeks are as red as the ketchup some guy's squirting on his slider.

"What are you doing?" she says through a clenched-teeth smile.

"Seizing the moment." It's my new motto. A new lease on life. Living large. Loosening Sadie up the best way I know how, by being ridiculous. "We're doing our dance."

"We haven't done our dance in eleven years. And everyone's watching."

An audience is gathering, couples and families eyeing us with friendly curiosity. I don't give Sadie time to overthink or freak out. *I* don't overthink or freak out. I grab her hand, pull her close, and try to remember how to sweep her around in a slow waltz.

Why does a not-so-great dancer—*me*—know the difference between a slow waltz and a Viennese waltz, you may ask? Simple. I wanted to make Sadie happy.

For her birthday one year, I surprised her with dance lessons, because she loved dancing, and I loved any excuse to have my hands on Sadie Jones. We tried to learn the rumba from *Dirty Dancing*—one of her favorite movies. With my lack of skill, we switched to a slow waltz and got pretty decent at it. But it's been eleven years.

We fumble our feet at first, the steps no longer second nature. Then we hit our stride. We do the gentle spins, rising and falling, our arms held at shoulder height, trying to get our posture right, the gold in Sadie's eyes shining with what's hopefully our bottomless well of fond memories. The song isn't an actual "waltz" song—the perfect three-four time that lets you glide effortlessly in circles. Still, we do our best and finish with a big dip, because Sadie always loved being dipped.

I drag her back up to the applause of our audience.

"Bravo!" someone shouts.

"Y'all are so cute." This from a woman to our left.

Sadie leans around me, addressing our fan. "He has a rare digestive disorder. If he doesn't dance when music plays, he's on the toilet all night."

The woman cackles. "That's it, girl. Keep him on his toes."

As long as Sadie keeps me, she can embarrass me all she likes. "You still love throwing me under the bus," I tell her, holding her close.

"You're still an obnoxious drama addict."

"If I am, it's your fault. You bring out my inner exhibitionist."

She scoffs. "Not true. You were a ham on the football field too."

I nose her ear and whisper, "Because I knew you were watching."

She shivers and takes my hand, leading us to icing heaven. "You changed me too. I mean, *God*. I was so cynical before we started dating. Angry all the time, assuming people were mean or had an ulterior motive. I was so rigid in my schedules. Then you blew into my life, all carefree and spontaneous. Being with you softened my edges."

"You were a cynical teen because your parents were awful."

"Sure, but you're what pulled me out of that funk." We dodge a couple of running kids, their hands full of mini donuts. "With you, I realized I was allowed to be happy, even if my parents weren't. That I didn't have to end up like them. Especially being around your family."

The wild and raucous Bower boys, relentless troublemakers until a hurricane blew through our lives. "Pretty sure my family isn't a benchmark."

"Not your father, who I hope I never see again or I might face charges, but you and your brothers." She smiles, knocking into my side with her lazy stride. "As much as you all fought, there was no denying how much you loved each other. This easy unconditional acceptance. It made me understand what a family really is."

We reach the cupcake line. The perfect opportunity to wrap my arms around Sadie and pull her back against my chest. "I've pushed them away plenty over the years, but I know I'm lucky. I'm working on being better with them and bringing more carefree spontaneity back into *your* life."

She nuzzles her head under my chin. "A single mom can't afford to be carefree and spontaneous."

My dancing afterglow dips. I mean, I have Sadie in my arms. She's running her fingers over the sparse hairs on my knuckles, turning my hands electric, but her words remind me how different we are now. Our lives. Our responsibilities.

"I almost forgot—how did the video meeting go? Did Sarah offer you the job?"

She stiffens again. Slightly. Enough that I feel her arms tense. "Yes, but it's not the job I was expecting."

"She doesn't want you starting the mentorship programs?"

"Not in the way I imagined."

"Shit, honey. I'm so sorry. It sounded perfect for you." When she stays quiet, I press my chin into the side of her head. "Are you negotiating with her or just turning it down?"

"Joseph wants to work with her." Her voice dims further. "He doesn't want to let it go."

"Well, if she doesn't see how amazing you are, someone else will. And when you win curator of the year at the annual curator festival, she'll regret her decision." And Joseph better not be putting pressure on Sadie to do something she doesn't want to do.

She laughs haltingly at my weak joke and . . . is that a *sniffle*?

Fuck. I desperately wanted this for her. She was so excited about the job, talking a mile a minute about the mentorship program, bouncing with excitement. Her tense shoulders now and subdued reply remind me of her tone when she admitted working from home was confining, that she missed seeing art and offices in person.

Unable to do a damn thing to help, I kiss the top of her head.

She runs her nail over my fingers, a light scrape I feel down to my toes. "Tell me about school," she says. "You must be dying to get back into law."

"Can't wait," I say. That's it. No excited boasting from me either, and I'm not sure why. Mom wired me the money. With her investments over the years, the sum is substantial. This is the stability Sadie and Max need.

"The syllabus is overwhelming," I admit, trying to figure out this ongoing edginess. "I have to repeat my first-year classes, but I can coordinate Friday afternoons and Monday mornings off." More weekend time for my three-hour drives back to Windfall.

She squeezes my hand. "I'm so happy you're finally getting your life back."

"I'm particularly excited to flash my ink and tell everyone my father laundered money for the Becerra cartel."

She pulls my arms tighter around her. "They'll shut up when they see how brilliant you are."

Whatever. Let them gawk and gossip. Sadie doesn't seem to care. "More important," I say, wanting to take Sadie's mind off of her job stress, "is our first menu choice. I can't decide between the chocolate chip cookie dough cupcake and the s'mores cupcake."

"Ooh." She pushes to her tiptoes and reads the chalkboard menu. "One of each, plus the maple bacon cupcake."

Have I mentioned how perfect Sadie Jones is? "It's a deal. I was also wondering if it's cool for me to take Max to a baking class. Delilah's hosting them in the café's kitchen. Since you mentioned Max loves cooking, thought it would be fun for him. And we'd get some one-on-one time together."

She spins fully and smiles up at me. "He'd love that. As long as you don't embarrass yourself by burning what you make."

"Yeah, no. I'll just be his sous chef. Let him bake however he wants."

She kisses the center of my chest. "You're already such a great dad. Before you know it, you'll be a Duke Law grad too."

As much as I appreciate the compliment, her vehemence on that degree sits roughly. Like she needs to keep convincing herself that's where I'll end up.

Preferring to stick to the topic of us, I lean down and nip her ear. "FYI, when we get those cupcakes, I plan to lick some icing off your neck."

Mischief sparks in her dare-me eyes. "Only if I get to lick some from your forearm."

Fair warning: the PDA is about to get intense.

We spend the next two hours being carefree and silly. As promised, I smear icing on her neck, then lick it off. She retaliates with two fingerfuls along my forearm. The second her tongue touches my skin, I grunt. Translation: *I'm aching to spread Sadie out on the nearest table and push into her with one mind-blowing thrust.*

We don't actually kiss, but man, do we *tease*. I tuck her into my side, wrapping my arm around her back, settling my fingers on the sexy place just below her breasts. She hooks her thumb into my belt loop and torments my hipbone. We eat falafel and pulled-pork sliders and fried avocado tacos while brushing against each other. We laugh about stupid things we did in school and marvel at Max's art talent. When we order pad thai, she asks for it without cilantro, which I hate, and eats the shrimp she knows I don't like. She doesn't need to ask my preferences because she knows them, and I'm struck by the ease of this. The history between us. So much bad, but so much good.

More good, I think. Like my talk with Olivia. The scales that tip from forgiveness to grudges, depending on emotional weight. Our slow waltzes and Bear Lake talks and french-fry-eating races are piled on one side, along with our amazing Max.

On the opposite end is a decade of hurt and heartache, but it somehow feels lighter now. Not gone. There's evidence of that weight.

Between our banter, Sadie occasionally goes quiet, like her stilted behavior when discussing her work and at the start of the night. Each time, a small wrinkle creases the space between her eyebrows. Then I make a joke, bringing her back to me, tipping us into playful territory.

"So." We're at her car, the end of a night I'd like to stretch out in. Stay here and inhale her intoxicating scent until I'm drunk with it: the Summer of Sadie Jones. I crowd her against her door, loom over her small frame. "Hope you had a nice second date."

A small sigh escapes her. "Thanks for planning such a perfect night."

"Guess this is the end, though." I hate saying goodbye here. I want to be at her home, asking to come inside.

She rests her hands on my chest, moves her fingers over my pecs, then down toward my abs. "You really have been working out a lot, Des." Her voice turns breathy, her hands splaying wider.

I clench and hold, because honestly, I'm not that strong of a man. One more shift of her fingers and I'm dropping to my knees, lifting her skirt, and capturing my first taste of her in way too long. "Sadie, honey. You're killing me."

It's dark on the street, the lamplights casting a soft glow as the odd shriek drifts from the food fair, reminding me we're in a populated area. My body's urging me to open her car door, coax her into the back seat like we're teenagers again, stealing privacy wherever we can. Tonight, though. So much was perfect, but there were too many distant moments. Rushing Sadie if she's not ready would only backfire.

"Des." Her hands press harder into my abdomen, then move around my waist to my back. "I . . ." She drops her gaze, but her fingers are strong and insistent, digging into the cut of my spine.

My hips move. I can't help it. They roll into her, the already hard line of my cock notching against her stomach. It's not classy or suave. I'm just a man, pressing his erection into the woman he loves, waiting to be told it's okay to blow her mind. "Just say the word, Sprite. Whatever you want, it's yours."

She pulls me closer, presses her nose to the dip between my collar-bones. She's smelling me, I think, threatening my already frayed composure. Then she returns her hands to my chest, creating space between us. "I should get home. Sitter and all."

Her voice has some husk to it, every syllable dragging across my oversensitive skin, but the worry line has returned to her brow. There's tension in her stiff shoulders.

I brush my hand down her hip. "When can I see you again?"

"You'll see me tomorrow."

"Alone." So we can work through whatever has her keeping me at a distance.

Her occasional stiffness feels bigger than her work issue. More upsetting and personal. Maybe to do with her law comment earlier—concern about where I'm at in my life now, the bartending I've done for a decade. I may have told her I'm going to law school, but she could be worried I'll get overwhelmed and quit. Or GQ Joseph could be putting moves on her, giving her another option to consider.

She leans onto her car, fiddles with her purse. "I'll check with the sitter about booking another night. Sorry I can't be more spontaneous."

"I don't need spontaneous." I dip my head and meet her eyes, trying to show my sincerity. "Just more time with you."

"Told you," she says tenderly, "the tattoos and hard exterior are just a disguise. In here"—she presses her hand to my chest again—"you're all marshmallow."

I cover her hand with mine, okay with my gooey center. "Can I get a kiss for the road?"

She breathes deeper, seeming torn. Then she nods.

I don't waste the gift of her consent. I lean down and slant my mouth over hers, pressing softly. Tender moves. Slow and languid kisses, like we have all the time in the world. Like I'm not worried Sadie's hesitancy will end with me on another wall-punching bender, bawling my heartache to Mirielle.

She moans and kisses me back, dragging her fingers through my short hair. And *Christ*. I'm done for. A pile of putty for this woman. The kiss turns deep and filthy, our tongues making up for lost time. I go from hard to harder, every muscle and tendon flexing with need—desperation I've never felt. I mean, I'm practically revirginized. I haven't been with a woman since the night I called Sadie and assumed she had a son with someone else. Nine months of self-pity and abstinence. But this is Sadie Jones. Only she could turn my body this haywire.

Pulling away is painful, but there's the issue of public indecency. I'd rather Max not see me in jail.

I squeeze Sadie's waist and finish with a soft kiss to her cheek. "You taste better than the cupcakes."

"You tasted better *with* the cupcake icing on you."

I groan, imagining painting her in icing—the dip of her collarbones, the tips of her nipples, the valley between her thighs. "You live to torture me. And when we're hiking tomorrow, don't go spreading lies about my digestive system like after our dance. Lactose intolerance is no joke."

She raises an eyebrow. "Says the guy who loved it when Lennon would dare him to drink milk or eat cheese."

"Sadie, Lennon's a menace. If I back down from a dare, the guy's intolerable."

"You boys were too funny together."

We were. Stupid boys doing stupid stuff. "Be warned, next time you throw me under the bus, I might have to share my photo of you with your anal-bead necklace."

She attempts to glare, but her twitching lips betray her. I wink at her, then head to my car, loving the cute amusement she can't hide. Our hike tomorrow can't come soon enough.

TWENTY-ONE

Fungus gets a bad rap. The name is obviously a kick in the pants, and some of them are nasty looking, but my preteen platoon is made of natural-born mushroom hunters. All six mini humans are zooming around the forest as we slowly make our way along the trail, constantly stopping for quick sketches. Using my handouts, they have to guess the varietal and write the name of the mushroom under their drawings. The kid with the most correct sketches wins a prize, and I've never seen them this intense. They know what's at stake today—the top mushroom hunter gets another of my braided bracelets.

I thought the homemade prize would be eye roll worthy. Then Olivia showed up this morning, all her other bracelets removed except for Monday's win, preening and showing it off. Not gonna lie, I think the heat in my face was actual blushing. Now they all want one.

Max runs up to me, breathless, shoving his sketchbook toward me. "It's a shaggy mane. It looks like a furry hat."

It sure does, because my son's a budding Michelangelo. He totally captured the lacy scales curving up the sides. "Maybe I should get *that* inked?"

"No way. I have plans." He runs off to join the others: the Sherlock Holmes Fungus Gang, scouring this new section of woods.

I wasn't sure what to expect with him today. We've talked on the phone plenty since my big reveal, and he likes his counselor, Samantha, but this is our first face-to-face time since I bawled into his neck on Monday. He hasn't called me Dad or, as far as I can tell, told anyone who I am, but he seeks me out often, shows me his sketches, asking which mushrooms are poisonous and which aren't. Even better, he's been laughing with his friends.

Learning who I am hasn't reverted him to his introverted ways. He hasn't seemed awkward or nervous. Unlike his mother, who's resumed her stiffness around me.

I narrow my eyes at Sadie's back, not making any sudden moves. She's done an excellent job of avoiding me today. Every time I walked toward her, she bolted off, saying things like, "Oh, Zoey! Careful near those trees," and "Olivia! Let me help you draw that contour," and "Carter, drop that right now!"

Granted, Carter dared Jun to eat a bright-orange *Amanita flavoconia*, and Sadie intervened before Jun landed in the hospital and Lennon murdered me for turning his business into manslaughter central, but I know what she's doing. She's avoiding me and her feelings, like during parts of last night's date. The question is *why*?

I walk as carefully as possible toward her, frowning at more annoying litter on the ground. Making a mental note to grab it before we leave, I forge on. Sadie's got her nose in my handout, which she's read sixty-seven times today.

Avoidance Queen.

When I'm close enough that she can't evade me, I say, "Have you memorized that yet?"

She jumps and squeaks. "You scared me."

Her avoidance is scaring me. "Sadie Jones, do I make you nervous?"

She waves her paper, laughing haltingly, like I made some kind of hilarious joke. "Don't be ridiculous."

"Ridiculous is you dodging me. Do I smell?" I make a show of sniffing my armpit.

There's the eye roll I missed from the kids. "You smell fine."

"I'm going for better than fine." I dig cologne. Smells can be sensual and intoxicating. Case in point, last night, Sadie took that extralong inhale at my neck. Eternity was my cologne of choice back in the day, classic and bold and manly. Opting for something fresher and lighter, I bought Cool Water recently and thought it was doing the trick. "So you *don't* like my cologne."

"That's not what I said."

"You said I smell fine. Fine's not good."

She drops her head back, mumbles at the sky, then skewers me with those ethereal eyes. "You look too good and smell too good and being around you is . . . difficult. I'm not ready for Max to know we're doing whatever it is we're doing."

"We're on the same page with Max, honey." And I don't think that's the reason she's acting cagey. I think she's worried I won't turn my life around the way I've promised I would. Needing to ease her mind, I walk forward until her back's pressed against a tree. "I got textbooks for school. Can't wait to crack them open."

The cracking open part is a lie, but the way Sadie brightens is worth it. "I'm so excited for you."

"Since I'll be spending more time prepping, I don't want to waste these minutes together. And we're being discreet. We're just two adults talking close so the kiddos don't overhear us. Isn't that what normal adults do around children?"

She tongues the corner of her lips, slaying me. "The way you're looking at me isn't normal."

She's probably right. All I feel around her is ravenous. "Speaking of our continued dating, have you organized a sitter for a night next week?"

"Des."

"*Sprite.*"

"Max can't know," she says again, but her gaze darts to my mouth. Something else she's done a few times today, along with launching a

Kelly Siskind

number of lingering glances my way, hopefully reliving that hot kiss at her car.

Since I can't outright touch her in our present circumstance, I scratch my hair and flex my biceps, remembering her throaty *You really have been working out a lot.* Can't blame a guy for showcasing his strengths. "Max doesn't know, honey. And I can't control how I look at you. I want to see you again. Alone. I thought you wanted that too?"

She breathes harder, looks about to speak.

Her damn phone rings.

She fumbles with her backpack, digs out her cell, then frowns at the screen before answering. "Chelsea, hi."

"My mom?" I mouth, unsure why she's calling Sadie.

She nods. To my mom, she says, "Sure, okay. That should be fine. Let me ask Des." She covers the phone. "Your mom and Lennon are in Windfall, visiting E and Delilah. They all want to swing by later and see Max."

"Of course they can." Though I'd hate not being there. Kind of resent Mom for not including me. "It's not my call."

Sadie shifts on her feet. "She wants to know if you'll come."

I should never have questioned my mom. Woman's always helping me out, even when I've been a bear. "I'll check my schedule, but I think I can make that work."

Considering the only things on my schedule are to flirt with Sadie and spend time with Max, it shouldn't be tough. I don't push the sitter issue and another date either. As far as I'm concerned, this is progress. It's time for me to check no one's eating poisonous mushrooms.

I turn to head over to the kids. But Olivia.

I thought I was past *But Olivia.* I assumed Monday's bracelet win and our talk about her dad pushed us past antagonistic territory. Apparently not. She's by a grouping of tiny white mushrooms. Instead of intently sketching her discovery, she's standing, arms folded, intently watching me. Her evil-mastermind expression doesn't bode well.

I go for evasion and try to beeline for Max.

She steps in my way, smug as ever. "You and Sadie, huh?"

"Me and Sadie nothing. And we're done with the questions. I don't care if the others hear about my past. You've lost your leverage."

Her smugness grows into a gleam. "Did you know straight men spend a year of their lives staring at women?"

"And?"

"You're going for the staring world record. There's no point lying. You and Sadie were basically making out over there."

Honestly. Why do I even bother? "Sadie and I were just talking over there," I say sternly, hunched lower, attempting not to growl. "Not making out. Maybe mind your own business."

She squints at me so intensely I start to itch. "Is Max your son?"

What in the actual fuck? I pat my suctioned yellow shirt, checking for a wire. I have no clue where she gets her intel. "Why would you ask that?"

"You were with his mom before your dad ruined your life." She holds up her thumb, counting off her first point with a hefty dose of condescension. "That was, like, ten or eleven years ago, and Max is ten." She ticks up a second finger. "Your eyes are pretty similar." Finger three. "And Max drew you in his sketchbook." Four. "If you're not his dad, I might have to call child services on that last one."

She's gunning for an extralong silent treatment from yours truly, but . . . "He drew me?"

Not only am I grinning like an idiot, but I've just given Olivia all the ammunition she needs to make my life intolerable. What else is new?

"He's really good at drawing," she says.

"He's fantastic. And you better not breathe a word to him about Sadie and me. It's too early to tell him."

She taps her chin, drawing out my pain. "Guess that leverage is mine again. Four questions a day, and you have to tell me your real name."

I grip the back of my hair, nearly yanking it out. I'm not sure if this leverage is better or worse than her last question-extortion stunt. With how cagey Sadie's being, possibly worse. But I have an edge of my own. "Zero percent of kids who get greedy when blackmailing receive more kickass bracelets. And my real name's Desmond. I was planning to tell the group about that and my WITSEC interlude at the end of today's hike anyway."

She makes a huffy sound. "Fine, *Desmond*. One question. So—"

I hold up my palm. "Not today, Satan. You wasted question number one at the start of this ambush."

Her irked expression is my reward for thinking on my feet. "Fine, but FYI, Sadie's doing that thing my mom does when she likes a guy, but she's worried he's a dick or thinks it won't work out."

"First, don't say *dick*. Second, what thing?" More to the point, I should not be on the proverbial edge of my seat, eager for advice from a twelve-year-old extortionist.

"The avoidance thing. You're chasing, and she's avoiding."

I glance at Sadie, who's flipping through Jun's mushroom book with him. A regular adult-kid interaction. My heart still does this strange squeeze-pinch-roll number. "How do these guys get her to stop avoiding?"

Forget eager. I'm downright desperate.

Olivia unleashes her evil-genius grin. "Two questions a day."

There we have it. I shouldn't be surprised. As painful as she is, I have to applaud her top-notch manipulation skills.

"Fine. Starting next hike and start talking." I make a swiveling motion with my wrist, encouraging her to get this over with.

"Simple. When those guys stop pushing so hard, she stops avoiding."

"That's a fast track to losing her." I sense it, how on the fence she is about us. All her worries over Max, concern he'll get hurt if we date and then split up. Valid, but I *know* we won't split up.

Olivia's sigh is pure exasperation. "According to *Psychology Today*, trust is the number one predictor of relationship success. That means reliability, dependability, and support," she says slowly, like English is my second language. "Stop pushing her and show her those things with your actions."

She walks off to join the mushroom hunters.

I rub my eyes, more confused than before. Enrolling in law school is the start of my dependability. Sticking with it will prove my reliability. Graduating will allow me to support my family. The whole point of earning that degree is to *show* Sadie I'm the right man for her and Max. But I have been pushing too, coaxing her to get a sitter and go out with me. Maybe that's part of the issue.

I'm shaking up schedules she's come to rely on. The important parts of being a mom. Maybe I need to alter my focus there. Quit pushing her to change her routine. Show her I can fit into her life. Prove spending time together with Max is as important to me as time alone with her. Major trust-earning behavior.

Or I should ignore Olivia. Last I checked, she has internet access, not a doctorate in psychology.

TWENTY-TWO

On the drive to Sadie's, I remind myself her concerns for getting involved quickly are valid. Finding our feet together will take more than a couple of dates and hot kisses. I listen to classic rock and switch my focus to today's hike. How engaged the kids were, the kick of my pulse every time Max ran up to show me his mushroom sketches. When Jasmine won the fungus contest and a bracelet, her excited squeal nearly broke my eardrums.

Even better, after I told the group about witness protection and my real name, they didn't get freaked out. I answered their questions while avoiding the subject of Max. They actually seemed more enthused than ever to chat with me.

By the time I'm parking on Sadie's quaint street, I'm more relaxed, looking forward to seeing her and Max and my family. I open my car door and wince at the grating screech. Fuck, do I need a new ride. Not the Porsche from my high school's Most Likely To list. A proper vehicle so I can shuttle Max around safely. Hell, I'll even drive a minivan. *That's* how committed I am to being a dependable family man.

"Desmond Bower?"

I crank my car door shut and grind my teeth. I should've prepared myself for running into a potential blast from my past. This is Windfall, after all. Home of the Scarecrow Scavenger Hunt, the Summer Art

Walk, and the nosiest townsfolk this side of Whoville. The fact that I visited Sadie once and didn't get accosted was a miracle.

I turn and sigh. There's my past, all right. Justin Bernardini. The dude who puked beside me at the Spring Fair, nearly causing me to puke too. A periphery high school buddy from my golden years, known for burping the alphabet. He failed his driver's license test four times and was voted Most Likely to Need the Jaws of Life. Honest to God, the guy had no depth perception. And here he is, his white skin extra tanned, his dark hair buzzed, looking fit and successful as he goggles at me.

"Man, almost didn't recognize you." He doesn't hide his shock at my appearance or the not-a-Porsche I drive. He's visibly stunned, his mouth gaping open.

"It's been a while," I grit out, my jaw feeling wired shut.

Not taking my get-lost glare as a hint, he plants his hand on my car. "Can't believe about your dad and the witness protection thing."

"Yeah, well." That's all I've got. No long diatribe about the life-ruining ways of money laundering.

He zeroes in on my neck and forearms. "The tattoos are badass."

I grunt. Translation: *Leave me the fuck alone.*

"And this car." He whistles.

I don't even grunt this time. I have no clue if he's purposely being condescending or if I'm more sensitive than I used to be, but I find my lats bunching. "Can't say the past decade's been easy."

"I'm doing real estate," he says, without me asking. "Sold the Goldstein farm last week. A hell of a lot of acreage, which means I'm one step closer to my dream vacation home in the Bahamas. And guess who bought the restored Victorian on Amber Street?" He points his thumbs at himself. "Married Ella May Saunders out of college and have two adorable girls. What about you?" He glances at my hand. "Still single?"

I run my tongue over my cracked tooth, a minute from launching my clenched fist into his nose, but I stay put and stay quiet. This idiot doesn't need egging on.

"Just can't get over seeing you, man." His attention keeps darting to my ink and the car. "Remember how you ruled school back in the day? You were *that* guy—every dude wanted to be you and every chick wanted to date you."

I was right about the condescension, and that he's about to get hit.

"There you are," Sadie says loudly from somewhere behind me, her voice overly cheerful.

I flinch at her proximity, unsure if she witnessed Justin Jaws of Life Bernardini driving his ego all over my dignity.

She joins my circle of hell. "Great to see you, Justin."

He grins a toothpaste-ad grin. "You haven't aged a day."

She puts her hand on my tense arm, gives me a squeeze. The sweet move doesn't make a dent in my agitation.

"Actually." She focuses on Justin, still sounding like an amplified version of herself. "Didn't you go to Duke? Des is heading back in August. Doing law. You could give him some tips on the best places to hang out."

"Oh, uh. No." He stuffs his hands in his pockets. "Didn't get in there."

"Really? I was sure you did."

He shrugs.

She gives him a condescending smile, letting Justin linger in his discomfort.

I know what she's doing. Purposely shoving that failure in his face, attempting to prove to him I'm more than my decrepit car and aggressive facade. Except there's nothing impressive about starting law school again at thirty-four, and the fact that she feels she needs to defend me proves what I've worried about: Sadie's embarrassed of who I've become.

"Anyway." She gives my arm another pat and heads for the house. "See you inside soon?"

"I'm coming now," I force out. An eject button would be helpful.

"Justin Berrrrrr-nardini!" Lennon saunters up before I can take off, bellowing Justin's name like he's an announcer at a boxing match. He punches Justin's shoulder. "You're the guy who puked at the Spring Fair, right? I think you peed yourself that night too."

Justin gives a stilted laugh and rubs his shoulder.

"Good times, my friend." Lennon loops his arm around my rigid back. "Gotta steal Des away for a sec—secret witness protection meeting with the government. President's on the line for us." He salutes the prick.

I'm verging on furious with a side of humiliation. Lennon's the second person in two minutes who's felt a need to save me. Like I'm a child who can't defend himself.

"Great to see you, Des!" Justin calls. "Wait until I tell Kyle I ran into you."

"Fan-fucking-tastic," I grumble as I strut away from him, pissed that the gossip hounds have been unleashed. Townsfolk might start staking out Sadie's home, desperate for a glimpse of how far I've fallen.

"Guy was always a douche," Lennon says.

"Bet he still can't parallel park."

We walk up the steps to Sadie's house, but Lennon blocks my way in. "It seems you aren't ruining my business."

I cross my arms and don't speak. I need to cool down, and Lennon attempting an apology should be amusing enough to leach my frustration.

"I've had calls," he goes on.

I raise a silent eyebrow.

"They've been surprisingly good."

I study my nails, uselessly analyzing my cuticles, making him work for this.

"A few were actually glowing. Said their kids have never enjoyed a program so much." When I continue stonewalling him, he heaves out a sigh. "What I'm trying to say is you're surprisingly good at running outdoor programs, and I maybe shouldn't have judged so harshly."

As entertaining as watching Lennon flounder is, there's no denying my chuff of pride at his compliment. "Guess I'm a natural at nature."

"You're also a natural at bad dad jokes. And FYI, I prefer gift certificates to small independent stores, not big box. I particularly like hat stores."

Says the guy who claims he's not a hipster. "Shouldn't *you* be the one buying *me* a gift certificate for giving your business a boost in this area?"

He waves me off. "The gift's not for that. You're here, at Sadie's home. Seems my dare worked."

Nothing's working at the moment. Sadie's being cagey. I just proved how low I land on the post-high-school success meter with Justin Jaws of Life Bernardini. The last thing I need is more Lennon interference. "Give it a rest."

"Do we need to play another—"

"Maggie Edelstein," I say.

He whips his head around and crouches. "What? *Where?*"

I step around him and go inside. When I see E in the hallway, I pound his back. "Dude, that Maggie trick is genius."

"Her name's like Lennon pepper spray."

I almost smile, thinking of the ways I can torment him. "Why exactly is he terrified of her?"

"More like secretly obsessed, and we can't figure it out. They both deny ever hanging out."

Good dirt, indeed. "Where's Mom?"

"Out back with Delilah, Sadie, and Max."

We walk into the kitchen, and I need to pause at the view through the windows.

Mom's on the grass with Max, the two of them playing with E's dogs, grinning up a storm. Sadie and Delilah are sharing a lounge chair, talking close. When they notice us through the window, the girls flip around and lean closer.

Lennon stomps in loudly, stalking by us to go outside. He doesn't say a word, just holds up his middle finger as he passes.

"You must be stoked about school," E says, ignoring Lennon as we normally do.

I rub my jaw and shrug. "Sure."

He stares at me in that penetrating way of his. "Sure?"

"Whatever. It's just school. A means to an end."

Last night, I grabbed one of my recently purchased law textbooks, ready to finally crack the spine and get ahead on readings. I barely got through two pages. I kept picking up my phone, scrolling through social media—even though I never post anything online. Then I decided I needed another workout.

E continues staring at me. "Interesting."

I don't know what's interesting, and I don't comment. I swear he doesn't exist on oxygen. E's brain thrives on overanalyzing every sound and twitch people make, the way Sadie analyzes art. Searching for deeper meaning.

When he gives up trying to read my mind for God knows what and grabs a glass from a cupboard, I exhale.

"Seems like Max took the dad news well," he says as he fills the glass with water.

"He's amazing." Except I haven't talked about Max with my family since then. Not even on the phone. I watch E's easy maneuvering around the kitchen, then glance at the girls seeming so friendly on the lounge chair. "You guys visit Sadie much?"

"Couple times this week, actually. She didn't mention it?"

I shake my head, wishing she'd invited me too.

"We stopped by for dinner once, and I've been teaching Max how to illustrate a graphic novel. He's been a lot more upbeat than when we first met him."

"I bet he loves the illustration stuff," I say, glad he's been more open with my family. "I signed us up for a couple of Delilah's Sunday baking classes starting next week."

Can't wait for those mornings, and I love that Max is getting to know his uncle better, but I'm also a bit jealous. Unlike E, I couldn't tell you where the glasses are kept in here, or the dishcloths, or where Max likes to sit on the big blue couch. I haven't seen Max's room yet. Or Sadie's room. I don't know if she still sleeps on the left side of her bed. If she still hogs the covers like her old cover-hogging days. If she still does that little body jerk when she's about to fall asleep.

E plants his hand on my shoulder. "She still has feelings for you, Des."

Feelings don't begin to cover my thoughts on Sadie Jones, but E's doing a mighty fine job of reading my likely pained expression as I stare at her through the window. "She's been a bit tough to read."

He sips his water, considering her. "Every time your name comes up, she blushes something fierce."

"She's holding back. Because of Max, she says, to protect him from getting his hopes up with us, but I don't know. I think something else might be going on with her. Reservations about me, maybe. Or her business partner might be into her. He said some stuff that didn't sit well."

"Did you ask her about him?"

"She said they're just friends."

"Then I suggest you believe her. Unless she also claims I told her you puked your guts out when you learned about Max. I swear I never said a thing."

Lip curled, I advance on him, but he's already jogging toward the door, laughing, trying not to spill his water. Pain in my ass.

I join my aggravating family outside and sit on the grass with Max and Mom and Lennon. Candy Cane bounds over and licks my face. Macaroon follows, getting in on the slobbery action. "Someone toss a toy before I get eaten."

Lennon picks up a ball and throws it at my head.

Max cracks up.

"*Lennon*," Mom says sternly, always being a mom.

Lennon does a body roll on the grass, grabs for the ball, and beans me in the head with it again. "He started it."

Hard to believe we're adult men.

"You better believe I'll finish it." I'm on him in seconds, grabbing him in a headlock. I jut my chin toward Max. "You need to noogie him."

Max laughs at our antics. "What's a noogie?"

"A kiss on the forehead," says a thrashing Lennon.

Nice try. "Knuckles," I say. "Grind your knuckles into his forehead."

Mom sighs.

"Get him good," E shouts.

"Children," Sadie mutters from behind us.

"I think it was WITSEC," Delilah says. "It stunted their emotional development."

She's not wrong.

Max crawls over hesitantly, like he can't believe he's allowed to torment his uncle. He glances at Sadie, then at me, then at Lennon, who bucks and squirms, trying to elbow me. Lennon gets in a solid jab to my ribs, but I've always been stronger. Guy doesn't stand a chance.

Finally, Lennon goes limp. "Fine. Get it over with. I can take it, Max."

Max sits beside him, still seeming indecisive. The opposite of me.

Growing up, if I caught any of my brothers vulnerable, they were getting a noogie or a wedgie or some form of torture. One time Callahan fell asleep in the old barn on the back of our property, so I ran around, searching for frogs to dump on him, but luck was on my side. I caught a four-foot black racer snake. You can imagine how his wake up went.

Max has a different gleam in his eye. Defiant, yet kind. He leans down gently . . . and kisses Lennon's forehead.

How the hell did I get lucky enough to have such a sweet kid?

We spread out and take turns roughhousing with the dogs. Except Max, who doesn't participate in the roughhousing. Being aggressive isn't in his DNA, which makes me regret pushing him to noogie Lennon, even though Lennon deserves to be noogied. What if he's worrying I won't like him because he didn't act like his buffoon father? What if he thinks there's something wrong with him for being gentle?

Parenting seems to be this constant battle between worrying I'm saying or doing the wrong thing and desperately wanting to do right by my son, but there's also *this*. An uncontrollable pressure in my chest as I watch Max laugh and toss balls for the dogs.

I turn to glance at Sadie, and that pressure expands. The way her hand is pressed over her heart, her expression tender and open as she watches us? If boasting about me going to law school is what she needs to deal with who I've become, she can have at it.

Her cell rings. She frowns at the screen, then hurries inside before answering. Once in the kitchen, her body language shifts to edgy. She paces, one arm wrapped around her middle, seeming to speak aggressively, or she's frustrated. She closes her eyes and firms her jaw. I almost go in to make sure she's okay, but Mom says something I didn't catch.

I flip toward her. "What?"

"School. Everything still on track for your first semester?"

"Yeah," I say distractedly, glancing again at Sadie's tense back. When Mom doesn't go on about my classes, prodding and gushing about how great of a lawyer I'll be—every conversation we had my first five years in WITSEC as she urged me to reenroll—I focus on her. "What?"

"I didn't say anything."

"Exactly."

She's no longer playing with the dogs. Her legs are tucked beside her, her head tilted in her mother-knows-all way. "If this is what you want, Des, I'm excited for you."

"Well, it's what I want."

"That's great." What's not great is that she and E share that over-analytical mind, and I don't like how either of them have been looking at me today.

"Max, honey." Sadie's back outside, standing by the door.

He doesn't glance at her, just pets Candy Cane's velvet ears and gives a careless, "Yeah?"

"I can't take you to the art walk on Sunday."

"What?" His head jerks her way, his expression crestfallen.

"I'm sorry, sweetie. I have a last-minute call for work scheduled. I need to be here. Unless . . ." She looks at Delilah and E, who are now snuggled together on the lounger. "Can you guys take him?"

Delilah cringes. "I wish. The café's too busy during the art walk, and E's signing copies of his graphic novels in the shop."

"We would," Mom offers, "but Lennon has to get back to Houston for work."

I never attended the art walk until I started dating Sadie, lover of all things art. Truth be told, I loved the festival. Vendors set up their wares in the town square. Musicians play throughout the streets. It's a fun, lively event, and I hate that she didn't ask me to take Max before seeking out Delilah and E.

"I'm free Sunday," I say.

"Really?" Max is back to beaming.

Sadie flips her phone in her hand. Twice. "The place will be packed."

"And?" Now I'm downright insulted. I get that I haven't earned a Number One Dad mug, but taking my son to a small-town festival isn't brain surgery.

"No. Not that." She shakes her head and holds up her hand. "I'm not worried you can't handle it. It's just, everyone from Windfall turns up to the event. People from your past."

Right. A parade of painful run-ins like with that knob Justin Bernardini. Not ideal. But attending an event that'll put me in the spotlight isn't about me. Going to the art walk is about being a good dad. "Not an issue." I turn to Max. "You good to go with me?"

He nods quickly and looks to Sadie. "It's fine, right?"

"Of course it's fine."

With Sunday's plans settled, Max resumes mucking around with Lennon and Mom.

I get up and walk over to Sadie. "You looked stressed in there. Everything okay with work?"

"Fine." She avoids my eyes when she says this—clearly not fine. Fucking GQ Joseph, creating drama even when he's not here. "Thanks for taking Max. It's a huge help."

"It's my pleasure, and I mean that. I want to spend as much time with him as possible." I also want to put Sadie first, make her life easier. She gave up a great job to raise Max, lost another opportunity recently. She has to choose now between her work and keeping a promise to our son. If she's choosing work, her art website's important to her, so it's important to me. As is flirting with Sadie.

My body's blocking us from my family's view. Enough that I can covertly brush my finger down the side of her hand. "It's also my pleasure spending time with you," I say quietly. "Even if we're not alone."

A tiny sigh escapes her. "You were always a charmer, Desmond Bower."

"No. I was an out-of-control braggart. Then I met you."

"Total marshmallow," she says.

With her I am. Problem with marshmallows is they burn easily, and I like standing close to flames. "In case you were wondering, I've relived last night's goodbye kiss all day."

The hungry swipe of her tongue against mine.
Her fingers dragging through my hair.
Her needy sounds and plump-soft lips.

"Des." She's trying to sound annoyed, but that red flush blotching her neck? The breathy tone of her voice? Not annoyed.

"Have you thought about kissing me?" I ask, pushing her, hopefully conjuring the image of me pressing her against her car door. "Or am I the only one fantasizing?"

She shifts, a subtle move from foot to foot. If I had to guess, I'd say her panties are getting wet. Now I'm picturing her stripped down, all her curves bared to me, and I nearly groan. But I keep myself contained. I'm not sure if pushing her to admit she's relived last night's kiss is working against me, the way mini-Freud Olivia told me pushing creates avoiding. I expect Sadie to brush me off, blow past me and my forwardness.

She gives me Saucy Sadie instead.

"I've thought about last night all day too." She leans forward, shrinking the small space between us. "That kiss reminded me what it feels like to be a woman."

She *does* blow past me then, not before she drags her fingertip along my abdomen, rendering me stupid.

TWENTY-THREE

Having Max all to myself is terrifying and exhilarating. His small hand is tucked in mine as we move from booth to booth, checking out watercolor landscape paintings and intricately carved pepper grinders. There's a bit of everything on display from a variety of artists. Quilters. Painters. Leather crafters. Knitters. Jewelry designers. All a reminder of how vital the arts are to Windfall—this creative and open-minded community that spreads beauty and positivity through its work.

As fun as the art walk is, I'm on high alert, wary of the Windfallians who'll remember me and make me look small in front of my son. Every time I recognize someone, I'm quick to maneuver, leading Max away from a possible ambush.

I've also barely let go of his hand.

This is the first time he's openly displayed affection toward me in public—yes, I'm overwhelmed and addicted—and it's busy here. I've seen one too many movies where a parent looks away for half a second, only to glance back and find their child gone. Max won't become one of Olivia's studied statistics. Not on my watch.

My other parenting skills, however, are clearly lacking. Max's T-shirt is covered with finger streaks from the caramel-sauce-topped popcorn he ate. I didn't think to grab napkins. He's also hopping while he walks with a tad more energy than seems normal. I blame his sugar high and the tons of junk I've let him eat, when Sadie expressly said, "Don't let him eat tons of junk food." He was just so cute when he asked to have that second bag of homemade licorice, looking at me with those pleading, thick-lashed eyes. What kind of monster would say no to him? Plus, I assumed the "homemade" part negated the "junk" part.

Now he's a jumping bean of energy.

"Oh my God." He yanks on my hand and points to a table of brightly colored jewelry. "That's Jasmine's mom's stuff."

Max leads us to her booth and shrieks when he sees Jasmine. Jasmine shrieks back. She probably overdosed on homemade sugar too. She says something about Camila Cabello—shocker—and holds up a pair of iridescent earrings, flaunting them. Max does the same, pretending he's wearing the dangling linked circles, swishing his head to show them off. Now I'm wondering how pissed Sadie will be if I take him to get his ears pierced.

"Desmond Bower?" says a guy from behind me.

Unsure who called my name, my facial muscles do that pinching thing I can't control. "Mind watching Max for a minute?" I ask Jasmine's mom.

When she agrees, I turn, and there's another blast from my past. Kyle Jackson. Former running back on our high school football team and prom king. He has dark skin and piercing eyes and no doubt got the lowdown on my crash landing from golden boy to rusted Camaro driver. He's holding out his hand to me, waiting on a shake.

I comply, expecting him to crush my hand in a show of overimportance. He gives my hand a friendly pump. "Heard you were in town."

I rely on a trusty grunt.

Two women, who look familiar from high school, walk by. They blatantly stare at me and whisper to each other.

"Seems like everyone heard I'm around," I say flatly, releasing his hand and rubbing the back of my overheating neck. Never imagined myself hating attention this much.

"This is nothing," Kyle says. "When E came back last year, it was all anyone talked about, trying to figure out why you guys left. Half the town was furious at him for returning before the WITSEC bomb was dropped. Place was on fire with gossip."

Considering E returned after the Becerra cartel was wiped out but before our father went public with his upcoming tell-all biography, the reaction's no surprise. From what he and Mom have told me, E suffered through a lot of angry backlash as he tried to keep our WITSEC history secret. Guess I can thank my little brother for being the first to break the Windfall seal, easing my return to town.

"Anyway," Kyle goes on, "I know it's been forever, but I'd love to catch up. Can't imagine how hard it's been for you, especially with Sadie and learning about Max. We should have a playdate."

I squint at him, wondering if he's going the condescending route after all. "A playdate?"

He grins. "I have a little girl—Kelsey. She's three and runs our house. I got married shortly after college to a goddess of a woman who somehow chose me."

Envy sneaks up on me. Kyle is so damn lucky to be married and present while his kid grows up, but the tension from my shoulders eases. My facial muscles actually relax. "I hope you didn't tell her you got stuck in a storm drain when you dropped your iPod and decided you'd become Indiana Jones to get it out."

He also did a backflip at graduation and missed the landing, then spent the entire night with a soggy pack of no-longer-frozen peas secured to his head. The pictures were hilarious.

Kyle huffs out a self-deprecating laugh. "My family has filled her in on my many embarrassments. Cearra deserves a knighthood for marrying me. And a vacation. Life's all about removing gross stains from clothes and not tripping on the mess in our house while we race around trying to get shit done." He shrugs. "Beer catch-ups have been swapped for playdates. Although, our kids are pretty far in age."

"Max is a sweet kid. Might even like teaching Kelsey some art. Count me in for a playdate."

Us and our kids. Honestly. Who even am I right now?

We shoot the shit about his frozen-pea-head incident and his current job as a website developer, the conversation so effortless I'm actually looking forward to hanging out with him.

"I better split," he says with a punch to my arm. "I'm helping my grandmother with her quilting booth. You should come by. She'd love to see you."

Seeing Mrs. Jackson might be another bright spot today. She was the leader of Mom's weekly quilting group, and the woman was a saint. She actually put up with Mom's horrible skills and didn't kick her out of the classes. Come to think of it, maybe I should sign up for a session. Except I'll soon be in law school, buried under textbooks and exams.

Shaking off my usual discomfort at the thought of school approaching, I swap numbers with Kyle, only to see Ricky and Aaron.

Ricky walks around me and analyzes my hair. "Gotta say, we did good work."

"All you did was heckle me." I nod to Aaron, who actually styled the top of my disaster head. "*He* did good work."

Ricky pshaws. "The heckling was part of the process. Can't have you getting too cocky with the handsome."

"Own the handsome," Aaron says, fixing my hair with his hand. "If you've got it, flaunt it. Ooh." He peers over my shoulder. "Bonsai trees. Excuse me while I marvel at the cuteness."

Ricky shakes his head as Aaron darts off. "He loves everything miniature."

"Is that a fact?" I look pointedly at his crotch.

His cheeks flame. "Not that, asshole."

I laugh. Guy made it too easy.

"Des!" Max waves and holds up the dangling earrings he was modeling. "Can we get these for Mom?"

He may not have called me Dad, but I love hearing him use my real name. And he said *Mom*, not *my mom*.

"Sure," I say, battling another overwhelming Dad Flush. Not sure what else to call these sudden floods of happiness. Emotion so strong I couldn't imagine letting him down the way my dad let me down. Having him hate or resent me for any reason is unthinkable, especially considering the websites I visited lately.

Determined to educate myself on being an open-minded parent, I read articles about kids coming out to their parents and parents dealing with their children's sexuality. The night I read that kids who aren't accepted by their parents have a higher risk of suicide, depression, and drug use, I barely slept.

Before I know what I'm doing, I turn to Ricky and lower my voice. "When you came out to your parents, was there anything you wish they did or didn't say? Anything they could've done better?"

He blinks at me. "Segue much?"

"Just, you know, hoping it all went smoothly for you." Even though *I'm* far from smooth or subtle with my abrupt question. But I don't feel right mentioning Max specifically, talking about him behind his back.

Ricky sneaks a glance at Max, who seems to be grilling Jasmine's mom on jewelry design, then he gives me an intense stare, proving how unsubtle I was. "For me, coming out to my parents was a bit of a bomb drop. I mean"—he points at his uniform of worn jeans and threadbare T-shirt—"I don't tick a lot of my-kid-is-gay boxes. I've always been a bit of a slob, and I'm a carpenter. Always liked typical 'boy' stuff like hammers and fixing things and rough sports, never got curious about wearing girl's clothes or playing with dolls like Aaron. So yeah—my folks were surprised."

"They didn't take it well?"

"My dad actually took the news pretty smoothly, but my mom got mad at first. Confused more than anything, I think. So if I had advice for *random* parents today," he says, half-heartedly pretending we're not talking about me, "I'd tell them that even if they think there's no chance their kid's gay, they should have the what-if conversation with each other anyway. Address how they'd deal with that news as a team—the best ways to make sure their kid feels accepted and loved, so if he or she or they are bi or ace or trans or gay or whatever, you bypass that angry shocked phase. All I wanted to hear from my parents was that they loved me no matter who I loved." He slaps my arm and gives it a squeeze. "If you ever need to chat, I'm just a call away."

Leaving me to chew on that nugget of wisdom, he joins Aaron at the miniature tree vendor. I'm about to grab Max and pay for those earrings, but a redheaded woman stops in front of me. Normally, I'd say this woman is beautiful—traffic-stopping gorgeous in a fashion-maga-zine way with fiery hair, a collection of freckles that puts Sadie's dusting to shame, glowing pale skin, and eyes so green they glint like jewels—but the only way to describe her intent expression is *spiteful*.

"Seems like we have a Bower boys epidemic in town. Y'all keep popping up like a rash."

I squint at her. "Do I know you?"

"Maggie Edelstein. Delilah's best friend."

I grin. Really fucking wide. *The* Maggie Edelstein. "You know Lennon, right?"

"Hardly." But she breathes faster, and an intense blush sears her cheeks. "We ran in different crowds."

"Interesting."

"Not really."

"I mean, the fact that you both deny hanging out together but have intense reactions to each other's names is pretty interesting." This whole Lennon-Maggie mystery is even more fun than I imagined.

She curls her lip, doing an excellent impression of my resting pissed-off face. "I have no idea what you're talking about. I was asked to find you and tell you E's busy signing books but would really like a grilled cheese from Marni's food truck. Do with that information what you will."

She lifts her head and marches off.

I smirk at her retreating back, then pay for Max's gift and take his hand, pleased with my interactions today, caring less if others gawk at me. There are plenty of judgy stares and whispers, along with a few too-eager-to-be-casual hellos from people I barely liked in high school, but we visit Mrs. Jackson's booth and joke about Mom's awful quilts. Max volleys curious questions at the artists we meet, like why they chose a certain subject when painting or how the colors in a work made them feel. Sadie-style questions, like the times we'd go to galleries and try to get into an artist's head. She's raised Max to be insightful and probing, and I love her even more for it.

We visit E in Delilah's cute coffee shop to drop off his grilled cheese. While there, a woman I don't know, who sports a retro eighties perm, stares at me so hard I give up all pretense of not caring, cross my arms, and stare right back. She actually wins.

By the time we've exhausted every art booth in town, I make a decision. Sadie hasn't invited me to stay for dinner, but it's time I show her I can adapt to her life instead of her needing to find sitters and adapt to mine. Max and I hit Duke's Market—Windfall's mom-and-pop grocery shop. He zooms around, helping me find the ingredients for my tried-and-true chicken, tomato soup, and rice casserole. Once we're back outside, walking the six blocks to his home, he gets quiet. Probably the sugar crash.

Switching the grocery bag to my left hand, I squeeze his shoulder. "Everything okay?"

He fiddles with the hem of his T-shirt. "Thanks for taking me to the walk," he says softly. After a beat, he looks up at me and adds, "Dad."

Someone get a medic. A defibrillator and oxygen mask. Pretty sure my heart just flat-out stopped. I quit walking and crouch beside him. "Thank *you*. I had the best time today."

He touches my arm, giving me a timid smile that flays me. "I wish you were staying over. That you lived with us."

My obvious gut reaction is *hell yeah, me too*, but that's an admission I need to hide. No way I'll paint Sadie as the holdout in our reconciliation. "Your mom and I were apart a long time. For now, we're just friends who are lucky enough to have an amazing kid together. I'll be seeing you more. Spending more time with you both, and taking you to that baking class, but staying over isn't in the cards right now."

Instead of harping on what we don't have yet, I stand and take his hand, searching for a new topic. Something so he doesn't feel too sad about our living arrangement or too vulnerable after calling me Dad. But hell. *Dad.*

"*Divergent*," I say once we're walking. We haven't held our second book club yet. He was too busy last hike sketching mushrooms and too pumped about the art walk today. "Which faction would you be in?"

He swings our hands and adds a hop to his step, recovering quickly from our talk. "Amity, I think. A peacekeeper. I don't like fighting. You'd for sure be Dauntless."

"Why Dauntless?" The Dauntless are the brave ones in that dystopian world, but they're also violent. The aggressors. Maybe it's my resting pissed-off face.

"You're big and strong, and you stand up for the little guy," he says matter-of-factly, like he didn't just compliment the heck out of me.

I should really buy a defibrillator and keep it close.

"And you're gonna be a lawyer," he adds. "Mom said you're gonna fight to make people happier. That's Dauntless stuff. The good kind of Dauntless."

I love that Sadie's been talking to Max about me. That they're both proud I'm going back to school, even though it's more than pride on her end. Like with Justin Bernardini, she's latched on to my future plans so my kid thinks I'm more than a stagnant bartender who sometimes leads hikes. Not that it matters. They're both looking ahead. Seeing what I can be, not what I have been. In their eyes, I have a promising future.

For the rest of the walk, we ask each other questions about the book—*Did Tris make the right faction choice? Why do you think Tris didn't forgive Al?* Max also tells me he has a surprise for me at home. Pretty sure it's the tattoo sketches, and I can't wait.

By the time we're at his place, I'm dying to see Sadie too. To tell her what an incredible kid we have. Hope to hell she lets me stay and cook her dinner.

Max runs inside ahead of me, clutching the earrings we bought. "Mom! We saw Jasmine and got you something. And there was this cool guy who painted animals on wood, and I ate caramel popcorn and two bags of licorice and the fudge was so good."

Dammit. Kid totally threw me under the bus.

Sadie steps from the kitchen into the hallway, her hands already planted on her hips. "What happened to not eating loads of junk?"

"It was all homemade," I hedge, even though I know I'm sunk. "Homemade doesn't count as junk."

Her raised eyebrow is more amused than upset. *Thank God.*

She takes the earrings from Max. "These are gorgeous, sweetheart. Thank you so much."

"I picked them out, but Dad bought them." He bolts toward the stairs. "Be right back with your surprise," he calls to me.

Sadie's lips tremble as she searches my face. "Dad?"

If an artist painted my portrait, it would be titled *Former Meth Dealer Look-Alike Turns to Goo.*

"I know." I drop the grocery bag and strut toward her, smoothing back the loose hairs from her messy bun. "I'm Dad now."

"Wow." She angles her face into my hand, runs her nose against my palm.

Definitely wow. That's a whole-body buzz. "Thanks for today. Loved hanging out with Max."

"No, thank *you*. This is the happiest I've seen him in ages, and the call was longer than expected. Max would've been nagging me to do stuff, and I would've spent the afternoon ignoring him and feeling guilty. This was a huge help."

"Speaking of." I jut my chin to my grocery bag. "I'm hoping you'll let me cook you two dinner." When she chews her lip, seeming indecisive, I step back and give her space. "If you don't want me to stay afterward to eat with you or hang out, I'll go. If you do, I'd be grateful and it doesn't have to mean anything. Either way, I just want to help."

"It'll mean something to Max."

"I'm his dad, honey. I *want* it to mean something to him. He knows I want to spend more time with him. I doubt he'll think it's anything more than that." Specifically, that I've fallen like a sack of bricks for his mother.

Sadie twines her fingers together and studies the floor.

Max jogs down the stairs, sketchbook under his arm, breathing hard. He grabs my hand and drags me into the kitchen, then clambers up on a stool and spreads out his book before Sadie can cut me down at the knees.

"Okay," he says, his cheeks bright. "I chose two sketches. This one"—he points to a killer drawing of his favorite Cessna 195—"would look awesome on your arm here."

He points to the inside of my left biceps, and he's right. I don't have any ink on my upper arms. The location is perfect and his shading brings the plane to life. If I pay for a half-decent tattoo artist this time, it would look sick.

"For the other one," he goes on, "I did more of a landscape. Like the nature hikes we do. But I don't know if you'll like it."

He flips the page, revealing a small summery scene with a butterfly and bold flowers—a colorful image some might associate more with a woman's tattoo. I couldn't love it more.

"It's perfect, Max. Might even like this one better. Where should I get it?"

He hops off the stool, crouches behind me, and lifts up the leg of my jeans. "You don't have much hair here." He presses his palm to my calf. "It would look cool when you're hiking."

"Sounds like a plan to me, but I can't afford both right away. Think I'll get the Cessna first."

He pops back up, still a jumping bean of energy. "Really? Like, when?"

"I have to find someone first. Good artists book up quick, so I might have to wait. But you can come when I get it done. As long as your mom's okay with that."

"Mom? Can I?"

I glance at Sadie for the first time since Max barreled down here, and the happy thud of my heart slows. Her expression's intense, but I can't tell if it's proud-mom-loving-this-sweet-bonding intense or he'll-enter-a-tattoo-shop-over-my-dead-body intense.

"As the artist," she says evenly, giving me nothing, "I think you should be there. Now go upstairs and take a shower. You have layers of caramel on you."

He says an enthused "*Yes*" under his breath and runs out of the kitchen.

Sadie's still intense, her nostrils flaring as she stares at me. Then she advances, reaches up, and tugs my head down. Before I know what's happening, she's kissing me. Hard presses of her lips mixed with needy sounds. My shock doesn't last long. I haul her against me, give back as good as I'm getting. Tongue. Hungry lips. A little roughness for good measure.

I drag my lips over her jaw, plant a wet kiss on the shell of her ear. "Does this mean I get to stay and cook you dinner?"

A shudder runs through her. Her ear was always a direct hit. "Only if you stay the night."

I pull back abruptly, too stunned and happy to act cool. "What about Max?"

"You'll have to leave before he gets up, and no open affection in front of him. But I can't keep fighting this. How much I . . ." She clamps her jaw shut.

I'm not sure if she was about to say *How much I still love you* or *How much I need to get laid.* I don't really care. While I did stash a just-in-case condom in my jeans, I didn't actually think I'd be spending the night with Sadie yet. If I'd known, I might have jacked off this morning. Taken the edge off so I don't come the second she touches me later. I'm already half-hard and might come from one hot look.

I step back, run my hand through my hair. "I'm making my chicken, tomato soup, and rice casserole."

She laughs. "So predictable."

"Sticking with my best moves." I lean down one final time and drop a kiss on her shoulder. "Including the ones I'll be showing you between the sheets."

Her pulse flutters. I'm wound so tight I might pass out.

TWENTY-FOUR

I don't let Max or Sadie help me cook. They're sitting at the counter—Max drinking apple juice and Sadie drinking white wine—having a blast while taunting me.

"See how he's ripping open that bag of frozen vegetables instead of cutting it?" Sadie says after a sip of wine. "Don't ever do that. That's how vegetables escape to inedible vegetable land."

On cue, pieces of broccoli and carrot scatter across the floor.

"Three-second rule," I say, collecting the runaway veggies and rinsing them under water.

"That's a thing," Max agrees. I pour the raw rice into the casserole dish, and he balks. "He didn't measure the rice. He's supposed to measure the rice."

I give a dramatic huff. "Not if I'm a master chef. Master chefs do it by feel."

"The only thing he's a master of," Sadie says, "is being a smart aleck. Your dad once managed to burn soup."

I'm officially *Dad* now. Excuse me while I remove the dust from my eye.

"Your mother's confused. She's thinking about the time she got distracted when cooking in her college apartment and set off the fire alarm, sending the whole building out in the pouring rain." Because I distracted her by stripping naked and lounging on her couch.

Her cheeks pink. Is she remembering how hard she rode me that night too?

"He doesn't need to be a master chef," Max says. "He's gonna be a Dauntless Duke lawyer who fights for the little guy."

Sadie squints at him. "Dauntless?"

"It's from a book," he says, his tone all *get with the program, Mom.*

"Well, whatever that is, your dad will be the best. Duke or die," she says and winks at me.

I said exactly that—*Duke or die*—the day we whispered our fears on the edge of Bear Lake, and she told me it didn't matter where I studied law. Except it did matter then, and it does now. For different reasons. People like Justin Bernardini and most gawkers at the art walk looked at me like I was a deadbeat. Duke is top tier. A degree from there comes with prestige. If I want to earn the pride on Sadie's face, not have her feeling like she needs to defend me in public, Duke is my ticket.

When my main ingredients are assembled and all that's left is covering it in canned tomato soup, I hold up my hands like a doctor prepping for surgery. "I need a can opener, stat."

"On it." Sadie leaves her heckling position at the kitchen island, grabs a can opener from her drawer, then runs around the island once before making a dramatic show of handing it to me.

Her antics coax a belly laugh from Max. She then lets her hand graze my ass, out of view from Max, and dips her fingers right between my thighs.

I nearly send the casserole dish flying.

"You look flushed," she says. Cheeky woman. "Feeling okay? Anything I can get you?"

I bite the inside of my cheek and clench my ass. No joke. I'm gonna last five seconds tonight. But if she wants to play dirty. Fine. We'll play dirty. "Think I'd like a glass of wine, if you don't mind. And Max? Could you grab your copy of the next book you plan to read? I'd like to see it."

"Sure." He pops off his stool and races away.

The second Sadie's at the fridge, attempting to pull out the wine, I spin her around and press her against the stainless steel. "You're playing with fire, Sprite."

She trails her tongue over her upper lip. "I've missed playing with your fire."

That's it. I kiss her thoroughly and palm her breast, groaning from my first feel of her, but I need more. I move my hand south, landing between the valley of her thighs. She's wearing soft sweatpants that allow me to feel her heat. I press my fingers exactly where she used to like, and *Christ*. The damp warmth she's giving off is intense and heady, as is the needy hitch of her breath.

"Dinner's just an appetizer," I murmur in her ear. "You're my main course. I'm gonna feast on you later."

She rubs herself against my hand, getting a bit frantic. I cup her harder.

Footsteps pound down the stairs, and we break apart. I quickly adjust myself in my jeans. Sadie pats her cheeks and hair, looking bewildered and turned on. Absolutely perfect.

"So," she says. "Wine. You wanted a glass of wine. So I'm just over here getting you a glass of white wine."

Max bounds in and slaps a book on the counter: *If We Were Us*, by K. L. Walther. "I want to read this for book club next."

"Book club?" Sadie asks, making her way back to her stool. Her T-shirt's twisted enough to make me smile, but the tease of a red bra strap has me biting back a groan.

"Dad and I started a book club. We have to read the books, then we ask each other book-club-level questions. Like, deeper stuff. We've done two so far."

I grab the box of Cheez-Its—Sadie's college favorite—from my grocery bag and put it on the counter for her. "Kid is a reading machine," I say as I move to heat the tomato soup on the stove.

"He is," Sadie says quietly.

I glance at her over my shoulder, and those eyes she's giving me? Like she's discovered a new star in the sky and isn't sure what to name it? My battered heart isn't prepared to deal with that look.

Clearing the scratchiness from my throat, I give the soup a stir, then move to start cleaning while it heats.

"Let me do that," Sadie says, already getting up.

I raise my hand. "No dice. I'm cooking and cleaning. You best get comfortable."

There's that discovered-star look again, and I dip my head, not liking that she feels surprised by me helping or that she needs to jump in. If I lived here, I'd do anything and everything to make her life easier. Cleaning. Laundry. Dusting. Seriously. *Dusting.* Sadie's spent years doing everything by herself. She deserves to rest for a change.

"I can help," Max pipes up. "I'm a top-notch cleaner."

I chuckle. "Top notch, huh?"

"I kind of like cleaning." He drops his voice, like he's embarrassed.

Not on my watch. "Well, Maximillian—"

"It's just Max."

"Right. Just Max, I'd dig some cleaning help after dinner, but your mother's not allowed to lift a finger. She'll have the tough job of lounging on the couch."

Sadie runs her finger around the lip of her wineglass, giving me sexy eyes. "I'm looking forward to all the *lounging* I'll be doing later."

I'll bet she is, but I doubt she's as revved up as me. There are no G-rated thoughts in my head. All I'm picturing are those swirling fingers pushing up my shirt, flicking the button on my jeans, dragging the zipper down . . .

I inhale deeply through my nostrils.

We chat and laugh more while I wash dishes and rescue my mind from a very pleasant gutter. Sadie and Max snack on the Cheez-Its. I sip my wine occasionally, enjoying relaxing with my family but still buzzing with anticipation. I've only kissed Sadie tonight, and my blood's already boiling faster than my tomato soup.

I grab the soup, pour it over my casserole, then cover the dish and slide my work of art into the oven. Pleased with my efforts, I return to the counter and grab Max's latest book.

Sadie's phone rings near me. I catch the name *Joseph* before she snatches it up and bolts away.

"Hey," she says into her phone, giving us her back. "Can we talk later?" Then, "Oh, sure. Just give me a sec." She waves her cell at us with a sheepish shrug. "Work thing. I'll be back in a minute."

She slips inside her office down the hall and closes the door.

I stare at the barrier between us, feeling uneasy. I mean, it's not odd to have so much weekend work. Smartphones have obliterated personal time, everyone constantly plugged in. I just don't get why she couldn't talk in here. Sadie doesn't work in the criminal justice system or as a therapist or some kind of finance job that requires discretion. She sells artwork and networks with artists.

Pushing her odd behavior from my mind, I focus on Max and his new book. A quick read of the back cover has me as moved as when he called me *Dad*.

If We Were Us is another contemporary read exploring relationships and sexuality.

Not only did my I'm-your-father reveal not revert him to his quiet and withdrawn ways, but he's openly sharing this book with me. Not afraid or timid. Just here you go. This is what's on tap next. He's either reading it for pure pleasure or to better understand himself. Regardless, I'm thankful these books are in the world. I'm thankful he doesn't hesitate to share them with me.

I tap the cover. "Looks like another stellar choice. Can't wait to dig in."

"Cool. And about your tattoos." He prattles on about some tweaks he plans to make to the nature scene—adding a mushroom from his mushroom sketches—then he sidelines to airplanes and air shows and something about an aileron roll he thinks is *just the coolest*. I have zero clue what he's talking about, but I love his excitement.

A few minutes later, Sadie joins us, looking decidedly less enthused. Her face is paler, her lips pinched tight.

When Max takes a breath from his airplane monologue and says, "Is it okay if I sketch for a bit?" I'm actually relieved to get Sadie alone.

She smooths her hand down his back. "Of course. We'll call you when dinner's ready."

He grabs his book and vanishes back upstairs.

I don't waste my time and crowd Sadie, pulling my stool next to hers. "You seem off after that call."

She shrugs a shoulder, keeping her focus on her wineglass. "Work's been stressful."

"Stressful how? Has something changed with the Sarah Lim job?"

She fiddles with the neckline of her loose T-shirt, pulling it up her shoulder, then she fixes her hair, staying quiet.

"Is this the type of stressful where if you tell me about it, you'll have to kill me?" I'm only half joking. She's being unpleasantly evasive.

With a half-hearted laugh, she relaxes on her seat. "Sara's been pushing about the job she offered, the aspects that are important to her. But it's still not what I envisioned. It's all getting more complicated than I expected."

"Are the issues negotiable?"

"Some aspects are flexible, but some aren't. There's more curatorship involved than first discussed."

"That doesn't sound like a bad thing. It actually sounds right up your alley. Unless you're worried you won't have as much time with Max?"

She scratches her nose. "Time with Max is a concern."

"Good thing you have me and my family here to help then. You can even travel if needed. See the spaces in person."

She nods but doesn't say more. Maybe she's nervous about the prospect. Concerned she doesn't have enough experience to work for a big gallery the way she did fresh out of college. Which is nonsense. Sadie has always lived and breathed art.

Standing, I rotate her on her stool and move between her spread thighs. "You, Sadie Sprite Jones, may be small, but you're mighty. Even if the specifics of the job are out of your comfort zone, I have no doubt you can rock it."

She splays her hands on my chest, moving them up until she's cupping my jaw. There's a whirlwind in her eyes I can't decipher. "I don't want to talk about work. All I want right now is you."

"And my chicken, tomato soup, and rice casserole?"

She pulls me down and kisses me softly. "And that."

An hour later, we're full of good food, and I'm on the verge of an orgasm. Sadie's beside me at the small square dinner table, and we've spent the entire meal secretly teasing each other. Like now, the way her lower leg is wrapped behind mine, her hand resting on my thigh—more inner than outer, the vixen—drawing small circles along the inside seam of my jeans? She lives to torment.

"Guess it's cleaning time," I say to Max. I don't look at Sadie, but I copy her hand movements, exploring her inner thigh, those soft sweatpants hiding nothing as I move up and up and . . . I abruptly stand, leaving her wanting.

She makes a tiny strangled sound.

"Something wrong?" I lean down and ham up my concern.

She bares her teeth at me in a forced grin. "Must be the wine. Feeling a bit overheated."

"Anything I can do to help?" I drop my voice. "Get you more wet. I mean, more water?"

"I'm pretty good at getting that myself," she says, beating me at my own game.

Now I'm picturing her slipping her hand under the band of those soft sweats, spreading herself open, touching herself. *Fuck.* She stands and brushes the back of her hand against my straining fly as she passes me. I'm too far gone to even attempt a comeback.

Somehow, Max and I clean our mess. True to my word, I don't let Sadie help. She'd only rile me up until the plates were in a shattered pile on the floor anyway. Still, she manages to light me on fire. She doesn't tease me verbally or find a reason to round the island and touch my on-edge body. She just sits there, watching us work, making Max giggle by reaching under the running water and flicking it in his face. It's some weird kind of foreplay—the domesticity.

I've never wanted Sadie like this. Not because I've been celibate so long. Not because I've fantasized about her for eleven excruciating years. She's still the smart, creative, caring, ball-busting woman I fell in love with at seventeen, but she's also more now. Stronger. Independent. An inspiring mother. I can barely contain my need to be inside of her, fracture her composure, show her just how incredible she is.

Also, kids are wonderful cockblockers.

After we clean up, Max asks to watch a movie. He apparently loves *October Sky*, an old movie about a young boy who designs and launches space rockets. He sits between Sadie and me on the couch. Cockblocker extraordinaire. Good thing he's cute. With him this close, I don't risk reaching behind to stroke Sadie's shoulder. She and I share a few I'm-going-to-ravage-you glances, along with one the-bed-will-shake smolder that has me dropping my head back, but we keep it clean.

When Max drifts off partway through—if this is a homemade-sugar crash, points to me—Sadie nudges him and tells him to go to bed.

He stands and rubs his eyes. "Will you be here in the morning?" he asks me.

I quickly shake my head. Sadie's rules. There's no way I'll test them at this particular juncture. "No, bud. I'm heading home in a bit. I'll see you at the hike tomorrow morning."

He nods and yawns, then leans down and cuddles into me, wrapping his arms around my neck. "Thanks for today."

Jesus Christ. This kid.

"Loved it. And I love you." I squeeze him and try to control my erratic pulse, but there's too much going on. Our fun day. This fantastic night. Max's heart-squeezing hug. The fact that I'm going to maul his mother the second his bedroom door closes.

I lift him off me and point him toward the stairs.

"Brush your teeth," Sadie calls. "Both—"

"Rows and all sides," Max finishes. Apparently their nightly banter. He gives a loose wave and drags his tired body up the stairs.

"How long until he's in his room?" My voice is no longer recognizable. This is how prisoners sound. Roughened men who've been in solitary confinement and haven't spoken in weeks.

She touches her neck and glances at the stairs. "About five minutes."

"Does he ever come into your room? Like, if he can't sleep or is having a bad dream?"

Now I'm a starving prisoner on death row.

"Hasn't done it in years, but we'll use the guest room down here."

I nod and stare at her. She stares at me. It's wild that we can sit here, a small space still between us, not touching, but I feel so damn much: my haywire pulse, the hot rush of my blood, this intense wanting that has my mouth going desperate-for-Sadie dry.

She glances at the TV clock, breathing harder. "Four minutes and counting."

The staring contest continues. She squirms in her spot. I think I might be made of that movie's rocket fuel, waiting to ignite. At minute two, I give in and rub my hand over my thickening cock, a few strokes over the rough denim that do zero to satisfy my growing hunger, but Sadie's eyes fall heavy at the move. Her neck and chest burn the color of ripe cherries.

My favorite woman, as desperate for me as I am for her.

Then she says, "One minute."

I don't move. I have no clue how my heart hasn't busted through my chest. When I hear the telltale sound of an upstairs door shutting, I do the only thing possible and *pounce.*

TWENTY-FIVE

I haven't made out on a couch since college. Not that what we're doing is any kind of making out I've ever done. This is full-throttle, full-body kissing. I'm on top of Sadie, grinding my hips against her writhing pelvis, one of my hands exploring her body while the other tangles in her hair. She alternates between grabbing my ass and tugging at my shirt, our mouths fused and tongues searching, teeth clacking as we go for broke. We'll probably walk away from this session with couch burns. Neither of us seems to care.

I whisper-growl the occasional, *"Fuck."*

She gasps for breath then kisses me harder, her restless thighs squeezing my hips. Her feet find my calves and dig in. I'm so turned on I can barely think, but this is too important to get lost in the moment. For years, I sleepwalked through life, existing instead of living fully, positive I'd never see Sadie again. Now she's here. We're all over each other, and I have no choice but to pull back and stare down at her. Remind myself this is real, not one of my painful fantasies.

We're both breathing hard, our eyes locked like before, but this staring is different. Deeper. Like she can see inside my broken soul, how lost I was without her.

"Sadie." I'm choked up, falling apart in front of her.

She presses her hand to my cheek. Her chin trembles. "I know."

She doesn't. Not really. There's this energy I can't contain. Potent waves pushing at my ribs, overtaking my throat. An overwhelming swell of energy—*love energy*—tearing me apart at the seams, and I can't do this on a couch. I untangle myself from her and scoop her up from the cushions, holding her against me, unable to give her space.

She kisses my ear, the scar on my neck, my jaw. "You better show me that ab ink soon."

I smile against the top of her head. "It's nothing special."

"Babe, I told you. I like the bad boy ink. It's hot."

"You're hot," I murmur as I deposit her by the foot of the guest room bed and give her another filthy kiss. I don't kick the door shut or bang her back into the wall how I might at my place. We need to be quiet. Careful. I *want* to be careful with Sadie Jones.

Slowly, I close the door until it clicks quietly shut, but she doesn't let me out of reaching distance. She's behind me, pushing up my shirt, kissing my bare back. By the time I yank off my top, she's somehow in front of me.

"Jesus, Des." She fondles my pecs, brushes her thumb over my nipples and the not-so-awesome penis-looking knife inked on my chest. Her busy fingers bump over my abs, down to the faerie tattoo beside my hipbone. "Why this?"

"It's a sprite." Like the rest of my ink, it's subpar. But I've always liked this one. An homage to Sadie's ethereal qualities. Her delicate cheekbones, like a Tolkien elf. Her pale skin and slightly pointed chin.

"For me," she murmurs and traces the edges.

My hips jerk, followed by a sharp pulse in my cock that has me clamping my molars, searching for some form of control. I find little.

Her focus moves to the ridges of my abdomen, her hands getting more frantic, exploring the sharp lines of hipbones, dipping below the waistband of my jeans. I'm a minute from embarrassing myself. No joke. I'm teetering on a knife's edge here, desperate to see Sadie, feel her skin against mine, but so close to coming in my jeans. I coax her

T-shirt up and off, revealing sinful red lace. The vixen lowers before I get a good view, moving down to her knees.

Houston, we have a problem.

"Sadie, wait."

She looks up at me, need and hunger in her searching eyes. "You want to stop?"

"No," I croak out. "I'm just really close. It's been almost a year for me." *And it's you,* I don't add. No other woman could dismantle me in seconds.

"If that's all"—she gives the button on my jeans an aggressive flick—"then I think I've waited long enough for you. Eleven fucking years," she murmurs, a hint of anger in her tone as she lowers my zipper and discovers I went commando today.

Just in case, I thought. Sadie used to love discovering I didn't have on briefs. The foresight is working against me.

There's no barrier between her hot little hands and the hard line of my cock. She yanks down my jeans, moaning as I spring free. I can't slow this down. Slow *her* down. I have no choice but to plant my palms on the closed door and brace. My dick's never felt this heavy, my balls already drawn up tight. She wraps two hands around my length, and I grunt.

Translation: *Don't you lose it. Don't you fucking break. Don't you dare last half a fucking second.*

When her tongue flicks out over the swollen tip, I almost black out. "Sadie."

It's the only word I can utter. My thighs are on fire, my ass clenched so hard I'm sure I'll pull a muscle. I lean heavier into my palms. She stretches her pink lips wide, taking in the head of my cock, her hum of pleasure shredding what's left of my self-control. I mean, I never stood a chance. The intoxicating rush of having her here, with me, is the only foreplay I need: her excitement to see me naked, the absolute hunger in her fiery eyes. The second she takes me deep, heat blasts up my rigid spine. I'm groaning and shaking and coming so fucking hard, keeping my sounds quiet, but there's nothing quiet about my hammering heart.

She makes a satisfied sound. "That was a record."

"Let us never discuss this again."

She laughs and helps me out of my jeans. As soon as my feet are free, I pull her up, holding her tight against me, kissing her hard, tasting myself on her tongue. Some life returns to my spent cock. Enough that I'm kind of thankful she went with the blow job first. I have time to explore her at my leisure now, getting us both ready, so when I do sink into her, I won't have another ten-second embarrassment.

I undo her bra clasp, slip the straps from her shoulders. The red lace drops, and I finally stand back and look. Breathe through the desire and reverence burning through me as I stare at this gorgeous woman.

"Des." She reaches for me. "I need to feel you."

Not a tough ask. I close the distance between us, crush her to me, trace the outer swells of her breasts, getting off on the softness of her pressed to my hard chest. She moans and explores the muscles of my back, her hummingbird heart beating rapidly against me.

"You feel so good," I whisper as I coast my hands down her silk-soft skin.

She digs her fingers into my spine, a place she seems to like, then traces the line to my ass. "Let's be naked together."

I chuckle, shaking us both. "Let's."

I carry her to the bed and lay her out, taking my time with her sweatpants and socks. When I discover a pair of red lace panties, I lift the edge and let it snap back in place. "Were you hoping I'd see these?"

She gives me sexy eyes. "Were you hoping I'd discover your lack of briefs?"

"One hundred percent." Instead of removing the sexy lingerie, I cage her legs with my knees. Kiss her elegant neck, the freckles on her slender shoulder, moving to her gorgeous breasts. They're larger than I recall, lush and soft, and I can't get enough of these pert nipples. Except

I need more. All of her. Endless nights like this, being hungry and thorough but quiet for our son. Cooking for her. Cleaning for her. Taking care of her, so she can be the best version of herself. The art curator *and* mother *and* lover she was meant to be.

She writhes under me, her fingers making a mess of my hair as she releases tiny *ah* sounds—music to my ears. I kiss my way down her belly, loving her softer lines, taking extra long nosing the clover-shaped birthmark on her hip.

"I missed this," I murmur against her skin.

"I missed *you*." More than desire infuses her whispered words. "So much."

I press my forehead to her abdomen, squeezing her hips with my fingers, trying to imprint myself on her. "I never stopped loving you," I say.

Her breath hitches.

I look up. "Every day. Every minute. I love you, Sadie. With or without Max, you're the only one for me."

A tear slips from the corner of her eye. She doesn't tell me she loves me back, just dashes the tear away. But I know Sadie Jones. The affection in her gaze, the trembling of her hands in my hair, her desperation when dropping to her knees before—she loves me too. She's just too scared to say the words. Worried for Max and probably for herself. Having me ripped out of her life has left its scars.

I don't dwell on her silence. I get back to work, teasing her around this sinful red lace. Feather-soft kisses. Tantalizing licks. When I blow air over all that damp fabric, her pelvis jerks and she swears. "Stop teasing."

I nip her inner thigh. "It's too much fun."

"*Des.*" She drags her nails along my scalp.

Sparks shoot across my skin. "Yeah, honey?" I press my mouth against her lace panties and flick my tongue.

She moans and gives my hair a harder tug.

Message received. I peel off her underwear and give her a hungry lick. Her enraptured "*Yes*" is a priceless gift. As is her heady musk and how wet she is. The way she spreads her thighs for me and thrusts her hips up, begging for more. I don't hold back. I flick and suck and work her over until her heels are digging hard into the mattress, her hands clutching the sheets as she shakes and jerks, the tiniest sounds vibrating from her.

She goes boneless, sighing and smiling a satisfied smile. "That was *wow*."

"We haven't reached *wow* yet." I'm hard again, my dick thick and flushed and ready. I give my shaft a couple of rough strokes while she watches—Sadie always liked watching me touch myself—then I look for my jeans. Earlier, I may have ejaculated as fast as a twelve-year-old watching his first porno, but I at least came prepared with a condom tonight.

When I turn around with the silver packet, Sadie's got her knees splayed apart, her fingers coasting over all that wet heat.

"Babe." I grip my shaft, give it a solid squeeze. "You can't do stuff like that."

Her lips twitch. "Because you'll premature ejaculate again?"

This woman. "Never happened."

"Oh, it definitely happened."

"You're gonna torment me over that, aren't you?"

Instead of admitting how much fun she's going to have with that ammunition, she says, "An artist should sculpt your hip bones. And your amazing ass. I can't look at you without touching myself. Also . . ." Her tone turns more bashful. "I've only ever been this comfortable with my body around you."

I love that she's this way with me. Open and experimental, willing to touch herself simply because it feels good.

I toss the condom on the bed and kneel between her legs, letting the weight of my cock rest against her pussy, hoping she takes my hint.

She does. She uses me instead of her fingers, pressing my length against herself, moving it around, in control of her own pleasure.

And of me.

For the rest of my days, I'll happily be her boy toy.

I move my hips, gliding over her slowly, not adjusting to sink inside her. Not yet. Just loving our subtle rocking. The tease of what's to come. (Mainly *us*, and the fact that I will not blow my load early.) Her attention's locked on my sliding cock. I keep trying to memorize the sexy part of her lips, that sweet slope of her nose, her womanly body open to me, ready to take me in.

Suddenly, she grabs the condom, rips it open, and rolls it down my length. I grip the root of my cock, position myself at her entrance, shaking slightly. I'm not about to lose my cool and premature-embarrass myself again, but that wave of emotion is back. *Love energy*, swelling so fast and hard I swear my ribs might crack.

I push in slowly, forcing myself to breathe. "Fuck, Sadie."

Her eyes drift shut, her back arching as she takes me in. "So good," she murmurs. When we're flush, she gasps.

My dick pulses. My lungs constrict. My heart isn't sure how it got trapped in such a confined place. It's suddenly too big. Too full. *Aching* with the need to thud its devotion to the woman under me. I pull my hips back, then thrust forward, rocking faster, grinding against her, caging her with my elbows as I suck on her neck and nip her collarbone and whisper how fucking *good* she feels. She locks her ankles behind my back, the two of us completely fused. Together forever, as far as I'm concerned. Sweat gathers between us. We pant and kiss and fuck like we need this to survive. I do, at least. I need this woman like I need to breathe.

She bites my shoulder. Her inner walls contract around me. "God, Des."

"Sadie," I whisper, still in awe that we're here. That she's mine again. "You have no idea how much I missed you."

Her body tightens under me, muffled sounds escaping where she's biting my shoulder, trying to keep quiet. I want to shout her name. Groan and swear and shake the walls, but we keep it contained. I feel it when she's spent, how she softens under me, her legs less secure around my waist. I move faster, pump harder, worried I'm crushing her under my weight, but I can't push up. Create distance. I'm surrounded by Sadie and her summer scent and second chances, and then I'm coming. Long, hard streams that steal my vision and send tremors through my body.

When my muscles recall how to function, I slip out of her and slide to the side, still keeping us close.

We kiss softly, then I nose her ear. "Let me deal with the condom. I'll be right back."

I'm extra quick in the adjoining bathroom and hide the condom in layers of toilet paper. Last thing I need is Max stumbling upon evidence of tonight's activities and asking awkward questions. I return to the guest room, relieved Sadie's under the covers, not hurrying me out.

I slide under with her and pull her against my chest. "Thank you."

"For what?"

"For being you. For being open to tonight. I'd have waited as long as you wanted, but I'm really happy this happened."

She snuggles deeper into me, kisses my chest. Our naked bodies are pressed together, our hands roaming. Not sexual. More like we can't believe we get to touch each other.

She trails her fingers through my chest hair. "Don't know why I bothered trying to fight this."

"Having orgasms with me?" I joke, even though she's being serious.

"That part's never been an issue with you. I mean, it might be different now that you can't always control yourself."

"Babe." I go for stern admonishment but crack a smile.

Her dancing eyes are all trouble. "I wonder if that was a record of some sort."

"Whatever. Take your shots. I got no shame here." I'm lucky that blow job lasted as long as it did. I smooth my hand down her back. "Do you still want to own a pigmy goat?"

She laughs quietly. "That's an abrupt question."

"There's still so much I don't know about you."

She presses two soft kisses to my pec. "No to the goat. Can you imagine the mess?"

"And the smell." I shudder. "So what does adult Sadie wish for? Something wild and frivolous just for you."

"Does wishing for an hour with nothing to do count as wild and frivolous?"

"Nah." I tickle her side. "You can do better than that."

She *hmmm*s and buries her head against me, then she perks up on her elbow. "Paris."

I grin. "Paris?"

"The Louvre. Spend a whole day with nothing to do but look at art. Or, oh—the Galerie Thaddaeus Ropac. It specializes in international contemporary art. Warhol. Katz. Sylvie Fleury and Tony Cragg. Four floors of mind-blowing work. God." She slumps into me with a happy sigh. "When I was younger, I wanted *things*. Now I want experiences. What about you?" She noses my neck. "What's your frivolous, selfish wish?"

"An experience for sure. Ten years ago I would've said a Porsche or a Rolex. But now . . ." I twirl her hair around my finger, try to see beyond wanting time with Sadie and Max. "Climb a mountain. Something big and challenging. Push myself to the limits." Feel the bite of physical accomplishment, the freedom of nature on a grander scale. "But it would be even better with you and Max at my side."

She tucks in closer to me, draws random shapes on my ribs, something she used to do when we were young and in love. "The night you took me on that date—to the food fair."

When she doesn't go on, I prod with a quiet "Yeah?"

She sinks heavier against me. "I thought it might be closure. That we were running on memories and history. One perfect afternoon in that clearing, throwing axes and kissing like we had no worries, then the shine would wear off. We'd realize what we had was in the past. That too much had happened to move forward together as a couple."

Her unpleasant admission tangles with that call I overheard outside the diner at our first reunion.

Won't like who he is now.

Won't be good for Max.

Won't recognize myself around him.

Not gonna lie. Remembering that gutting moment and hearing her recent hesitancy stings. I've got Duke on the horizon, though. Now more than ever, I need to prove to Sadie she made the right choice letting me in. "I know I'm not the man you thought I'd be, but I'm getting there. Once school starts, I'll be on my way to a great job. Security for you and Max."

"Des, you don't have to convince me." She lifts her face, intensity in the depths of her eyes. "I'm *thrilled* for you—that you're going to Duke, reclaiming the future your father stole. You deserve your fresh start. My worries were more abstract."

"Abstract how?"

"Just." She nestles back into my chest. "Pulling myself together these past years has taken so much work, and I'm proud of who I am. Proud of what I've accomplished. But it's been so easy to get caught up in these moments, in *you*, and I think I've been scared to lose myself in you too. Lose some of my independence, having to share the decision-making and this little world I've created with Max."

"You had a long-term boyfriend, though. Didn't he become part of your lives?" The last thing I want to think about right now is Sadie with another man, but there's no denying the time we've spent apart. The experiences we've had, good and bad. I want to know all of hers, no matter how unpleasant.

She slips her leg between mine. "Trevor met Max and came over for dinner occasionally, but our lives were still separate. Not fully enmeshed. It's part of why we didn't work out. I couldn't picture him as more."

"And me? Do you picture me as more?" I hold my breath, terrified having sex wasn't as life altering for her as it was for me. She didn't say she loved me back. This could just be attraction for her—a mother needing to feel like a woman, as she once admitted.

She shifts off of me, lining us up so we're sharing the pillow, facing each other. "You're *more* than more, Des. If I picture myself touring Paris, I picture that fantasy with you. That's why this has been so scary. Dating you, wishing for a future together, means opening myself up to possibly being hurt again. To Max being hurt if we don't work out. And I think I was worried about sharing him with you." When I frown, she says, "Not in a bad way. I knew he'd love you. I think I was jealous. Afraid of the time I'd lose with him. That he'd maybe like you more than me."

"That's not possible, honey. You two have a bond I'll never share. Ten years without me."

"And you're the drama king who makes everyone laugh. But I realized something else tonight."

I tug on her hip, bringing us closer. "That everything's more fun when I'm around?"

She smooths her hand over my ass. "Can't argue with that. But no. I realized most good things in life come with sacrifice."

My brow pinches. The word *sacrifice* isn't giving me the warm fuzzies. I want to skip to the part where she says we'll build a life as a family because she's happier with me in the picture. More fulfilled. That we're better together. "Can I have the fine print to this realization?"

She pulls her hand from my ass and traces the edges of my collarbones. "Being with you means losing some of the independence I've fought for, which is tough for me. And there will be times when Max might like you better, when you'll have fun outings I'm too busy to join, or book club moments that are special for just you two. And." She firms her jaw, as though readying to do battle. "Sometimes we have to let go of old dreams to make room for new ones."

I'm not sure why she's suddenly so intense, or what dreams she's spent her years working toward. All I've been doing is trying to get through each day without tattooing my face. But maybe she's right about sacrifice. I've been ambivalent about returning to law, procrastinating over the prep work, lacking the excited determination I had coming out of college. I've realized I don't want it as much, but the sacrifice of these tougher years will lead to better days ahead. Financial stability. Now that I'm a parent, all my choices aren't about my happiness alone. Parents need to plan and provide.

"Whatever your plans are," I say, "count me in. I don't even need a vote. I promise not to undermine your independence, and I'll never knowingly hurt you or Max. I just want to be with you both, any way I can."

She nods, emotion shining in her eyes. "You get votes. You're his dad."

"Does that mean I get to see you more often? Spend time with you both as a family?"

"No sleepovers yet. I don't want to tell Max until he's more used to having you around, and we've had longer to find our feet together, but we'd both love it if you were here more. And I want to spend more time alone together too. Do more fun stuff like axe throwing and that street food night. But I have a condition."

"Anything." She can have the skin off my back. Every horrible craft I've ever created, which isn't saying much about my worldly possessions.

The corner of her lips tilts up. "We need to work on your stamina."

At least she's not too emotional to tease me.

"It might take months of practice." I pull her flush against me, guiding her arms around my neck. "At regular intervals."

"We might need to do a whole series of studies. Controlled situations with multiple positions. For science." She kisses me, soft and slow.

"Right." I smile against her lips, unsure when I developed a resting-grinning face. "For science."

TWENTY-SIX

I am a baking disaster. Three other groups of two are in the kitchen of Delilah's shop, Sugar and Sips. Two are moms with their daughters. One is a mom with her son. I'm the only dad, and I'm the only one covered in flour and smears of scone batter.

"How much longer?" Max asks, stirring our cooling pot of jam.

I finish wiping our section of stainless steel and check our timer. "Eight minutes. Is the showstopper almost ready, Captain?"

He giggles. "Why do you keep calling me captain?"

"Aren't you the leader of this mission? Also, you're cleaner than me."

He glances at me from the corner of his eye and snorts. Yeah, I'm a sight. A six-foot-two man, tattooed neck and arms, wearing a too-short apron, looking like I had a fight with a scone and lost.

"The scone batter isn't supposed to be used as shampoo," Delilah says, coming to our table, her amused expression locked on my head.

I cringe. "There's some in my hair too?"

She pats my shoulder. "I already took a picture and sent it to E."

Fucking great. That asshole will go to town with that ammunition, but spending time with Max is worth the ridicule.

"What do you think?" I ask Max. "Should I stick my head in the oven and see how it bakes?"

He smirks. "Only if we sprinkle it in chocolate chips."

"Chocolate head scones. We'll be famous for a new invention."

"Dipped in strawberry jam." He lifts a spoonful of our homemade jam, his smile so wide my chest feels like it *is* in the oven.

He's been awesome today, relaxed, joking with me. Chatting with the other mini bakers as we watched Delilah demonstrate how to mix the lemon blueberry scone batter.

"School starts soon," I say, leaning my elbows on the table. "You feeling nervous about starting fifth grade?"

He lifts a shoulder, staring more intently into the jam. "Jasmine's in my class, I think. It's her birthday the first week. She's having a party at her house."

"Do you think Camila Cabello will be invited?"

"Yeah." He grins up at me. "She sent her an email and everything but hasn't heard back."

Gotta give her points for trying. "If you want, I could come dressed as Camila Cabello. Set up karaoke and perform for your friends."

He drops the spoon in the jam, splattering strawberry on the table.

"No." His look of abject horror is too cute.

"But I was great on the hike when we played name that tune."

"No, Dad. Please, *no*."

I chuckle, unable to keep up the charade. "Maybe next time. And if you're having any issues with school, or with kids there, you know you can talk to me about it, right? Or your mom. Or Samantha, if that's easier."

"Yeah, I know," he says quietly. "Thanks."

I cup the back of his small neck and give it a tender squeeze.

The timer dings. He jumps up, nearly falling over as he hurries to the oven with the group. Delilah pulls out two trays and places them on the cooling racks. Our scones are easy to spot. They're the ones shaped as hearts.

"They smell so good," he says eagerly.

"They'll be even better with the whipped cream and strawberry jam," I say.

"But we have to save some for Mom."

That's a no-brainer. If I let Max eat more than two of those heart-shaped beauties, dripping with strawberry jam and whipped cream, Sadie would take me to task.

Twenty minutes later, I have a wet cloth in my hand, wiping strawberry off of Max's cheek, when Sadie appears in the kitchen. She glances between us, laughing. "I'm not sure which one of you is a bigger mess."

"Him." Max points at me.

I laugh. "Buddy, I thought you were on my team."

He smiles at Sadie, ignoring me. "We saved you some scones. And Dad almost overwhipped the whipped cream, and he got batter all over his apron and even in his hair. And the strawberry jam almost bubbled over the pot."

Sadie rubs his back and studies our box of baked goods. "They look delicious, and it sounds like you had a fun morning."

"So fun," he says, slaying me with a beaming grin.

Delilah calls the kids over for a final chat and to hand out the recipes to take home.

I face Sadie, keeping my batter-smeared self a distance from her. "I thought I was meeting you at the house."

"Change of plans. Delilah said she could spend the afternoon with Max. You and I have something else to do."

"Is there nakedness involved?" I ask, dropping my voice.

"No." But her upper chest turns red. "You've just done so much for us, cooking and helping around the house. I wanted to do something for you."

"Sadie, I don't need anything but you and Max."

It's been a week since we first made love, and true to her word, she's invited me over most nights. I don't sleep over, and we've kept the intimate aspects of our relationship secret from Max, but I help her cook and clean, going out of my way to make her life easier. The only thing missing in my life is a permanent place in their home.

She gives me a soft look. "When's the last time someone did something special for you? Something nice just to make you happy?"

I frown, pretty sure that person was Sadie. A birthday or something from before WITSEC. "That day you washed my car and left your underwear for me to find in the glove box?"

She blushes. "That was eleven years ago."

I shrug. "It was an awesome surprise."

She laughs under her breath, shaking her head. "I promise this will be better. I told Max we have errands to run for the hiking program, but we're heading to a spot in Ruby Grove, so we'll stop by your place on the way. You can shower off that mess, and we need to grab your bathing suit and a book if you want. I have to be back for dinner, but the only thing on tap for the afternoon is wild and frivolous fun."

I look down at her, wishing I could run my fingers through her hair. "Sounds perfect," I murmur as my phone chimes.

I grab it from the table and see Mirielle's name. I tap on the text, and there's one word:

DESMOND.

Another message pops up quickly:

But you'll always be Walter to me.

"What are you smiling at?" Sadie asks.

"Just realizing how fortunate I've been to have such great people in my life." For longer than I truly realized. "I'll say goodbye to Max and meet you outside."

∼

An hour and a half later, we're at Emerald Lake—Ruby Grove's popular swimming hole, surrounded by the Rough Ridge Mountains. Sections of smooth rock encompass the sparkling water, perfect for lounging on a hot summer Sunday.

Sadie left her planned picnic and our towels and books in a quieter spot. Now we're clambering up the rocks, both of us being careful in our bare feet.

I'm fortunate enough to have her bikini-clad ass in my face. "The views here really are spectacular."

She peers over her shoulder, giving my chest a thorough once-over. "They certainly are."

I move up a step and cross my arms, making sure my pecs flex for maximum viewing. "Is this why you brought me out here in my bathing suit? So you can ogle my body. Am I just a piece of meat to you?"

Her gold-flecked eyes shine with mischief, then she fondles my chest, moaning dramatically, totally hamming up her performance. "The hottest meat I've ever seen."

She may be teasing me, but my body doesn't care. Heat swells between my thighs. She drags her hand lower, shoving apart my crossed arms, charting a course south until I'm hard and my eyelids are drifting shut.

"Also," she says in a seductive whisper, "I'll race you to the top."

Grinning madly, she darts off, leaving me turned on and flustered. Cheeky woman. I catch up just before the summit and pick her up by her waist, carrying her the last few steps while she half-heartedly smacks at my arms.

With my feet firmly planted at the top, I turn and place her so she's one level down. "Guess I won."

She rolls her eyes, then joins me several steps back from the cliff edge. She wraps her arms snugly around my waist. "We both won."

Amen to that. "This place really is stunning. Almost as nice as Bear Lake."

"I actually think it's nicer." She takes in the majestic vistas and ancient rocks reaching for the sky. "The mountains are so dramatic."

"Visually, sure, it's beautiful. But Bear Lake is where you and I used to swim." I blink through memories of us splashing each other and skipping rocks at the water's edge. The nights we used to lie by the lake, cuddled together, talking quietly. "Memories make a place special."

She doesn't tell me we'll go back there soon, where we can openly display our relationship in Windfall, but she tucks in tighter to my side. "I like this too. Creating new memories together."

"Yeah. I love this too." I play with the string of her bikini bottom. "I'm pretty sure people jump off this cliff, don't they?"

She leaves my side and walks hesitantly toward the edge. "They do."

Her tone sounds surprisingly nervous. The Sadie I knew had no issues taking a running leap off the thirty-foot cliff at Bear Lake.

I join her and peer down at the water. "It's not quite as tall as the jump we used to do."

She leans back a bit. "I think it's taller."

"Sprite." I face her and cock my head. "Are you afraid of heights now?"

"No," she says quickly. "I'm fine. I'd jump." But she takes another step back.

"You're afraid of heights."

She looks ready to keep lying, then her shoulders sag. "I'm *maybe* a bit more freaked out by heights now."

"So why'd you bring me up here?"

She shrugs a shoulder and scrunches her cute nose. "You used to love jumping off the cliff into Bear Lake. I wanted to do something fun with you."

Just when I didn't think I could love her any more. "You're facing your fear for me."

She doesn't reply, just knocks into my side and rests her head on my chest.

"You don't have to jump, honey." I breathe in the fresh air, loving the heat of the sun on my skin. The heat of Sadie leaning on me, while learning new things about her . . . so I can use that intel to rile her up. "I can just jump on my own and heckle you from the bottom."

She smacks my stomach. "Still so obnoxious."

"It's a gift," I say and pinch her side.

"Coming through!" a guy bellows, then blows past us in a running leap, hollering as he launches into the air and falls down, down, down, *smack* into the water.

Sadie gasps and clutches her chest.

I laugh at her horrified expression. She may have developed a fear of heights, but I don't think she just came up here for me. I think she wants to remember what it's like to be wild and youthful. Not think before she acts, when all she's done for the past decade is think and plan.

I drop my head to her eye level. "Jump with me, Sprite. I'll hold your hand."

She worries her lip. "I don't know. I mean, I want to. I'm just . . . *ugh.*" Her wide eyes find mine. "Why does this scare me now?"

"Because you have more to lose." A son she loves. A great job. Adult responsibilities. Hopefully *me.* "But that's just your adrenaline talking. You're a badass who slays at axe throwing. And we're safe here. I won't let anything happen to you. Trust me. We'll do it together."

She blinks a few times, then nods and firms her jaw. "Yep. *Yes.* I used to do this all the time. I'm being silly, freaking out over nothing."

"That's my girl."

I check that the water below is clear, then I take her hand and lead us away from the edge, preparing for a running launch. "Ready?" I ask.

Her face is on the pale side, but her body is pitched forward, determination in her tense expression. "I was born ready."

God, I love this woman.

I give her hand a squeeze, then we're running and jumping, the air rushing at us as Sadie screams and I whoop, my grin almost as wide as her shell-shocked eyes. We hit the water with a *crack*, the force of it pulling us apart. I kick up, breaching the surface with a gasp, and there she is, the center of my world, grinning and laughing, my chest so full and warm I'm sure I swallowed the sun on my way down.

We swim over to a shallower section and laze about for a bit, floating and swimming around each other as we talk and laugh. A few families are nearby, along with other couples on the surrounding rocks. Regular people out in the Sunday sun, having fun and relaxing, and I'm struck by how long it's been since I've done something like this. Just enjoyed a day for the sake of it.

"I want a do-over on my wild and frivolous wish," I say.

Sadie kisses my wet neck, fits herself behind me as we balance on a rock. "What's your new choice?"

"This."

She sighs happily. "It's a slice of paradise."

I pull her arms around my chest. "We should do a family cook-off night."

"I have no clue what that is, but it sounds fun."

"Max really loves cooking, even just watching what someone's doing. We could make an activity of it, you and me doing our own versions of the same meal. He gets to help and chooses the winner."

"I love that." She jumps off the rock and swims in front of me, treading water. "When did you get so into activity planning?"

I join her, switching to floating on my back, the sun hot on my face. "Not sure. Feels like it happened by accident. Or out of necessity, maybe. I was so determined to make the hiking program fun for Max. Make up for that shitty first effort." Chasing my shadow games. Treating Max like a six-year-old.

"Well, it suits you. Like being in the wilderness. But so does wearing a suit and carrying a briefcase," she adds brightly, "like you'll be doing soon. You're a chameleon."

For the first time today, agitation edges my movements. Briefcase. School. The way Sadie keeps mentioning the man she hopes I'll be. Unfortunately, when I think about Duke these days, all I think about is the time I'll be missing with her and Max.

"Right now," I say, splashing her lightly, "I'm just a man, swimming with the woman he can't stop thinking about."

She splashes me back, laughing as we float on our backs again, holding hands this time.

"When I'm with you," she says quietly, "nothing else seems to matter. It's like the rest of the world floats away."

"Yeah. I feel that too." *When* we avoid the topic of school, which reminds me of Sadie's unresolved job offer. "Where are things at with the big gallery job?"

She gets quiet, a sudden frown marring her forehead. "Still the same back-and-forth—Sarah asking for things that don't work for me. Which is fine. The website is doing well."

Except she seems as bothered by the topic as I am about school, and I hate this for her. She deserves this chance and has the talent to pull it off. "I bet she'll come around. Cave just to get you on board."

Sadie doesn't reply. Just stares up at the sky. I try to read her mind, figure out exactly what's concerning her.

Abruptly, she points up at a cloud. "*Congregation of a Dynasty*."

I smirk at the cloud she's turning into a work of art. "I'll need an explanation for that name."

"It looks like a wolf howling at the moon, calling to his pack and bringing them together."

I study the cloud. Try to see what she sees, but my interpretation isn't quite so uplifting. "Or he just lost his loved ones and he's roaring out his pain: *Cry of the Last Wolf*."

My self-portrait, floating in the bright-blue sky.

Sadie tugs on my hand, guiding me back toward the rock until we're standing on it, half in and half out of the water, her arms circling my waist. "You're not alone now. Not anymore. You have me and Max."

"I know, honey." I stroke her wet hair. "I still have rough thoughts sometimes, bad dreams about losing you and Max. Then I wake up and realize everything's different."

Mostly different. There's still a barrier between us she hasn't lifted, subtle but there—moments where she gets quiet and seems lost in thought, like just before. Usually work related, but not always, and it doesn't sit well.

I kiss the top of her head, get lost in the feel of her wrapped around me.

"I'm on the pill," she whispers into my chest.

I go rigid. "Yeah . . ."

"And I've been tested." She lifts her eyes to mine. "If you have been too, we don't need to keep using condoms."

It's a good thing the lower half of my body is in the water, although my suddenly rigid cock might poke a fish in the eye. "I've been tested too," I say roughly.

"Good."

That's all she says. *Good.* And jumps off the rock, dives down, then breaches the water's surface in a graceful move. She swims toward the shore, giving me flirty eyes as she stands and sways her hot ass toward our towels.

I bite down on my cheek and slow my breaths, too turned on but also overwhelmed. The last time we thought the pill was infallible, Sadie got pregnant with Max. She doesn't seem to care about our history, and I stay quiet. Fact is, if she gets pregnant again, I'll be thrilled. If she forgets a pill or messes up the timing, and our inability to keep our hands off each other produces another child, I'll get to be here when she learns she's pregnant. Watch her belly grow. Be her anchor in the delivery room, hold my child the second they are born and witness all the firsts and seconds and thirds and everything I missed.

For now, I'm all for practicing our baby-making moves. "Get back in here," I call to her.

She gives me a saucy smile. "I'd like to lounge around a bit, preferably with you beside me. Hang out until we have to leave—read and soak up the sun. Maybe think about what we'll do next time we're alone." She winks.

I grunt.

Fuck like rabbits is what we'll do, but with her needing to get home soon, that won't be tonight. Still, I kind of dig her plan. Spending the afternoon flirting and teasing, getting turned on just by the idea of knowing I'll be sinking into her one day soon, no condom between us. I'm also craving more from her. Real alone time, without Max in hearing distance, so I can hear Sadie scream my name while I utter filthy words in her ear.

Regardless of when that happens, I'm guessing this was part of her day's plan: infiltrating my waking fantasies until I'm putty in her hands.

TWENTY-SEVEN

"How can you feel this fucking *good*?" I pull my hips back and thrust forward, pushing into Sadie from behind, mesmerized. Those dimples above her rounded ass. The dip of her spine as she arches. All that marble-smooth skin. Heat barrels through me, that telltale sizzle gripping my balls.

"God, yes." She matches my relentless rhythm. "Harder."

"How hard, baby?" I dig my fingers into the curves of her hips and pump. The bed shakes. "Like this?"

"Fuck, *yes*."

"Louder, Sprite." Max is spending his Saturday afternoon with Uncle E and Aunt Delilah. No one's home but us—our first time with no one in hearing distance. We've made it our mission to be as noisy and filthy as possible. "I want you to fucking *scream*."

The headboard smacks the wall. She pushes into me harder. "Fuck me with that fucking gorgeous cock, you fucking gorgeous *man*."

I growl and slam into her, giving her what we both need, fighting my release. Which, in case you were wondering, is no longer a challenge. I've had plenty of practice improving my stamina, even without condoms, the past two weeks. Quiet sessions in the guest room downstairs. One impromptu car marathon where we left Max home with E and Delilah, who were over for dinner, and we pretended we needed to go to the store to pick up ice. When we returned without the ice, E shook his head at our flushed faces and muttered, "Amateurs."

I lift Sadie so we're both kneeling, her back pressed to my chest, giving me full access to her body. "Your sweet little pussy was made for me. So tight and wet." I cup one of her breasts and circle her swollen clit with my free fingers. "Let me feel you squeeze my cock."

I give her pussy a light slap. She gasps, and yeah. There's that contraction I was after.

A few more strokes is all it takes. She knocks her head back, reaches over her head, and grips my hair as she shouts and moans and falls apart around me. I'm seconds behind her, grunting loudly, coming so hard I lean into her, my weight taking us to the mattress as I gather her in my arms. "Jesus, woman."

She laughs, blissful and loose. "Can't believe I said those things."

"With me, you get to be whoever you want. Say whatever you want. No judgment ever."

Rain pelts the roof. Our breathing slows and evens out. I pull her closer.

"Being with you again"—she rotates in my arms and strokes my cheek—"it's like that saying: you don't know what you have until it's gone."

I run my fingers through her hair, eliciting a sigh from her. "I'm not gone, Sprite. I'm right here."

"Let me rephrase." She traces a vein on my forearm. "Being with you again is the opposite of that saying—I didn't know what I lost until I got it back. I forgot how free you make me feel. What it's like to just let go—jumping off a cliff or being wild in bed. I've never felt as safe with anyone as I do with you."

I rub our noses together, unable to speak through the burn in my throat. After what I put Sadie through, her feeling safe with me is everything. Safety is the feeling of home. It means trust—the number one predictor of relationship success, according to future psychoanalyst Olivia. But we still have a distance to go.

A few mornings this week, I've found myself pulling out the engagement ring I never gave Sadie, staring at it, wondering when we'll feel solid enough for that next step. Which might still be a while. She's gone out of her way to do things for me, like our impromptu cliff jumping, and smaller gestures like hugging me for no reason and pulling me into "our dance" after Max has gone to sleep. But she still hasn't told me she loves me. I haven't said it again since that first time, either, worried she's not ready for that level of emotion.

I skim my knuckles down the side of her breast, loving this ease between us now. Her complete surrender. Still, I want more. I want everything with Sadie and Max, which means talking about the tough stuff too.

I kiss her nose and give her some space, needing to read her expression for this conversation. "You know I've been doing that book club with Max."

She nods. "It's incredibly sweet."

"And fun. But the first book was a bit of a surprise, and I'm not sure if you've seen his blue sketchbook, the personal one he showed me on the first hike?"

When she shakes her head, looking less amused, I wind our hands together. I'm not sure if now's the right time to discuss Max's sexuality. I'm not sure there's a right or wrong time or why I've kept quiet to date. I just suddenly need to share my thoughts with her. Work toward being better parents together, like Ricky suggested at the art walk. "Have you ever wondered if Max is gay?"

She doesn't suck in a surprised breath or frown or tell me I'm being ridiculous. She nibbles her lip and searches my face. "I have, but I'm not sure. Why? Did he say something to you?"

"Not exactly. Some of his sketches in that book are . . . sad? Like he's struggling with knowing who he is." A boy standing separate. A boy escaping Earth. A boy divided into pieces. "Our first book club novel was *Simon vs. the Homo Sapiens Agenda*—a book he chose about teenage drama and a boy coming out—and I asked him how he thought Simon might have felt when he was younger, before that book, when he was figuring out he was gay."

"What did he say?" Her whispered words are so timid, so full of emotion and worry.

I exhale through the tightness in my chest. "That he thought Simon might have been afraid people wouldn't like him. That his mom maybe wouldn't like him."

Sadie gasps and covers her mouth.

I cup her cheeks and kiss her forehead. "It's okay, honey. They're normal fears."

"Did I do something to make him think that? Say something without thinking?" She grips my wrists, tears filling her eyes. "I'd never love him less. He's perfect no matter who he loves."

"I know, and I think deep down he knows you'd support him. There's just so much on social media these days. There's no telling what he's seen or read."

Her fingers dig harder into my wrists. "What did you say to him?"

My absolute, undying truth. "I told him if I was Simon's dad, I'd be sad if I knew he was upset or scared when he was younger. That I'd wish I could go back in time and tell him he's loved unconditionally."

Her tears fall unchecked as her lips tremble. "How are you so amazing?"

"I'm not amazing, Sprite. I said some careless things to him before that. Off-the-cuff hetero comments that were stupid. And I might be wrong on this. He's still young. Reading a book about a gay teen and drawing sad pictures isn't evidence of anything. I just think it's an important conversation for us to have. Together. So if he does come to us one day with big news, we aren't shocked. We're a solid support he knows he can lean on."

She kisses me, hard and needy, her salty tears mingling with our tongues. "I love you. God, I love you so much."

I freeze for a beat, overwhelmed, then kiss her with all I have, sinking into the words I've been waiting to hear, letting them wash over me with their sweetness.

"Love you so fucking much," I whisper back, hugging her while we cling to each other and kind of laugh and kind of cry, eventually talking about what a great kid we have. How proud we are of his talent and kindness. How relieved we are he likes his counselor, Samantha, and has someone outside of family to confide in.

"I should've told you about his sketches right away," I say into this intimate space we've created. A safe bubble of whispered words. "Should've let you know he was struggling with something. I was scared, I think. Worried I'd lose his trust. I was thinking about myself, how much that would hurt, instead of about what was best for him."

"Oh, Des." Her sigh is full of gentleness. "You became an instant dad to a ten-year-old. If he has drawings that concern you, I need to know, but you're learning. You told me now. We're all learning how to be a family together."

That *How to Parent for Dummies* book needs a chapter for men shoved into WITSEC unaware that they were dads.

"I promise to do better," I say against her forehead. "No matter what Max's future holds, we'll make sure he's happy. We'll make sure he knows he's loved."

"He's so lucky to have you as a dad."

"And you as his mother, but I'm the lucky one." Everything in my life finally falling into place.

A door slams, and we stiffen, still naked under the sheets.

"Let's get you some water," E says loudly, stomping into the house earlier than expected.

Like an hour earlier.

At least they didn't walk in half an hour ago and get an earful of *Your sweet little pussy was made for me.*

I rub my hand down my face. "Guess that's our cue."

I roll away to get up, but Sadie places her hand on my waist. "Move in with us."

I whip around and search her face. "You want me to move in?"

She traces the contours of my lips, the edges of my stubbled jaw. "I'm tired of not kissing you when I want to kiss you. I hate not sleeping with you at night. I want you here when Max is being a pain in the ass and when he's being funny and sweet. I want him to have his father, because he needs you. *I* need you. I want us to be a family."

"You're sure?" When she nods, I don't test my luck and ask again. I kiss her hard and smile against her lips—seriously, this resting-grinning face is taking over—breathing more freely than I have in an eternity. "We'll tell Max when E's gone."

Her eyes shine. "He'll be so excited."

I'm so excited, except for the fine print. "When school starts, I'll stay at my apartment in Durham Tuesdays through Thursdays." The less exciting part. "Come back here Fridays to Mondays to be with you. Studying will be intense, but this changes everything. We'll get as much time together as possible."

"You're on your way, baby." She presses her lips together, like she's fighting another wave of tears. "Duke or die."

It's only *Sadie and Max or die* now, but I don't correct her.

We rush to get dressed and cleaned up, stealing a few more kisses along the way, then Sadie swats my jeans-clad ass. "I need to make a work call. Be down in a few."

I head for the door but decide I need another kiss before I go, because I'm a Sadie-obsessed motherfucker. When I turn, her face is resolute, like she's readying for a tough call.

"Is this about the gallery job?"

She pauses. The strong lines of her cheekbones sharpen, then she sags. "It fell through in the end, and I need to tell Joseph. I've been putting it off."

My stomach twists. "Sarah wouldn't adjust the job the way you wanted?"

She runs her thumb over her phone and bounces her heel. "We weren't on the same page, and she decided to hire someone else. Which is fine. She's demanding and works crazy hours. It was turning into a headache." She flicks her hand, as though the matter is done.

Unwilling to let her brush off this setback, I crouch in front of her and grip her calves. "It's okay to be upset. You were excited about it. I'm sorry it didn't work out."

More than sorry. I thought that job was her chance to fulfill her dreams. Reclaim an aspect of her life she lost because of me.

She strokes her thumb over my cheek. "I'm not sorry. If I got that job, we wouldn't have as much time for us."

As much as I love our time together, I'd happily swap a portion of it for Sadie to have a fulfilling career. "Something else will come up. Your eye for talent is a commodity."

She shrugs, as though unaffected, but I know Sadie. The pinch of her brow, her fidgetiness and eye contact avoidance—she's disappointed. I give her calves a reassuring squeeze and plant a soft kiss on her shoulder, then leave her alone to call Joseph.

The second I'm downstairs, my frustration melts into contented warmth. Max is at the dining table with E, the two of them poring over one of Max's sketchbooks. I'm here so often these days, Max doesn't question what Sadie and I were doing upstairs. He just waves distractedly, consumed by his art. And I need a minute. A breath to let my good fortune sink in.

From this day forward, there will be no more pretending. I'll be living in this house, part of Max's daily life, when I'm not at Duke. I'll have Sadie at night and time with my family. I'll actually miss leading hikes, and law will be an uphill battle, but I never imagined a life as fulfilling as this.

Joining them, I cup the back of Max's neck and kiss his head. "I assume you're early because Uncle E's incredibly boring, and you couldn't wait to shake him."

E taps his fingers on the table, unamused. "Your dad can't fold paper without cutting himself, so I'd suggest not taking his advice. Ever."

Last time we saw E and Delilah, we joked about Mom's horrible creative genes, and I made the mistake of mentioning I shared her awful crafting DNA. Now E's relentless.

Max does that belly giggle I love. "I forgot this sketchbook here. Uncle E's helping me with my graphic novel layout."

"Don't rely on him too much," I say. "His novels are color by number."

E purses his lips. "This from a guy who drank a bottle of hot sauce because Lennon dared him."

"And your point is?"

"You have bad judgment and can't be trusted."

Max snorts at our friendly sparring.

"What's so funny?" Sadie comes into the kitchen, drops her cell on the counter, and grabs a bowl of grapes from the fridge.

"E's attempting to never get invited here again." I scan her for signs of distress, but she's stoic, her chin lifted and shoulders squared.

She puts the bowl of grapes on the table and rubs Max's back. "You're working on the giant eagle comic?"

"It's a condor, Mom. *A vulture*," he adds with a dose of get-with-it exasperation. I think he's been spending too much time with Olivia, but I love that he's developing a drawing from our first hike. My talented kid took his initial sketch—the angry boy flying away from the world—and is turning it into a kickass comic, thanks to my insanely talented brother.

Sadie gets in Max's face and plants a loud kiss on his cheek. "I love the condor, and I love *you*, more than anything in the world." Her voice shakes slightly.

My heart decides to swell and squeeze at the same time.

Max lifts his shoulder, nudging her away, too focused on his art to care about his mother's professions of parental love.

She and I lock eyes. I mouth, *I love you.*

She blinks and fans her face, rolling her eyes as though annoyed with herself for being emotional. I wouldn't want her any other way. Showing her love to Max, even if he doesn't fully know why, is the safety net our son needs to be brave in life. To be experimental and open and trust himself.

Her phone rings from the counter, and Joseph's name flashes. She glances at it, flattens her lips, and cancels the call. When it rings again, she shuts off her phone.

I rub my jaw. "He knows losing the job isn't your fault, right?"

"He just likes to overthink and overtalk things. I'd rather spend my Saturday with my favorite men than deal with work. Especially when we have an important talk ahead of us."

The moving-in talk with Max. Another swell-squeeze number happens behind my ribs. "Fine, but if you need to vent or anything with me, don't hold back."

She nods, then I help her tidy the kitchen and living room. A similar routine to our past couple of weeks, but I keep thinking, *This is my home now.* I belong somewhere. I'm no longer drifting without an anchor. A crack of thunder rings out. Heavy rain pelts the roof and windows, but in here we're safe and dry. I even imagine inviting Kyle over with his daughter for the playdate we haven't arranged yet, meeting his wife, making deeper friendships. Maybe I'll walk through Windfall one day, enjoying its quaint charm as a Dauntless Lawyer, not as That Guy People Whisper About.

When E grabs his raincoat and announces he's leaving, I pull him into a hug at the door. "Thanks for being such a good uncle and brother."

He pounds my back. "Thanks for having such a great kid."

"You can thank Sadie for that."

E pulls back and gives me one of his intense stares. "Sadie's done an amazing job with him, but Max is part of you too. He's happier now because of *you*, so quit it with the self-sabotage. And his drawing skills are clearly from me."

I bristle at his "self-sabotage" comment. All I did was compliment Sadie. But whatever. I don't have the energy to analyze my overanalytical brother. Not when I'm about to give my kid the gift of a lifetime.

E darts out in the rain, and I mentally rearrange Monday's hiking plans. Even with the recent rain, we've had fun getting muddy. To a point. Sadie won't tolerate more puddle jumping (which I encourage). With only two sessions left, I want to end on a high note.

For now, I clap my hands and strut back to the kitchen. "Who wants ice cream?"

Max looks up from his sketchbook, his expression a mix of excitement and skepticism. "We can't have ice cream before dinner."

"We can when we have something to celebrate." Except. Shit. I guess I don't know the house rules. Basic adult rules, really. One hour into living with my family, and I'm already messing things up. I glance at Sadie and mouth a contrite, *Sorry*.

Instead of giving me hell, she shakes her head and grabs a tub of cookies and cream from the freezer. "We'll make an exception today. But *only* today."

Max slides off his chair and hurries to his counter stool, lest she change her mind. "What are we celebrating?"

"You have three guesses," I say.

He scrunches his face and taps his thumb on the counter. "Did we win a trip to the National Air and Space Museum?"

"Nope." Sadie scoops ice cream into bowls, the corners of her lips betraying her amusement.

Max goes still, his dark eyes managing to get even wider. "Are we getting a *dog*?"

"Double nope," I say, but I make mental notes of my son's wishes: trip to the Air and Space Museum, cute dog to cuddle.

He chews his lip, his gaze darting between Sadie and me. "Am I getting a baby brother or sister?"

Sadie freezes, her mouth partway open. I choke on nothing and pound my chest. I don't know if that's a theoretical wish or if he's heard us when we thought we were being quiet. Either way, Sadie's cheeks flame. Pretty sure mine match hers.

"No sibling." *Yet*, I don't add. I drag my stool closer to his and place my hand on his back. "Remember after the art walk, we were heading home, and you said you wished I'd stay over and that I lived with you and your mom?"

He nods, his small chest swelling and falling faster.

Sadie leans over from the other side of the counter and grabs Max's hand. "Your dad's moving in, sweetheart. We're gonna be a family."

His eyes fill and his chin trembles, but he sits so stiffly I start to worry this news isn't as welcome as I imagined. Then he's all over me, hugging me and shaking and crying, not speaking, just holding on for dear life. I'm getting that this is a thing for him. How he processes feelings. Internalizing like his Uncle E, going quiet, then exploding in a rush of emotion.

My heart just ballooned to three times its size. I squeeze him back, cup his head and kiss his cheek. Sadie gives her own waterworks performance, then gets in on the action, hugging me from behind and kissing us both, while I shake slightly and hold on for dear life. Because honestly. This much happiness terrifies the living shit out of me.

TWENTY-EIGHT

The sky has a leak in it. Or a faulty drainage system. Whatever the cause, the constant rain is feeling more Noah's ark and less family-nesting cozy. Tomorrow's my last hike with my Littlewing group, and I have no doubt there will be a few sulking troops in my preteen platoon.

To compensate and earn my official Happy Hiking Leader merit badge, I decided to make my mini squadron matching braided bracelets in the Littlewing colors of green, white, and exhausting yellow. (Olivia can complain all she wants.) Which means I need to get my naked ass in gear.

I grab jeans and a T-shirt from my drawer in *our* room—mine and Sadie's, because my disaster life somehow became awesome. I can't imagine ever getting used to falling asleep with her. Keeping her tucked close into me. Loving on her. Waking her up by kissing my way down her body. Cooking Max the breakfast I've learned he likes—egg-in-the-hole toast with a side of fresh berries. I have only five days left before I head to my Duke apartment and start school. I plan to make every second count.

Case in point, the second Jasmine's mom picked Max up for a movie in town, I abducted Sadie from her office, tossed her over my shoulder, and proceeded to defile her on *our* bed.

I pop my head into *our* bathroom and whistle. "That's my favorite outfit of yours."

"I'm not wearing clothes," Sadie deadpans from the shower.

"Exactly."

She wipes condensation from the glass, then puts on a show, soaping up her breasts and swaying her hips.

A feral noise escapes my throat. "If I didn't have three more bracelets to make, I'd be in there with you."

"You actually weren't invited, because *I* have to get back to work. But for what it's worth, watching your man hands attempting to craft is shockingly sexy."

Guess I'll be saving a bracelet for later tonight.

I quit pestering Sadie and head downstairs, stopping to tidy the shoes by *our* front door. I grab my bag of colored thread and sit on *our* sofa, then kick my bare feet up on *our* coffee table.

Trust me. I'm annoying myself. But I can't stop.

I glance at the stack of textbooks on the end table and debate cracking those open instead of crafting. The prospect has me doing a full-body sigh. I'll have plenty of hours to fill when I'm living on my own next week. Braiding string seems like a much better use of my time.

I gather the colors and twist a knot at the top, then pin it to my jeans, smiling as I picture Sadie getting hot watching me doing something as simple as braiding string. I gather the first threads, ready to get these bracelets done, but *our* phone rings.

A week ago, I wouldn't have answered. Sadie's house. Sadie's phone. Now that I'm living in *our* territory, I grab the cordless from the end table and hit talk. "Jones and Bower residence."

Silence greets me. Then a deep voice says, "Everything's starting to make more sense."

I squint, trying to place the familiar voice. Then it hits me—*GQ Joseph*. The guy hasn't stopped nagging Sadie since they lost that gallery job. I've caught her turning down his calls several times. Like clockwork, she gets quiet afterward, and stress lines sink into her forehead.

No matter how often I suggest she tell him to back off, or remind her losing the job wasn't her fault, she introverts and shuts down.

Guess it's time to step in on her behalf. "I'm not sure what your problem is, Joseph, but jobs come and go. I get that this was a big one, but Sadie's upset about losing it too. Guilting her and harping on it isn't helping anyone."

"I assume you're living there," is all he says.

"I am," I reply forcefully. Not only did he avoid the topic at hand, he's focusing on Sadie's personal life. *My* personal life. Maybe he was into her after all.

"What did Sadie tell you about losing this job?" he asks.

"That Sarah was being difficult, not willing to negotiate the terms Sadie wanted, and Sarah wound up hiring someone else."

This next pause feels unpleasantly weighted. "Sarah didn't choose someone else as head curator for this once-in-a-lifetime opportunity. She chose Sadie and me, and Sadie turned it down."

I frown, sure I heard him wrong. "Sadie wasn't applying for the head curator position."

"No, she wasn't. But Sarah was blown away by our presentation. She wants the mentorship program to be helmed by the curator, and she likes thinking out of the box, giving people chances, even if they have less experience. So she offered Sadie the career opportunity of a lifetime, and Sadie turned it down."

"Why the hell would she do that?" I'm on my feet in seconds, struggling to process what he said.

Sadie lied.

Sadie was offered her dream job.

A job a million times better than the one she was after.

And she turned it down?

Joseph blows out a rough breath. "The job requires her to move to Arizona."

My gut bottoms out. Drops to my goddamn feet.

Arizona is across the country, eight states away, and I'm here, about to start classes at Duke next week. Which means, *fuck*. The only reason Sadie would ditch the job of a lifetime would be to keep us together, settling for less, when she deserves to dream big and chase those big-league opportunities.

I start pacing, torn between what this job means for Sadie personally and what it means for us. If she goes, I can't follow. Not while I'm in school. If I want to make something of myself and be the Dauntless Lawyer that Max and Sadie expect and deserve, I have to get that degree. We'll be reduced to computer chats and phone calls. Long-distance hell. After sampling the real thing—living together, working together, movie nights, cliff jumping, cooking classes, Max's belly laughing at my antics, Sadie's warm body pressed to mine beneath the sheets—I'm not sure how I'll survive.

My fingers twitch to end this call. A quick hang up is all it would take. I could pretend I never picked up the phone. Let Sadie make the sacrifice so I can have more *our*. *Our* home. *Our* family. But it wouldn't be ours, would it? That future would be mine. *My* selfish needs steamrolling hers, and I can't do it. I can't let Sadie lose herself because of me again.

"You still there?" Joseph says. I swear there's sympathy in his voice.

"Can Sadie still get the job? If she changes her mind, will she be hired?"

"Only if we act fast. Sarah's speaking with another candidate today. This was my last-ditch effort to convince Sadie to change her mind."

The sound of Sadie's hair dryer carries from upstairs. She often has a soft smile on her face when she's blow-drying her hair, like she's daydreaming while getting ready. The other morning, when I asked what she was smiling about, she turned those big faerie eyes on me and said, "You."

A sharp pang cuts through my chest. I seriously might pass out. The notion of losing those special moments kills me. Sucks the air right out of my lungs. But I picture Sadie giving up that museum job after I left, suffering through her parents' cruelty and carelessness, living with them when she first had Max, all that helplessness and fear stealing her bravery before she realized she deserved better and forged her own path.

Now she has the chance to grow, thrive. Be everything she ever wanted to be.

I plant my ass on the couch back, slump forward, and rub my eyes. "Tell Sarah she'll take the job."

"Desmond, I can't tell her that unless it's true. There's a lot in play here."

"Can you give me time? Another few days to convince Sadie?" I'll just cut out my heart and find a way to get through the next few years as a zombie version of myself. Like the old me. Except no. I'll never be that guy again. I need and want more from life, and I'll have school. I have to make myself better for my family . . . who will be across the country until I can be with them again. For *three* excruciating years.

"I'll speak with Sarah," Joseph says. "Ask her to extend their deadline for us. But it won't be long."

"Just do what you can."

The second we hang up, I drop the phone on the couch, feeling both ill and determined. I won't let Sadie give this up. I can't. She's given up too much already.

She comes down the stairs looking happy and fresh.

My insides pitch violently.

"I'm making tea," she says brightly. "Let me know if you want a cup. After which, you will not interrupt me in my office again." She smiles at my legs. "That's a cute look on you."

I glance down. The damn bracelet's hanging off my jeans, unfinished and getting tangled. Pretty much how I feel. When I don't reply, Sadie searches my face. "Everything okay?"

Not even a little. "You can't turn down the job."

She scrunches her nose. "What job?"

"The Arizona gallery job. Joseph just called, and I answered."

Her loose posture stiffens, the amusement on her face twisting into panic. She resembles Max when he's processing big emotion: breathing hard, freezing up, eyes getting watery and wide. "It's not your choice to make."

"You can't throw away such an amazing opportunity."

"So loving my family and wanting to keep us together isn't an amazing opportunity?"

I cross my arms. Not to intimidate. I need to hold myself together. "I won't let you lose the job of a lifetime because of me. Not again."

"Except this is *my life*." She jabs at her chest. "Mine. You don't get a vote in this."

"I do when I'm the reason you're making the decision."

"Not everything's about you!" Her complexion reddens, anger firing in her eyes. "Max is finally happy here in Windfall, making friends, coming out of his shell. I moved here after a lot of thought, before your family even found you to tell you about him. I wanted to set roots down in this town, for me and my family. If I move Max again so quickly, take him away from his new friends and you after just getting you in his life? How do you think that will affect him?"

I cover my mouth with my hand, at a loss. Max is sensitive and sweet and emotional, and I wasn't thinking about him. I was thinking about Sadie. And about me—*my* need to see her succeed. I was being an inconsiderate parent who didn't consider his kid.

Now I'm the one who's frozen, internalizing, eyes stinging, trying to think my way through this. "I won't go to school then. I'll ditch law and come with you to Arizona."

"Not up for discussion."

"So you get to make all the decisions, and I get to make none?"

"Didn't you promise not to undermine my independence?" She fists her hands and closes her eyes, then exhales, focusing on me as her shoulders drop. "When you went into witness protection, you lost as much as I did. Probably more. You lost your career and me, and you lost Max. So it's Duke or die, Des. It always has been. If you want to stay together, you're getting that degree."

I could tell her I don't care about the degree. Not if I'm choosing between law and being with my family—between law and most things these days. But she just admitted what I already knew: she needs me to be the future Duke lawyer she fell in love with at seventeen. Not the guy Justin Bernardini laughed at. Or the guy who slings drinks for a living and cuts his fingers on paper when he's trying to destress. If I don't get that degree, I'll always be an embarrassment to my family. I'll probably lose her down the road.

"Then we do this long distance," I force out.

"I'm not taking the job." Obstinance has nothing on her.

"You can't give up your dreams, Sadie. I won't allow it." My jaw's clenched so tight my molars might crack. "My stipulation's the same as yours. If you want to stay together, you're taking that job."

"You would seriously leave me and Max over this? After promising you wouldn't hurt us."

I'm shaking now. A terrified, spineless leaf of a man. Of course I wouldn't leave her and Max. That pathetic bit of posturing was nothing but a knee-jerk reaction. The only solution is convincing Sadie to change her mind. "If I weren't in the picture, would you have moved Max and taken the job?"

She stares at me. I stare at her. A contest of wills I won't lose. I love her too much to watch her give up this vital part of who she is.

"Sadie," I say quietly. "Tell me honestly—does the idea of being head curator excite you?"

She drags her teeth over her bottom lip, breathing harder, weighing, assessing. Then she deflates. "It's an unreal opportunity. I'd be working with brilliant creators, the space will be breathtaking, and Sarah's budget means we wouldn't be strapped for cash when pulling together exhibits and installations. Not to mention the pay is . . . a lot. But even wanting this makes me feel so selfish. Max is happy here. And you're here. I won't lose what we're building or hurt Max. I just . . . won't." She flattens her lips. "The sacrifice is worth it."

No, it isn't. Not again. Not this time. And she didn't answer my question. "But if I wasn't in the picture. If I never came back—would you have taken the job, even if it meant moving Max again?"

Her chin quivers, a near-silent sob making her heave. "Yes," she whispers.

"Then you have to take it." I close the distance between us and brush an errant tear from her cheek. "Max has your blood running through his veins. He's strong and resilient. If he made friends here, he'll make friends there." The idea of moving him away from Jasmine and Zoey and my family pains me, but there's no mistaking the anguish in the admission Sadie tried to hide. She wants this job desperately. If she turns it down, it will eat at her. "You've said yourself how uncreative you feel cooped up, working from home, not seeing the office buildings you decorate, or most of the art in the flesh. You can't pass this up."

"I won't lose you again." She grabs my wrist, her fingers digging in. "Max can't lose you."

"You're not losing me. We're not breaking up. I'll be at school, talking to you both all the time."

"But we need you with us. These are such important years for Max."

Low blow. Not fair. She knows that's a direct hit to my heart, but I won't falter. Max *is* resilient. The two of us have to be strong for his mother.

I press my forehead to hers. "I need you two as much as you need me, but I need you to be happy more. I *need* to know I didn't steal your career from you again."

I'm not as strong as her. I can't live with this knowledge. Seeing those quiet moments where she looks frustrated and resigned, knowing why now. Knowing I'm the cause.

"Please, honey. Take the job."

We breathe like that for several long moments, our foreheads touching, hands clutching. I feel her softening, the tension in her arms giving way. *Thank God.*

Then she pulls away. "You pushing for this means the world, but the decision's done. I'm not taking the job, and that's final."

There's no missing how she's biting the inside of her cheek, trying not to cry. I debate suggesting I ditch Duke and reapply to a school in Arizona, but admissions are done for the year. Sadie would probably think this is my way of delaying, quitting. Giving up the way I have the past decade. She'd look at me with less love in her eyes.

She marches to her office, shutting herself inside without making her tea or giving me a second glance. An ache lances through my chest, harder this time. Breath-stealing pain. Like something bigger happened here. A fault line carved between us. Broken ground I won't be able to bridge. Sadie's strong and stubborn and fiercely devoted to our family. I love her for it, but that admission—how perfect this job is, that she'd have taken it if I hadn't returned—how do we live with her letting that go?

I force a swallow. Blink at the home that had started to feel like *ours.* Everything looks different.

I somehow get my three bracelets done, my fingers moving by rote, my heartbeat thick and sluggish. Max comes home, and I manage a smile, hugging him tighter than normal, trying to pretend my seams aren't fraying. Sadie and I move around each other in the kitchen, cooking and cleaning, but we don't brush against each other like usual, stealing small touches and tender looks. There's distance between us. Awareness of each other's stance on this huge decision.

We don't talk while we get ready for bed. I watch her brush her teeth. Stand beside her, searching for words to mend our divide. All I manage is to graze my hand down her back and whisper, "We'll be okay. We'll figure this out."

She stiffens at my touch. "There's nothing to figure out. I'm not taking the job, and you're going to school."

She leaves me in the bathroom alone.

I brace my hands on the sink counter and hang my head, force more air into my lungs. Six hours into this disagreement, and I can barely stand upright. I lean heavier onto my palms, stare at myself in the mirror: the scar on my neck, the unprofessional ink, my thick eyelashes, and the sharp cut of my jaw, so much like my father's, who never put anyone before himself. Another reason why I need to change her mind.

I can't be a selfish bastard like him.

I leave the bathroom, needing to hold Sadie, feel her in my arms, ask her again to reconsider. Drill it in to her that we're still together. But she's under the covers already, her eyes closed and bedside light switched off. Shutting me out.

My throat constricts so forcefully I can barely drag in a breath.

Wetness is pushing from her closed eyes, and her lips are pressed tight. Intense emotion that hints at my biggest fear: this is a no-win situation. If she keeps the job, she'll end up resenting me for breaking us apart and hurting Max. If she gives up the gallery job, she'll end up resenting me for missing this opportunity. A sacrifice that big will fester and infect. It's already starting, and I'm not sure how to cauterize the growing wound.

I'm not sure how to make this right.

TWENTY-NINE

Today is off to a predictably horrible start. I barely slept last night. I spent a portion of my restlessness watching Sadie pretend to sleep. An effort she gave her all, but she can't fool me. I've memorized the tiny whistle her nose makes when she's fully passed out, the slow rise of her chest, how her lips part slightly and her body softens.

Last night she gripped her sheets in a tight fist, and there were no sweet whistles. The creases at the corners of her eyes were anything but soft and relaxed.

So I stewed. Wound up staring at the ceiling, despising my father all over again for stealing Max and Sadie from me. For putting this mess in motion so he could earn cash. I berated myself for not finishing law school during WITSEC like I should've. If I had that degree, I wouldn't be attending Duke now, forcing Sadie to choose between her job and us.

Such an utter moron.

Now we're nearing the meeting point for today's hike, and Sadie and I have barely said a word on the drive. Mud churns under the car's tires. Sadie's leaning against the passenger door, staring out the window, giving off wafts of silent misery. Max is drawing in the back, doodling in his sketchbook. Every time I glance in the rearview mirror, his worried eyes dart between Sadie and me. As hard as I've tried to be positive this morning, there's no hiding the heavy mood in the car. He's a smart, intuitive kid. He knows something's wrong.

"Mom," he says sharply. "My cookies aren't in my bag."

Sadie mutters a quiet "Shit," then faces him in the back. "Sorry, sweetie. I totally forgot."

Because she was distracted by her sadness and our fight.

"I have extra granola bars in my bag," I offer, trying to catch his eye in the rearview.

He mumbles, "Fine," and continues drawing, his head hung lower.

My mind takes a deep dive into treacherous waters.

Yes, Max is resilient. Yes, he'll have our support no matter where he is. But he's been so happy in Windfall with his new friends and his extended family, with me in his life. Now there's a hint of change—discord between Sadie and me—and he's curling in on himself. Maybe Sadie's right and moving him is a horrible idea. All this upheaval in a short time might sap his confidence in a damaging way. Which leads us back to Sadie's upsetting solution of her giving up her job. The best thing for Max likely, not the best thing for Sadie.

By the time I park her Honda at the site of today's final hike, I've clenched my jaw to the point of having a headache. Sadie abruptly gets out and waits for Max to join her, not sparing me a glance. Probably worried I'll jump at the chance to push my opinion on her, convince her to take that job. I don't even know what I want anymore. How to make her *and* Max happy.

I sit in the car and grip the wheel, trying to get ahold of my spiraling thoughts. Another sinkhole forms in my stomach, widening at an alarming rate. I grab the door handle to get out and get this day going, but my heart beats faster. Scary fast. Face-planting-in-the-mud fast.

Before I hyperventilate, I grab my phone and call E.

Three rings later, he answers. "Is there a nuclear strike I'm not aware of?"

I squint out the windshield and attempt to slow my breathing. "What?"

"Did they announce they're discontinuing that brand of tomato soup you use for that one dinner you know how to make?"

"What the fuck are you talking about?"

"You never call me during the day. Figured it was world-ending stuff."

I lean the back of my head into my seat and press the heel of my palm against my vibrating sternum. *World-ending* sounds about right. "Sadie has a job offer from Arizona."

"Since when?" The teasing vacates his tone.

My voice turns stone-cold devastated. "Since a while ago. She's been lying to me, telling me she was negotiating a different job, then that someone else got the position. Probably started lying to me about it before that. And it's the job of a lifetime. She'll never have another opportunity like this. I can't stand by while she loses herself again because of me. So I told her to accept it, but she won't take it. Insists on staying here while I'm at Duke, and she doesn't want to move Max. Which I get, she's probably right. I just know this will eat at her. She's already pulling away from me, resenting me for what she's giving up. I'm totally, completely *fucked*."

"And you're still starting Duke?"

Pretty sure I already summed that up. "I told her I'd ditch school. She wouldn't consider it, and it doesn't solve the Max problem."

"So you're listening to her and going to Duke." His tone morphs from questioning to downright accusatory. "While Sadie gives up this once-in-a-lifetime job."

"Yes, *again*, that's what I said."

His laugh is far from amused. "Don't take this the wrong way, but you're an idiot."

This is why I've shut my family out for the past decade. They never fail to rile me. "It's been fun, but I gotta go."

"No, you don't. What you need to do is stop hating yourself."

"I don't hate myself. Not anymore, at least."

"Kind of, but kind of *not*." When I don't hang up or rebut his comment, he says, "If you think something enough, you start believing it. And that was your mantra for most of WITSEC. *I'm worthless. I'm a loser. I'm nothing without Sadie.* All of which is bullshit, but, even now, your brain keeps slipping into that rut."

My lip curls. "You weren't exactly busting with self-confidence without Delilah."

"No, I wasn't. But I still found enough in me to like that I could move forward. I took hold of my art. Made a career for myself. You purposely wasted away your days for years, because you didn't think you deserved better."

"Which is why I'm going to Duke." I gesture angrily at nothing. "To fix that part of myself so I can finally move forward and be what Sadie needs."

"Duke isn't forward, Des. Duke is *backward*."

I blink through the car's windshield. Jasmine and Zoey have arrived. My favorite psychoanalyst pops out of an unfamiliar car. I'm surprised when a man gets out of the driver's side and says hi to Sadie. He has similar features to Olivia with less unnerving intensity. He doesn't talk long to Sadie, but Olivia grins brightly at him, waving when he leaves. My best guess is she decided to give her father a second chance. A reconciliation I helped orchestrate.

As happy as I am for her, I can't muster a smile. I'm not picking up what E's putting down. My overanalyzing brother is seeing things I don't understand.

"Sadie told me I have to go to Duke, E. Said she'd leave me if I didn't. If that's not a neon sign saying she can't see past what I've become unless I get that degree, I'm seriously missing something."

He sighs. "At the risk of sounding insensitive, you're missing everything."

"Fucking asshole," I mutter.

"Sadie thinks *you* want Duke. She's pushing you because she thinks you're devastated that you lost your law degree and future and feels like she's the cause. That losing *her* caused you to lose your drive, and that knowledge devastated her. It still devastates her."

Like her giving up the assistant position at the art museum in Raleigh all those years ago devastated me. All well and good, but he's missing a big part of this picture. "You didn't see her with Justin Bernardini boasting about me going back to law. She talks to Max about it all the time, telling him what a great lawyer I'll be. She may think she's pushing me for my sake, but she's also gripping onto that image of me. She needs me to be the guy she fell in love with before WITSEC. Not the stagnant bartender I became."

E's next sigh holds little patience. "The hiking program you're running, has it been successful?"

I squeeze my eyes shut, rubbing at my forehead, remembering our first session. Chasing shadow games. Coloring books. "Started off brutal. Embarrassed myself in front of Sadie and the kids."

"Honest to God," he mutters. Then louder, "I didn't ask you how it started. I asked if it's become successful—if the program you created, with no guidance and no help from Lennon, even though he offered it, has been enjoyed by the kids?"

I watch my preteen platoon comingling, Carter and Jun having joined the rest of them. All the kids hang out in a circle, mud already crusting their sneakers, hands and arms moving animatedly as they talk. Max is more subdued, glancing at me and nibbling his lip, no doubt wondering why I'm holed up in the car, but there's no denying the group is tighter. There's no phone surfing and yawning as they wait for me. We've had fun in the wilderness together. The kids have been engaged and enthusiastic.

"The hikes have been good," I admit grudgingly.

"And you and Max—have you formed a bond with your son? Does he seem happier to you than when you first met him?"

I think back to how sullen Max was that first day, avoiding Carter and Jun, scratching his mosquito bites and hanging his head. I think about our book club talks and him pretending to wear earrings with Jasmine at the art walk, about baking with him in Delilah's class, and how fiercely he hugged me when I told him I was moving in. The opposite of how he'll be if he moves to Arizona.

I exhale roughly. "He's been amazing lately."

"Open your eyes, Des." E's voice is so full of sympathy my throat tightens. "WITSEC changed us all, and not just for the worse. You understand loss and pain now. You're more compassionate than you were. I mean, you *were* secretly caring growing up, doing stuff like fixing my bike and letting me think Cal did it. And I know you had words with bullies who picked on me."

More like uttered vicious threats. The only asshole allowed to rough up my brother was me. "I was no saint."

"Far from it. But the untouchable golden boy who you thought could do no wrong before WITSEC wouldn't have put Sadie first the way you're trying to now."

"I *always* put Sadie first. Then and now."

"Remind me again why you didn't propose to her?"

I startle, frowning at the implication, searching my memory for that life-altering night. The sex we had in Windfall's town square under the cover of night, my debilitating nervousness—Male Moron Syndrome—as I procrastinated asking her for forever. The flood of what-ifs that plagued me: the possibility that she'd steal my concentration from school, or I'd get too focused on law as it got more in depth and hurt her, or she'd meet someone better down the line, or we'd get married and get tired of each other. I worried that proposing was rushing us, that I'd somehow derail my plans, slow my path to success.

Not *our* plans. Me and *my* plans.

"Des!" Sadie's voice cuts through my rising discomfort. She points to her empty wrist, miming that it's time to get my ass in gear.

"Gotta go," I tell E.

Go lead this last hike.

Go untangle the swirl of thoughts making me queasy.

"Quit sabotaging yourself," he says, like it's the easiest thing in the world. "You deserve to be happy."

He hangs up, and I give my head a swift shake. *Hike. Kids. Get my shit together.* These kids are under my care. My focus needs to be on them, not on my anxious energy as E's words ricochet through my mind.

I unzip my backpack and shove in my end-of-hike bracelets. *Hike. Kids. Get my shit together.* I go to the trunk and grab my bag of equipment for today's activity of trash collecting. And yeah. I know asking them to clean the trail is risky. These kids might take one look at this chore and groan their faces off. Except I have a pep talk planned and a killer prize up for grabs.

I turn, determined to slap on a grin and entertain my preteen platoon. But Olivia.

I'm not sure I can handle But Olivia today. Unfortunately, ditching her is like trying to shake off Krazy Glue. "Get it over with," I say.

She does one of her unnerving staring numbers that has me considering getting back in the car and locking the doors. After a painful beat, she says, "Are you leading the fall hikes?"

"I . . ." Was not expecting that question. During recent hikes she nailed me with torpedoes like "Did you kill anyone during WITSEC?" and "Did the cartel just sell weed and cocaine, or did they push Dexies and molly and smack?" at which point I flat-out panicked and told her the only Molly I'd heard of was Molly Fingold, who ran my high school pep rally. Honestly. Someone needs to install child locks on this kid's internet access.

So yeah. Her hiking question is jarring for a couple of reasons. I didn't know Lennon planned to continue the program. He must be leaving Houston, moving his business here. Or he's hiring someone new. A possibility that makes irrational jealousy flare behind my ribs. Like someone's stealing my job from under me, which is ridiculous. This was only ever a temporary gig. A pitstop on my way to Responsible Dad. I also barely recognize *this* Olivia. She's twisting her fingers and has diverted her attention to her hot-pink sneakers.

"I have law school starting," I tell her. "Witness protection's over. Finally time for me to be an adult and get my life together. School's too far to do both."

Too far for me to be with my family.

Her expression falls, and my stomach does a disconcerting dip. Olivia's never looked so much her age. Young and worried, openly upset and vulnerable. Then the scary know-it-all who told me 67 percent of men are liars resurfaces. "Did you know you don't need a valid driver's license to compete in NASCAR?"

"Okay . . ." I lean away, waiting for her surprise strike.

"You also don't need law school to be an adult." She swivels and marches back to the group.

Olivia's emotional intelligence is as frightening as always. No, I don't need law to be an adult. I need something steady, though, and Sadie needs the lawyer version of me. Unless E's right and she only wants it because she thinks I want it, and I'm the one undermining us both by clinging to the last vestiges of the man I was because I don't trust the guy I've become. Maybe the guy I was *before* WITSEC wouldn't have been good enough for Sadie in the end. Too self-obsessed. Too insular to propose or make lasting friendships with guys like Kyle. Maybe the man I've become is more compassionate. More loving. More aware of the people he loves.

Wading through my mental swamp, I join my hiking group. Sadie and I lock eyes for a second. Immediately her eyes glass over. Mine burn, and my fingers twitch.

Not reaching for her is a physical ache.

Blinking hard, I inhale the post-rain smells of sweet grass and damp earth. If my past eleven years had a scent, this might be it—decay and growth. The unexpected results of WITSEC, like E suggested, and I *have* been too focused on the negative to see the positive. But there's no denying the eager faces turned toward me, the way Max nudges Jasmine, whispering something to her, the two of them giggling and smiling.

Another puff of pleasure warms my chest. He's happier and has new friends because of *me*. Because I've helped orchestrate this hiking program and his joy, building all these kids up along the way, even helping nudge Olivia and her father to reconcile.

Decay and growth.

Maybe that's what I've been missing all along. Not Duke Law and prestigious credentials. I haven't allowed myself the room to change. To be a success *and* a failure and accept that my inside doesn't have to match my outside.

Breathing through this new awareness, I focus on my group—these great kids who've shown me what it truly means to be an adult. "I have something fun planned for our last day."

"Did you hide pictures of Camila Cabello for us to find?" Jasmine's still dedicated to achieving fan-club president.

"I did not."

"Are we sketching animal poop?" Carter snickers. The kid's obsession with bodily functions will no doubt lead him far in life.

"No sketches today." I give them my full attention, setting aside my dizzying thoughts for now. "We're cleaning up trash."

Their collective groan has birds scattering, but I don't falter.

Two months ago, at the start of these hikes, their disappointment would have had me berating myself for screwing this up. Today, I stand taller. "Carter, would you like it if I dumped garbage on top of your dad's Porsche?"

His lips shrivel. "No."

I turn to Zoey and Jasmine. "Would it be cool if someone dumped garbage on Camila Cabello's house?"

"Oh my God." Jasmine gasps in horror. "No freaking way."

Zoey repeats the same omg-gasp-no-freaking-way routine.

"Max." I smile at my sensitive son, who's quieter today than usual. "Would it be as fun drawing scenery if it's covered in litter?"

He shakes his head.

"Jun, what would happen if I dumped garbage in your yard, where your adorable new dog hangs out?"

He cringes. "Newton eats everything. Even poop."

Carter cracks up. The girls roll their eyes.

"And he might get sick," I say, then I zero in on my personal psychoanalyst, Olivia. "How much trash do Americans toss in a single day?"

She opens her mouth then closes it, frowning, probably shocked she doesn't have this statistic on the tip of her tongue.

Suck on that, mini Freud. "One point four billion tons. In case any of you are wondering, that's a lot, and this forest is a dumping ground for careless people. The beautiful land you've used all summer is getting disrespected regularly. So think of this forest as your Porsche. It's Camila Cabello's house and your artistic inspiration and the woods where Newton and lots of other animals hang out. It's precious and fragile, and we're gonna do our part keeping it alive and healthy, so we can hike here for years to come."

Their pinched faces clear. I get a few nods.

"Also, whoever collects the most trash gets the bag of candy I've stashed in my car. It's as big as a horse."

As expected, they explode into motion, grabbing bags and gloves and pick-up sticks in a flurry of darting arms. Carter and Jun fight with the sticks like they're lightsabers. They of course make *pew-pew* sounds. Max and Zoey and Jasmine and Olivia are already zooming around like two-footed hoovers, snatching up scattered paper and cigarette butts near the trailhead trash cans.

Another shot of pride lifts me up, because I *like* running these hikes. These preteens are fun to be around. The work isn't frivolous, like I kept telling myself—my constant, droning self-sabotage. Teaching kids makes a difference. And I'm good at this. Actually, scrap that. I'm not good at organizing activities. I'm fucking *great* at it. I'm a grunter and a happy hiking leader and a father willing to lay his life down for his kid, and I don't want to go to law school. Not anymore. It's not who I am now.

I want to run these programs, work harder at them, help Lennon build his business. Access my drive and determination and convince him I have good ideas and value and can work as a team with him. I mean, *yes*. I'll also pester him and toss Maggie Edelstein's name out on a whim, but I love my brothers. Working with Lennon would be fantastic.

I cut a glance at Sadie.

Her back is to me, but she's not watching the kids. Her attention is on some middle distance, her expression so despondent my chest twists.

She barely ate this morning. She hasn't smiled once today. She ignored me on the drive. She forgot to pack Max's snacks. She's avoiding my eyes now, evading talking to me. Wiping the edges of her eyes. Not even interacting with the kids. She's biting her lip so hard I'm worried she'll break the skin.

Jesus.

That's not one subtle reaction to our tough situation. Those are ten glaring signs that I need to grovel. Show her I've finally figured out who I am. That we're a family who makes decisions together, instead of me going off half-cocked, forcing my opinion on her without fully understanding myself or her motivation.

I need to pull out all the stops and grovel so thoroughly my knees are skinned from the effort.

An idea forms, the perfect way to apologize and reach Sadie. Accomplices will be needed to pull this off—Max and E and Delilah— and I'll have to grab some stuff from my rental house. If all goes well, Sadie and I will have brighter futures than we'd ever imagined. At least, that better be how this ends.

THIRTY

Lying to Sadie is worse than drinking milk. After the hike, I told her I needed to do school prep at my Ruby Grove apartment, which is still rented until the end of this month. The only thing I'm prepping is my groveling, and my stomach is now cramping something fierce.

I keep picturing her on this morning's hike, how despondent she was, going through the motions of participating, barely interacting with the group. Except when I declared Max the garbage-collecting winner.

He ran in circles screaming, "Oh my God! I get *all the candy!*"

Sadie finally smiled, laughing at his antics. Then I handed out the end-of-program bracelets to everyone, and Olivia nearly knocked me over with a rib-cracking hug.

And Olivia. Not *But* Olivia. Wonders will never cease.

After that tearjerker, Sadie approached me for the first time all morning and touched my arm. "I'm not sure I told you, but you're amazing at this. In all the after-school programs Max has been in, I've never seen kids get so involved and care so much."

I took her hand in mine and laced our fingers together, exhaling through the heaviness in my chest. "That means more than you know. And we'll get through this, honey. Everything will work out as it should."

She bit her lip and nodded, still looking heartbreakingly sad. I nearly broke and explained my plans, but I needed to do groundwork first. Speak to people and make sure my proposition had legs. Hence my lying and gut cramping since this afternoon.

Freshly showered and wearing a nonsuctioned, nonyellow T-shirt, I hop in my Camaro and put my phone on speaker to call Mom, since my piece-of-crap car doesn't have Bluetooth.

"To what do I owe the honor," Mom says when she picks up.

"I've made a decision and need to talk to you about it," I say as I drive, aware I'm about to disappoint my mother for the millionth time. But I have to start honoring myself. "I'm not going back to law school. I'm pulling out before classes start, which means I get a full refund. And I know you wanted this for me, but I've been doing what I thought everyone wanted me to do, not what *I* wanted to do. I was afraid to let go of who I was, worried about what people would think of me. But it's not what I want anymore."

Her pause has me gripping my steering wheel tighter.

"Thank *God*," she finally says.

I blink at the stoplight in front of me. "What?"

"I've been biting my tongue for the past two months, dying to tell you I don't think you should go back but not wanting to undermine your choice."

A car behind me honks. Right. Green light.

I ease forward, grappling to follow Mom's revelation—an echo of E's not-so-subtle talk this morning. "You don't think I should go back?"

"You've just changed so much. The idea of you being confined in an office all day, working that grind after all you've been through, doesn't feel right. You've become so kind and thoughtful during WITSEC, worrying about me in your quiet way. Reading books you wouldn't normally read just to get my mind off my worries. I pictured you doing something more motivational like that. Kind of how you were as a quarterback captaining your team."

Seems my family knows me better than I know myself.

"I actually have a new plan," I admit, completely at ease with this decision. No weird freezing up or procrastination putting this into effect. Talking faster, I explain my plan to ask Lennon to consider joining forces with me, building his business together, along with the more complicated issues concerning Sadie's job, and the possibility of me using the school money for this new business venture.

By the time I'm done and Mom agrees about the cash, she sniffles. "You're finally doing it."

"Doing what?"

"Letting go of all your hate and letting in the light."

I nod as I drive, because she's right. I'm not sitting here comparing myself to the guy I was before WITSEC. I'm finally figuring out who I'm meant to be now, taking strides to claim my life, instead of plodding blindly through my days as a Walter. It feels pretty damn great.

After we hang up, I call the next person on my list, who will no doubt give me a lot more attitude than Mom.

"Did you bribe the parents from your hiking group?" Lennon says when he answers.

"No?" I hedge. I did bribe the kids with prizes. Last I checked that wasn't a crime.

"They all want to reenroll for the fall, and they're telling people you ran an excellent program." Instead of sounding thrilled, there's tension in his voice. "I'm getting calls, Des. Like, a lot of people want to sign up."

"That's a good thing, right?"

He makes an annoyed huff. "My business has been struggling in Houston. E keeps telling me I should move back to Windfall, that the outdoor scene there is ripe for what I do. I keep telling him starting over and rebuilding a reputation is too hard. Now you've gone and proved me wrong."

I squint at the passing farmland that stretches between Ruby Grove and Windfall, not connecting those errant dots. "I thought you loved Windfall growing up. That you missed living there."

"I did," he mumbles. "I do."

"I feel like I'm . . ." *Missing something,* I'm about to say. Then I recall the feisty redhead at the art walk. "What happened with you and Maggie Edelstein?"

"Nothing," he says quickly, followed by a sigh. "It's complicated."

I feel a twinge of compassion. Being ripped away from your friends and lovers without so much as a goodbye has a tendency to ruin relationships. Otherwise known as the Bower Boys Curse. I could tell him rearranging his life over one woman is ridiculous. He should live how he wants and where he wants, but I didn't exactly lead by example. Until recently.

I tap my thumb on my steering wheel and attempt to channel a portion of our brother Cal's soft understanding. "I won't ask again what happened with Maggie. It's your business. But we've spent a decade running and hiding from who we are. If you miss living in Windfall, suck up what went down with Maggie and face her. Don't let your past dictate your future."

"Wow, Des. That was deep."

Such a pain in my ass. "Don't let my newfound maturity fool you. I'll still noogie your head until your scalp bleeds."

He laughs. "I expect nothing less."

He probably won't expect this. "About your business, I actually have a proposition."

Half an hour later, as I roll into Windfall and park on Main Street beside the town square, I relax into my seat and soak in the view. The afternoon sun has burned off the remnants of this week's rain. Massive barrels still line the street, bursting with flowers and greenery, soon to be replaced with the fall decor of pumpkin-filled wheelbarrows and hand-sewn scarecrows on the lampposts for the Scarecrow Scavenger Hunt, assuming they still do that. People are walking their dogs and pushing carriages, stopping to talk to one another.

My rusted car is getting the odd wary glance, but the mood in Windfall is jovial and welcoming, and I really hope Sadie digs my plan, because I *want* to live here. I want to let these positive vibes rub off on me and my son.

When Sadie drives by in her red Honda and slows, trolling for a parking spot, my stomach resumes its nervous cramping.

I hop out of my car and strut toward Delilah's shop, Sugar and Sips. As per my request, she closed the shop early. E's been in there setting up the space for me, following my instructions. Everything should go smoothly, but this is Sadie. My everything. A strong woman with her own drives and desires, who's been deathly quiet the past day and a half. I don't know where her head's at and if I'm about to derail us further.

As I wait, Maggie Edelstein pushes out of Duke's Market down the block and saunters toward me, a bag of groceries in her hand. "If you're panhandling," she says, "word to the wise: looking like you're about to puke isn't helping. Neither is the scowl."

Guess my resting pissed-off face resembles my I-love-Sadie-and-am-terrified-to-lose-her face. "Lovely to see you again, Maggie. And your sarcasm."

While I don't get the Maggie-Lennon conundrum, I like the idea of them together. Specifically, of her sassing the hell out of Lennon.

She stops beside me, gripping her bag with both hands. "I heard you're ditching law again."

What in the actual *fuck*? The gossip in this town is always impressive, but the speed of that intel verges on creepy. The only people who know my plan are Mom, Delilah, E, and Lennon. Delilah's for sure the weak link here, seeing as she's best friends with Maggie, but the Lennon angle is too fun to let slide. "Did Lennon share that detail with you?"

"What? No." Her face gets that hit-the-deck look Lennon acquires when he hears her name. "As I told you, I don't talk to Lennon. I barely know the guy."

Likely story. "In case you were wondering, the Bower boys epidemic you were so concerned about at the art walk is about to get worse. Seems Lennon's moving back to Windfall."

Her cheeks flame the color of her red hair. So bright I'm sure her freckles will catch fire. "Whatever. He's not my concern. I don't care where he lives."

Her huffy glare as she storms off says otherwise.

"Des?" Sadie's voice sends my gut on another deep dive. I swivel, and she's there, standing beside Max, her brow pinched. "I thought you were at your apartment in Ruby Grove."

Instead of answering, I squeeze Max's shoulder. "Thanks for bringing her here, bud."

He grins. "She didn't suspect a thing."

"Because you're a superspy."

A superspy who seems less worried about me and his mom. *No,* I haven't gone and undermined Sadie by explaining the source of our ongoing tension to Max without her. I'm not that big of a moron. I told him I have a surprise for Sadie and asked him to be my wingman. He, of course, didn't disappoint, begging her to take him to visit Aunt Delilah and Uncle E at Sugar and Sips.

Her calculating eyes ping-pong between us. "What are you guys up to?"

Hopefully making her the happiest she's ever been.

On cue, Delilah and E slip out of the shop, doing a pitiful job of hiding their conspiratorial smiles and not-so-subtle thumbs-ups.

"The place is yours," Delilah tells me, practically vibrating with excitement. "And you're mine." She points to Max, mock scowling. "I have two dogs who need to lick someone."

He giggles and skips ahead with them, disappearing down the alley toward their apartment entrance.

Sadie raises her eyebrows, no longer wondering if something's up. My accomplices suck at discretion. "What have you done?"

I swallow hard and hold out my bent arm, attempting old-school chivalry. "We have an art exhibit to attend."

The tiny lift of her lips is a good sign. "Since when is there an art exhibit in Delilah's shop?"

"Since one minute ago? And we're late."

"Des." She doesn't say more, just looks kind of overwhelmed, fiddling with her purse strap. Then she ducks her head shyly and puts her hand through the crook of my arm. "Guess we shouldn't be late."

I'm hoping it's better late than never.

I hold the door open for her and exhale in relief. The pretty pastel décor is the perfect backdrop for my groveling. Delilah put instrumental jazz music on her stereo, something romantic and light, quiet enough not to overshadow our conversation. The lights are dimmed, and E brought down the bright studio lamp he uses when sketching. It's aimed at the wall beside the pastry display, illuminating a row of hastily installed framed artworks, which are actually my horrible crafting relics.

I lock the door behind us and place my hand on the small of Sadie's back, leading her to the first framed piece. We stand in front of it the way we used to ponder art in galleries, our heads tilted slightly, expressions intent.

"You did this." Something like wonder infuses her quiet words. "These are the crafts you've been doing this year."

"They are." The first one's my mutant origami triceratops. It's stuck in a simple black frame, reminding me of how I was stuck in my boxed-in world back then, barely making strides to pick myself up, while Mirielle badgered me in her good-natured way. Hard to believe that was nearly four months ago. Feels more like four years. "I call this one *Buried under History.*"

The café still smells sweet, remnants of baked sugar and roasting coffee beans in the air. The backs of our hands brush, and I link my fingers with hers lightly, testing her boundaries, asking with my tentative touch if this is okay.

She winds our fingers more firmly together. "What do you think the artist was feeling when he created it?"

I smile at the question. She's catching on to what I'm doing here. Presenting myself to her, letting her dig through my head.

"Well." I rub my thumb over her knuckles. "This piece was done after he learned he no longer needed to be in witness protection but before he knew he had a son."

"So . . ." Her lips twitch, but I'm not sure why. "Before he puked in a bar bathroom when he learned he was a dad."

Goddamn E. The guy has no sense of self-preservation. "Yes. Before *that*. Swear to God, my brother's gonna end up breathing through a straw."

She laughs. "E loves you. I think you're his favorite brother. But back to this accomplished artist." She nudges me with her elbow. "What was he feeling while making this piece?"

"I'd say he was feeling stuck. Terrified to look for the lost love of his life, assuming she'd moved on with someone else and worried he wasn't good enough for her anyway. And . . ." I replay my talks with my pain-in-the-ass brother and my mother, this undercurrent that's been sabotaging me since Sadie's been back in my life. "I think he was depressed and didn't know how to name that. I think he'd forgotten how to have fun and pushed his family away so he wouldn't drag them down too. He was lonely and lost, even though he had people who loved him and an awesome neighbor who taught him crafts."

Sadie's looking at me now, not the painting, her expression brimming with compassion. "I'm so sorry."

"So am I. It wasn't a good place to be." I don't talk over the experience with light quips or brush it off with a grunt. Hiding how I struggled then doesn't serve me or us now.

She squeezes my hand, a gentle pulse that travels up my arm, then she pulls me to the next piece. "What was the artist feeling here?"

Certainly not patient. My attempt at needlepointing a grouping of flowers lasted approximately twenty minutes. Hardly anything's done on the piece, and what is there looks as jagged as I felt. "That was done after the artist met a terrifying girl in a diner, and he was petrified she'd join his hiking program."

Sadie snorts. "You and Olivia are priceless together."

"She's still frightening, but God help me, I dig that girl." Using my free hand, I trace a slow line from Sadie's bare shoulder downward, letting my fingers rest inside the smooth divot of her elbow. "The artist also made that piece before he met his son. He was convinced he wasn't father material. That he'd end up hurting his son somehow. He didn't trust himself to be a good role model."

Sadie blinks up at me, moisture clinging to her eyelashes. "And now?"

"We're getting there, Sprite." I lift her hand and kiss her fingers. "We still have three pieces left."

She nods and presses her lips together.

I gesture to the blind drawing I did with Max, where we drew each other's faces without looking at the pages. My sketching skills are pitiful. "This one was done after the artist met his son. He was desperate for his kid to like him, to do right by him. He was also mesmerized by the kid's mom, falling harder for her by the minute, but drawing this was his first taste of what it was to feel connected to another person in a deeper, unbreakable way. That first awareness of fatherhood. Of realizing life was bigger than his own regrets."

Sadie places a kiss on my shoulder. I run my nose along the top of her head, breathing her in. The Summer of Sadie Jones.

"And this?" She moves us along to the next frame of a hanging embroidered bracelet.

It still baffles me that my thick fingers can wind thread that tightly. "This particular bracelet was done this afternoon."

She faces me fully and wraps my hands in both of hers. "What were you thinking while making it?"

She's no longer pretending we're at a posh gallery. We're Desmond Bower and Sadie Jones, former high school sweethearts, parents of one fantastic kid, desperately trying to figure out our future.

"I was thinking about how sorry I was that we fought. That I didn't really listen to your worries or consider Max's feelings. But also that life's short, and I'm tired of trying to be something I'm not. It's like I've been living with this unsettled panic under my happiness, worried you'd realize I'm not worth loving and that I wouldn't be good enough for you and Max. Thinking Duke Law was the answer to everything, because it represented who I was before. Who I thought I was supposed to be. Truth is"—I free a hand from Sadie's grasp and brush her hair behind her ear, letting my hand come to rest on her neck—"I don't want to go to law school. Not anymore."

She shakes her head, frowning. "Des, you can't do this for me."

"That's the thing, honey." I cup her neck harder. "I'm not doing it for you. I reapplied to Duke because I wasn't happy with myself. Because I thought it was what *you* needed, so you'd see me as a success."

She rears back. "I don't care what you do for a living. That's never mattered to me. *You're* what matters to me."

I smile at her tenderly, letting the vehemence of her words sink in and settle. I'm done second-guessing her motivations and undermining myself. Tonight is about laying ourselves bare. "What I want, Sadie, is to be a full-time father and dedicated partner to the woman I love. Which is you, by the way." She lets out a watery laugh. I run my thumb down her neck. "I also decided to start seeing a therapist. Took a cue from our kid to finally talk through the mess of my last eleven years. And I want to do more as a group leader, planning outdoor activities and that kind of stuff. Which brings me to us. To your job, and a new suggestion I have on how to plan for the next few years."

Her next swallow is long and slow. "Okay."

"I agree that Max is happy here in Windfall. He has friends and extended family he won't have in Arizona, but I still desperately want you to take that job so you can live your best life. Fulfill yourself professionally in a meaningful way. So." I lick my parched lips, readying to take this next leap. "I suggest he lives here with me. We set up our home base here, and I step in as his full-time parent."

"Des, no. I'm so happy you've decided to see a therapist, and working with Lennon is a great idea, but—"

"*And*," I go on, jumping in before she completely squashes my plans, "you'll probably be pissed I did this, but I called Joseph and talked to him about logistics. Asked him if you can work blocks of time in Arizona and blocks here remotely. He said it shouldn't be a problem, except when setting up new exhibitions. Otherwise, you can split your time between Arizona and Windfall. And since I'll be here now, we can make it work. He also said getting Sarah to add a travel budget to your contract is no issue. *That's* how much she wants to hire you. Because you're that good, and your perspective is that unique."

I study her tense expression, unsure which way she's leaning, terrified she won't give the idea a chance.

She focuses on the floor, squeezes my hand tighter. When she looks back up, there's fire in her eyes. "Being a full-time dad is hard. It's not all fun art walks and cooking classes."

"I know," I say quickly, thankful she's even considering my plan. "I don't expect it to be easy. I also know it'll be worth every tough day, every frustration." Every time Max decides he hates me for wielding parental law.

"I want this, Sadie. I want to be the stay-at-home dad while you work." Let assholes like Justin Bernardini make all the cracks they want. I'll hold my head high, knowing how goddamn lucky I am. "E and Delilah said they'd help out as much as I need. I've even spoken to Lennon and can work with him on Littlewing part time or however much I can do. Continue leading programs and help build the business."

We'll be adding an adult component with certifications offered and skill-building events—corporate programs and trust exercises. My mind's been spinning with possibilities, but the most exciting aspect of this plan is the idea of living with Max full time. Helping raise him and shape my son into the strong man I know he'll be.

"I would miss so much," Sadie whispers, her voice cracking.

"Honey, I know. Being away will be hard. I'm not pretending it won't. But lots of parents travel for work, and your entire life the past ten years has revolved around being a mother and doing for others. This is your time, Sadie. Your chance to spread your wings and see what you can accomplish, and the I-miss-you sex will be fucking fantastic."

She covers her mouth and laughs. "Am I really doing this?"

"*We're* doing this. Together." I nudge her hand away and kiss her, a soft press that ricochets through me. Yeah, the I-miss-you sex will be mind blowing.

"With that settled." I guide her toward the final frame on the wall. "We have one more artwork to discuss."

She's still shaking slightly, stealing glances at me as we approach the wall, probably overwhelmed with all we've discussed. It's about to get more intense. Like, forever-and-a-day intense.

She gives her head a small shake and appraises the piece. "It's a purple envelope, and by the perfect angles and folds, I'd say you didn't make it."

"Maybe there's something inside," I say not so smoothly. I'm buzzing with nervous excitement, not bothering to hide my wide grin.

She scowls at me, but her eyes are dancing. "Desmond Bower."

"Sadie Jones."

"What are you up to?"

I nudge her forward. "You'll find out shortly."

"If there's something gross in there, you're dead." Tentatively, she pushes to her tiptoes and lifts the envelope flap. When she peers inside, she gasps. "Oh my God."

By the time her head whips my way, *happy* tears are shining this time, and I'm already on bended knee. "This only works if you actually take the ring out."

"Oh my God," she says again, softer this time, glowing as bright as I hoped.

Reverently, she pulls the engagement ring from the envelope and stares at the small round-cut diamond. The stone is shiny and clear, perched on a slim white-gold band. Nothing fancy. Simple elegance. My entire soul captured in a time-honored gesture.

"It's gorgeous," she breathes.

"You're gorgeous. Now get over here."

Instead of taking my offered hand, she gets on her knees too, holding the ring between us. Her eyelashes flutter. "What was the artist thinking when he bought this?"

I clasp my hands around hers, both of us holding tight to the ring. "He was thinking he was too young to be so in love."

She crinkles her nose. "I wouldn't call thirty-four too young for love."

"I bought this ring eleven years ago, Sprite."

Right there. *That* expression—how her mouth softens and eyes widen, the pink on her cheeks growing deeper. I'd like to frame that look. "Before you left?"

I give a sheepish shrug. "Carried it around with me for weeks, scared of how much I loved you, worrying about stupid things. Planned to propose our last night together, but I obviously chickened out and missed my chance to ask you for forever. But I'm not worried anymore. I mean, I'm still a stupid guy who'll make stupid mistakes, but you're it for me, Sadie. You make me a better man. You're the reason I'm here now, finally pulling myself together, and I love you so much I *ache* with it. I want to spend forever putting you first and making you and Max happy."

I take the ring from her trembling hands and slip it on her finger. "Sadie Jones, will you do me the absolute honor of being my wife?"

She nods, tears escaping. "Yes," she says against my lips, cupping my cheeks and kissing me hard, tugging me closer.

I don't need the encouragement. This is everything. My promise to quit letting my past dictate my future. Her finally allowing herself to follow her dreams. Us working together to raise a happy, healthy kid, while figuring out the logistics as we go.

Sadie Jones and me, eleven years later, but at the exact right time, finally promising each other forever.

EPILOGUE

Two Months Later

"Does it hurt? Do you feel the needles? Oh my God, is that actual *blood*?" Max is transfixed, pushed to his knees on the stool beside me, slack jawed as my tattoo artist does her work.

"It hurts, but I'm tough." Except this is the first tattoo I've gotten sober (second if you count the simpler one Cearra already did this morning—a surprise for Sadie), and I don't remember the process hurting this much during those drunken WITSEC nights. "The blood's no big deal," I tell Max.

Finally getting Max-designed ink *is* a big deal—the Cessna 195 on the inside of my left biceps. From an actually talented tattoo artist.

When Kyle was over for our first playdate, and he told me his wife was a tattoo artist about to open a local shop, Max and I scrolled through her impressive online shots, goggling at the realism in her colorful work. I booked her the next day.

"How do you do the shading?" Max's eager gaze latches onto Cearra. "Do you use the same needles or switch to the ones with more lines stacked together? And does the color fade over time or stay the same? Like with the sun and stuff? Mom tells me if I leave my shirt on the clothesline in the sun it'll fade. And how come the purple outline doesn't smear off?"

"Those are a lot of questions, Max. But since you're the artist of this cool piece, I'll answer every one."

I'm thankful for the reprieve. Keeping up with Max's inquisitive mind is tough when I'm trying to breathe through the dig of those vibrating needles. The kid's art obsession has actually saved me more times than I can count when Sadie's been away.

If I need a couple of hours to make dinner and do the laundry, I get him going on an art project. If I need an hour to talk to Lennon and discuss Littlewing's expansion, I get Max going on an art project. If I need to shut myself in the bathroom so I can talk dirty to Sadie on her lunch break, I get him going on an art project.

Give this kid's mind a creative outlet, and he's instantly obsessed.

Cearra somehow maintains her focus on her work while answering his question barrage. I can't help but smile at him. My resting pleased-as-shit-father face these days. I mean, it's not all roses, as Sadie warned. His art obsession has led to skipped homework and a punishment I had to reluctantly dole out. And the cooking is intense. Like, three meals a day, *every day* intense. Seriously. Every. Day. Not sure how my mind skimmed over that duty, but here we are. Max also mopes around at times, missing his mom when she's away, possibly blaming me for her new job. Granted, I *am* partly to blame for her living in Arizona for short stretches, but I don't regret one second of that choice.

When I speak to Sadie, she talks like Max asks art questions, going a mile a minute, praising the gorgeous gallery space, telling me about the caliber of artists she's working with, gushing about their mentorship program, how it will incorporate a yearly exhibit she's heading.

She *loves* what she's doing, and I couldn't be prouder.

We're on a countdown now. She's been gone two weeks, with one more to go. The calendar in our kitchen has a big fuzzy heart sticker on it, chosen by Max, indicating the day she's back. So far, two weeks is the longest we've been apart, and I was right about the I-miss-you sex. Fucking *intense*.

The tattoo machine buzzes. Max watches, entranced.

The front door jingles, signaling a newcomer. E saunters into Cearra's small one-person shop and stands over us, arms folded across his chest. "Max. I thought we agreed on the poop emoji tattoo."

Max giggles. "No, we didn't."

I stare blandly at my brother. "I debated getting your portrait but decided I didn't want Sadie to run screaming when she saw it."

E blinks at me, then leans down toward Cearra's ear, feigning a whisper. "If I slip you a fifty, will you turn that plane into a worm?"

She rolls her eyes. "Get lost, E. Unless you want your face inked."

"It's incredible work," he says more seriously. "Can't believe my brother's finally gonna have decent art on his body. And although I know you love having me here heckling you, I'm actually here for him." He points at Max. "Delilah has a chocolate banana cookie experiment that needs tasting. What do you say we help her out for a few, then you can come back here?"

Max is up and moving before E finishes. "Is it one of the big plate-size cookies?"

"Face-size. Think you can handle it?"

Now he's running and dragging E, pushing out the door.

"He's a great kid." Cearra wipes a section of ink, glancing between Max's art and the outline on my arm. "Super talented and smart. Kyle and I will be lucky if Nyah turns out half as sweet."

"Nyah's a doll. Max loves playing with her."

"Your Dad Dates are adorable."

And informative. Thanks to Kyle and our Dad Date afternoons, I now know how to remove an ink stain from a shirt: a combination of hairspray, soaking time, elbow grease, plus a few prayers that Max's favorite shirt won't be ruined, because he gets seriously upset when his favorite clothes are ruined. Lennon and I also hired Kyle to design our website for our newly branded business. We've changed the company name from Littlewing Outdoor Camp to Littlewing Adventures. Its adult-geared sister company is Bigwing Adventures. Aside from revamped websites, my first order of business was ordering new, nonyellow, nonsuctioned T-shirts.

"We'll do a family night soon," I tell Cearra. "With all of us. Maybe when Sadie's back next week."

She hums her agreement and resumes her work. The machine buzzes as rock music plays. Pain flares in my arm, but not unbearably. I close my eyes, breathe through the discomfort that dulls slightly as she works.

The bell on the front door jingles again. I open my eyes and almost jump out of the chair.

Sadie's at the reception desk, not in Arizona where she's supposed to be, waving a hand at me nonchalantly, like she hasn't given me the best surprise.

"Cearra," I say, with minimal control and a hint of a growl. "We need to take a break."

She laughs. "I'll grab a coffee. Be back in ten."

The second she leaves, I have Sadie against the back wall and I'm kissing her senseless, keeping my partially inked arm and secret rib tattoo at a distance, but *hell*. It's been two weeks since I've had my hands on her. I'm hard in seconds, not even talking, just kissing and nipping and pressing closer, needing to chart every inch of her.

"You're here," I whisper into her ear, then give it a lick.

"I'm here," she breathes, arching into me. Then she ducks her head and studies my arm. "It looks *unreal*."

"That's what happens when I have a top-notch designer and killer tattoo artist. But back to you." I skim my hand down her side. "How long do I have you for?"

"Three weeks."

I pull back, sure I heard her wrong. "Three weeks?"

She nods, beaming. "I'm working on behind-the-scenes mentorship stuff for a bit, things that can be done remotely. So you have to share the sheets with me for twenty-two whole nights."

"Oh, honey." I plant my palms on the wall, caging her in. "You're gonna get fucked so good."

"Jesus, Des." She palms my ass, pulling me flush as we tangle our tongues and share a moan. When she grazes my newly inked ribs, I flinch. She looks down, frowning. "Are you hurt?"

"Not exactly." I lift the edge of my T-shirt, showing her the writing across my ribcage. "Had something extra done this morning."

She traces the edge of the plastic bandage covering the scripted words. "What does it say?"

"They're my wedding vows."

Her eyes widen and dart to my face. "But we're not getting married until the summer."

I shrug. "Couldn't wait to have a permanent reminder of my love for you. As far as I'm concerned, we're already hitched."

"Des." Her eyes go dreamy—my favorite in-love look from my favorite woman.

She pushes me farther back and crouches, reading the elegant script Cearra tattooed:

> When I'm lost, you light the way.
> When I'm down, you lift me up.
> My life is full because of you.
> Friend. Lover. Wife. Beautiful mother.
> A partner in this life we're building.
> When you need me, I'll be there to hold you.
> Support you. Encourage you.
> Find you when you're lost.
> Lift you up when you're down.
> No obstacles are too hard for us to conquer together.
> I am forever and always yours.

"God, I love you." She's up and kissing me again, so much emotion in each fervent press of her lips.

"Love you so much," I murmur, still awed she's back in my life. That her lips are mine to devour, but I slow us down. "I plan to prove those words with my actions. Every day. But if we keep making out, I'll bust a hole through my jeans, and we'll have visitors soon."

She laughs and plants a last kiss on my lips. "To be continued later."

"You can count on it." I release her, pleased with the deep flush in her cheeks. "Guess whose winter roster is three-quarters full?"

"I knew kids would eat it up."

"Kyle's website design helped a ton, and I did a presentation at Max's school. We're definitely off to a solid start."

The fall and winter kids' programs run once a week instead of twice, but the demand has been high enough that we've hired another part-time leader to help out. We even have plans for expansion next summer, offering more programs and building a ropes course.

I'm not sure how I would've felt working as a lawyer, but I love developing this business, planning and organizing and being outside, getting kids hyped up and active. I love being Max's dad. And I love welcoming Sadie home with promises of ravaging her between the sheets. I truly love my life, and I'm not sure if the hell I went through is partly why. Either way, I don't take one second of my happiness for granted, hence not waiting to get my vows inked.

I pull Sadie to the tattoo chair with me, guiding her onto my lap. "There's one drawback to the winter programs."

She cuddles in close, running her fingers over my stubbled jaw. "Do tell."

"Olivia has informed me she's now my assistant on all future hikes." No joke. This is the shit I have to deal with. The "sacrifice" part of having everything I want. "It's horrible," I go on, feeling itchy just thinking about how she'll scare the new recruits with her terrifying statistics. "She actually sewed a patch on her shirt that reads, 'Assistant to Grouchy Hiking Leader.'"

Sadie cracks up. "Oh my God, I love that kid."

I smile. "She's pretty great. As is ours." I trail my fingers through her hair. "I love you, Sadie Jones, soon to be Sadie Jones-Bower."

She sighs and noses my neck. "I love you, Desmond Bower, soon to be Desmond Jones-Bower."

In eight months, during a quieter time in Sadie's schedule, we're taking each other's names. Binding our promise to be partners and lovers. Retaining our identities while growing together. That's how we do things now. Loving big, supporting big, and living big. Our kind of big on our terms, and I have no plans on settling for anything less ever again.

AUTHOR'S NOTE

Thank you for reading Desmond and Sadie's story!

If you miss them already, I have a treat for you! Visit my website, www.kellysiskind.com, and look for the Bower Boys series page for a *free* bonus chapter. You get to experience one of their fun master chef cook-offs, followed by a spicy interlude, all from Sadie's point of view.

And keep an eye out for Lennon's book. Details will be on my website when available. That man puts the comedy in rom-com, and wait until you find out why he's secretly obsessed with Maggie!

ACKNOWLEDGMENTS

Readers! As always, none of this would be possible without you. Thank you for reading my words and escaping into Windfall and Ruby Grove with me. I can't wait for you to get swept away with Lennon and Maggie next. I cackled to myself while writing half of that book. Lennon doesn't disappoint in the fun department, and his chemistry with Maggie is singe-your-eyebrows hot!

Huge thanks to all the reviewers, bloggers, vloggers, Instagrammers, and BookTokers who read early copies of this book. You're why Desmond and Sadie's story is making it into so many hands.

Fun fact: I'm one of those nutty writers who prefers revising to drafting. Desmond Bower—my sweet, grumpy, grunting hero—took some drafts and rewriting to get right, but I loved every second of shaping him. I owe a massive thank-you to my acquisitions editor, Maria Gomez, and my content editor, Angela James. You opened my eyes to Desmond's complexity and pushed me to bring out all sides of him. While revisions were a ton of work, the process was a pleasure.

Without my copyeditors and proofreaders, you would've read things like "my crock swelled" instead of "my cock swelled," so I think we're all thankful for Stephanie Chou's, Megan Westberg's, and Heather Buzila's hard work. Without their expertise, some scenes in this book would've read much differently.

The Amazon Montlake team is a powerhouse I'm thankful to have in my corner. Jillian Cline, Cheryl Weisman, Patricia Callahan, and Anh Schluep are the collective backbone that lifts a book and its author up. Thank you all for your incredible work.

My agent, Maria Napolitano, deserves all the wine and chocolate. Signing with the Bookcase team was one of the best parts of my writing journey, and working with Maria is the cherry on that sundae. Thank you for having my back, for championing my work, and for looking at hot guy pics with me, even when our eyes are bleeding from the repetition.

When it comes to drafting and revising, I'd be lost without my early beta readers and critique partners. Brenda St John Brown, J. R. Yates, Heather Van Fleet, Shelly Hastings Shur, Nena Drury: you all gave me tough love as needed and cheered for the parts you loved. I'm forever in your debt.

Exploring Max's sexuality and a parent's reaction to that journey was a topic I've wanted to write about for a while. I don't have children, but several of my relatives have come out at different times in their lives, and, afterward, I recalled moments I said the types of blanket heterosexual comments Desmond made to Max. I've used those experiences to learn and grow, and I'm thankful there are more and more books in the world featuring LGBTQ2S+ kids, so anyone struggling can feel seen and understood. Thank you to my sensitivity readers, whose children came out at young ages. You know who you are, and I'm grateful for your candor on the subject.

All my love goes to my husband, whose patience while I spend oodles of time in my office and my head is astounding. You're my go-to when I hit plotting roadblocks, but I'll always roll my eyes when you tell people you inspire all my heroes. Thanks for putting up with my writing obsession and for making me laugh.

I'm excited to see you all (and Lennon!) again soon in the quaint town of Windfall!

ABOUT THE AUTHOR

Photo © 2015 Eirik Dunlop

Kelly Siskind writes romantic comedies and contemporary romance novels for daydreamers and fantasists everywhere. She is the author of the One Wild Wish, Showmen, and Over the Top series, among other titles. Kelly's novels have been published internationally, and she has been featured on the Apple Books Best Books of the Month list.

Kelly lives in charming Northern Ontario, where she alternatively frolics in and suffers through the never-ending winters. When she's not out hiking or home devouring books, you can find her, notepad in hand, scribbling down one of the many plot bunnies bouncing around in her head. Sign up for Kelly's newsletter at www.kellysiskind.com and never miss a giveaway, a free bonus scene, or the latest news on her books. And connect with her on Twitter and Instagram (@kellysiskind) or on Facebook (@authorkellysiskind).